DIANA
and the HERO'S
JOURNEY

WRITTEN BY
Grace Ellis

ART AND COLOR BY
Penelope Rivera Gaylord
WITH JERRY GAYLORD

LETTERING BY
Lucas Gattoni

Wonder Woman created by
William Moulton Marston

DIANA and the HERO'S JOURNEY

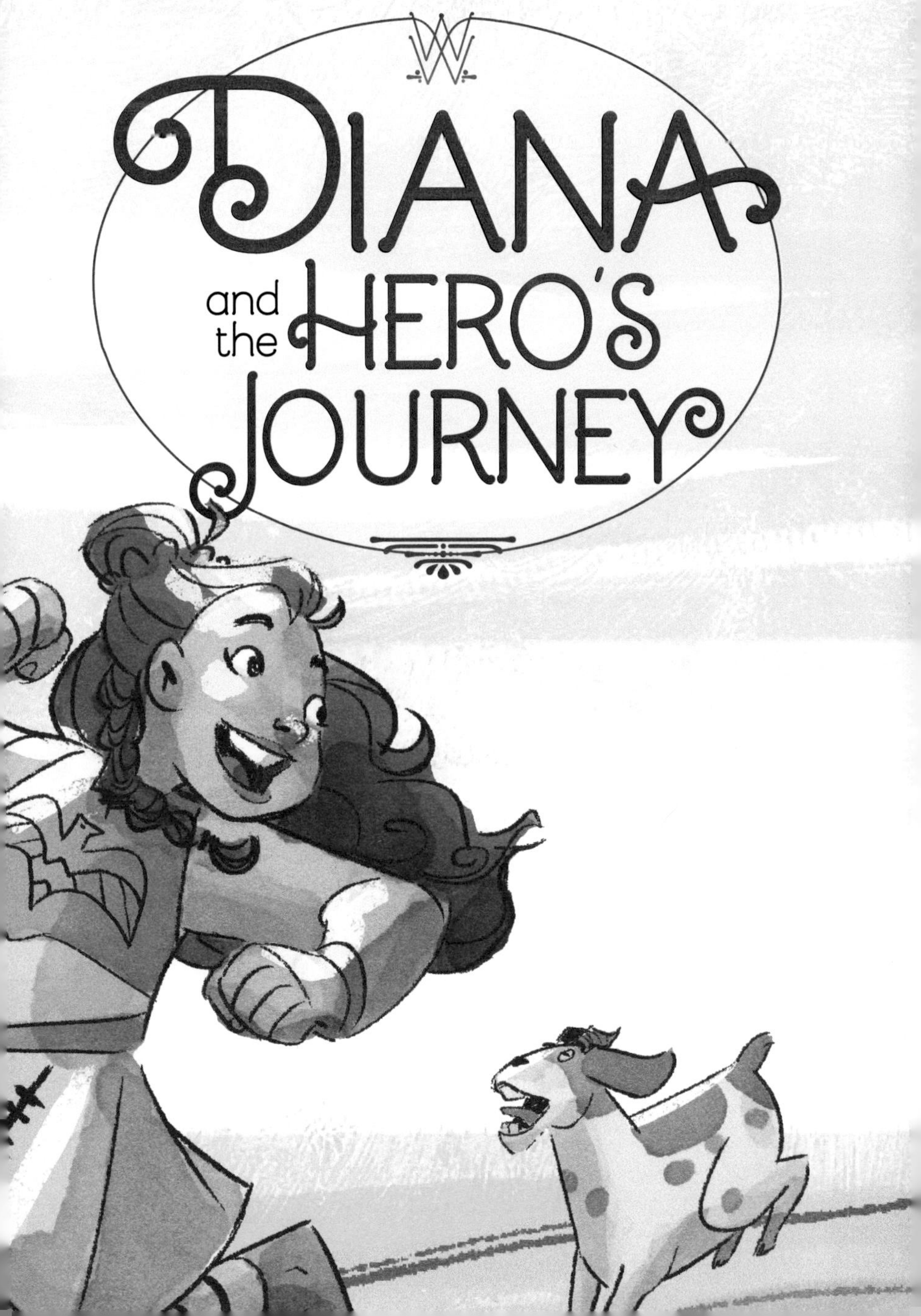

SARA MILLER Editor
STEVE COOK Design Director – Books
AMIE BROCKWAY-METCALF Publication Design
TIFFANY HUANG Publication Production

MARIE JAVINS VP – Editor-in-Chief

JIM LEE President, Publisher & Chief Creative Officer
ANNE DePIES Senior VP & General Manager
LARRY BERRY VP – Brand Design & Creative Services
DON FALLETTI VP – Manufacturing & Production
LAWRENCE GANEM VP – Editorial Programming & Talent Strategy
ALISON GILL Senior VP – Manufacturing & Operations
NICK J. NAPOLITANO VP – Publishing & Business Operations
NANCY SPEARS VP – Sales & Marketing

DIANA AND THE HERO'S JOURNEY

DC Comics, 4000 Warner Blvd., Bldg.
700, 2nd Floor, Burbank, CA 91522
Printed by Worzalla, Stevens Point, WI,
USA. 8/18/23.
First Printing.
ISBN: 978-1-77950-969-7

MIX
Paper from
responsible sources
FSC® C002589
www.fsc.org

Library of Congress Cataloging-in-Publication Data

Names: Ellis, Grace, author. | Gaylord, Penelope R., artist. | Gaylord,
  Jerry, illustrator. | Gattoni, Lucas, letterer.
Title: Diana and the hero's journey / written by Grace Ellis ; art and
  color by Penelope Rivera Gaylord ; layouts by Jerry Gaylord ; lettering
  by Lucas Gattoni.
Description: Burbank, CA : DC Comics, 2023. | Audience: Ages 8-12 |
  Audience: Grades 2-3 | Summary: After accidentally destroying the
  Amazons' hard work preparing for a festival celebrating the story of
  Hero, the first hero in Greek mythology, Diana and her goat pal,
  Phyllis, embark on a journey to clean up their mess, soon embracing the
  support of her community to learn what it truly means to be a hero.
Identifiers: LCCN 2023027837 (print) | LCCN 2023027838 (ebook) | ISBN
  9781779509697 (trade paperback) | ISBN 9781779509703 (ebook)
Subjects: CYAC: Graphic novels. | Heroes--Fiction. | Amazons--Fiction. |
  Princesses--Fiction. | LCGFT: Fantasy comics. | Graphic novels.
Classification: LCC PZ7.7.E447 Di 2023 (print) | LCC PZ7.7.E447 (ebook) |
  DDC 741.5/973--dc23/eng/20230620
LC record available at https://lccn.loc.gov/2023027837
LC ebook record available at https://lccn.loc.gov/2023027838

TABLE OF CONTENTS

Chapter 1 9

Chapter 2 48

Chapter 3 68

Chapter 4 98

Chapter 5 112

The Story of Hero 141

CHAPTER 1

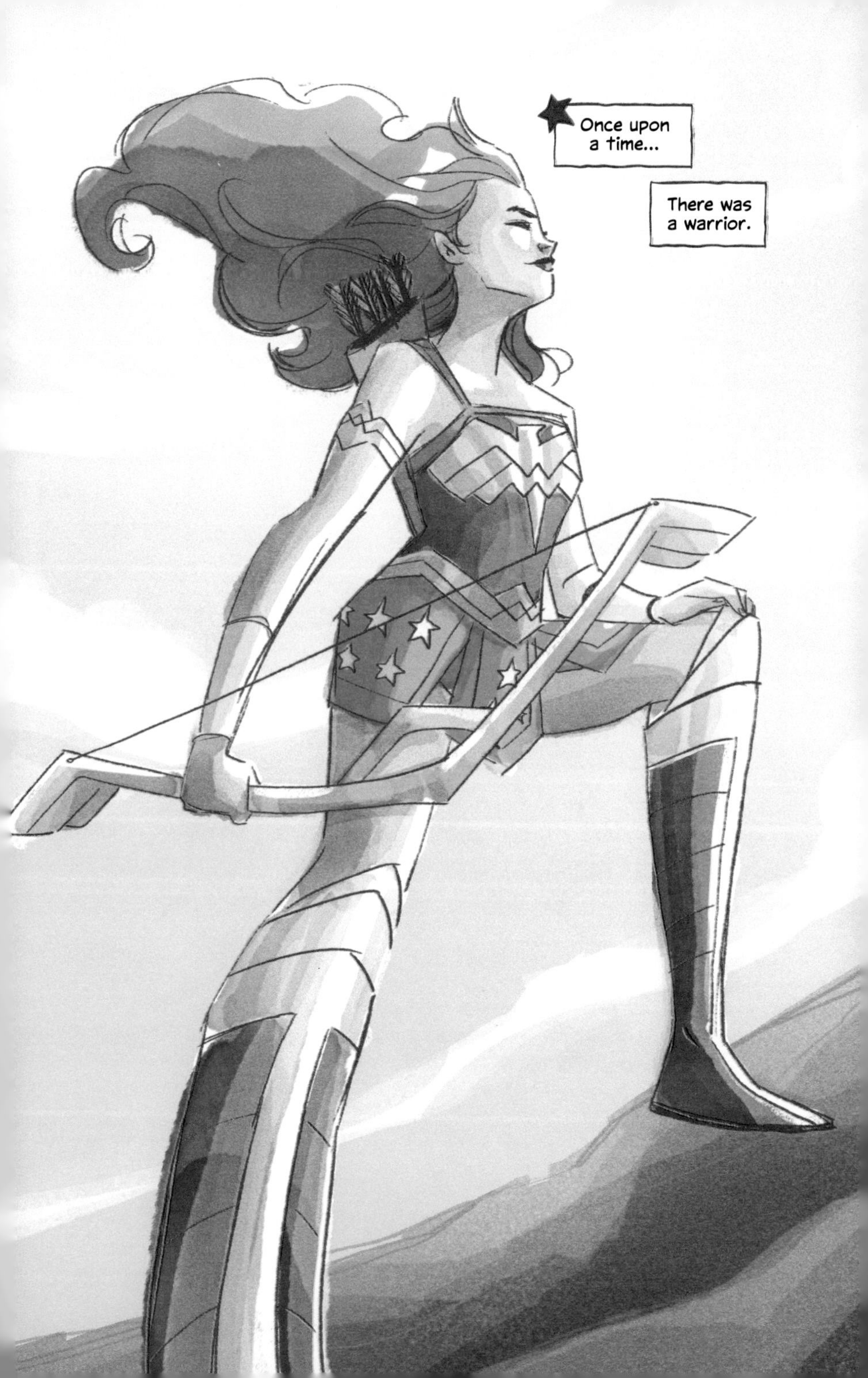
Once upon a time...
There was a warrior.

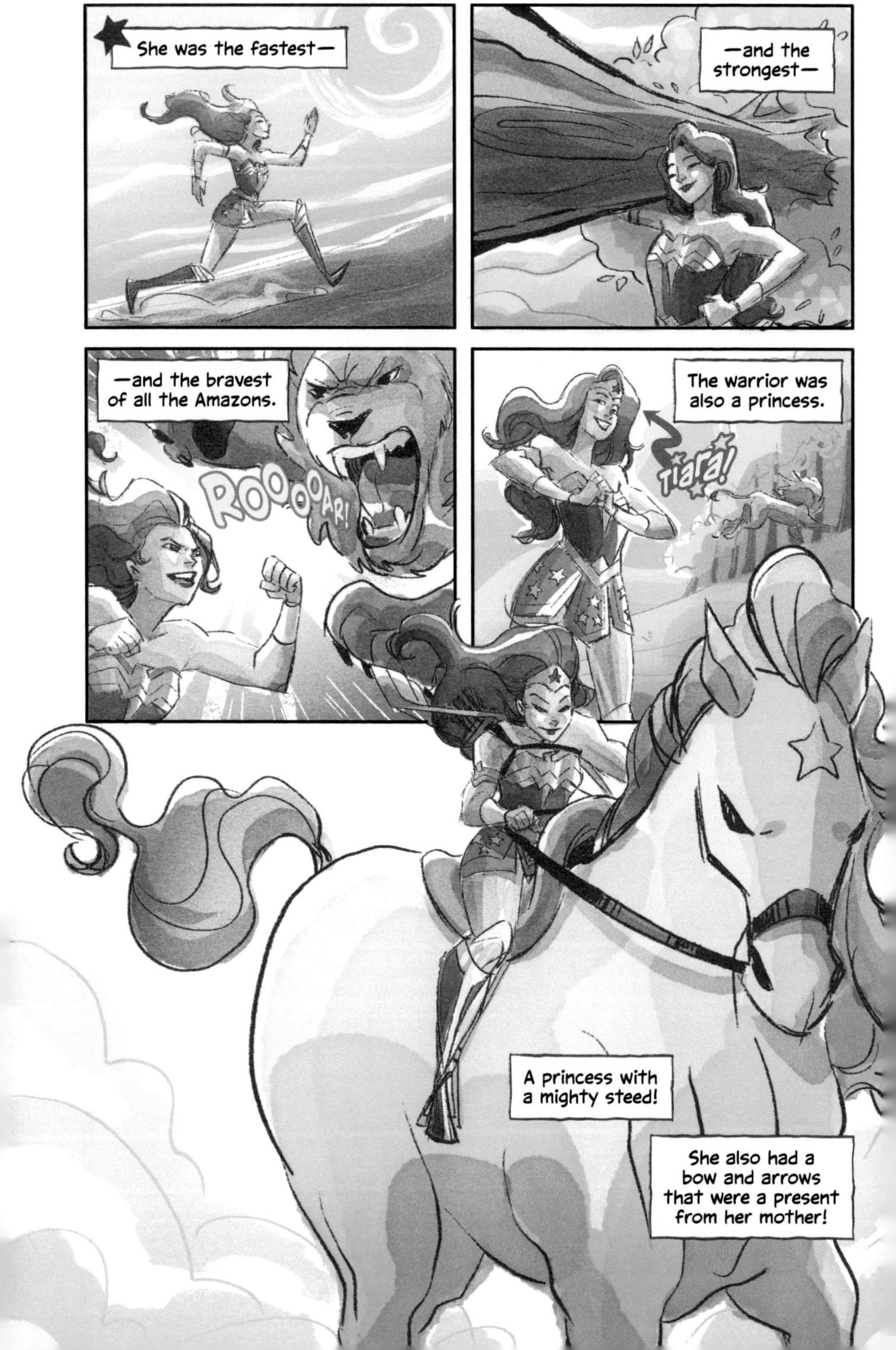
She was the fastest—
—and the strongest—
—and the bravest of all the Amazons.
ROOOOAR!
The warrior was also a princess.
TIARA!
A princess with a mighty steed!
She also had a bow and arrows that were a present from her mother!

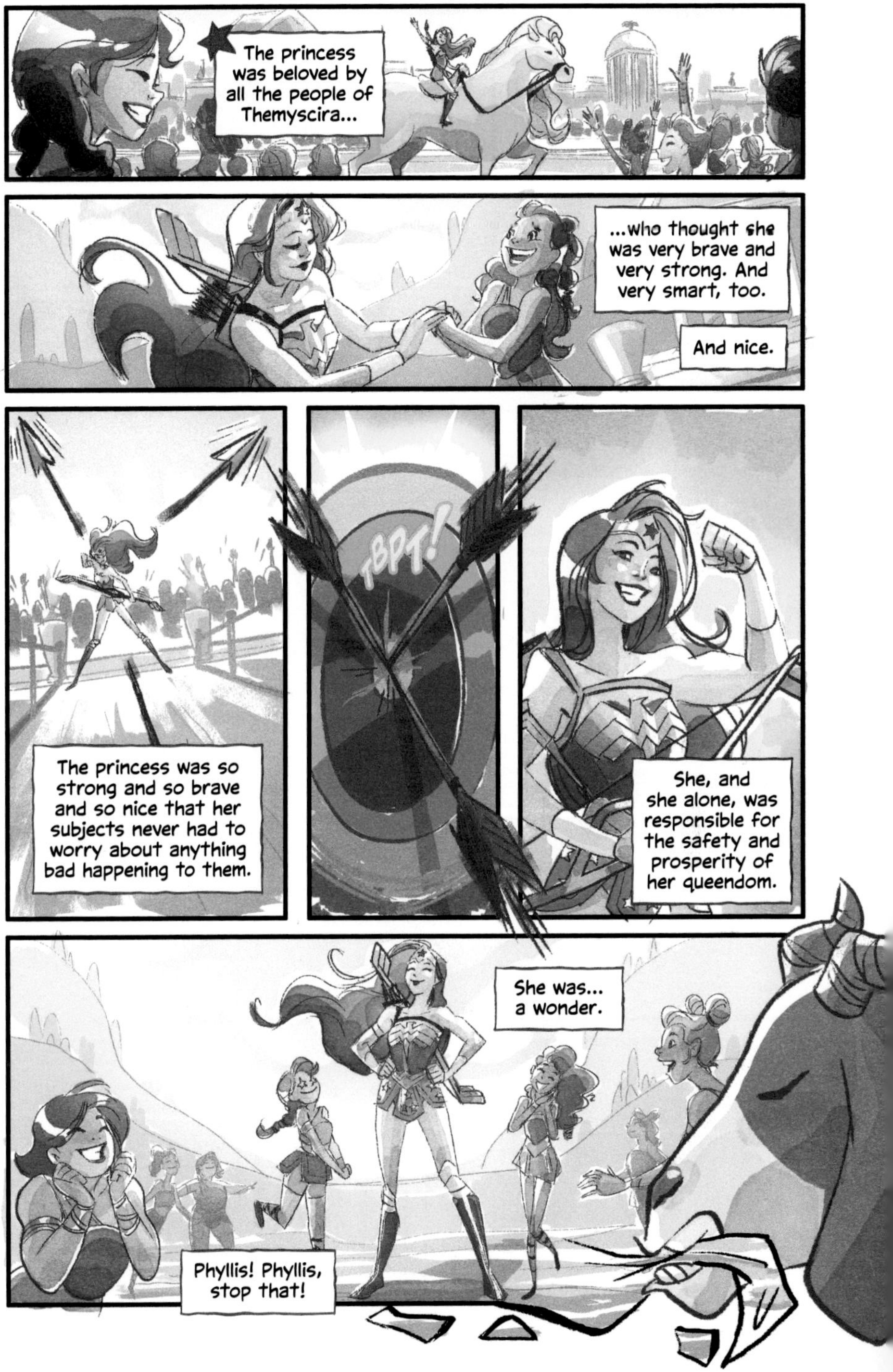

The princess was beloved by all the people of Themyscira...
...who thought she was very brave and very strong. And very smart, too.
And nice.
The princess was so strong and so brave and so nice that her subjects never had to worry about anything bad happening to them.
TBPT!
She, and she alone, was responsible for the safety and prosperity of her queendom.
She was... a wonder.
Phyllis! Phyllis, stop that!

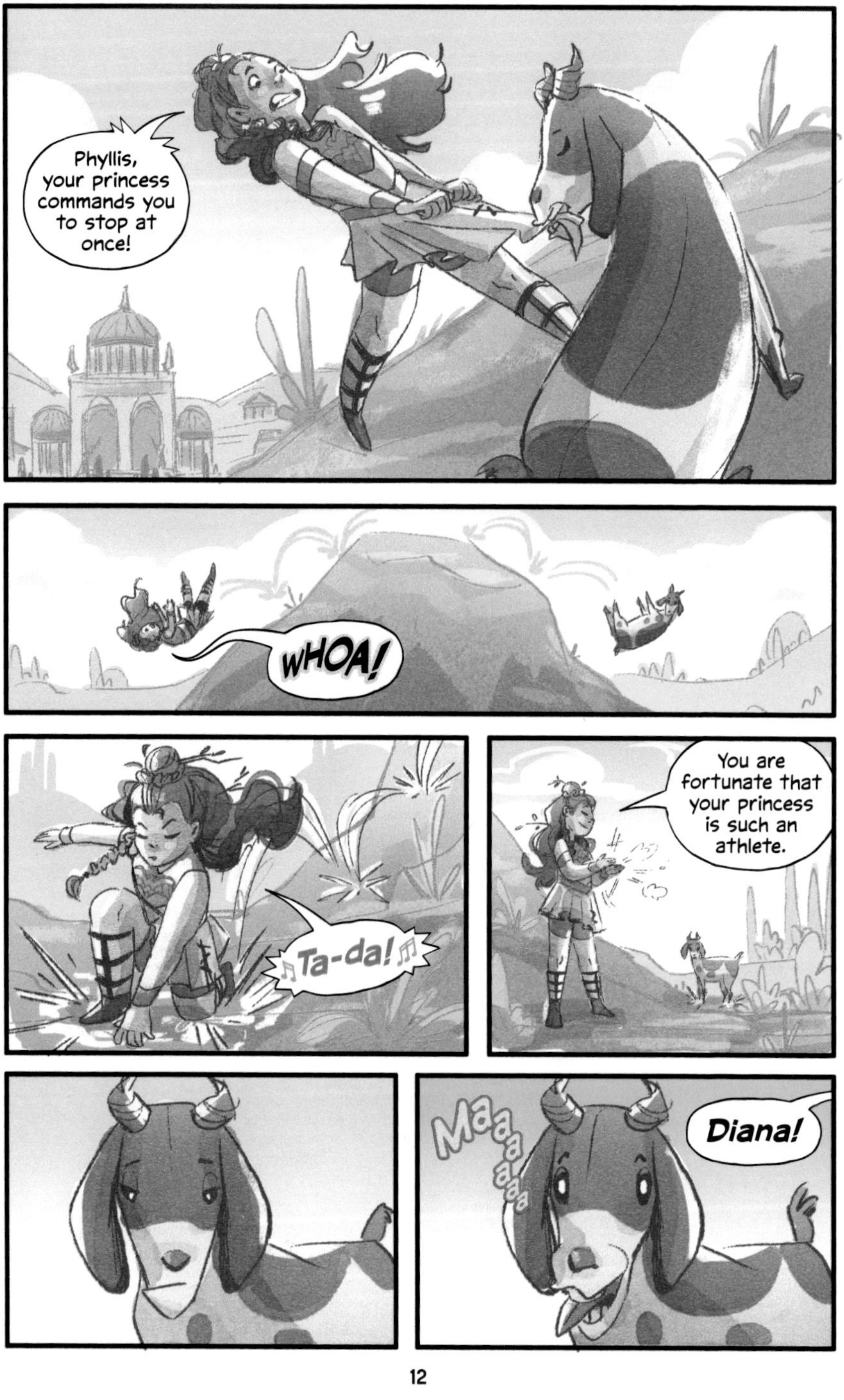
Phyllis, your princess commands you to stop at once!
WHOA!
Ta-da!
You are fortunate that your princess is such an athlete.
Maaaaaa
Diana!

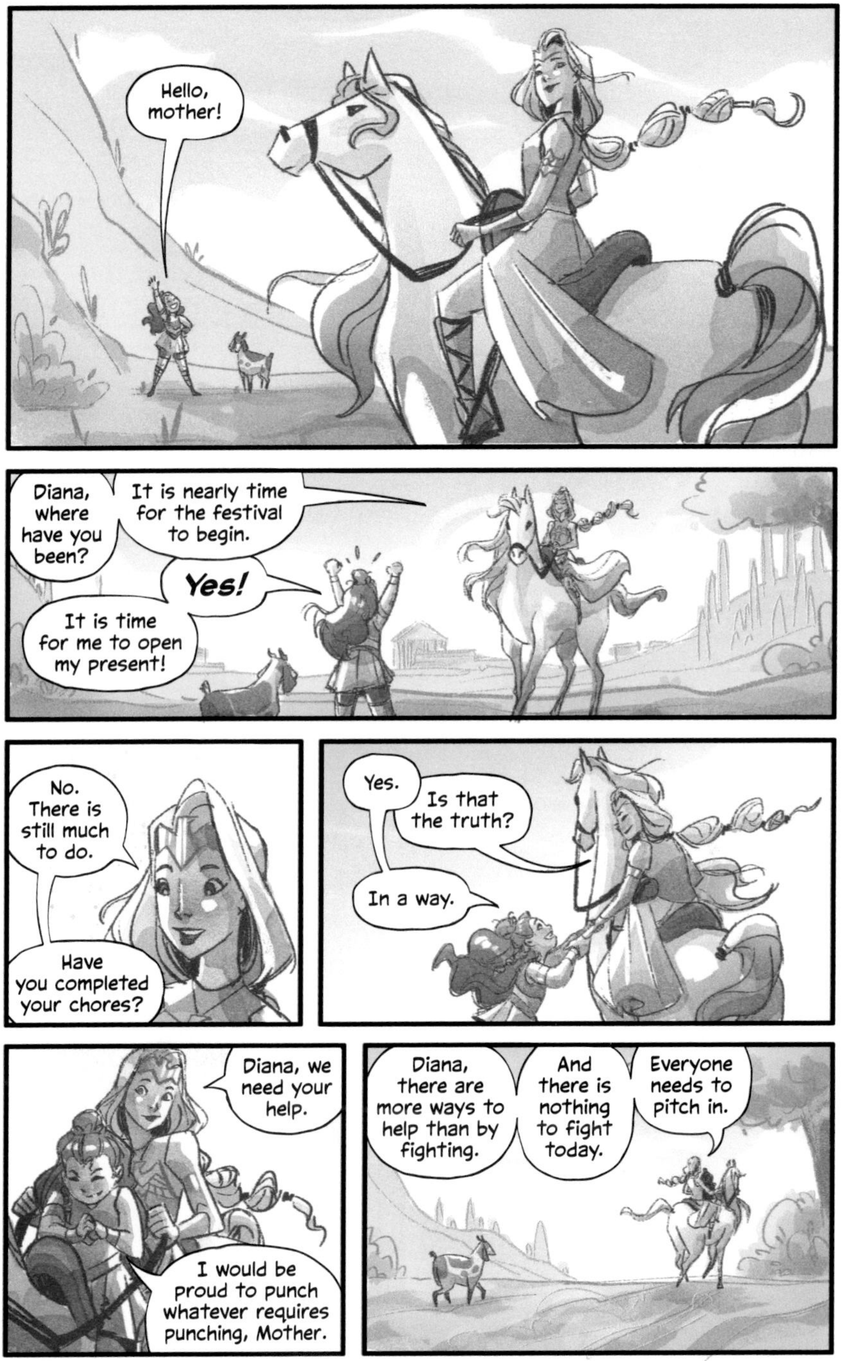
Hello, mother!
Diana, where have you been?
It is nearly time for the festival to begin.
Yes!
It is time for me to open my present!
No. There is still much to do.
Have you completed your chores?
Yes.
Is that the truth?
In a way.
Diana, we need your help.
I would be proud to punch whatever requires punching, Mother.
Diana, there are more ways to help than by fighting.
And there is nothing to fight today.
Everyone needs to pitch in.

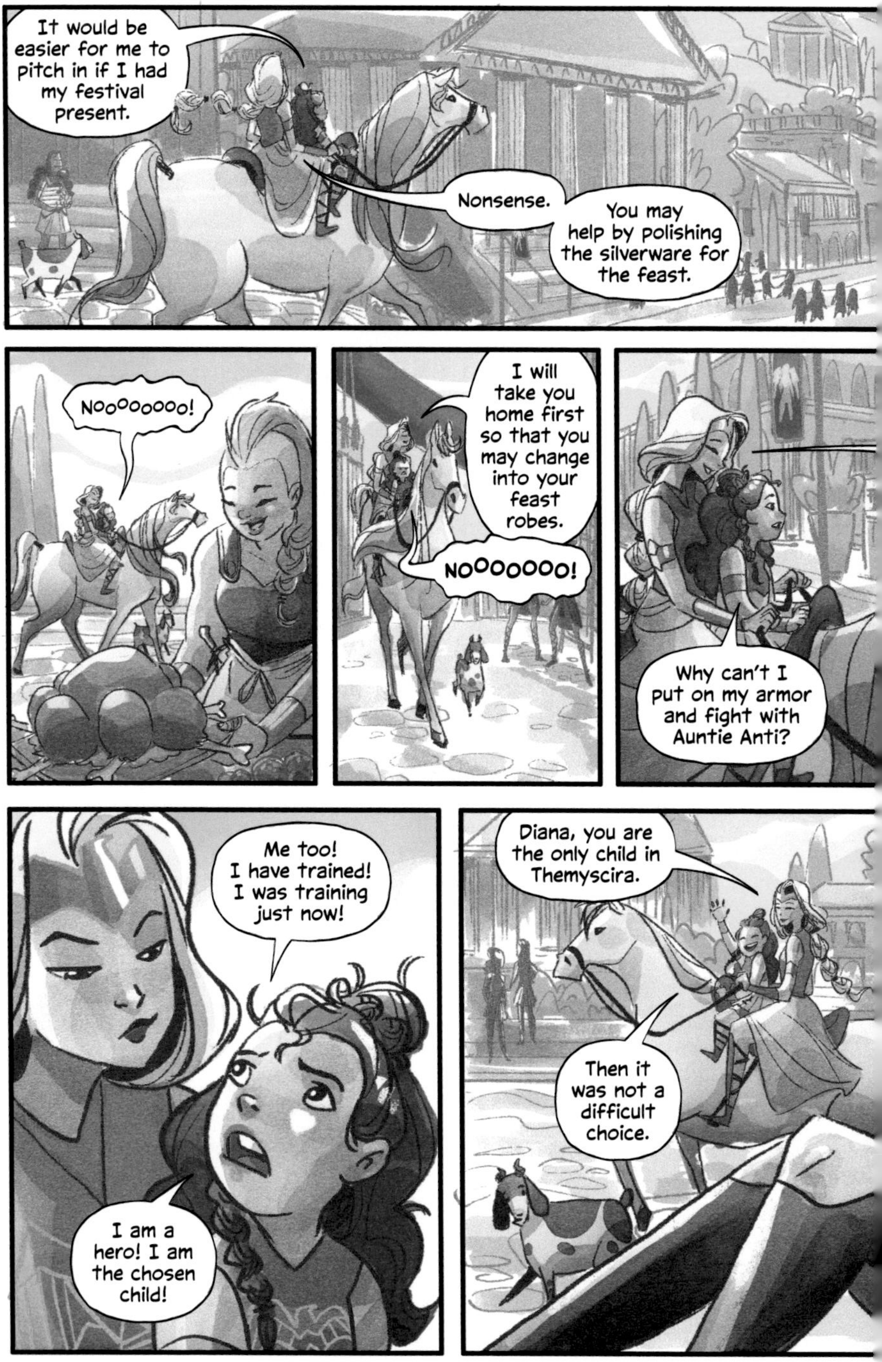
It would be easier for me to pitch in if I had my festival present.
Nonsense.
You may help by polishing the silverware for the feast.
Nooooooooo!
I will take you home first so that you may change into your feast robes.
NOOOOOOO!
Why can't I put on my armor and fight with Auntie Anti?
Me too! I have trained! I was training just now!
I am a hero! I am the chosen child!
Diana, you are the only child in Themyscira.
Then it was not a difficult choice.

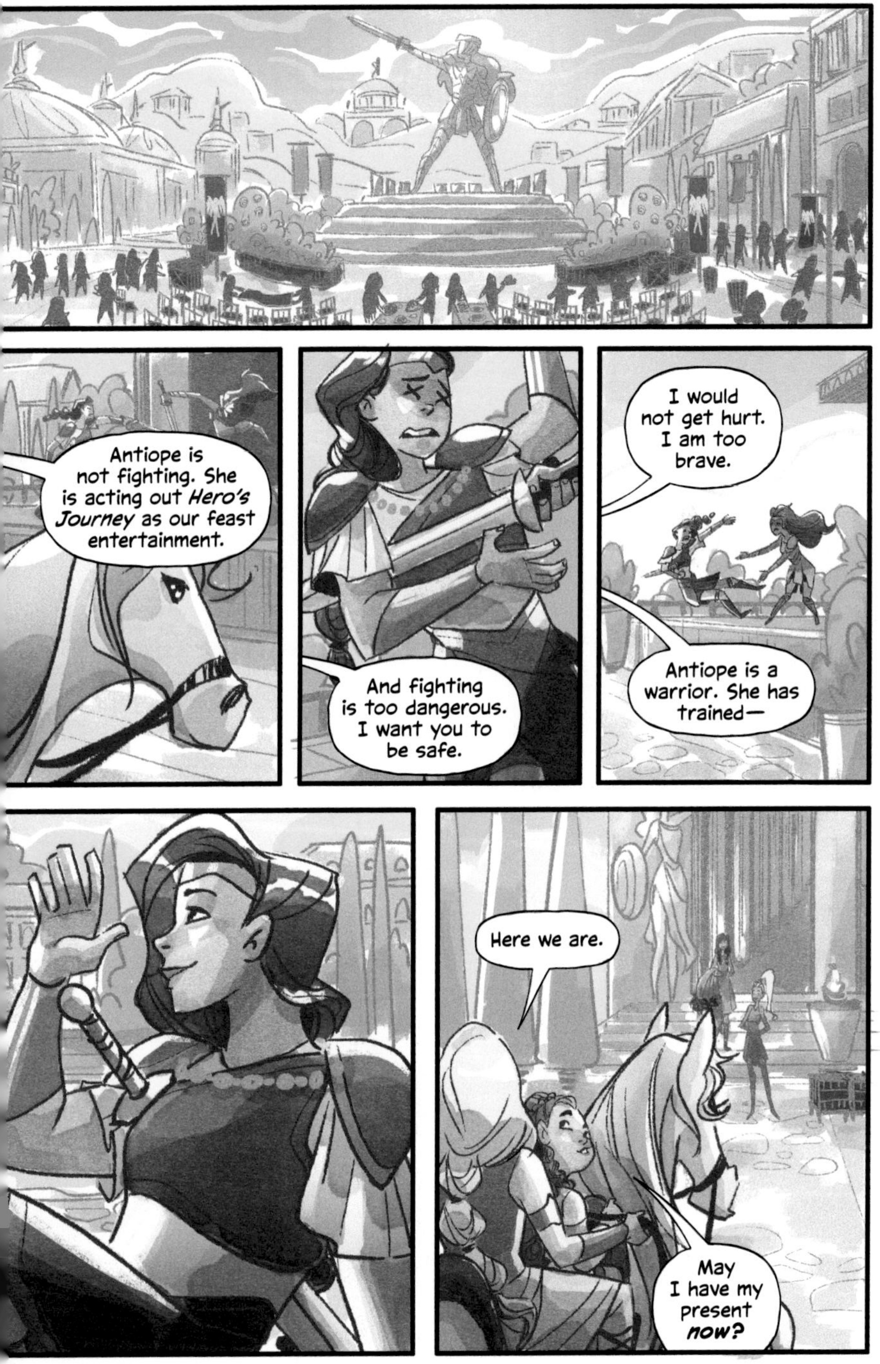
Antiope is not fighting. She is acting out *Hero's Journey* as our feast entertainment.
And fighting is too dangerous. I want you to be safe.
I would not get hurt. I am too brave.
Antiope is a warrior. She has trained—
Here we are.
May I have my present *now?*

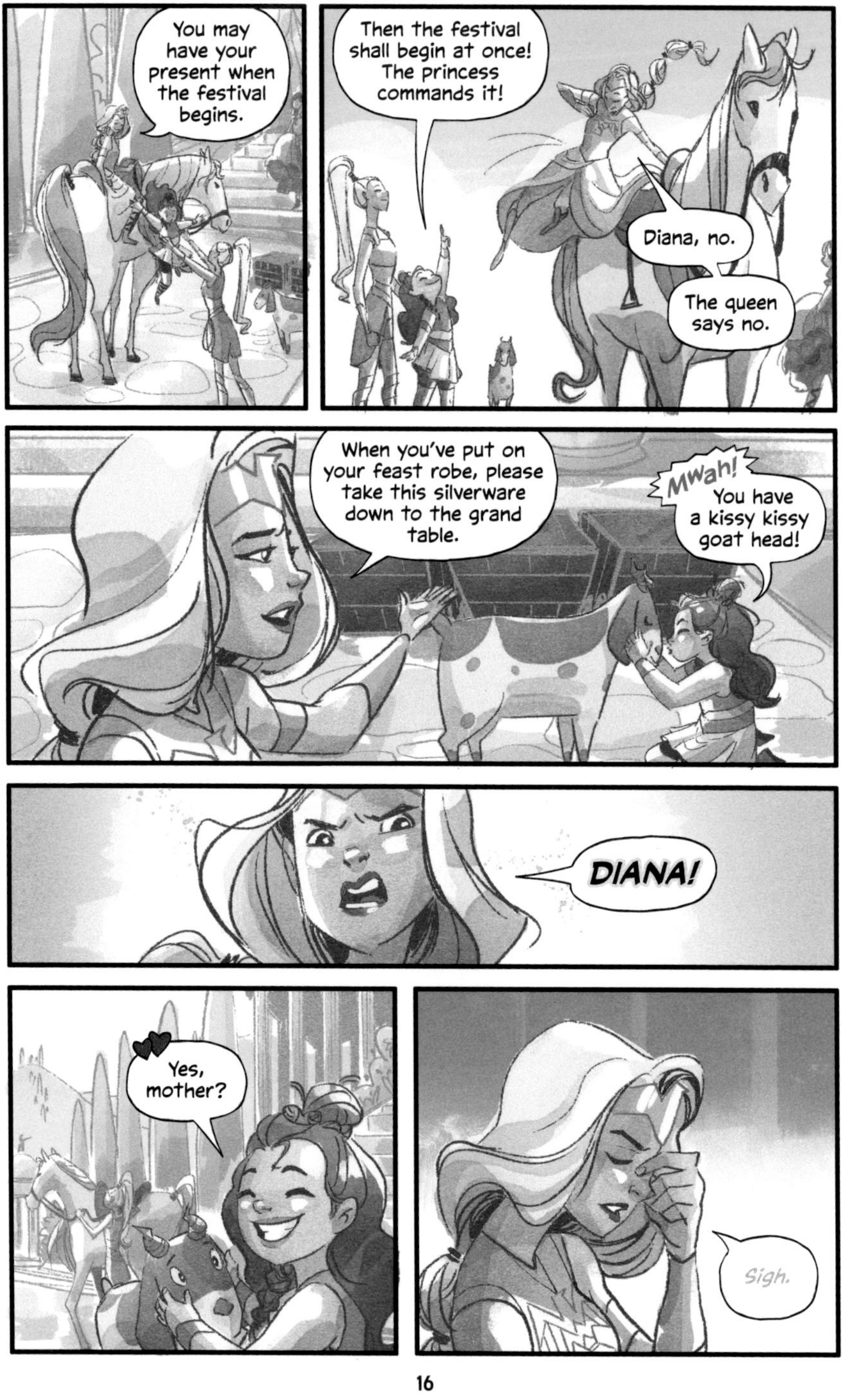
You may have your present when the festival begins.
Then the festival shall begin at once! The princess commands it!
Diana, no.
The queen says no.
When you've put on your feast robe, please take this silverware down to the grand table.
MWah!
You have a kissy kissy goat head!
DIANA!
Yes, mother?
Sigh.

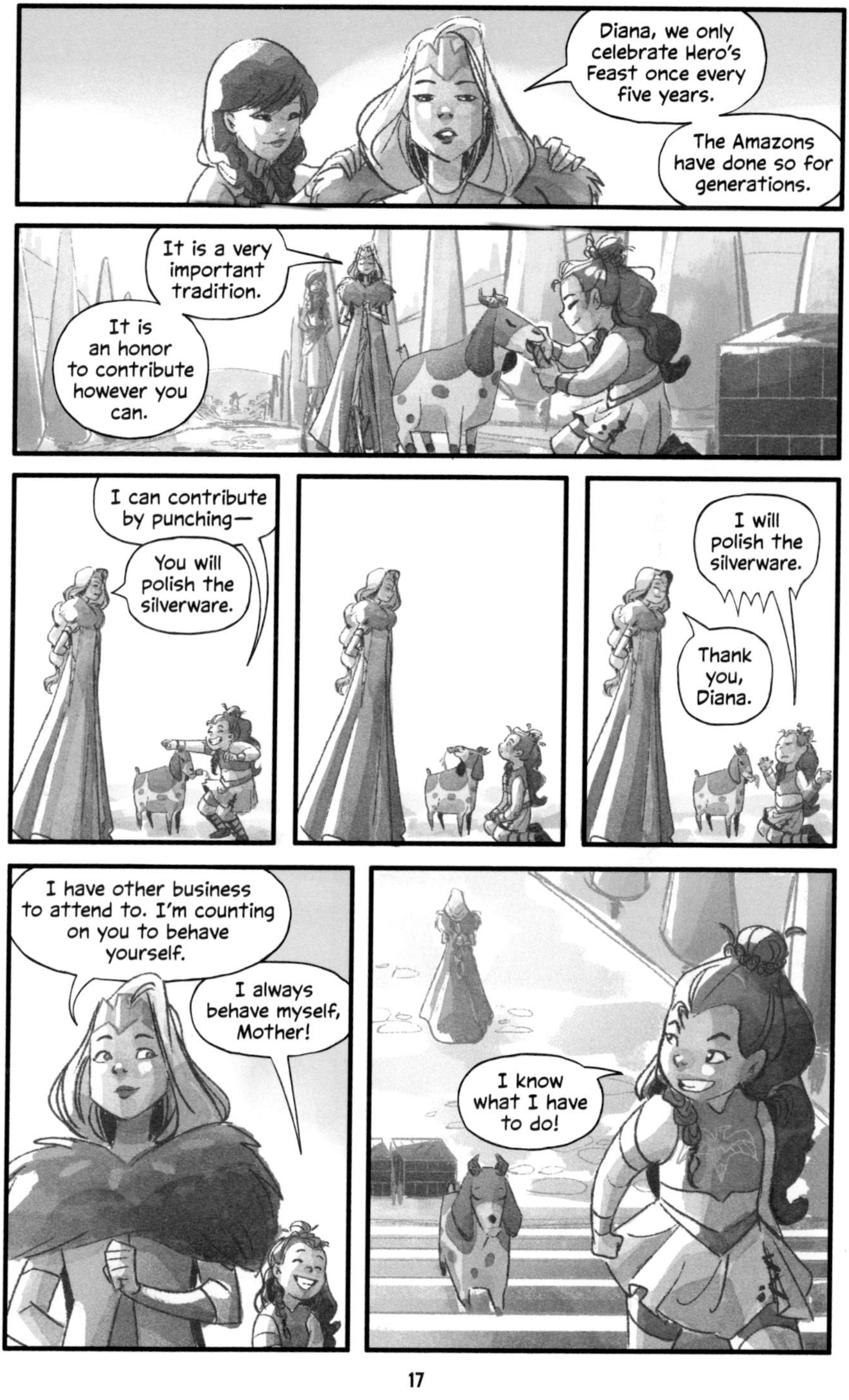
Diana, we only celebrate Hero's Feast once every five years.
The Amazons have done so for generations.
It is a very important tradition.
It is an honor to contribute however you can.
I can contribute by punching—
You will polish the silverware.
I will polish the silverware.
Thank you, Diana.
I have other business to attend to. I'm counting on you to behave yourself.
I always behave myself, Mother!
I know what I have to do!

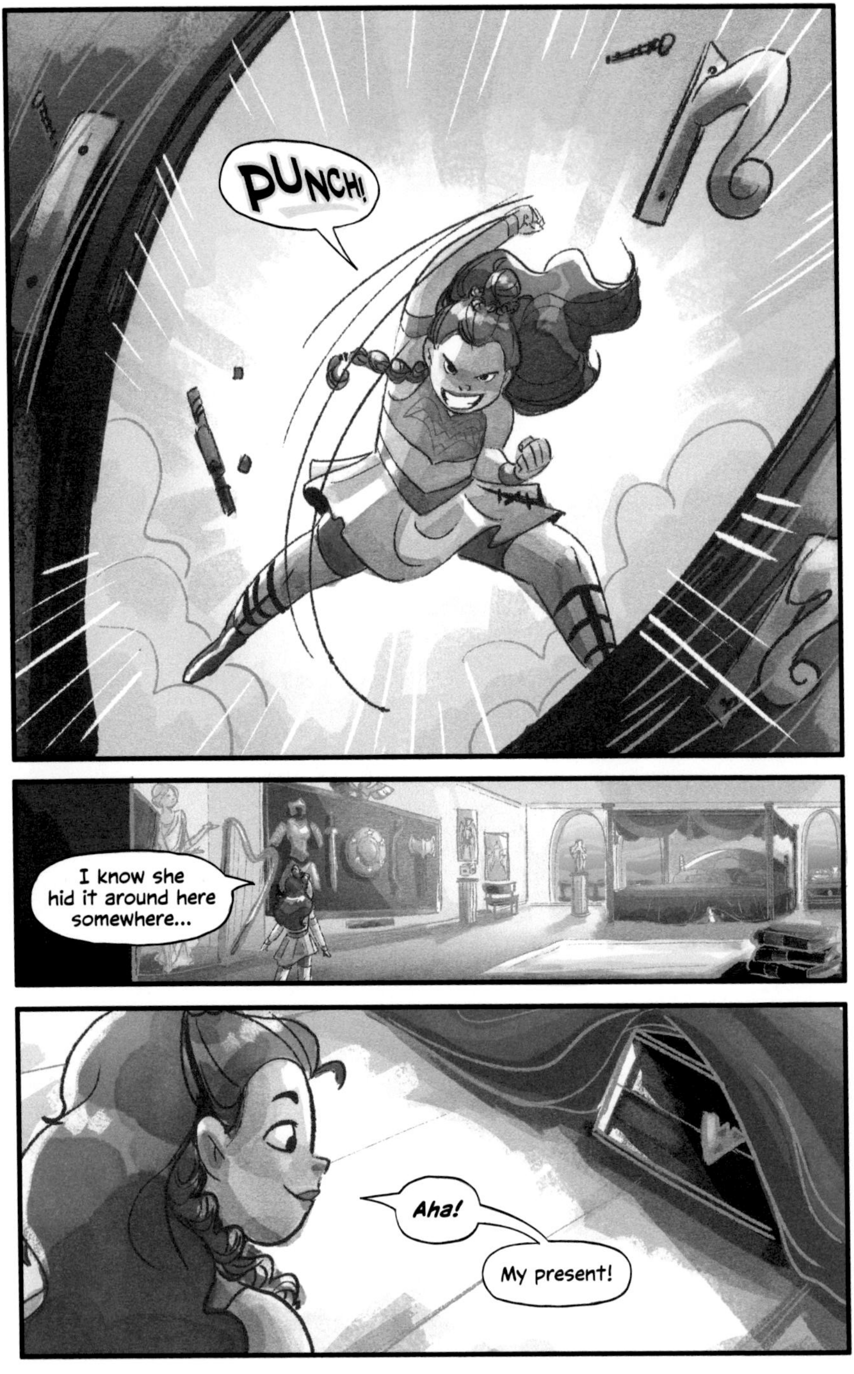
PUNCH!
I know she hid it around here somewhere...
Aha!
My present!

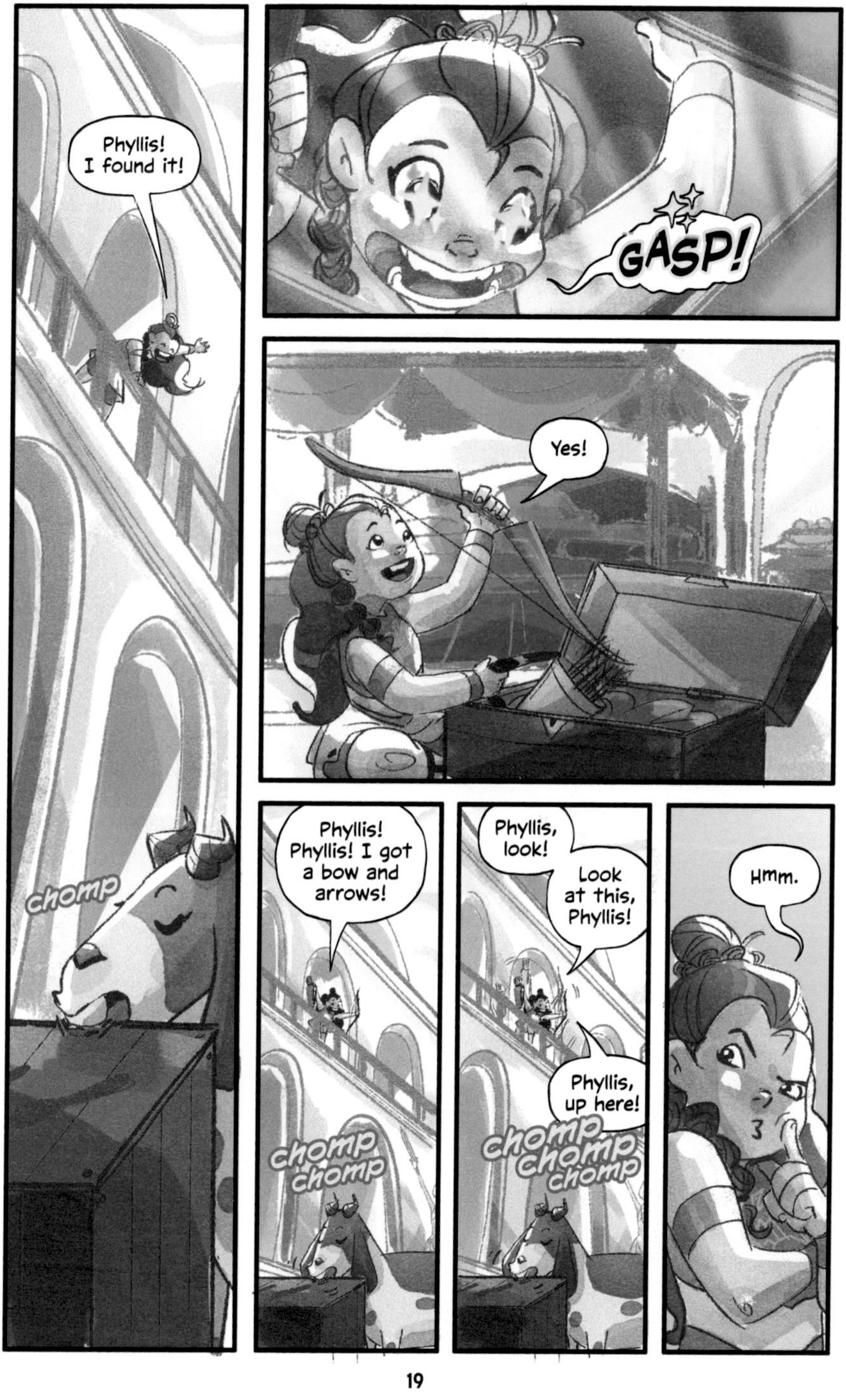
Phyllis! I found it!
GASP!
Yes!
chomp
Phyllis! Phyllis! I got a bow and arrows!
chomp chomp
Phyllis, look!
Look at this, Phyllis!
Phyllis, up here!
chomp chomp chomp
Hmm.

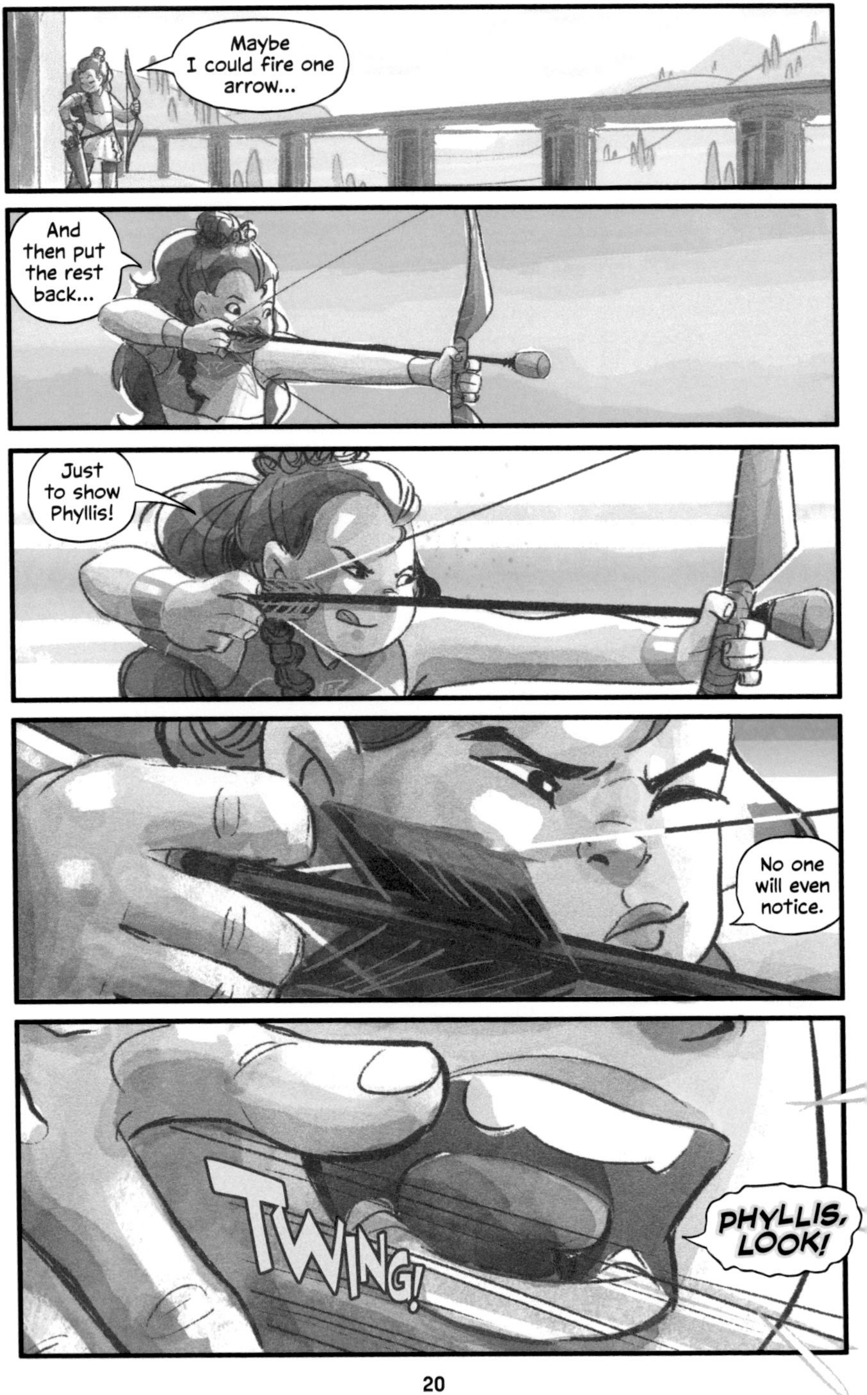
Maybe I could fire one arrow...
And then put the rest back...
Just to show Phyllis!
No one will even notice.
TWING!
PHYLLIS, LOOK!

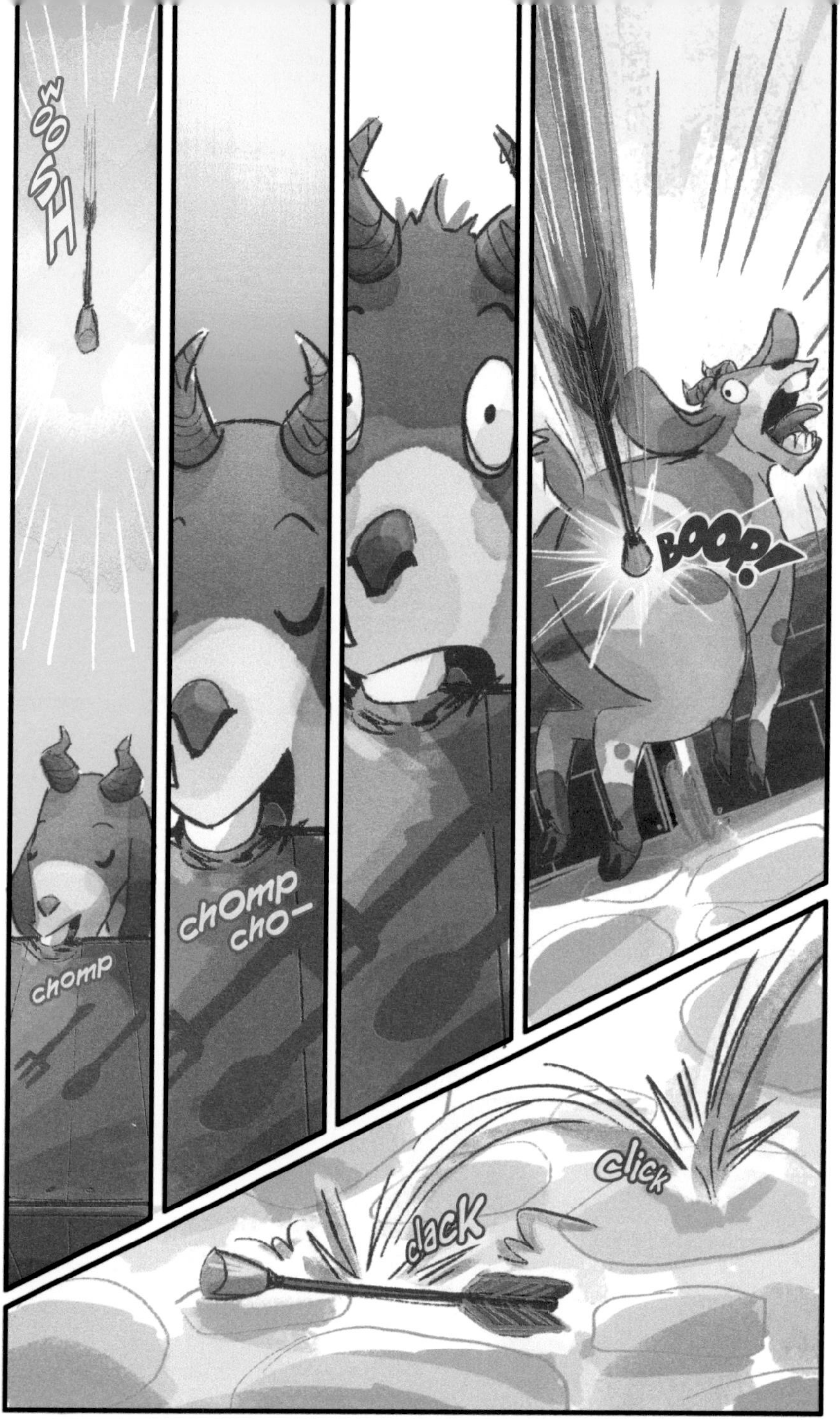
WOOSH
chomp
chomp
cho-
BOOP!
click
clack

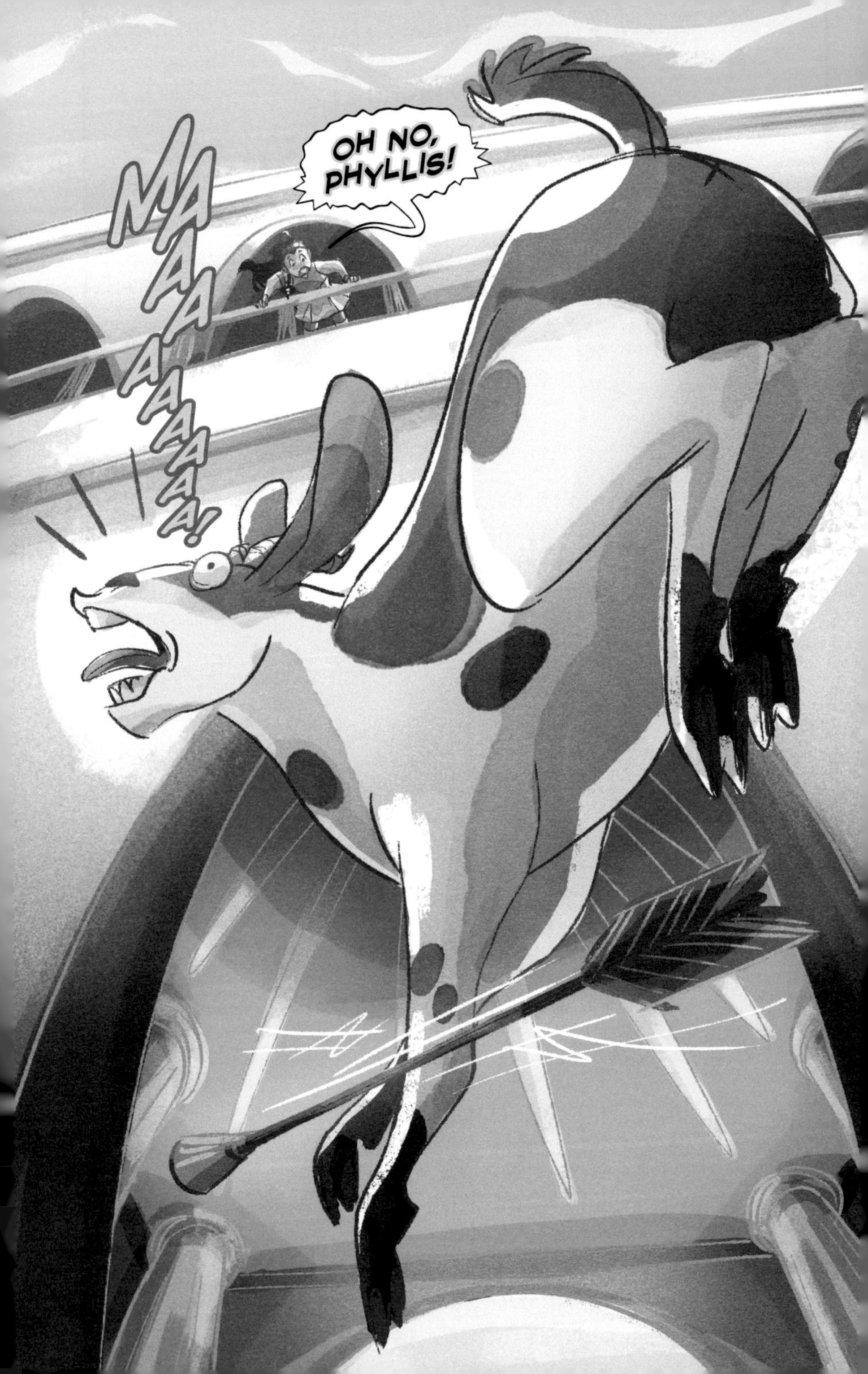
OH NO, PHYLLIS!
MAAAAAAAAAA!

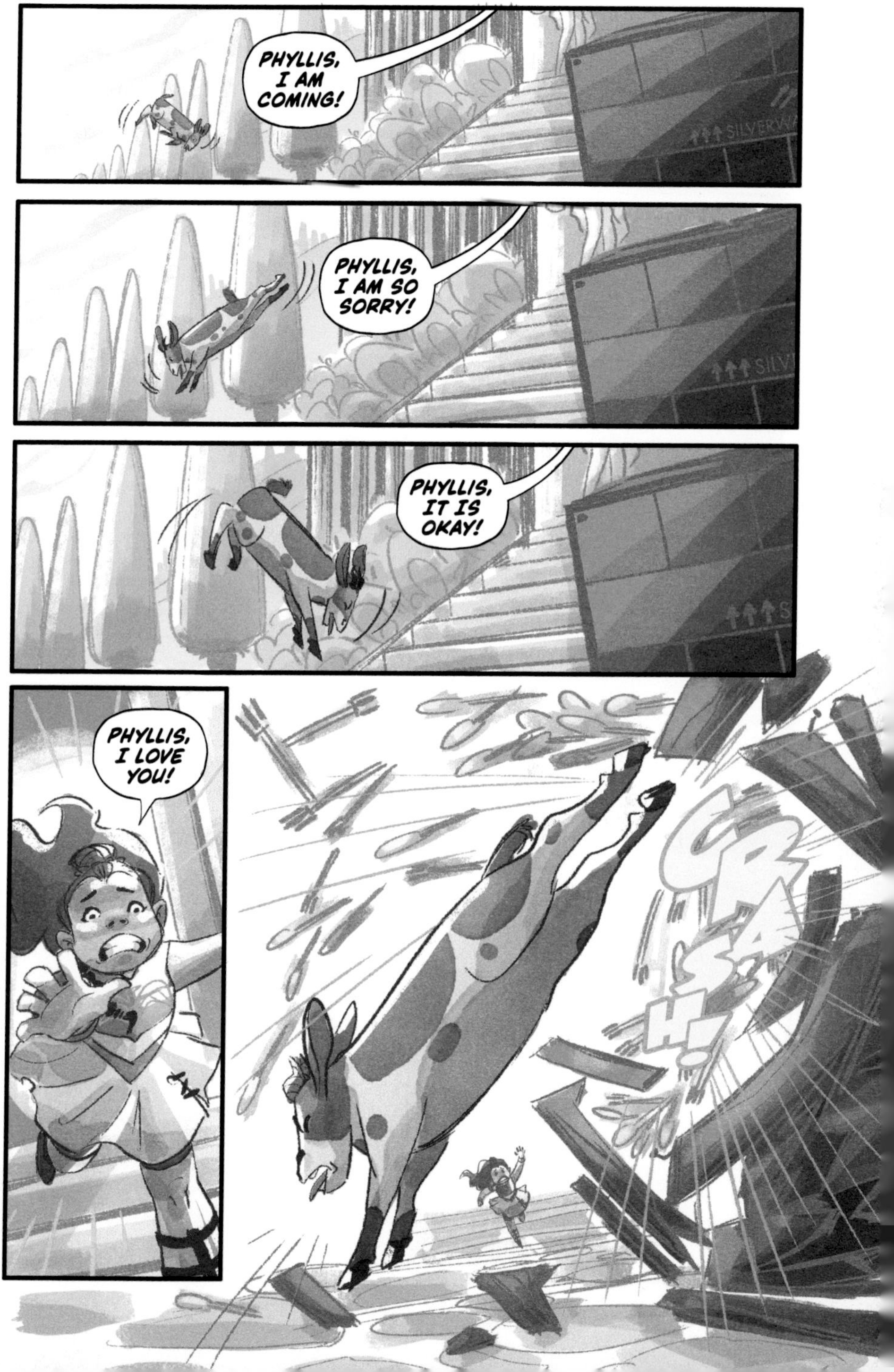
PHYLLIS, I AM COMING!
SILVERW
PHYLLIS, I AM SO SORRY!
PHYLLIS, IT IS OKAY!
PHYLLIS, I LOVE YOU!
CRASH!

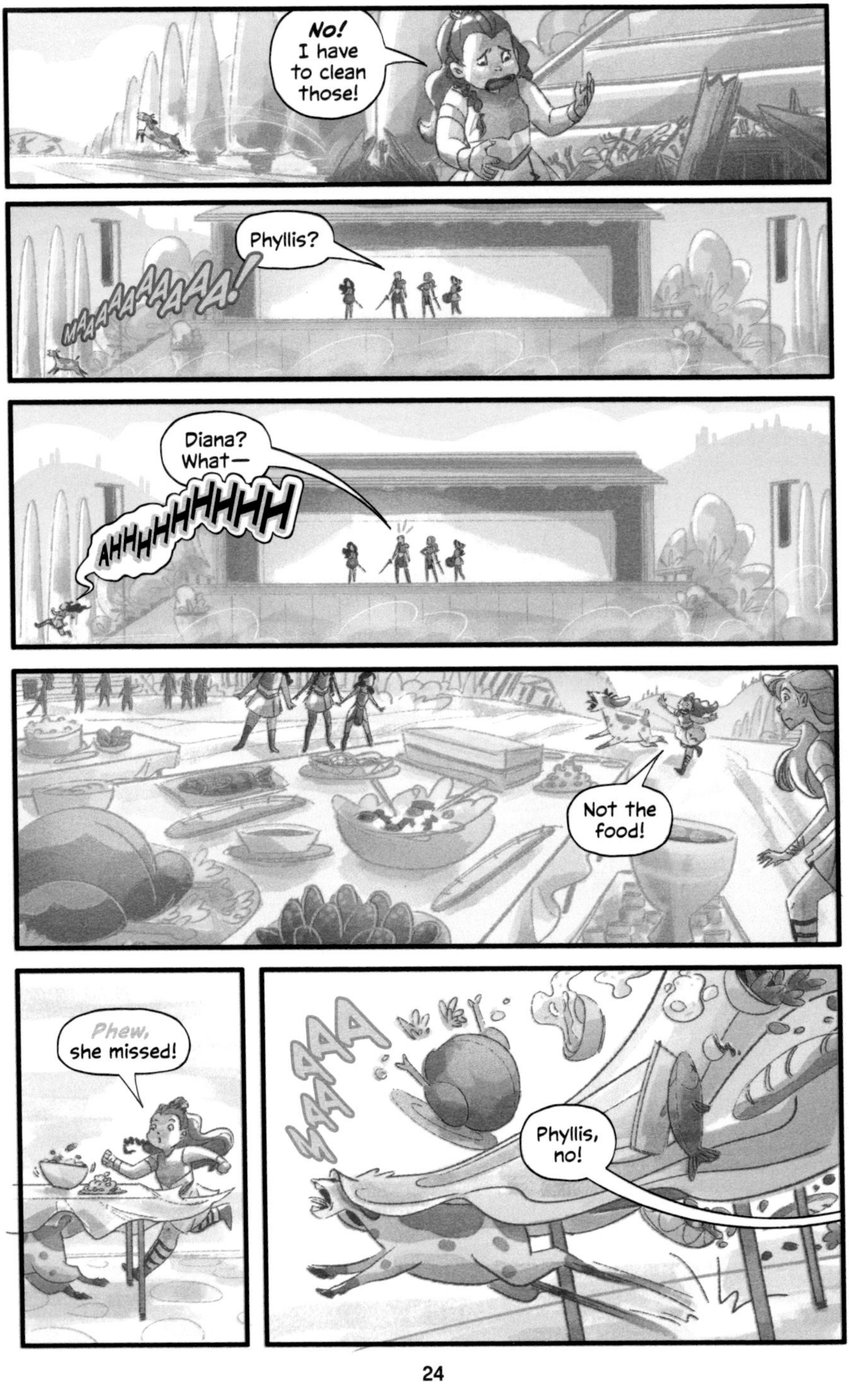
No! I have to clean those!
Phyllis?
MAAAAAAAAAA!
Diana? What—
AHHHHHHHHHH
Not the food!
Phew, she missed!
MAAAAA
Phyllis, no!

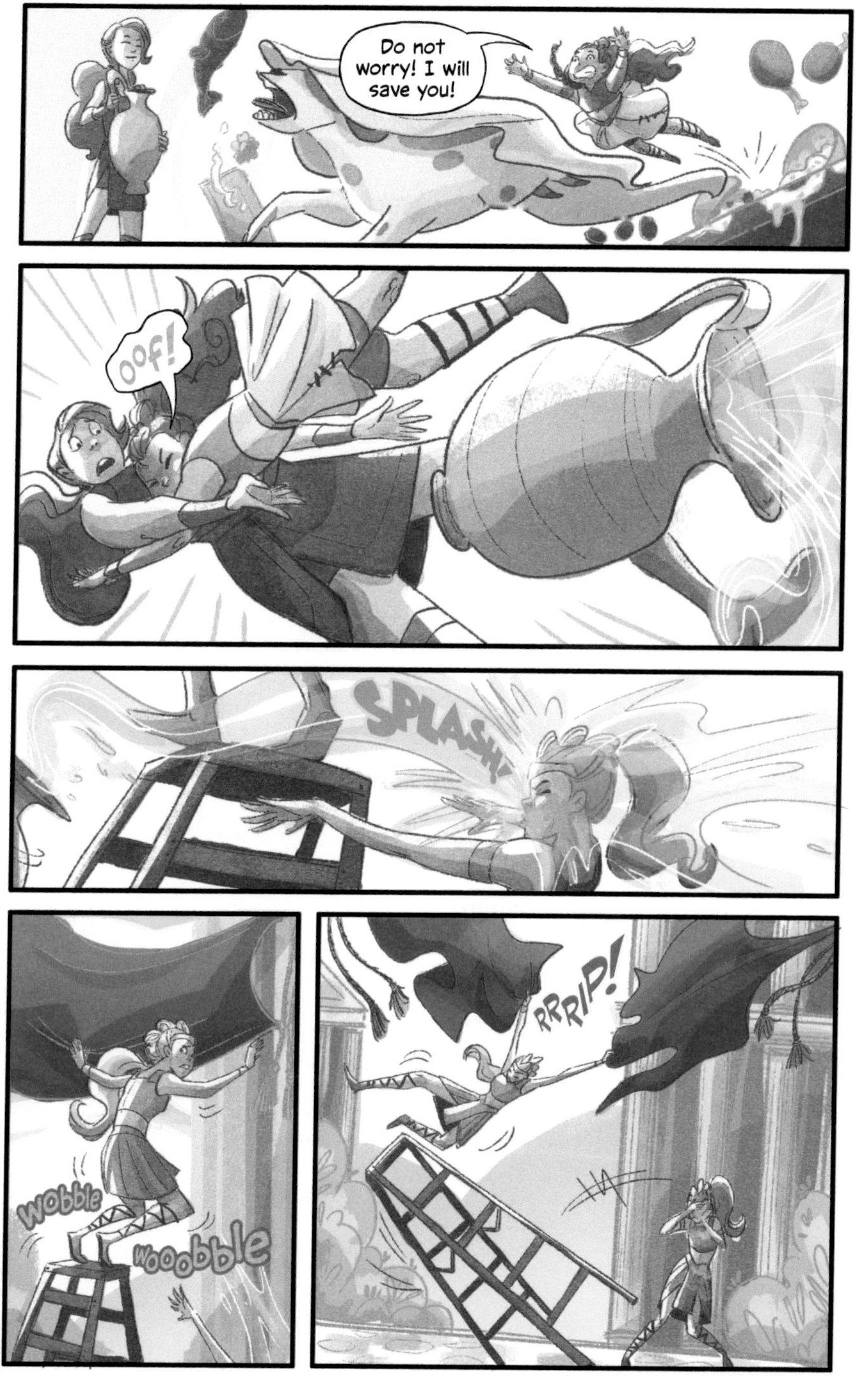
Do not worry! I will save you!
OOF!
SPLASH!
wobble
wooobble
RRRIP!

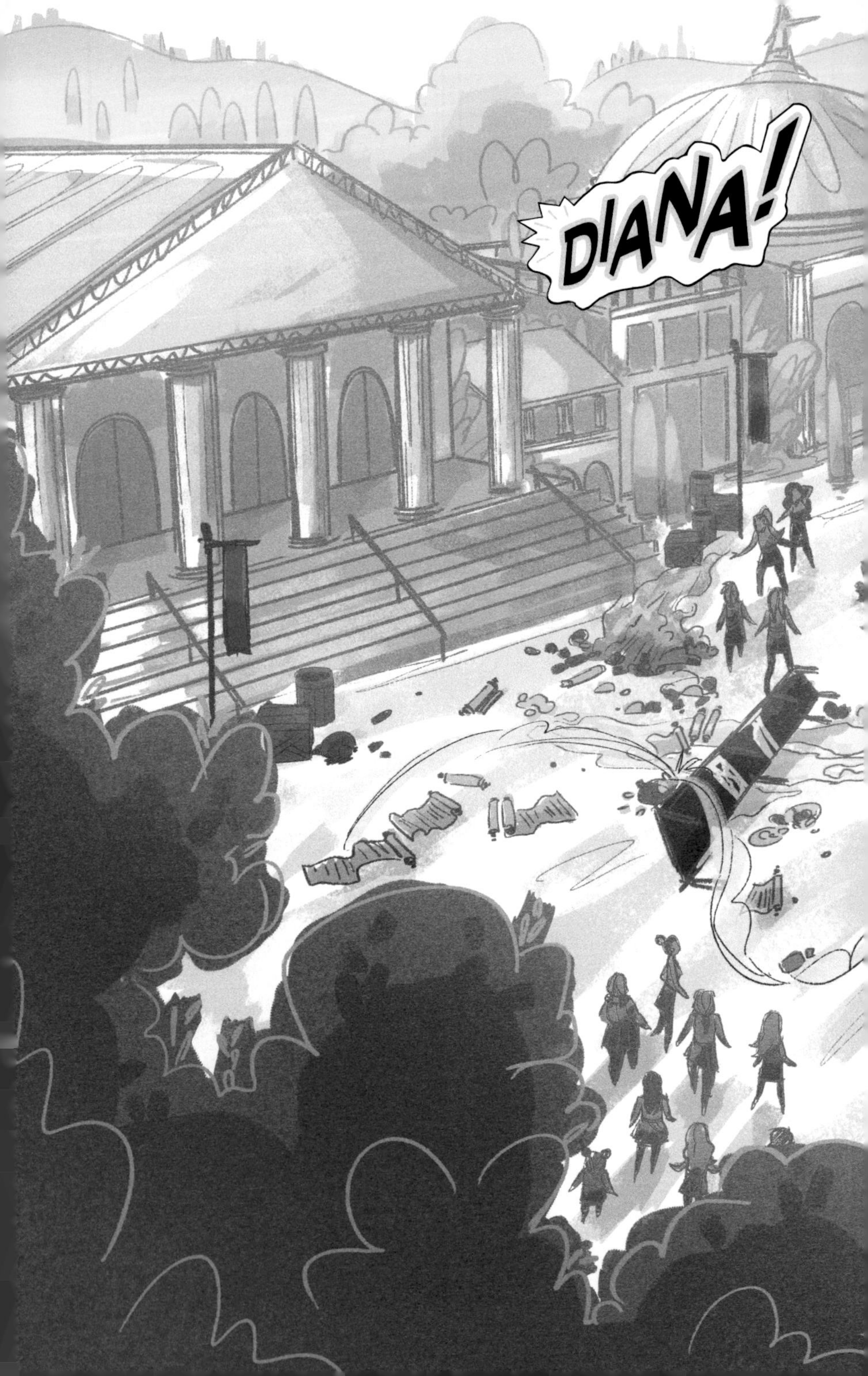
DIANA!

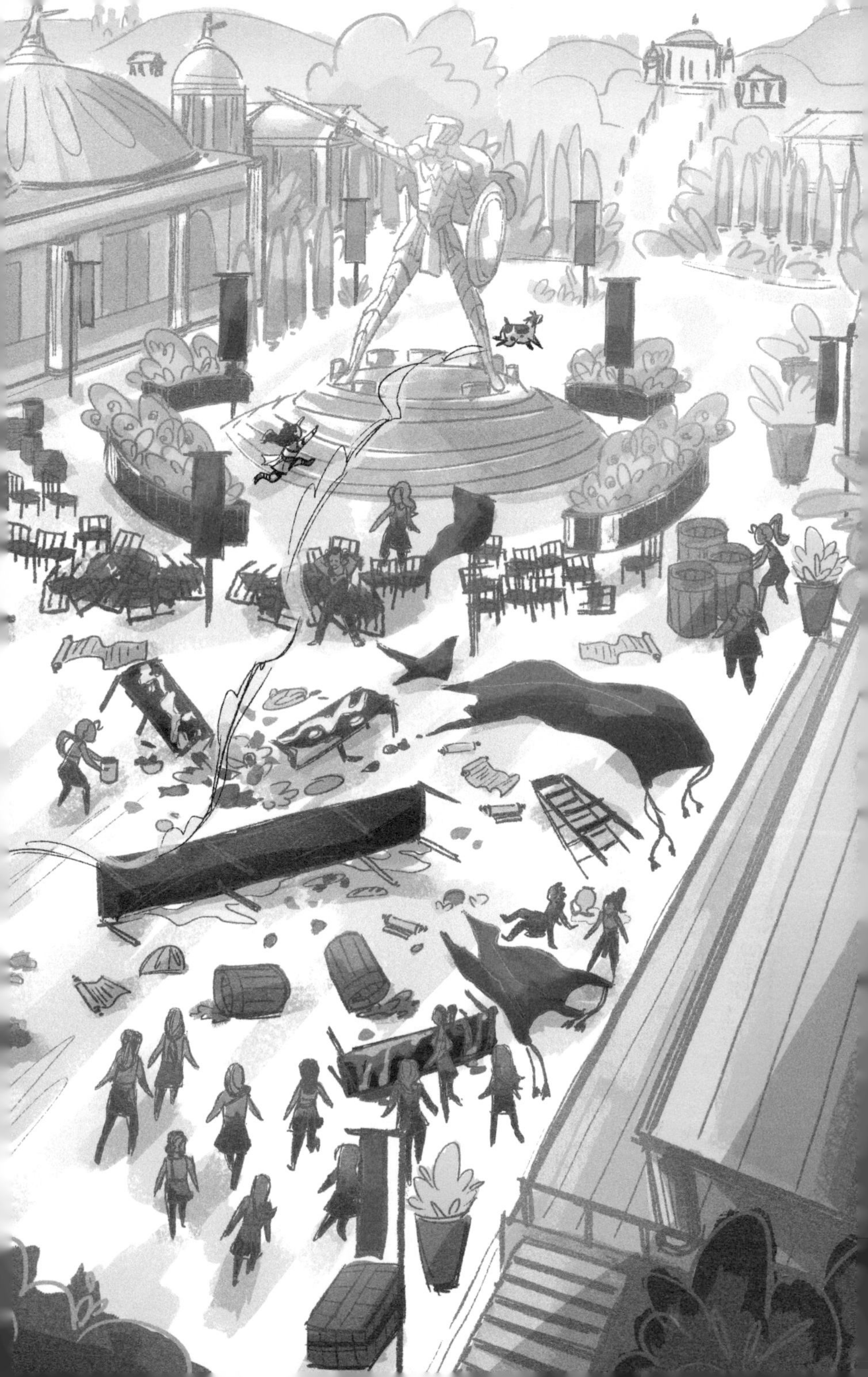

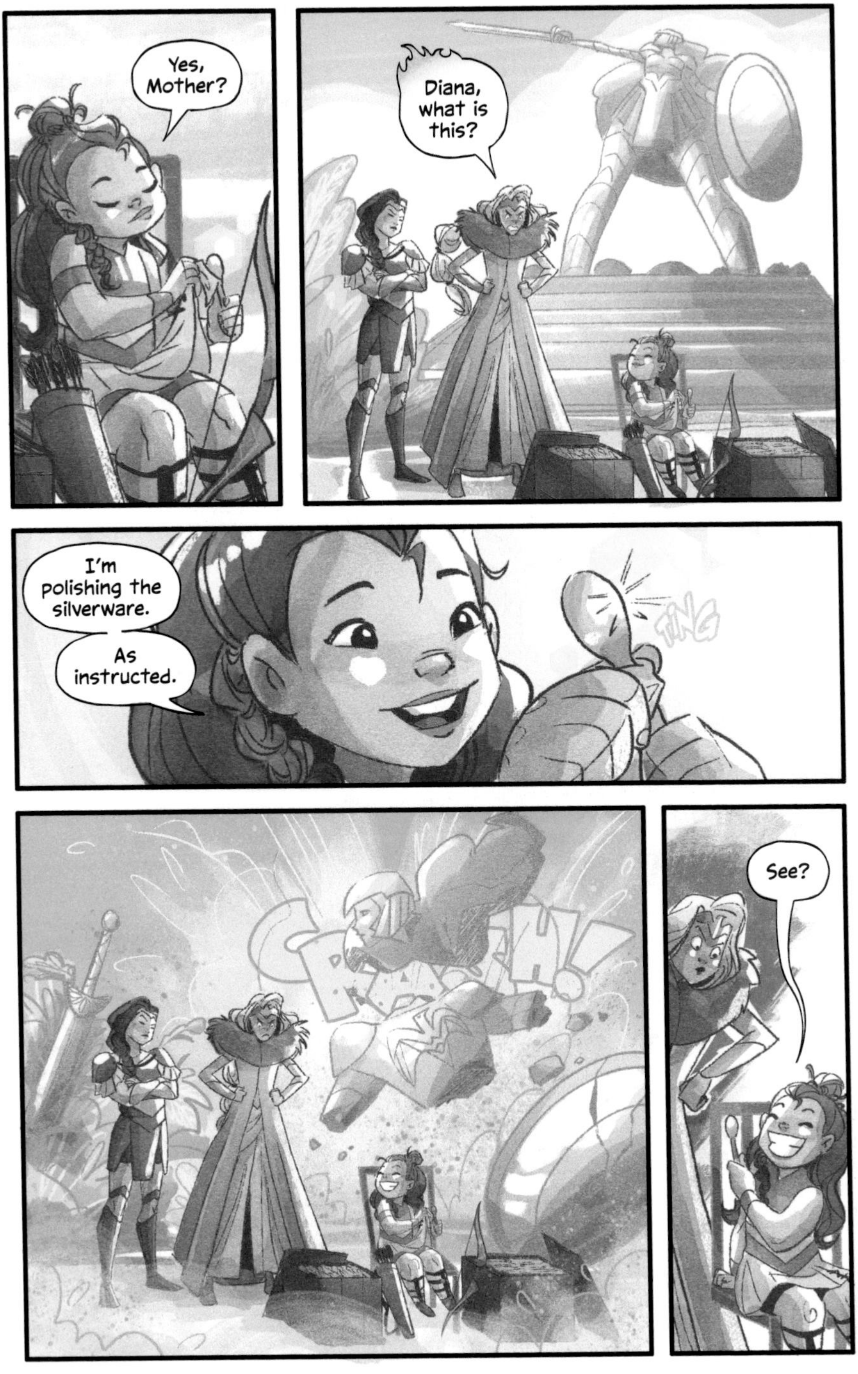
Yes, Mother?
Diana, what is this?
I'm polishing the silverware.
As instructed.
TING
See?

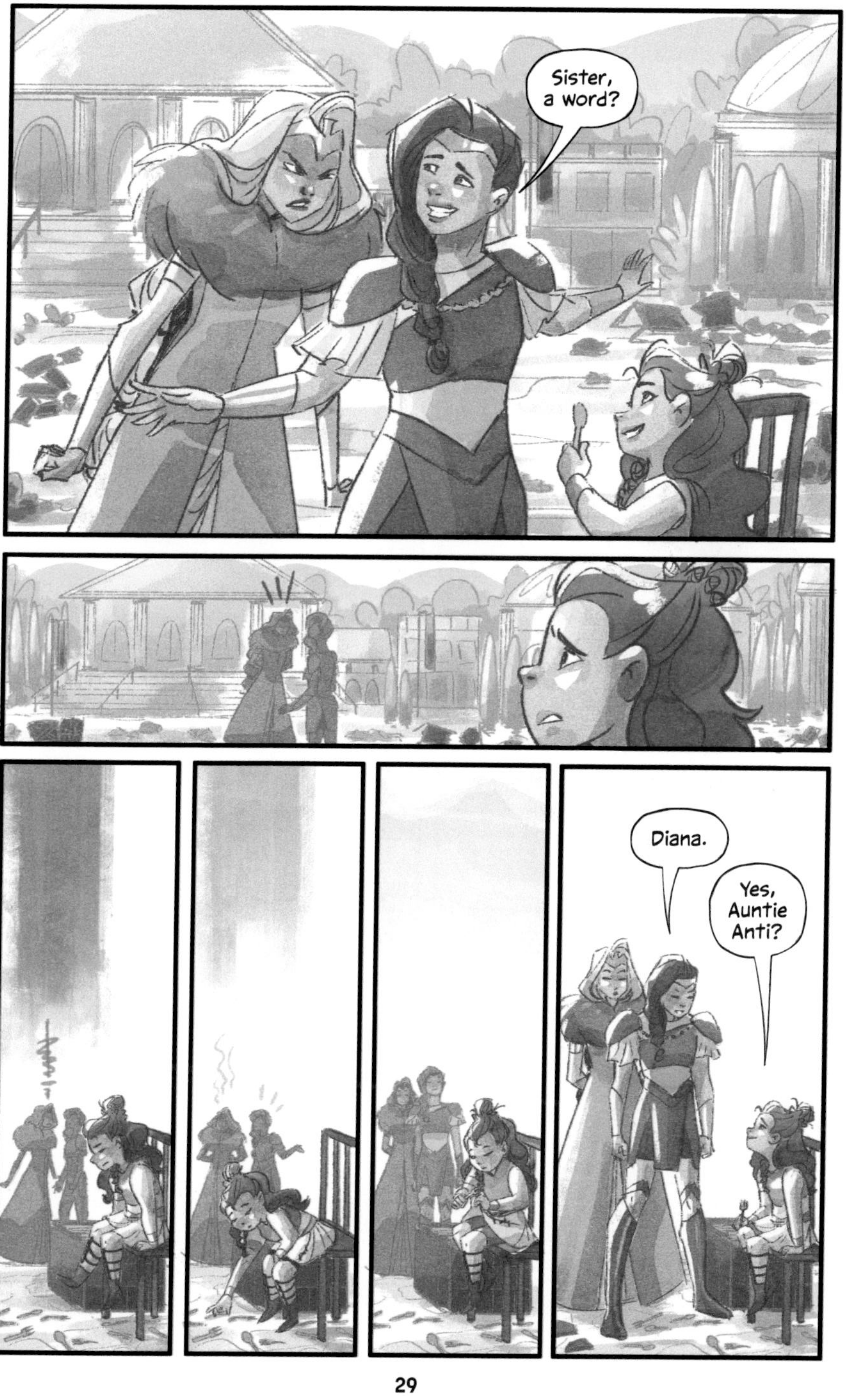
Sister, a word?
Diana.
Yes, Auntie Anti?

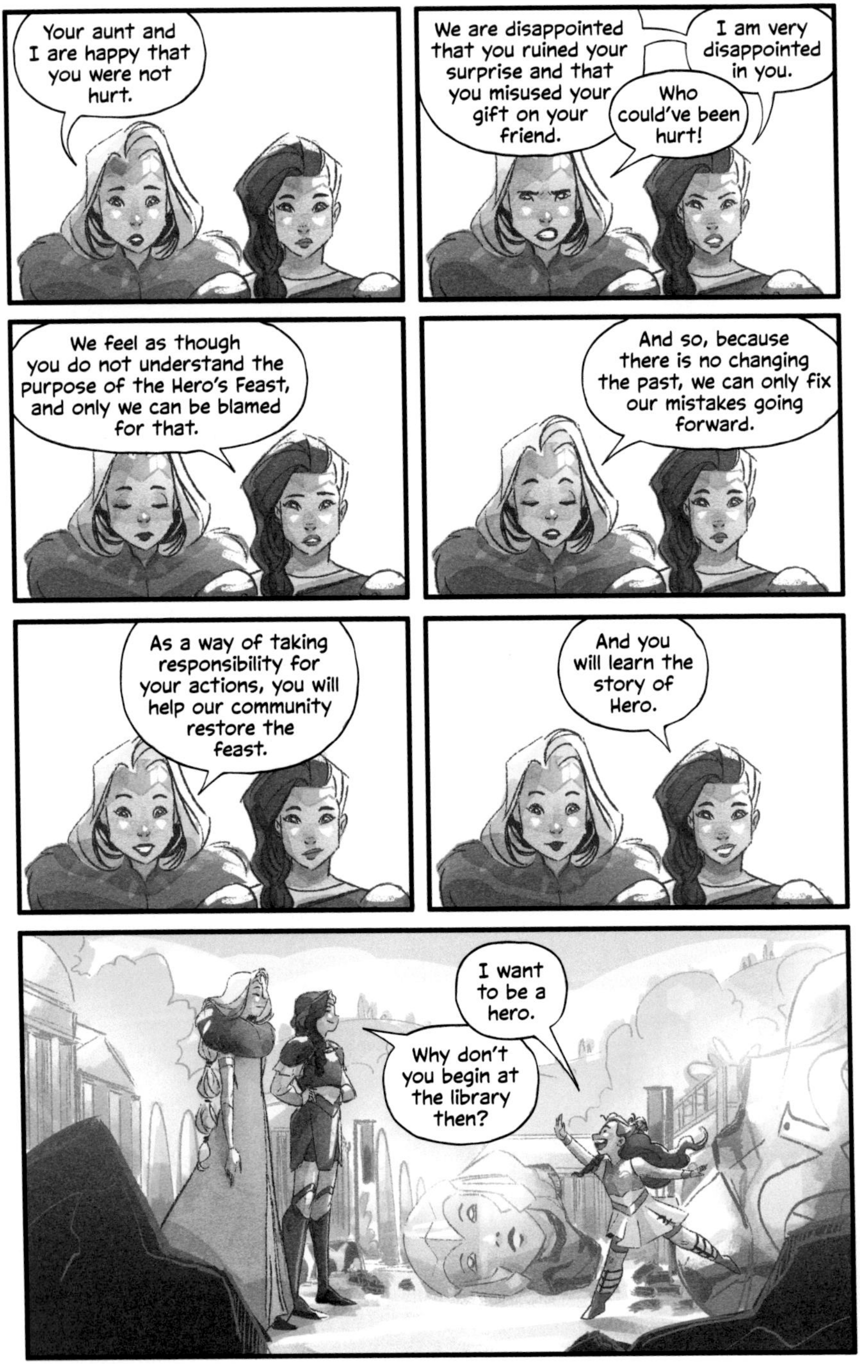
Your aunt and I are happy that you were not hurt.
We are disappointed that you ruined your surprise and that you misused your gift on your friend.
I am very disappointed in you.
Who could've been hurt!
We feel as though you do not understand the purpose of the Hero's Feast, and only we can be blamed for that.
And so, because there is no changing the past, we can only fix our mistakes going forward.
As a way of taking responsibility for your actions, you will help our community restore the feast.
And you will learn the story of Hero.
I want to be a hero.
Why don't you begin at the library then?

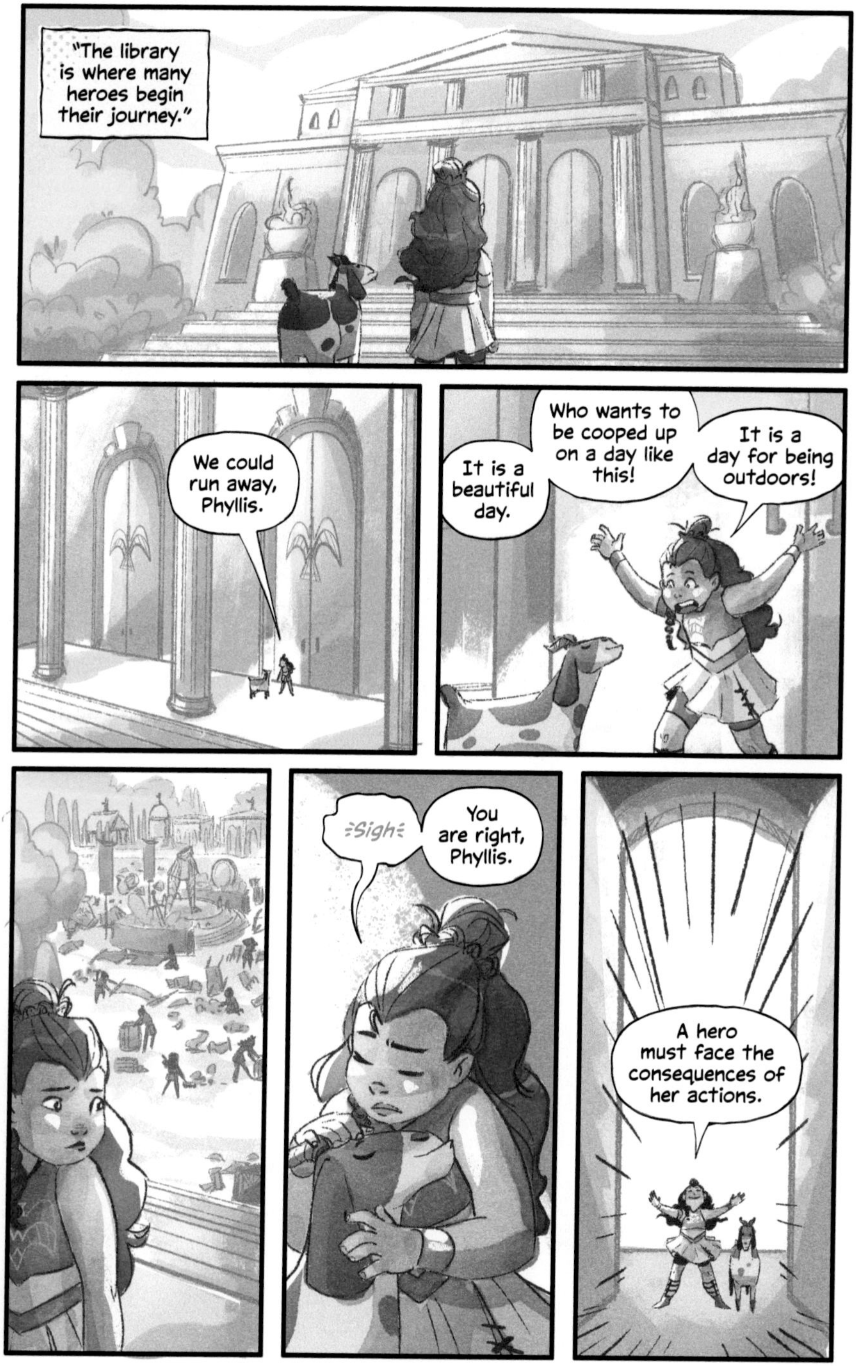
"The library is where many heroes begin their journey."
We could run away, Phyllis.
It is a beautiful day.
Who wants to be cooped up on a day like this!
It is a day for being outdoors!
Sigh
You are right, Phyllis.
A hero must face the consequences of her actions.

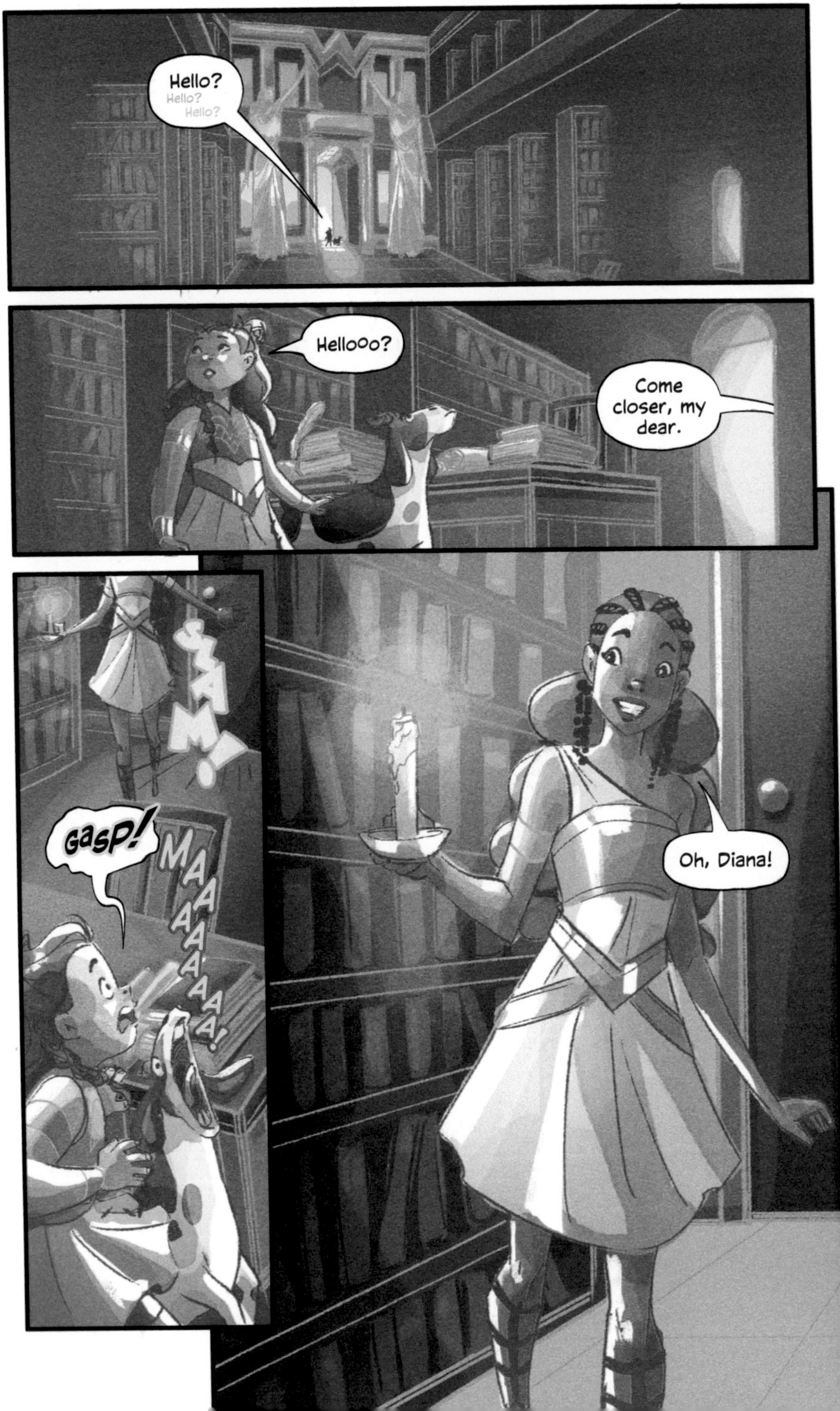
Hello?
Hello?
Hello?
Hellooo?
Come closer, my dear.
SLAM!
GASP!
MAAAAAAAA!
Oh, Diana!

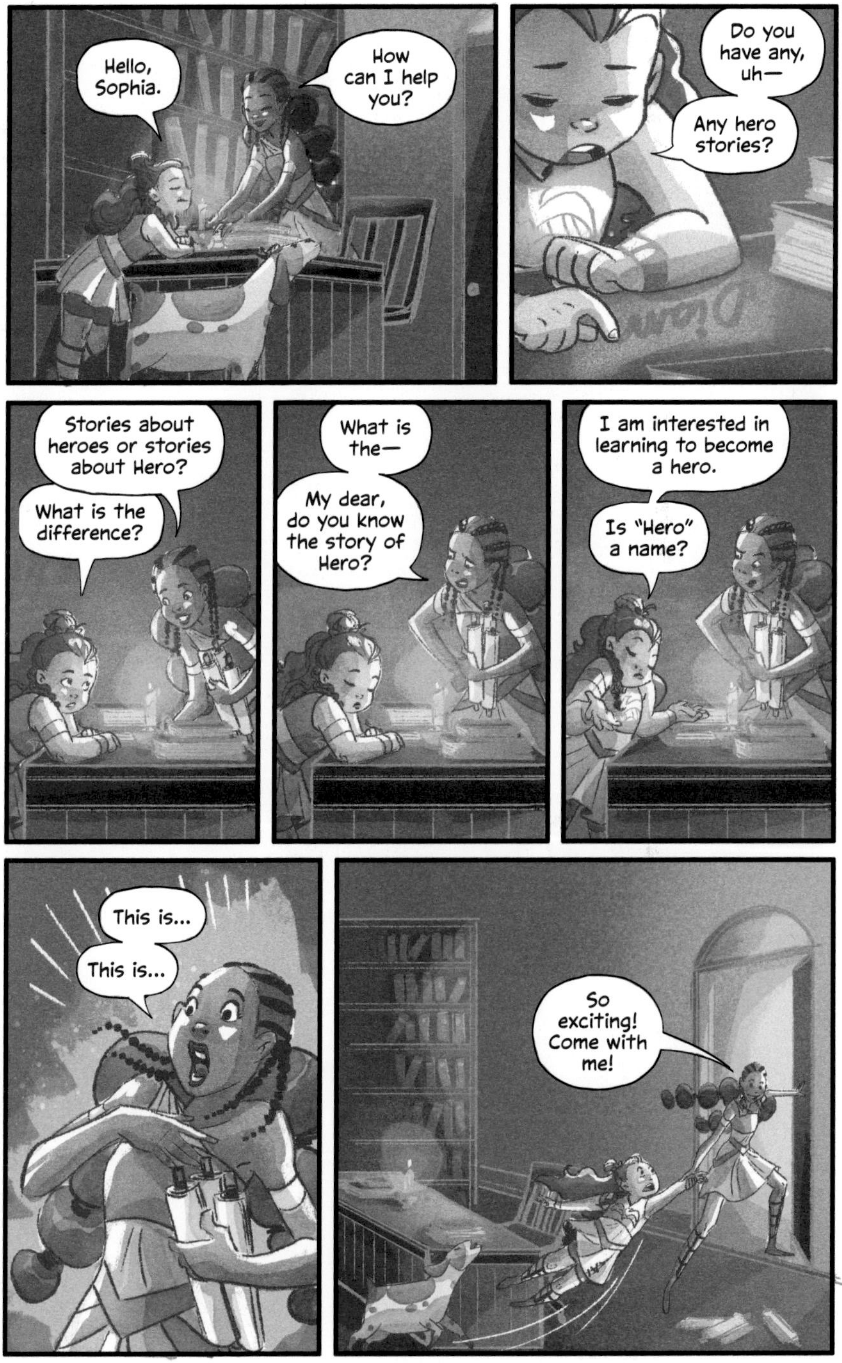

Hello, Sophia.
How can I help you?
Do you have any, uh—
Any hero stories?
Stories about heroes or stories about Hero?
What is the difference?
What is the—
My dear, do you know the story of Hero?
I am interested in learning to become a hero.
Is "Hero" a name?
This is...
This is...
So exciting! Come with me!

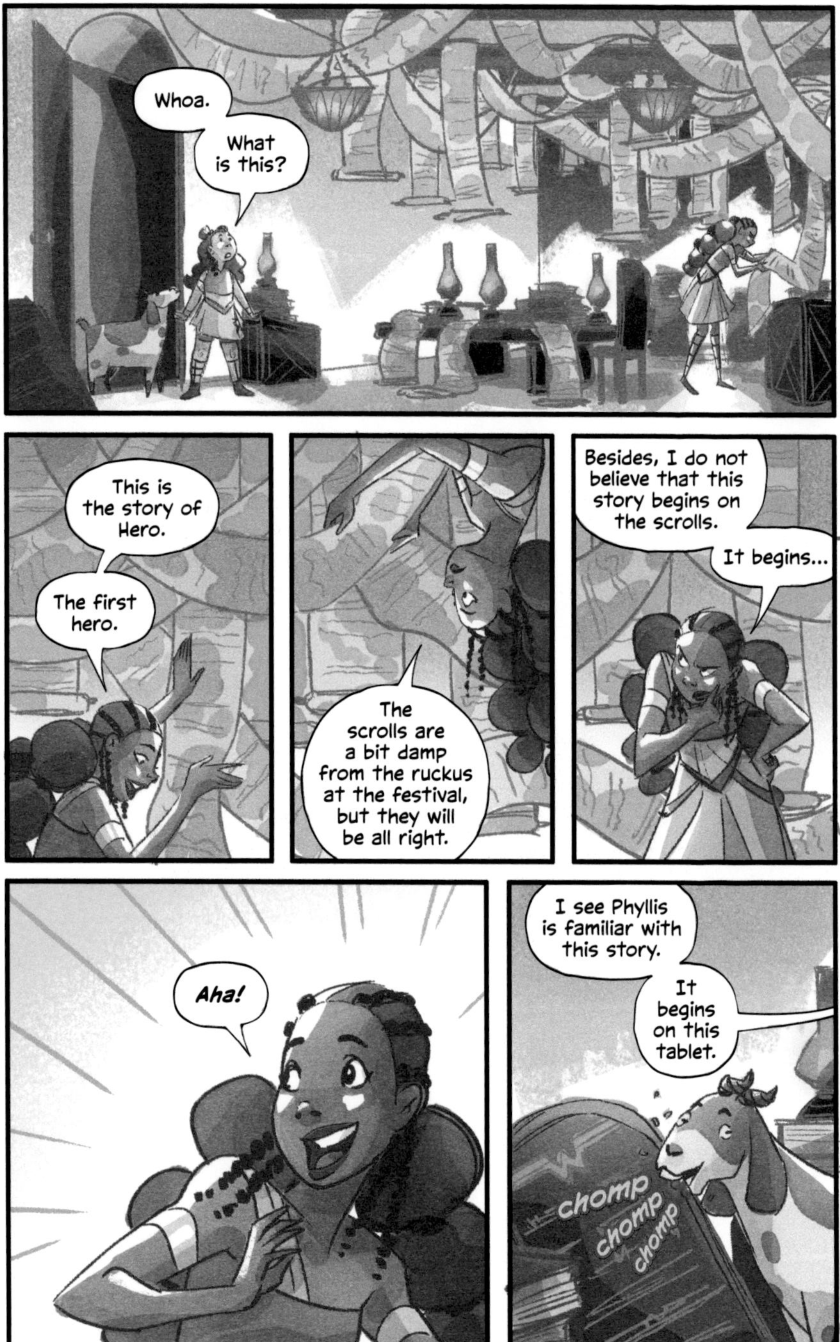
Whoa.
What is this?
This is the story of Hero.
The first hero.
The scrolls are a bit damp from the ruckus at the festival, but they will be all right.
Besides, I do not believe that this story begins on the scrolls.
It begins...
Aha!
I see Phyllis is familiar with this story.
It begins on this tablet.
chomp chomp chomp

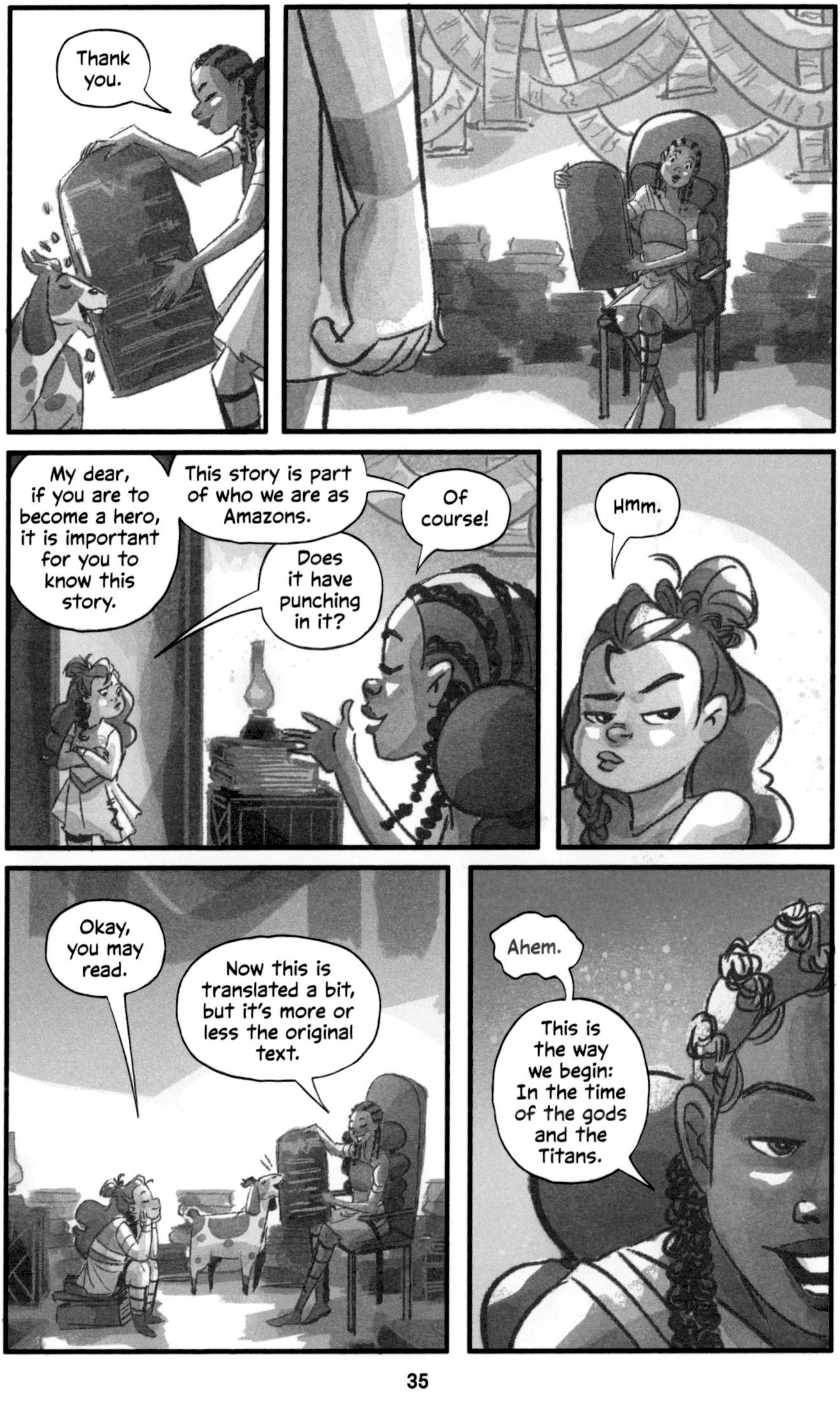
Thank you.
My dear, if you are to become a hero, it is important for you to know this story.
This story is part of who we are as Amazons.
Does it have punching in it?
Of course!
Hmm.
Okay, you may read.
Now this is translated a bit, but it's more or less the original text.
Ahem.
This is the way we begin: In the time of the gods and the Titans.

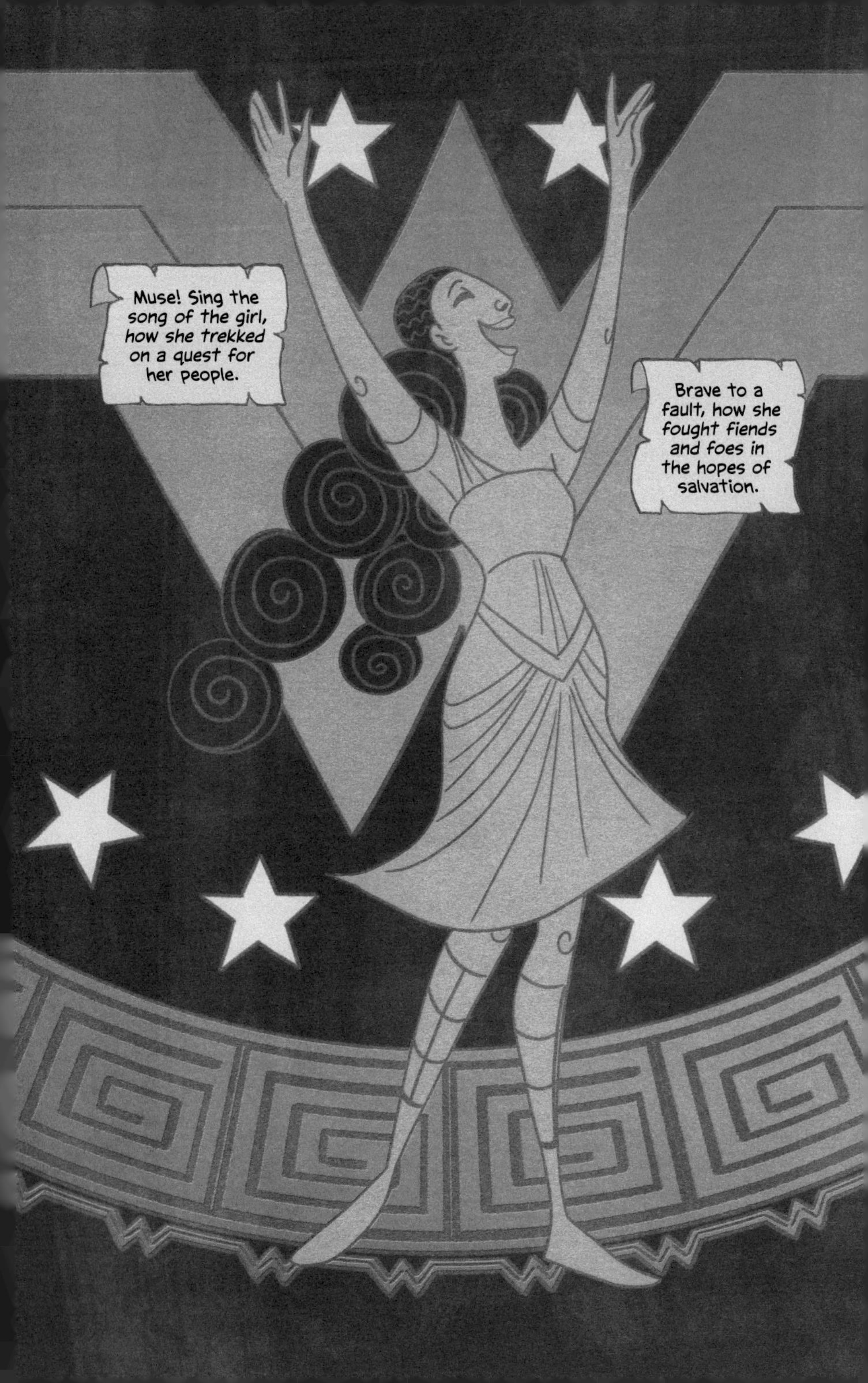
Muse! Sing the song of the girl, how she trekked on a quest for her people.
Brave to a fault, how she fought fiends and foes in the hopes of salvation.

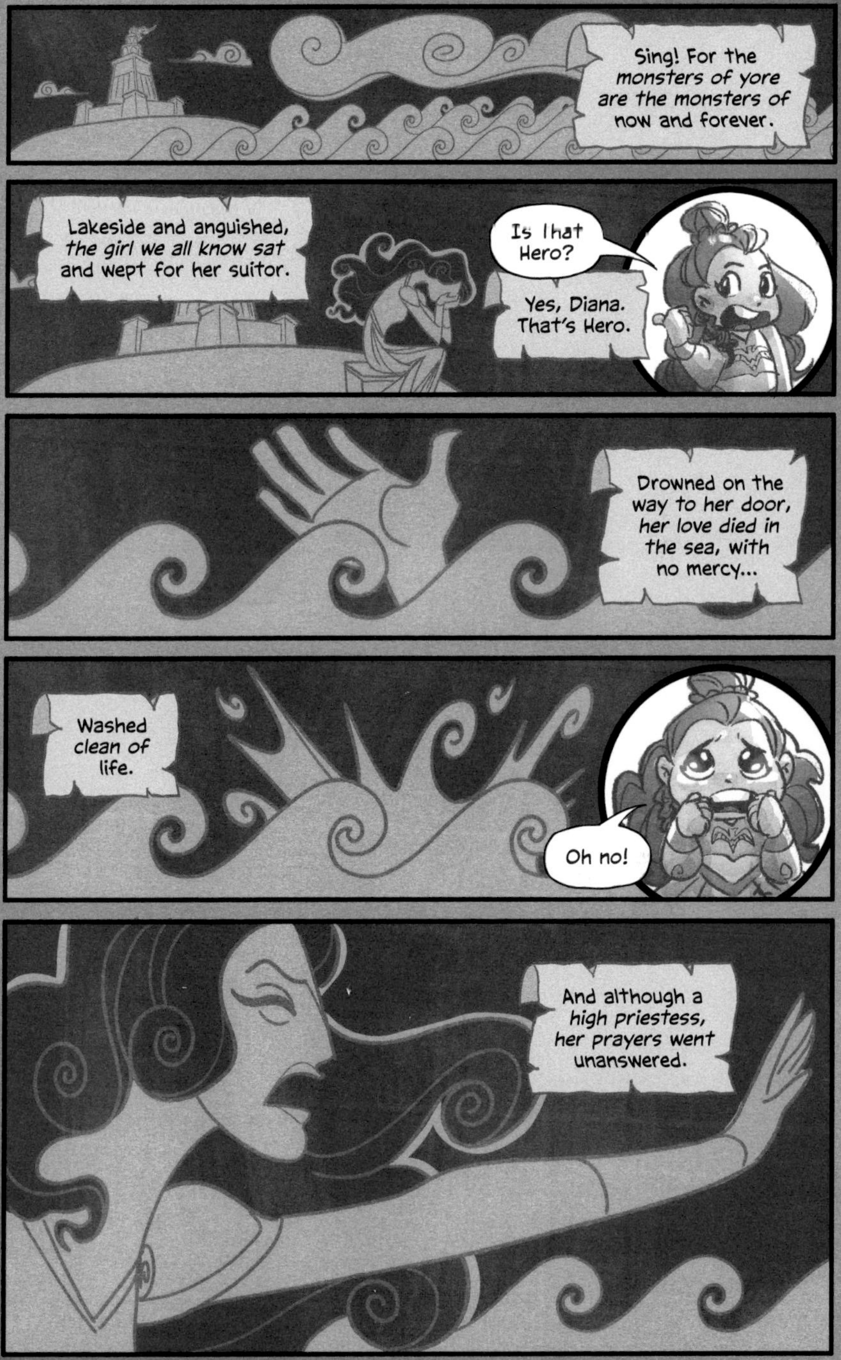

Sing! For the monsters of yore are the monsters of now and forever.
Lakeside and anguished, the girl we all know sat and wept for her suitor.
Is that Hero?
Yes, Diana. That's Hero.
Drowned on the way to her door, her love died in the sea, with no mercy...
Washed clean of life.
Oh no!
And although a high priestess, her prayers went unanswered.

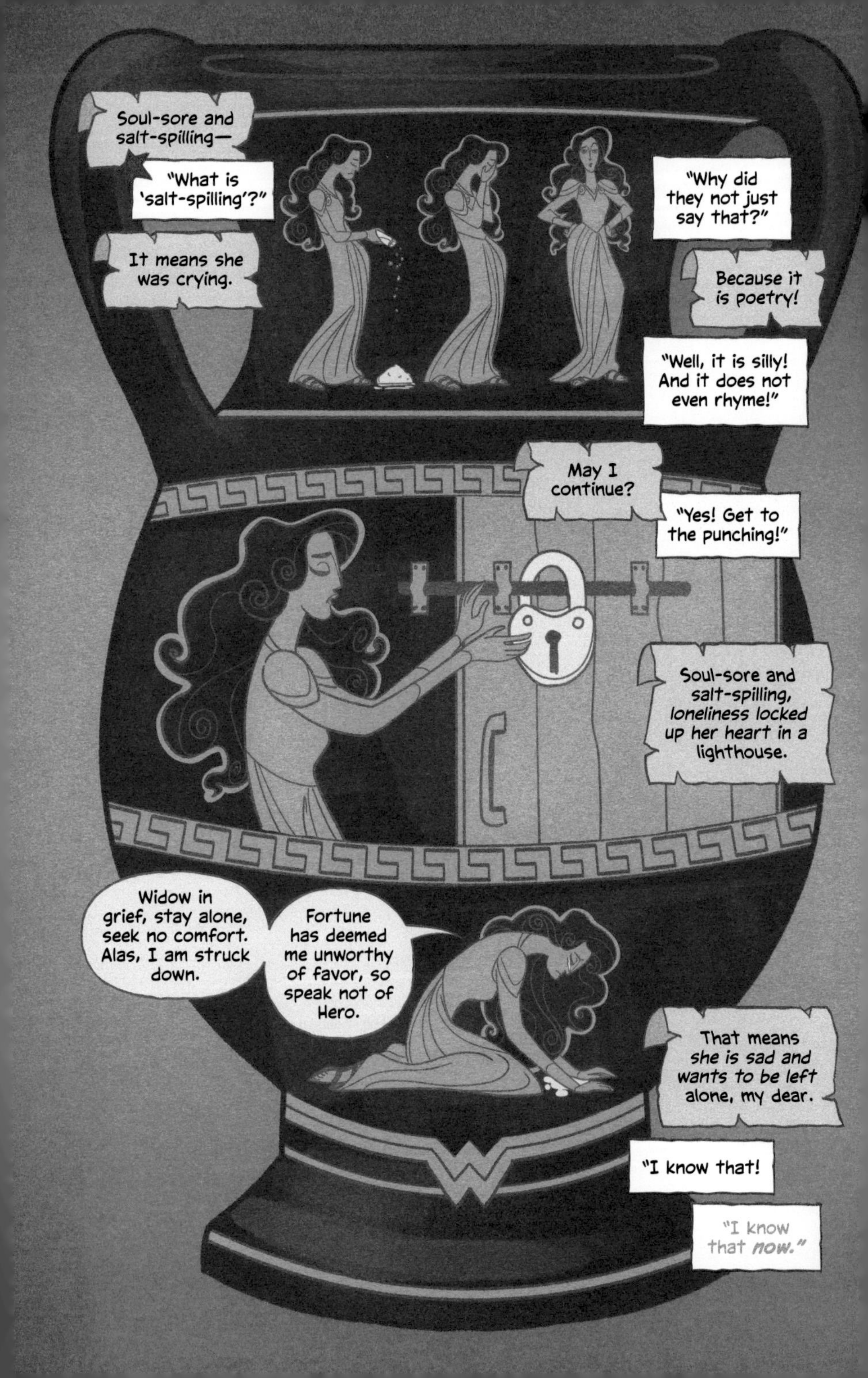
Soul-sore and salt-spilling—
"What is 'salt-spilling'?"
It means she was crying.
"Why did they not just say that?"
Because it is poetry!
"Well, it is silly! And it does not even rhyme!"
May I continue?
"Yes! Get to the punching!"
Soul-sore and salt-spilling, loneliness locked up her heart in a lighthouse.
Widow in grief, stay alone, seek no comfort. Alas, I am struck down.
Fortune has deemed me unworthy of favor, so speak not of Hero.
That means she is sad and wants to be left alone, my dear.
"I know that!
"I know that now."

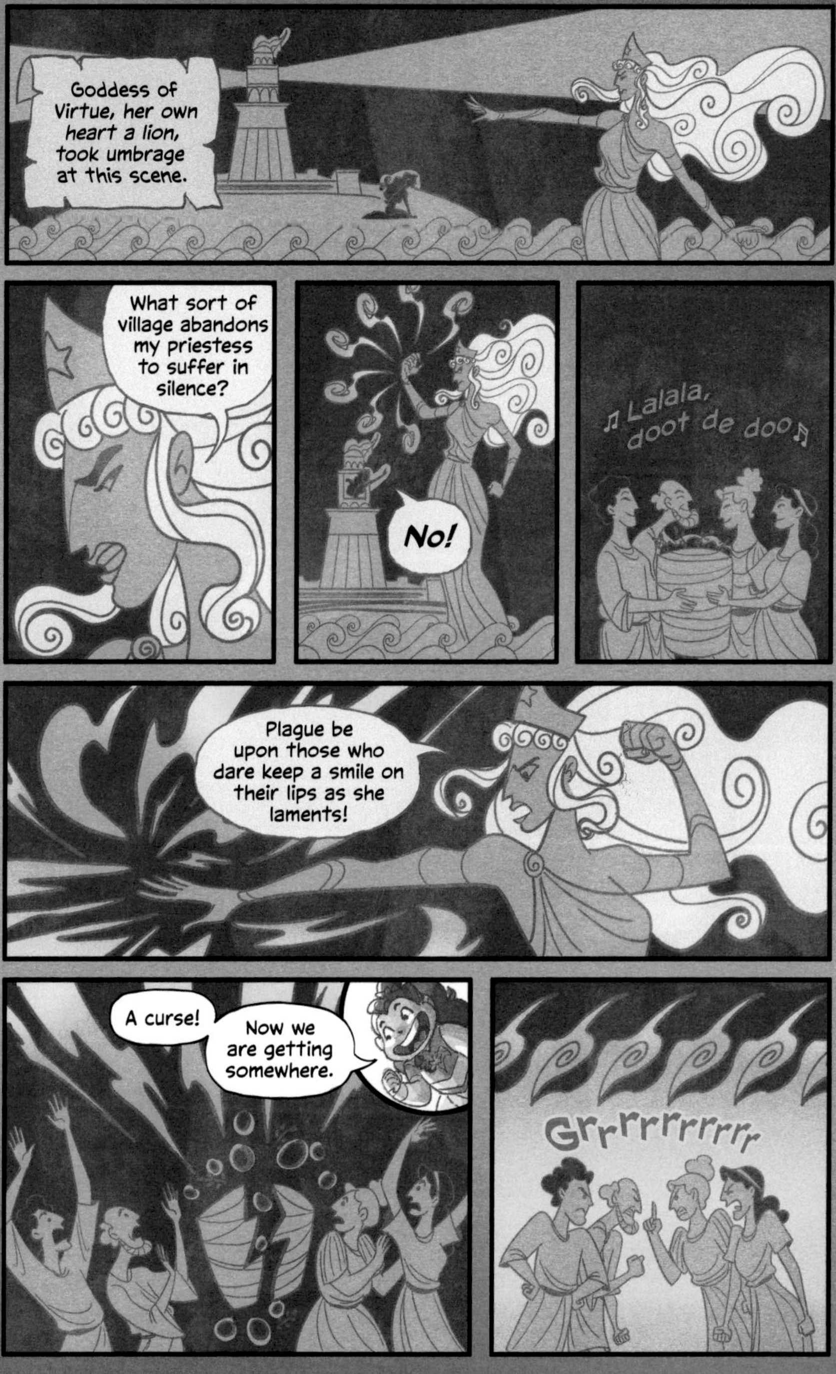
Goddess of Virtue, her own heart a lion, took umbrage at this scene.
What sort of village abandons my priestess to suffer in silence?
No!
♫ Lalala, doot de doo ♫
Plague be upon those who dare keep a smile on their lips as she laments!
A curse!
Now we are getting somewhere.
Grrrrrrrrrr

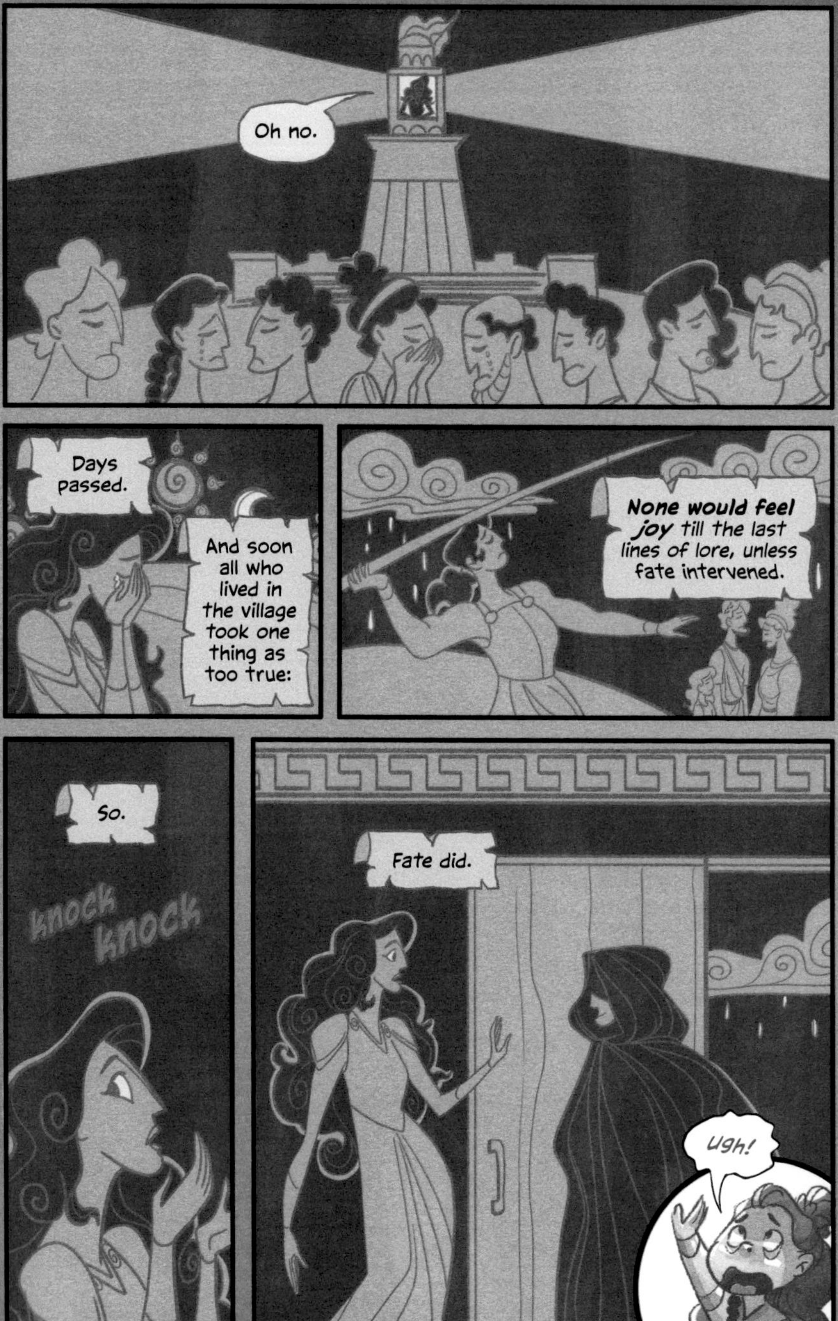
Oh no.
Days passed.
And soon all who lived in the village took one thing as too true:
None would feel joy till the last lines of lore, unless fate intervened.
So.
knock knock
Fate did.
Ugh!

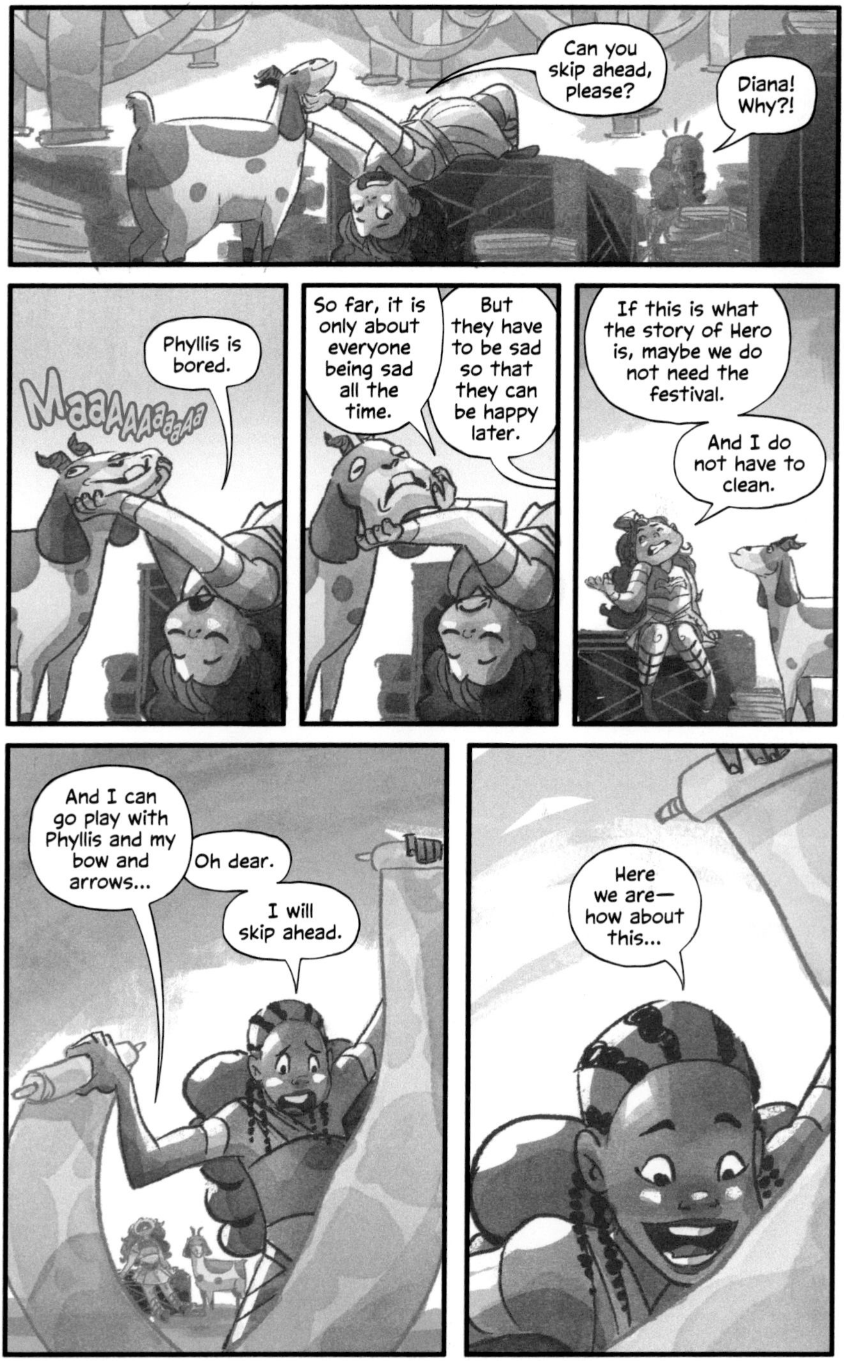
Can you skip ahead, please?
Diana! Why?!
Phyllis is bored.
MaaAAAaaAa
So far, it is only about everyone being sad all the time.
But they have to be sad so that they can be happy later.
If this is what the story of Hero is, maybe we do not need the festival.
And I do not have to clean.
And I can go play with Phyllis and my bow and arrows...
Oh dear.
I will skip ahead.
Here we are—how about this...

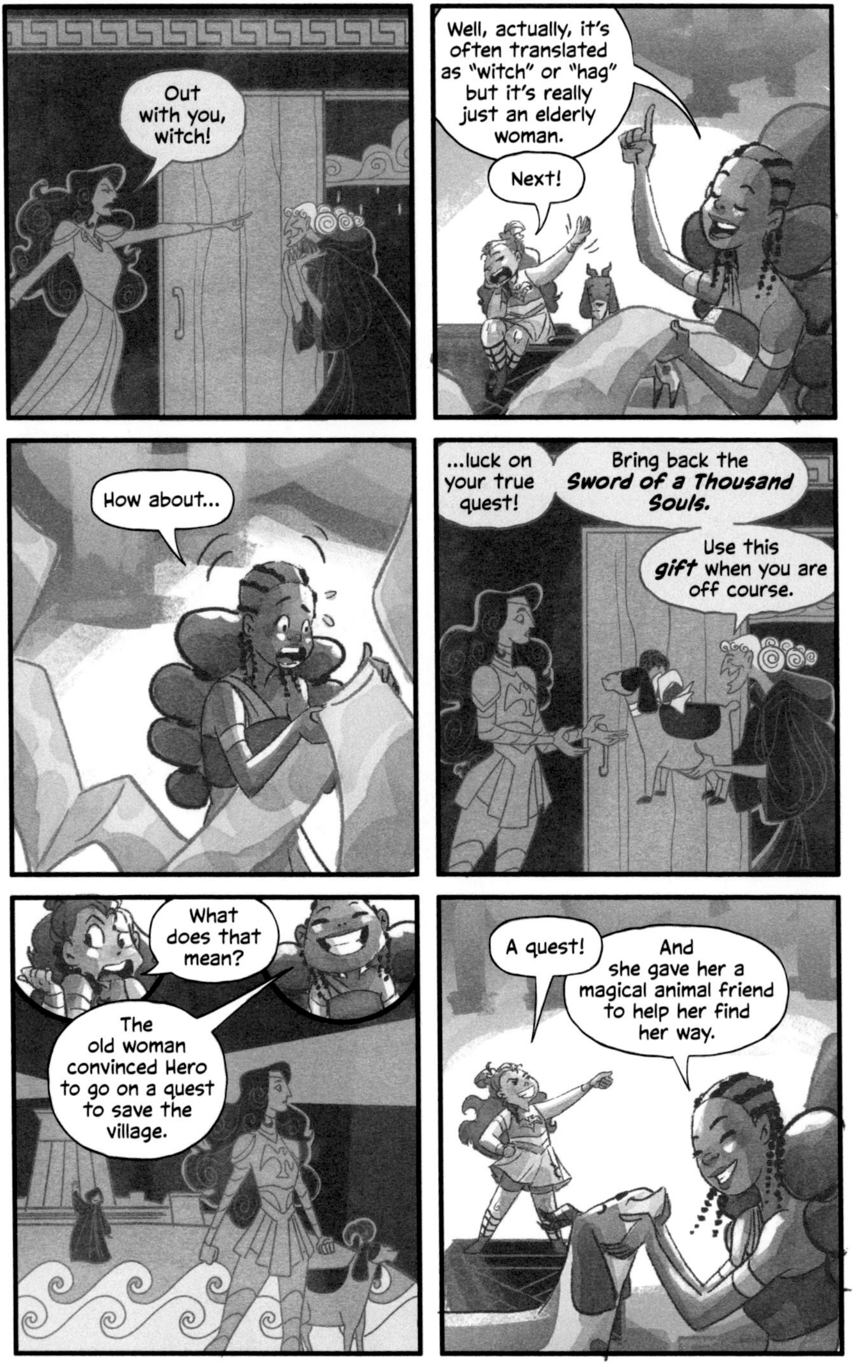

Out with you, witch!
Well, actually, it's often translated as "witch" or "hag" but it's really just an elderly woman.
Next!
How about...
...luck on your true quest!
Bring back the ***Sword of a Thousand Souls.***
Use this ***gift*** when you are off course.
What does that mean?
The old woman convinced Hero to go on a quest to save the village.
A quest!
And she gave her a magical animal friend to help her find her way.

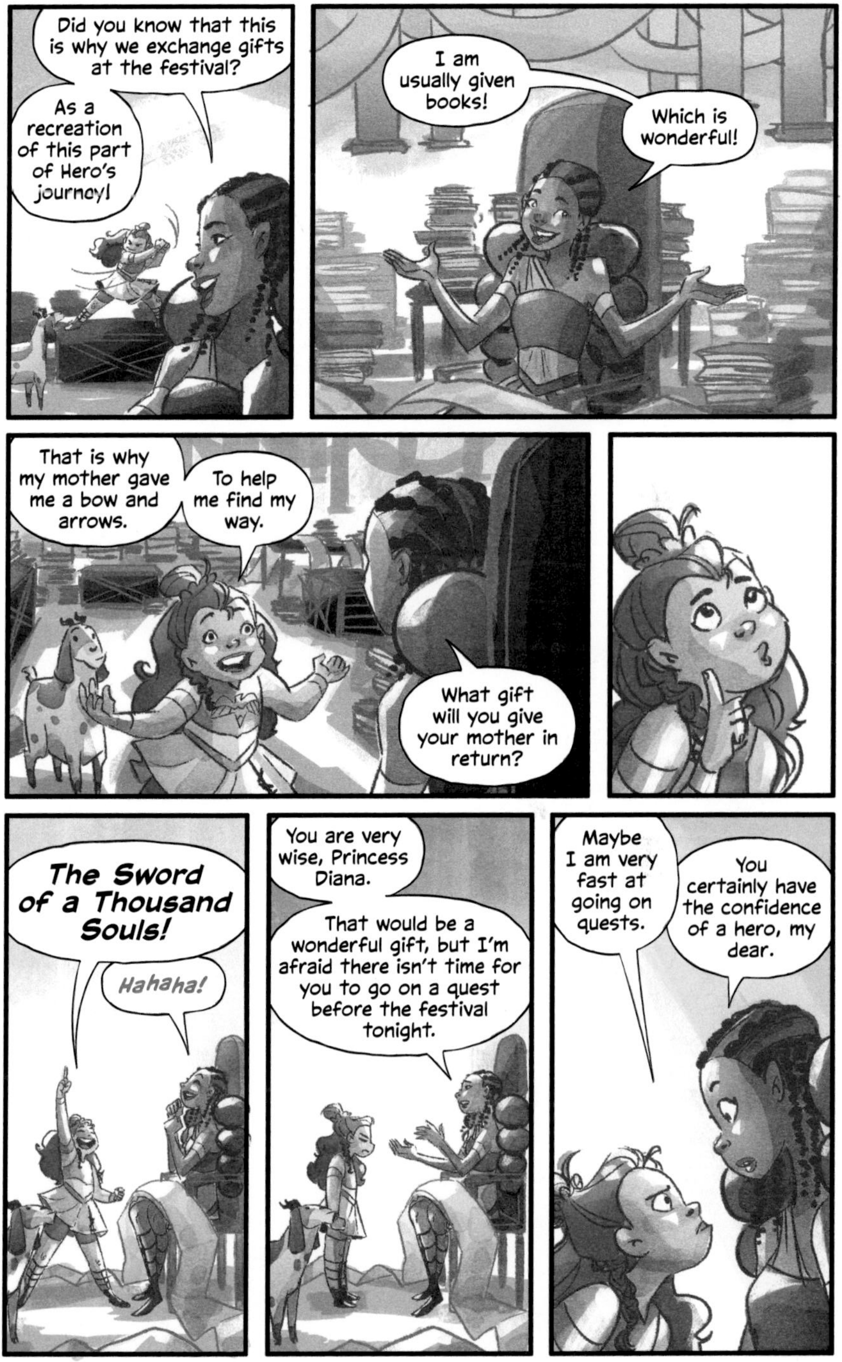
Did you know that this is why we exchange gifts at the festival?
As a recreation of this part of Hero's journey!
I am usually given books!
Which is wonderful!
That is why my mother gave me a bow and arrows.
To help me find my way.
What gift will you give your mother in return?
The Sword of a Thousand Souls!
Hahaha!
You are very wise, Princess Diana.
That would be a wonderful gift, but I'm afraid there isn't time for you to go on a quest before the festival tonight.
Maybe I am very fast at going on quests.
You certainly have the confidence of a hero, my dear.

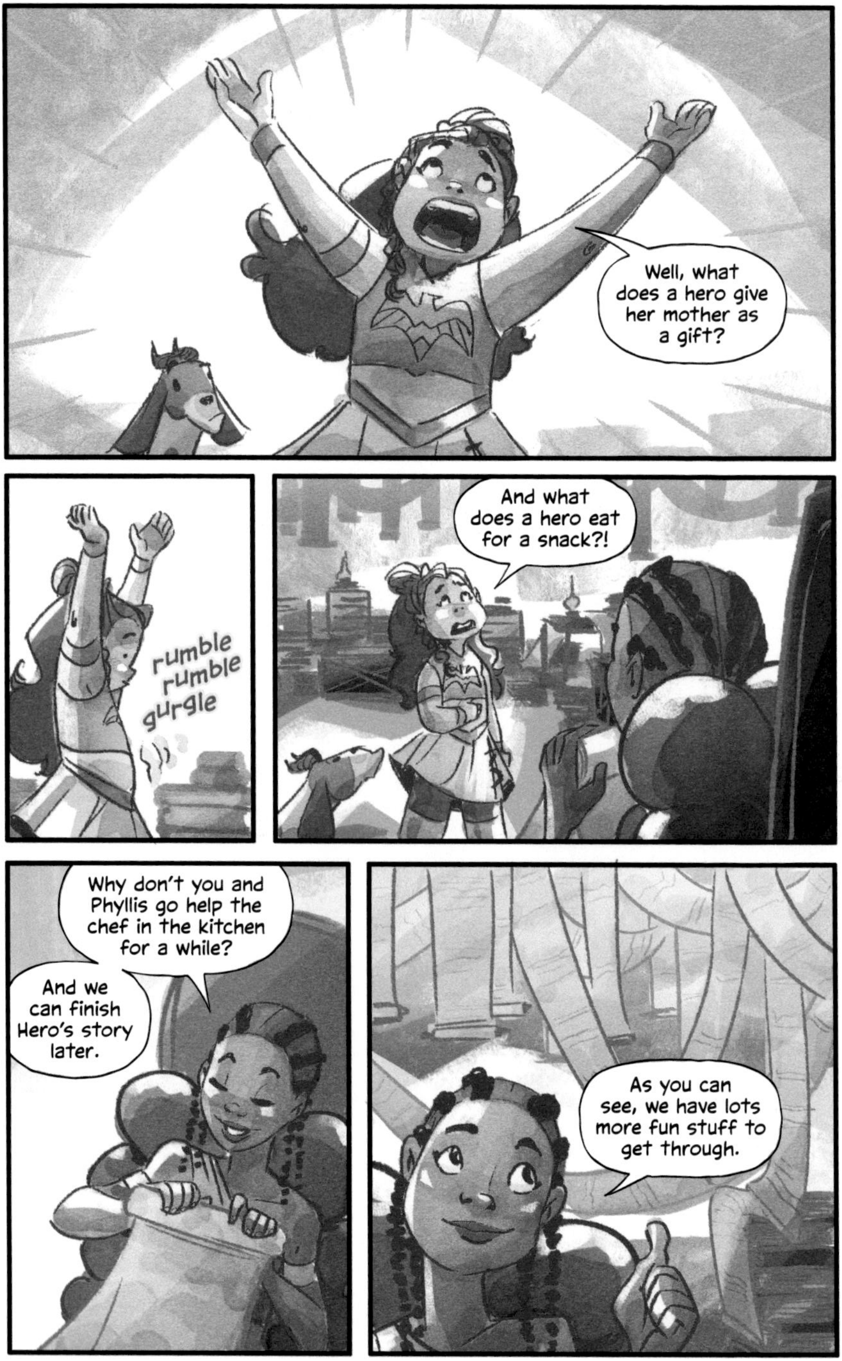

Well, what does a hero give her mother as a gift?
rumble rumble gurgle
And what does a hero eat for a snack?!
Why don't you and Phyllis go help the chef in the kitchen for a while?
And we can finish Hero's story later.
As you can see, we have lots more fun stuff to get through.

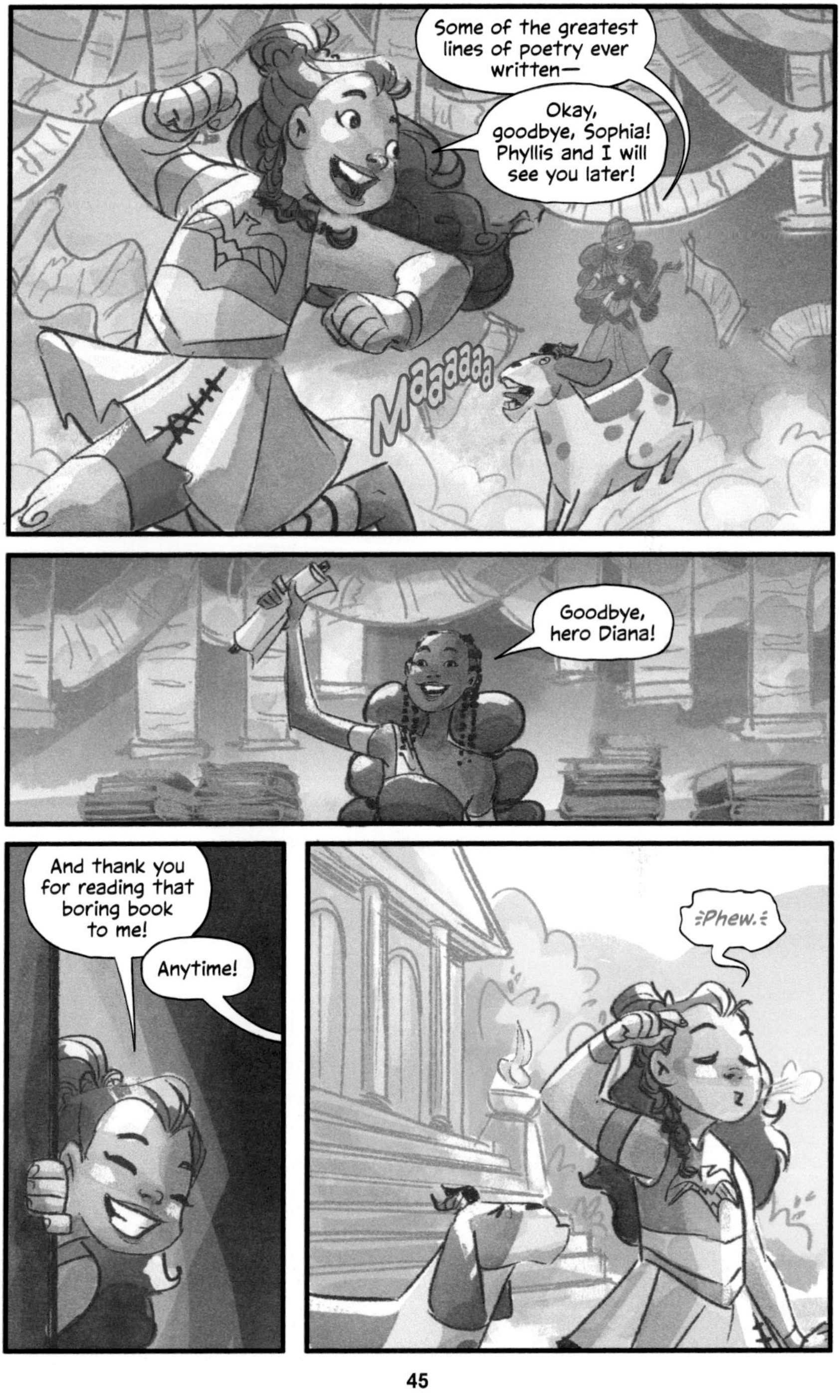
Some of the greatest lines of poetry ever written—
Okay, goodbye, Sophia! Phyllis and I will see you later!
Maaaaaa
Goodbye, hero Diana!
And thank you for reading that boring book to me!
Anytime!
Phew.

CHAPTER 2

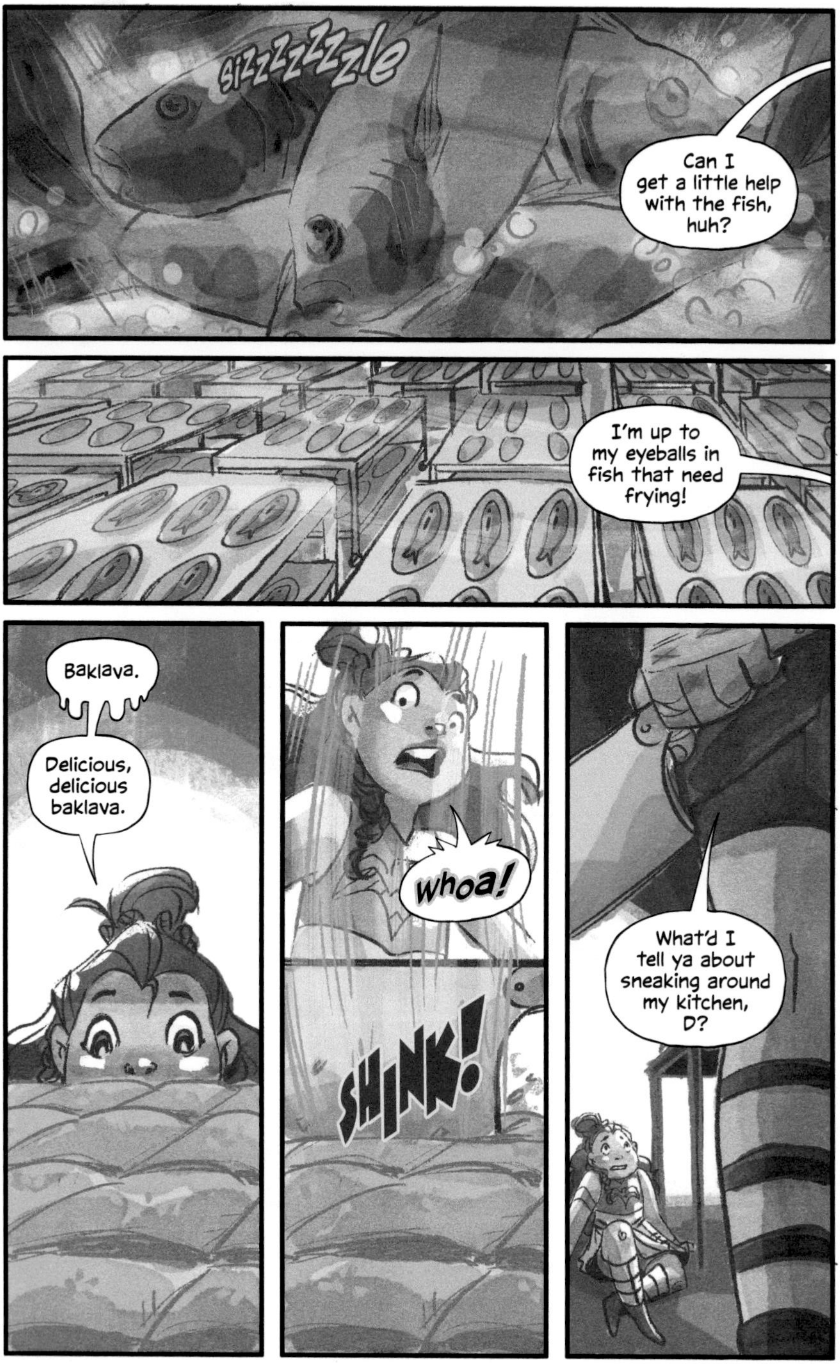
SIZZZZZZZLE
Can I get a little help with the fish, huh?
I'm up to my eyeballs in fish that need frying!
Baklava.
Delicious, delicious baklava.
Whoa!
SHINK!
What'd I tell ya about sneaking around my kitchen, D?

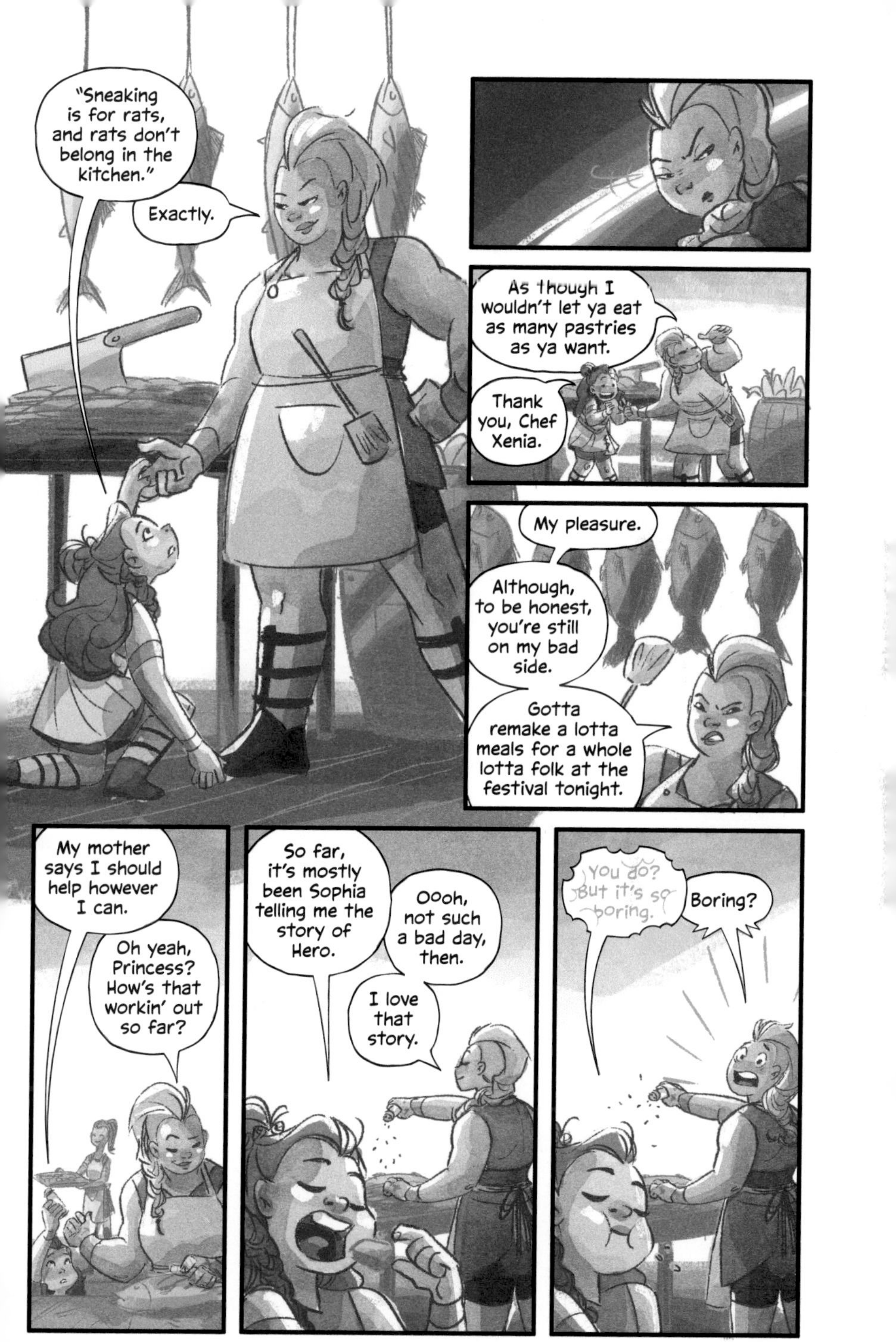
"Sneaking is for rats, and rats don't belong in the kitchen."
Exactly.
As though I wouldn't let ya eat as many pastries as ya want.
Thank you, Chef Xenia.
My pleasure.
Although, to be honest, you're still on my bad side.
Gotta remake a lotta meals for a whole lotta folk at the festival tonight.
My mother says I should help however I can.
Oh yeah, Princess? How's that workin' out so far?
So far, it's mostly been Sophia telling me the story of Hero.
Oooh, not such a bad day, then.
I love that story.
You do? But it's so boring.
Boring?

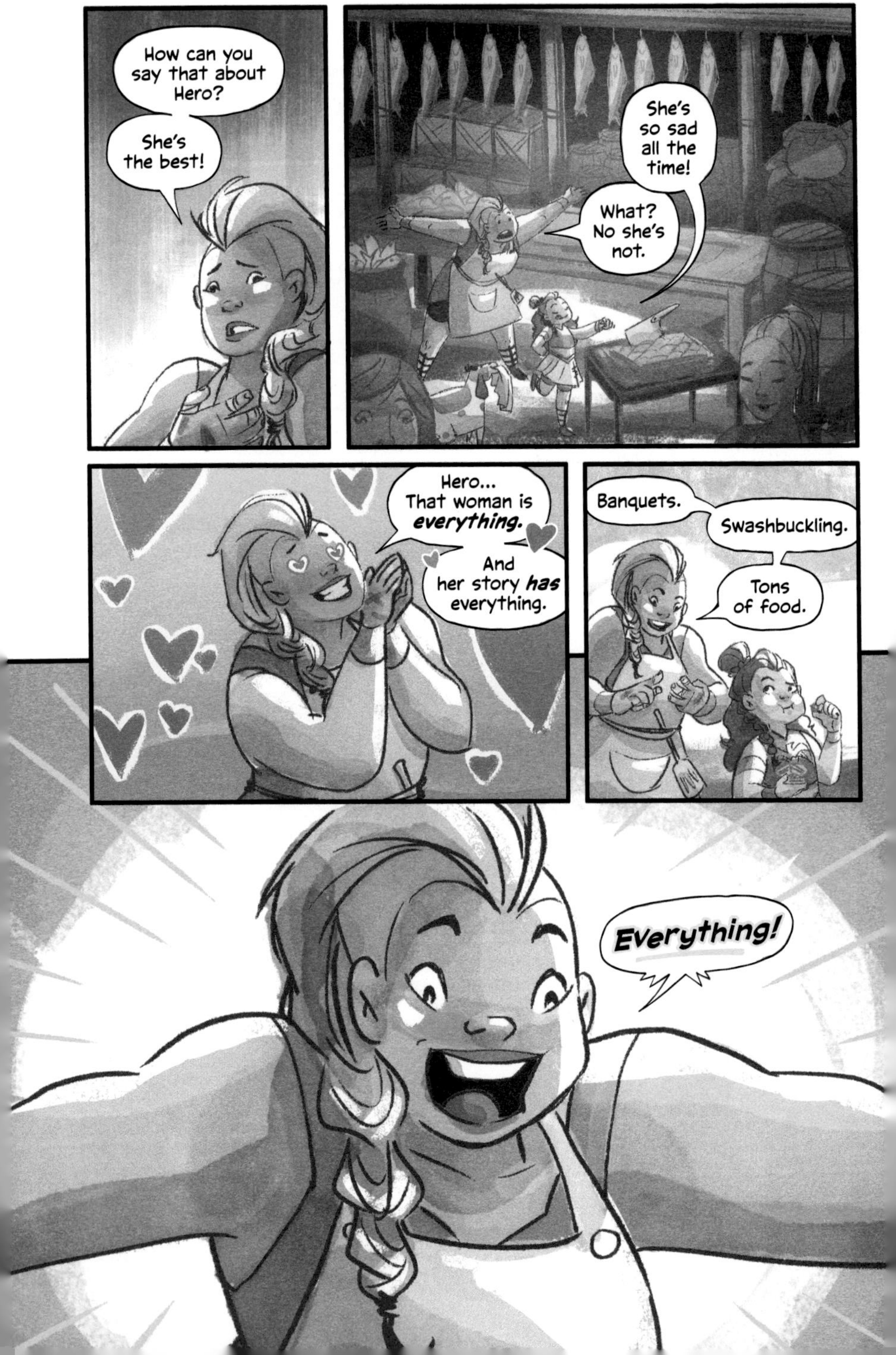
How can you say that about Hero?
She's the best!
She's so sad all the time!
What? No she's not.
Hero... That woman is *everything.*
And her story *has* everything.
Banquets.
Swashbuckling.
Tons of food.
Everything!

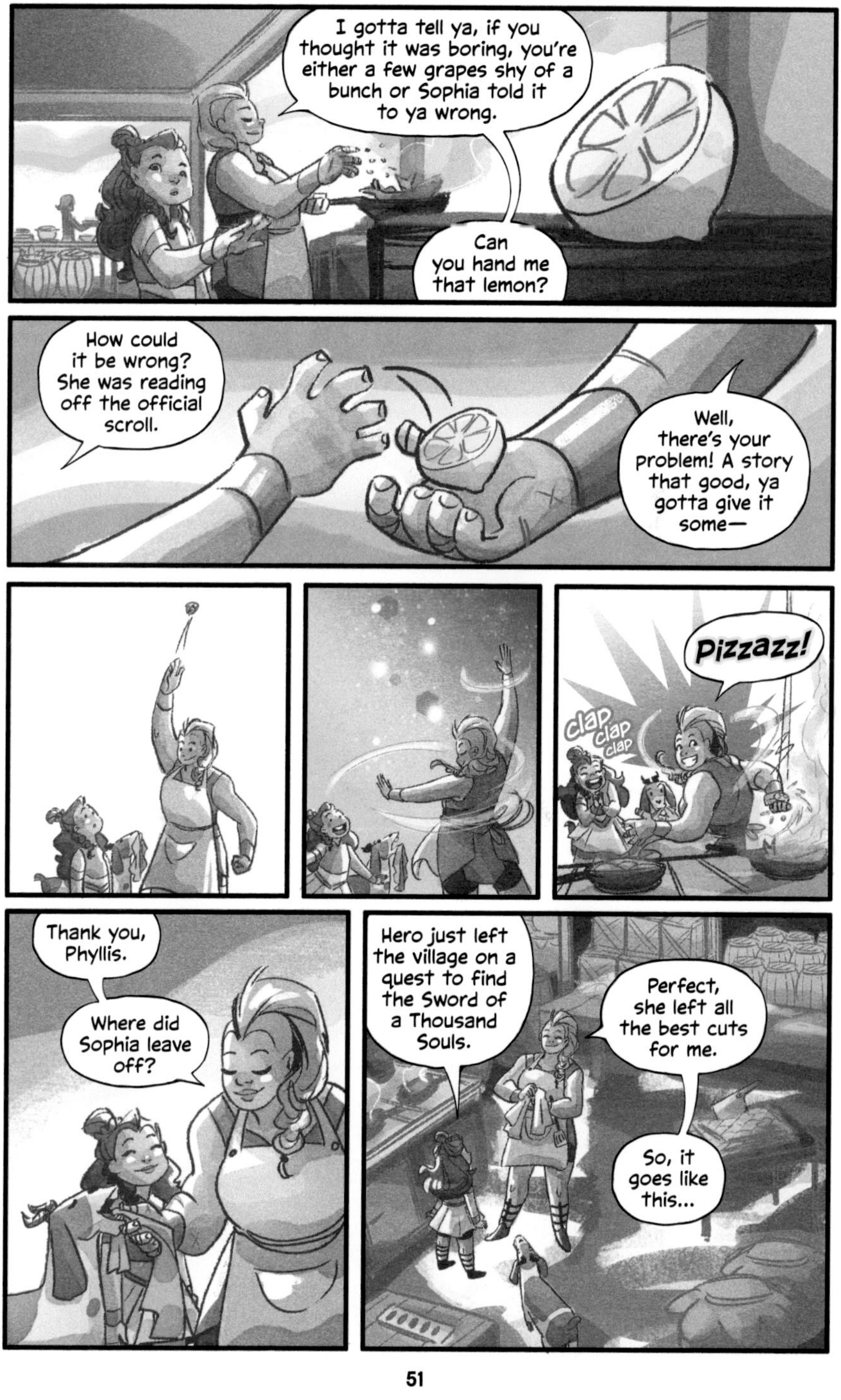
I gotta tell ya, if you thought it was boring, you're either a few grapes shy of a bunch or Sophia told it to ya wrong.
Can you hand me that lemon?
How could it be wrong? She was reading off the official scroll.
Well, there's your problem! A story that good, ya gotta give it some—
Pizzazz!
clap clap clap
Thank you, Phyllis.
Where did Sophia leave off?
Hero just left the village on a quest to find the Sword of a Thousand Souls.
Perfect, she left all the best cuts for me.
So, it goes like this...

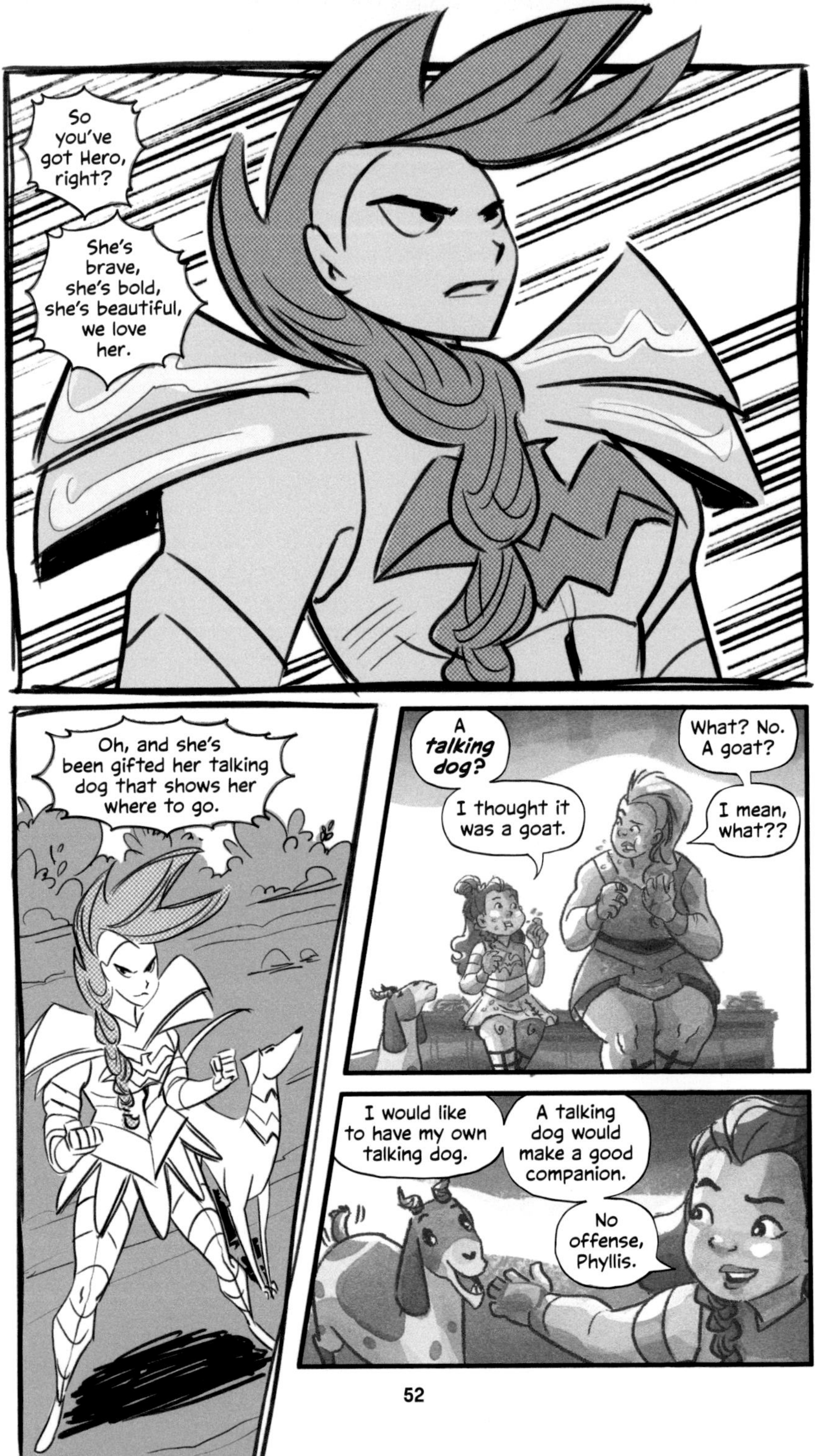
So you've got Hero, right?
She's brave, she's bold, she's beautiful, we love her.
Oh, and she's been gifted her talking dog that shows her where to go.
A *talking dog?*
I thought it was a goat.
What? No. A goat?
I mean, what??
I would like to have my own talking dog.
A talking dog would make a good companion.
No offense, Phyllis.

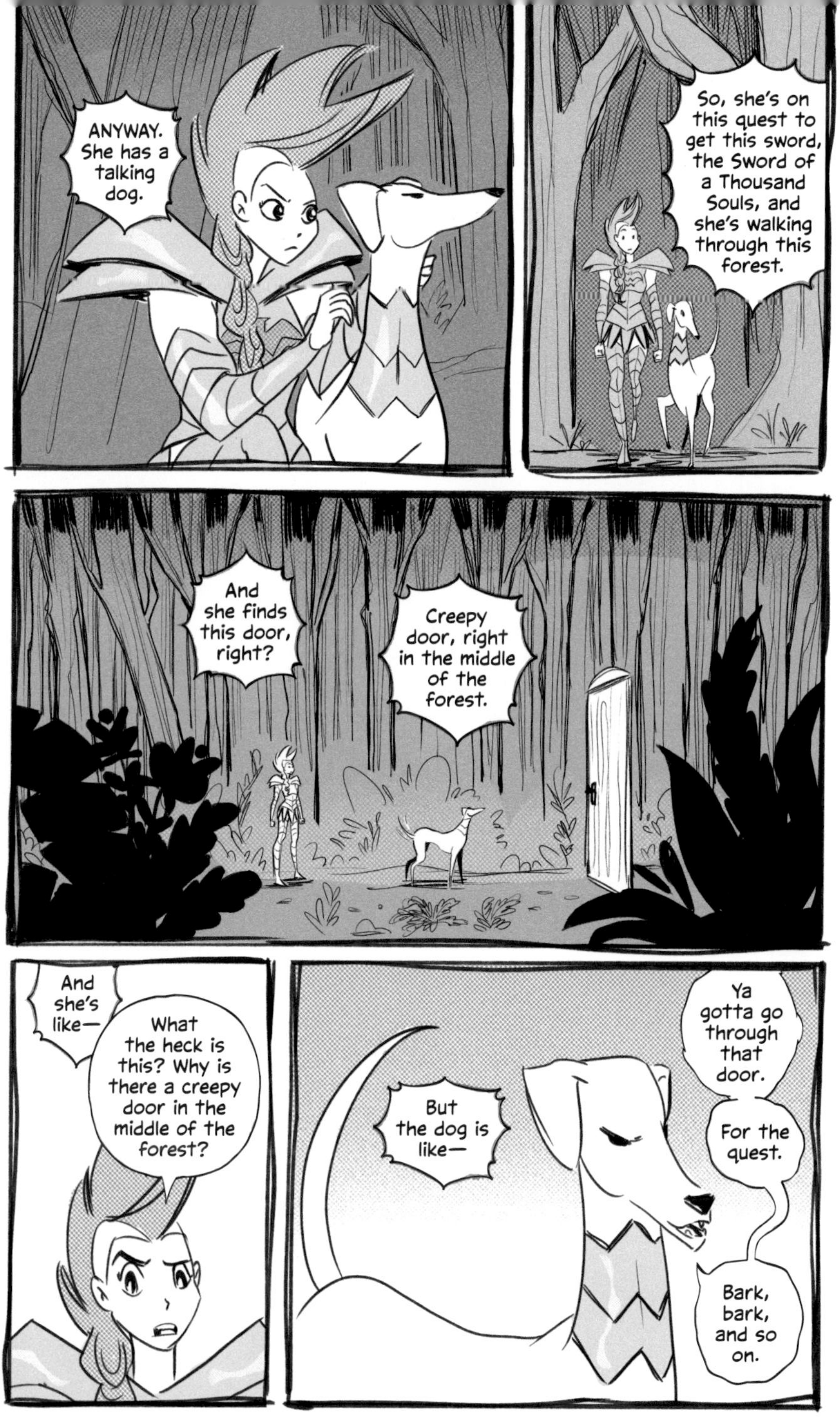
ANYWAY. She has a talking dog.
So, she's on this quest to get this sword, the Sword of a Thousand Souls, and she's walking through this forest.
And she finds this door, right?
Creepy door, right in the middle of the forest.
And she's like—
What the heck is this? Why is there a creepy door in the middle of the forest?
But the dog is like—
Ya gotta go through that door.
For the quest.
Bark, bark, and so on.

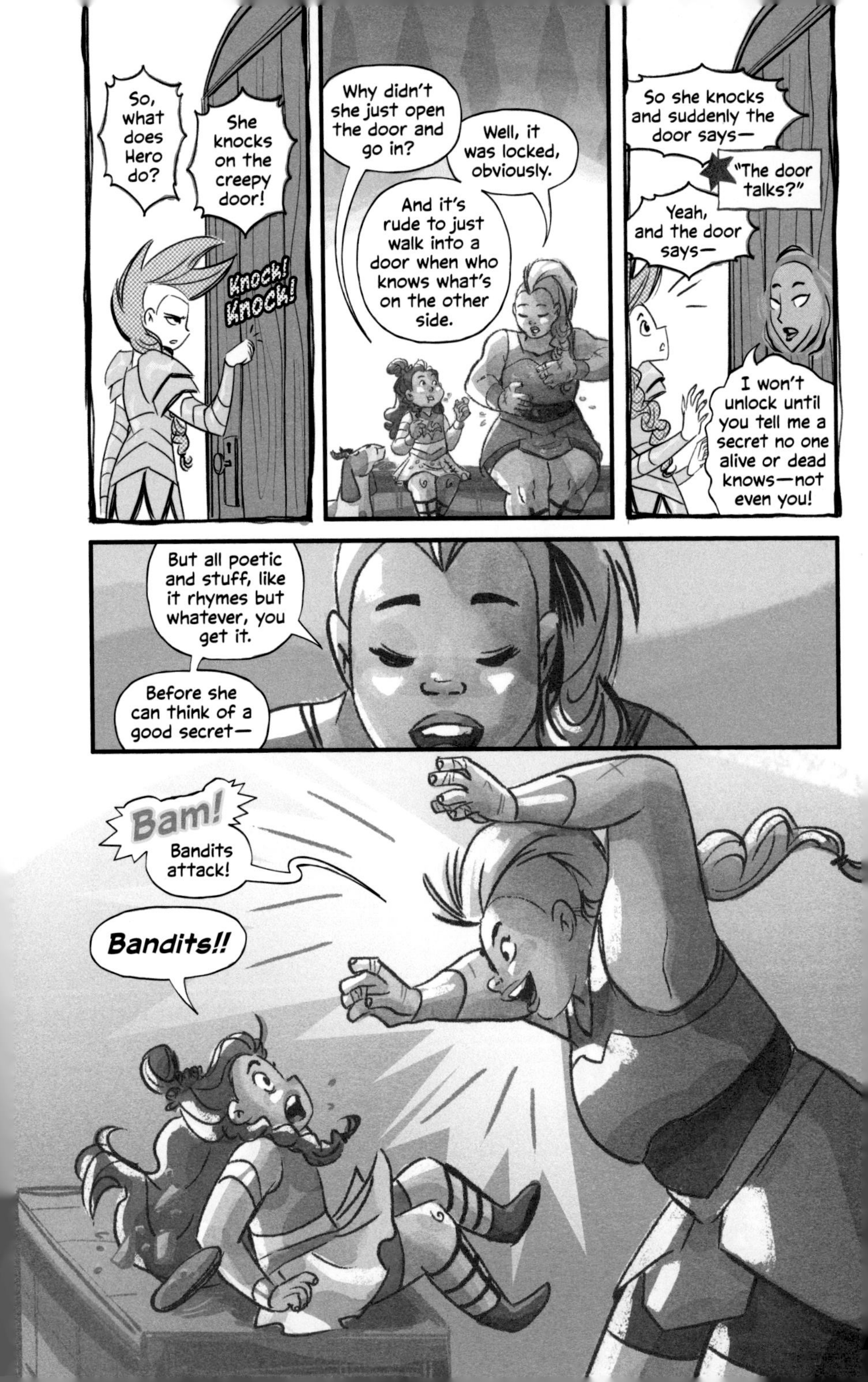

So, what does Hero do?
She knocks on the creepy door!
Knock! Knock!
Why didn't she just open the door and go in?
Well, it was locked, obviously.
And it's rude to just walk into a door when who knows what's on the other side.
So she knocks and suddenly the door says—
"The door talks?"
Yeah, and the door says—
I won't unlock until you tell me a secret no one alive or dead knows—not even you!
But all poetic and stuff, like it rhymes but whatever, you get it.
Before she can think of a good secret—
Bam!
Bandits attack!
Bandits!!

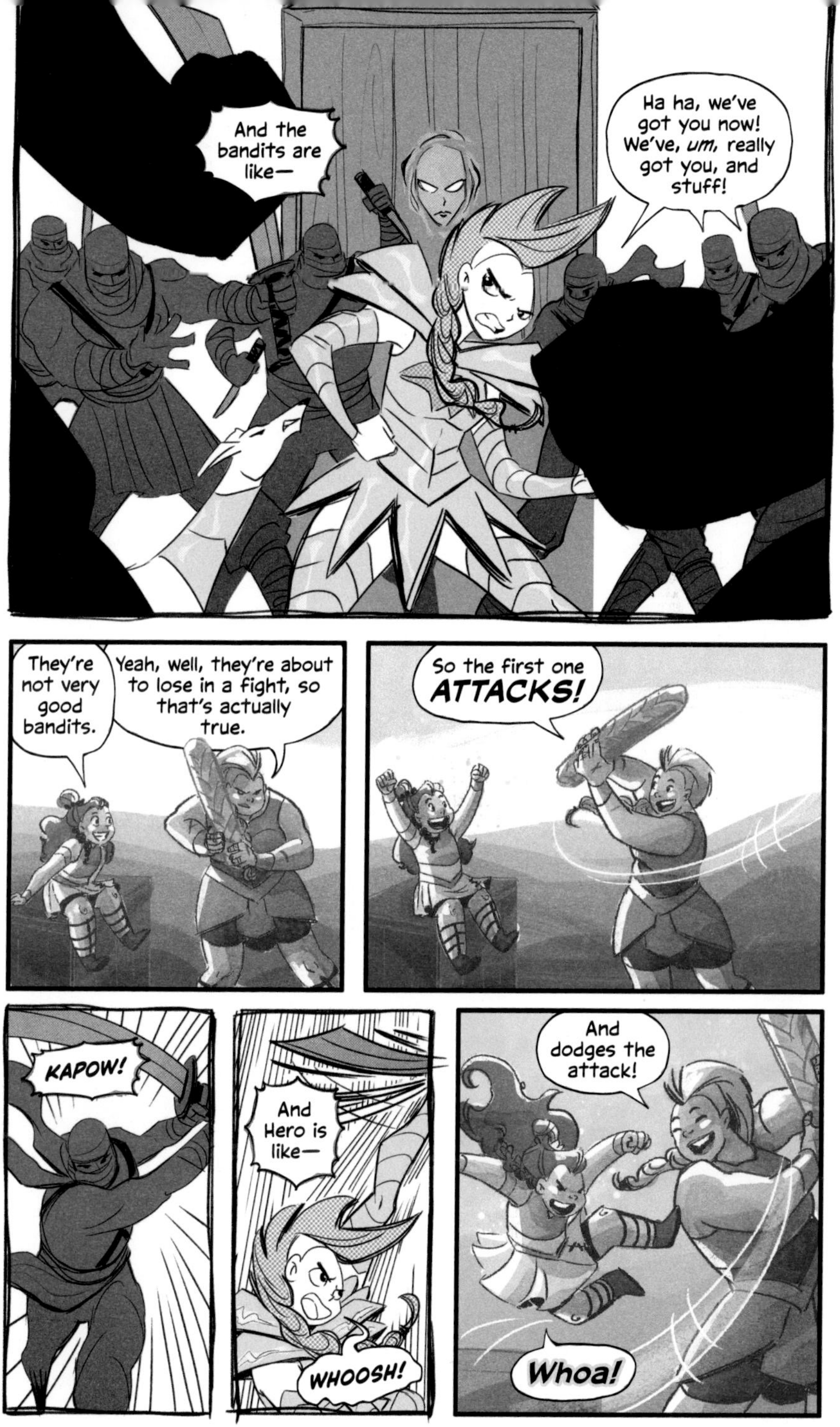

And the bandits are like—
Ha ha, we've got you now! We've, *um,* really got you, and stuff!
They're not very good bandits.
Yeah, well, they're about to lose in a fight, so that's actually true.
So the first one **ATTACKS!**
KAPOW!
And Hero is like—
WHOOSH!
And dodges the attack!
Whoa!

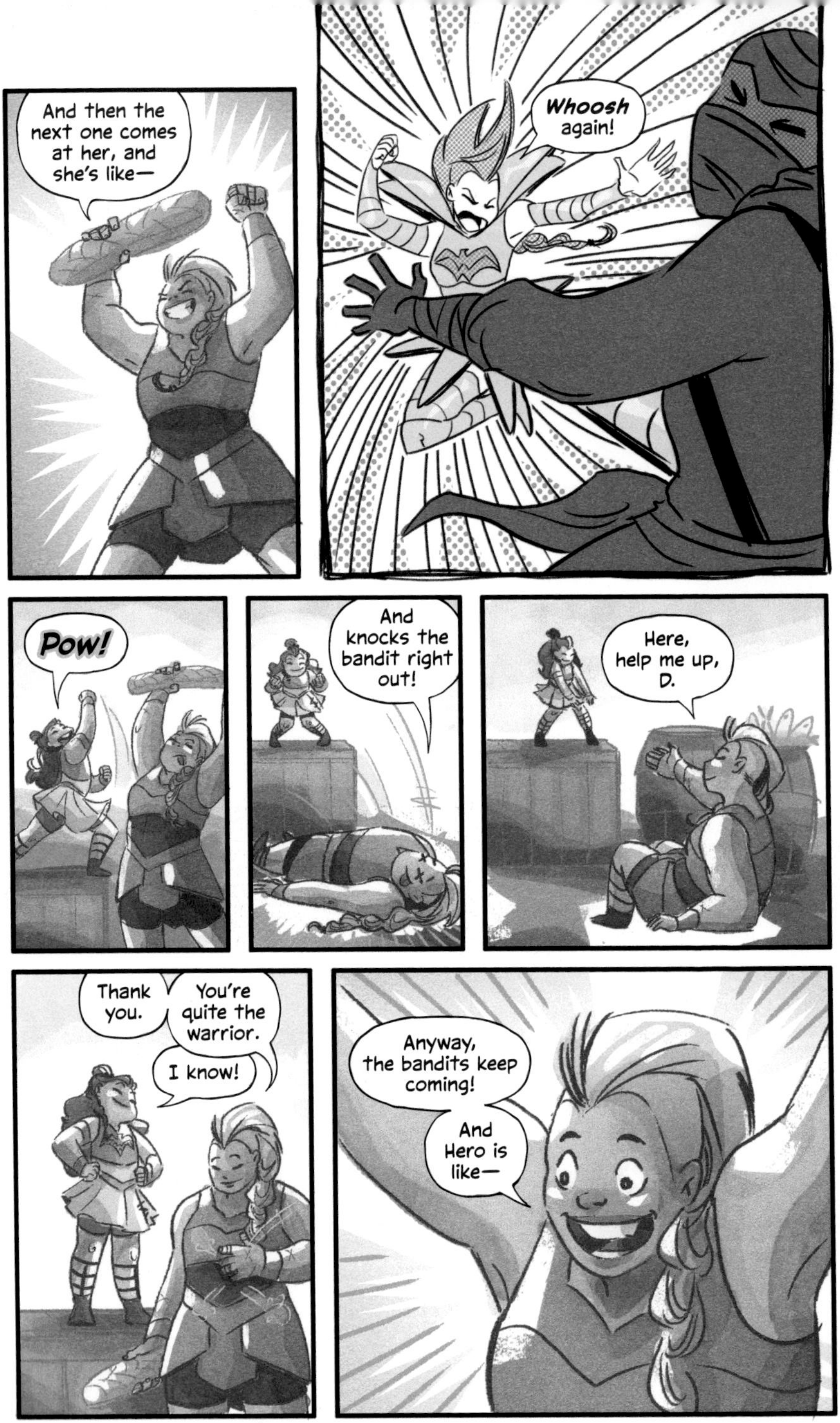

And then the next one comes at her, and she's like—
Whoosh again!
Pow!
And knocks the bandit right out!
Here, help me up, D.
Thank you.
You're quite the warrior.
I know!
Anyway, the bandits keep coming!
And Hero is like—

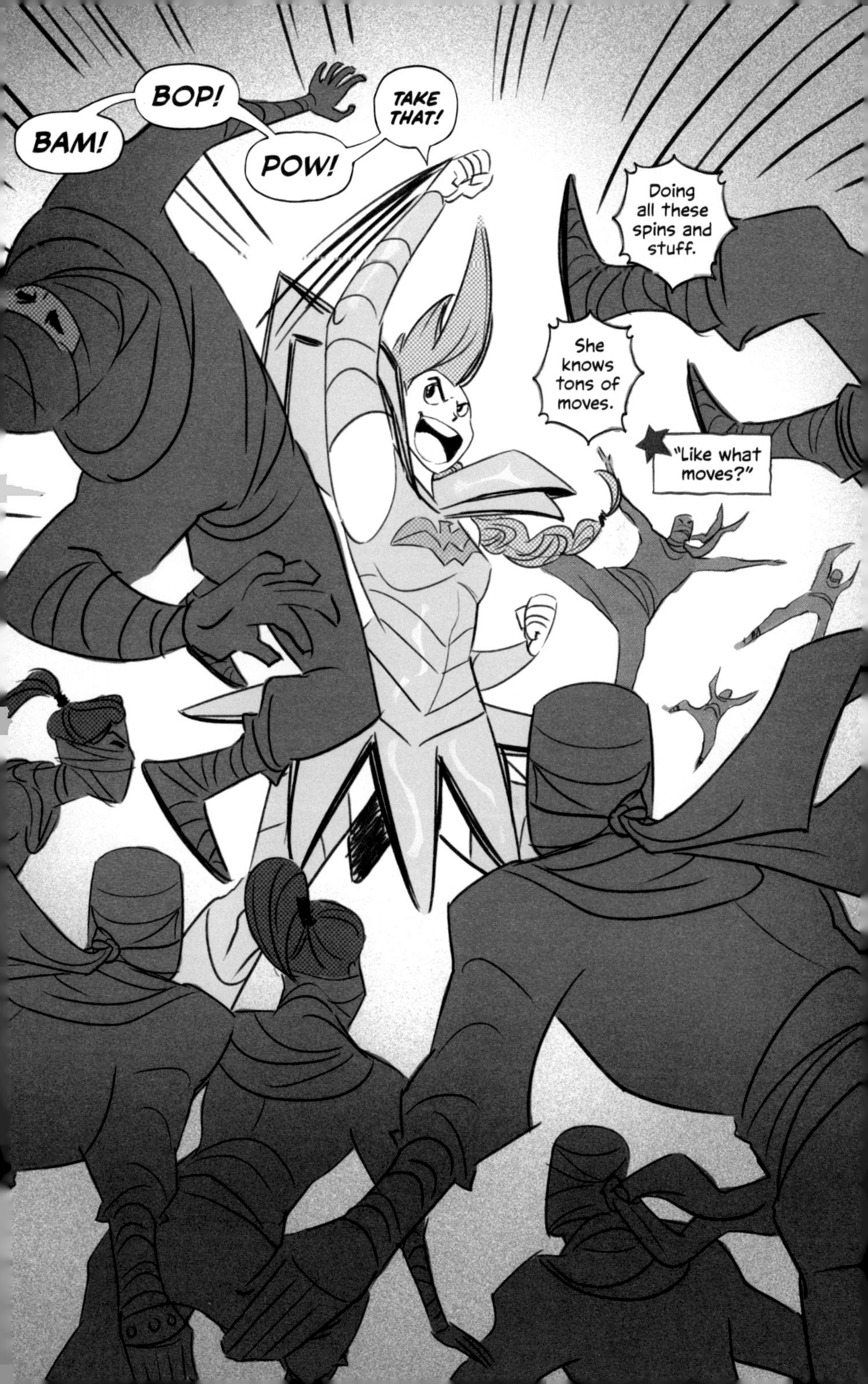
BAM!
BOP!
POW!
TAKE THAT!
Doing all these spins and stuff.
She knows tons of moves.
"Like what moves?"

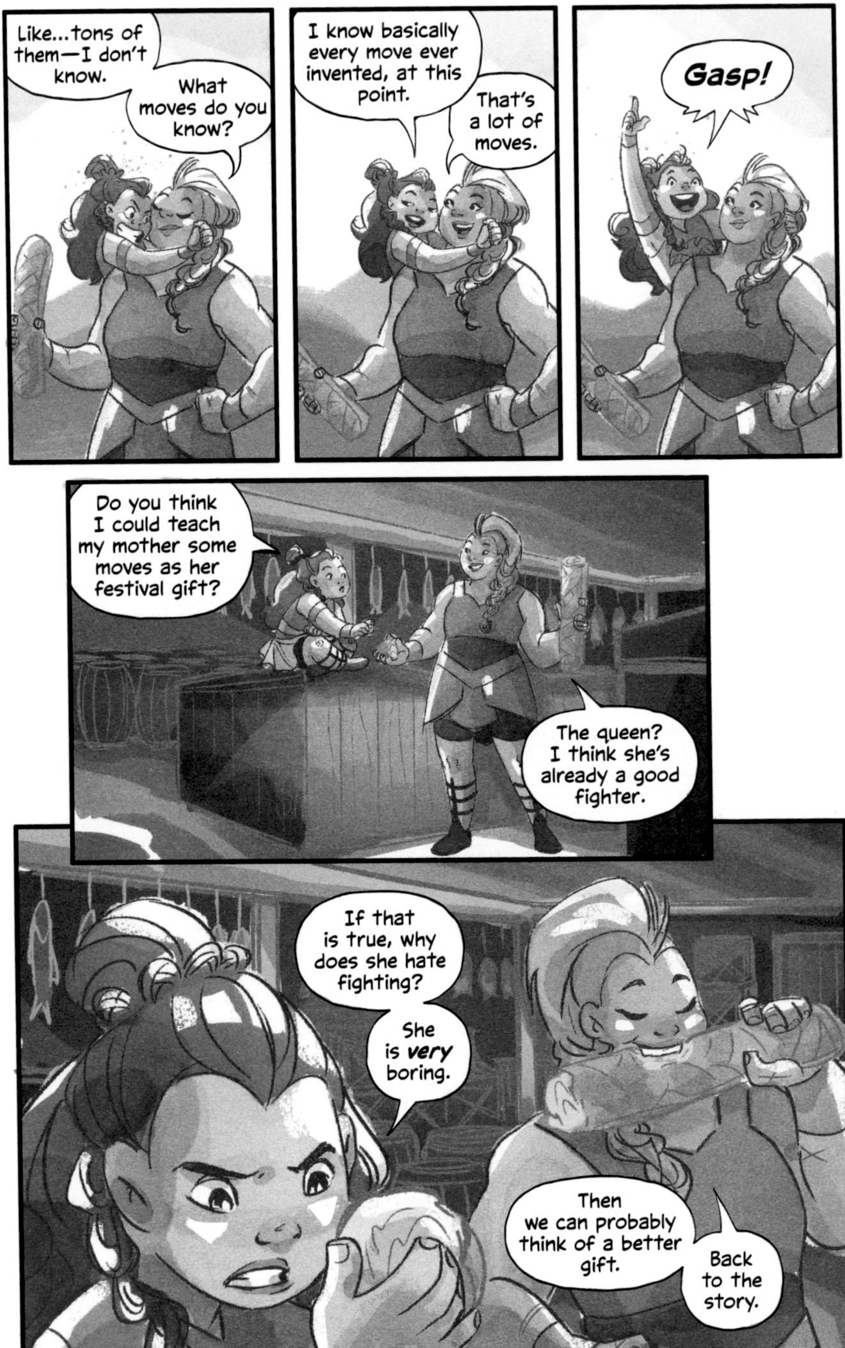
Like...tons of them—I don't know.
What moves do you know?
I know basically every move ever invented, at this point.
That's a lot of moves.
Gasp!
Do you think I could teach my mother some moves as her festival gift?
The queen? I think she's already a good fighter.
If that is true, why does she hate fighting?
She is *very* boring.
Then we can probably think of a better gift.
Back to the story.

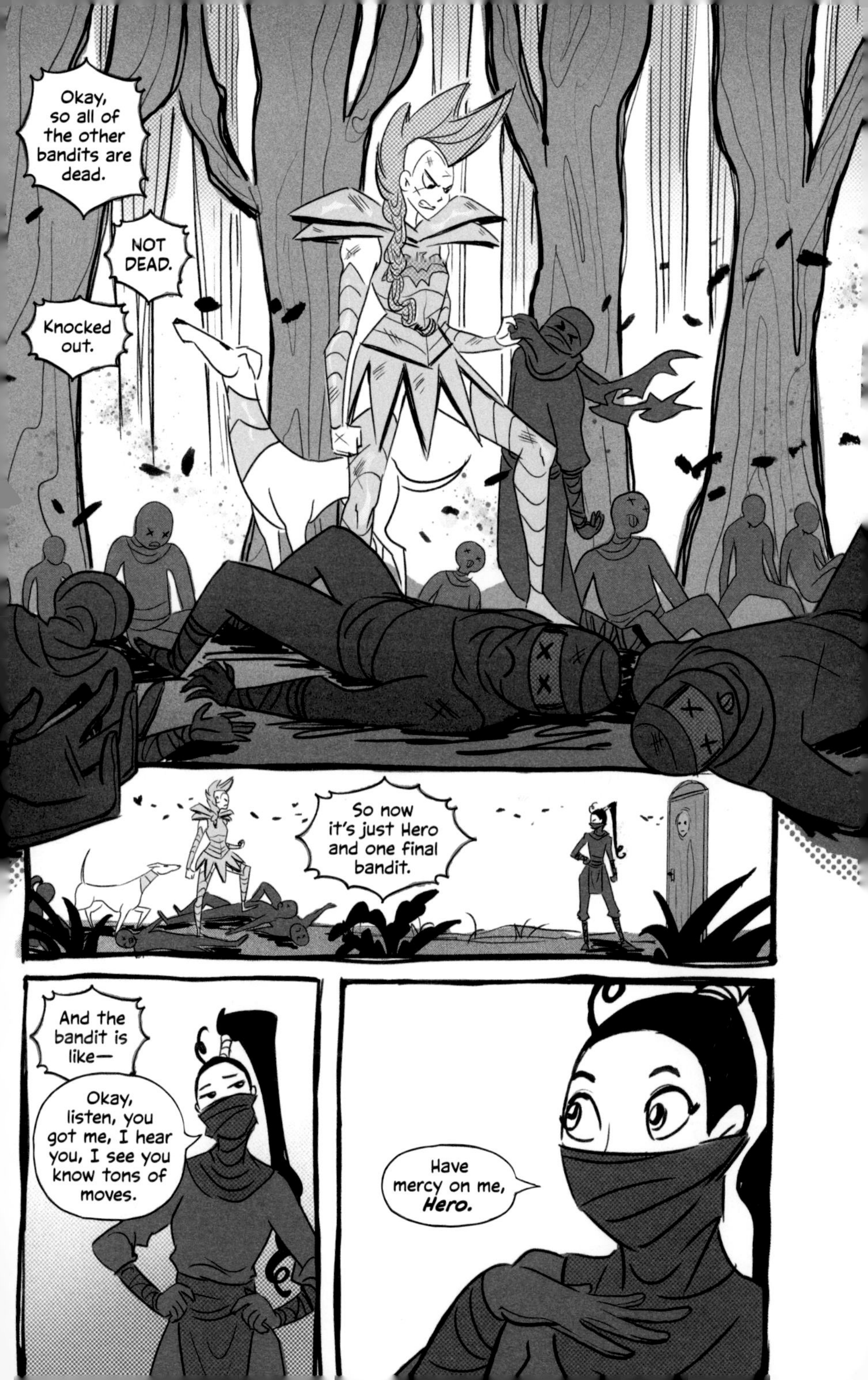
Okay, so all of the other bandits are dead.
NOT DEAD.
Knocked out.
So now it's just Hero and one final bandit.
And the bandit is like—
Okay, listen, you got me, I hear you, I see you know tons of moves.
Have mercy on me, *Hero.*

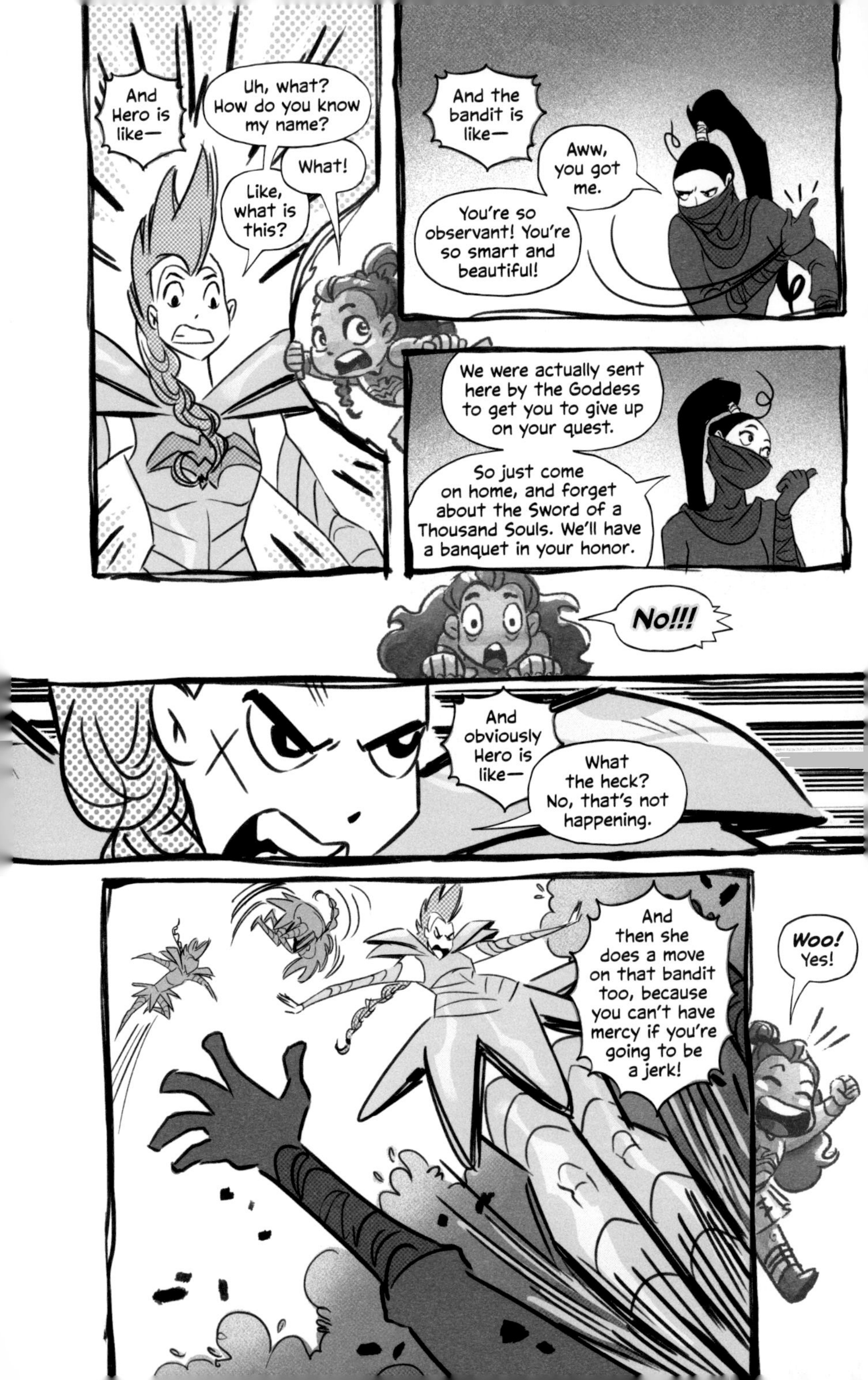
And Hero is like—
Uh, what? How do you know my name?
Like, what is this?
What!
And the bandit is like—
Aww, you got me.
You're so observant! You're so smart and beautiful!
We were actually sent here by the Goddess to get you to give up on your quest.
So just come on home, and forget about the Sword of a Thousand Souls. We'll have a banquet in your honor.
No!!!
And obviously Hero is like—
What the heck? No, that's not happening.
And then she does a move on that bandit too, because you can't have mercy if you're going to be a jerk!
Woo! Yes!

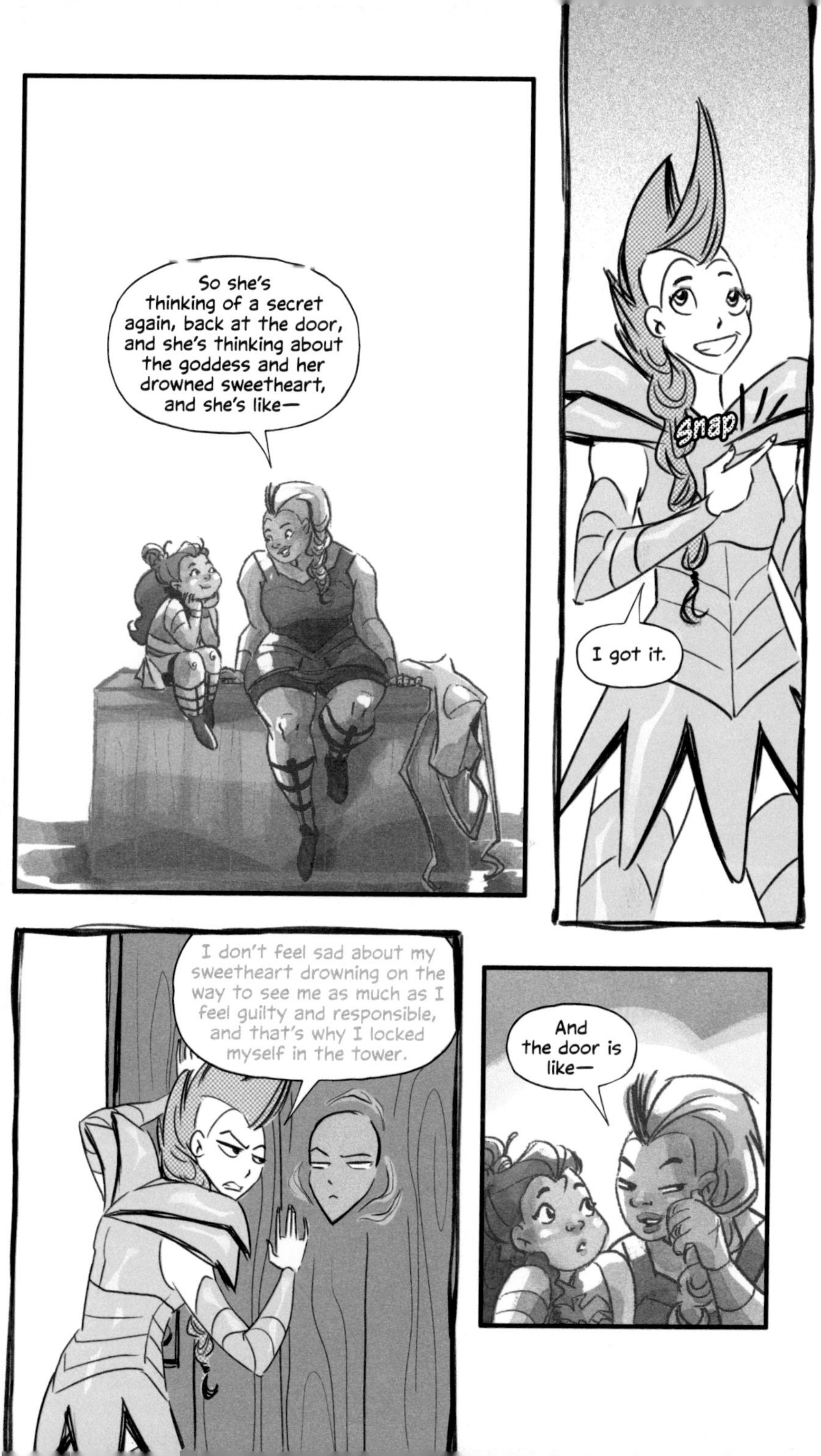
So she's thinking of a secret again, back at the door, and she's thinking about the goddess and her drowned sweetheart, and she's like—
SNAP
I got it.
I don't feel sad about my sweetheart drowning on the way to see me as much as I feel guilty and responsible, and that's why I locked myself in the tower.
And the door is like—

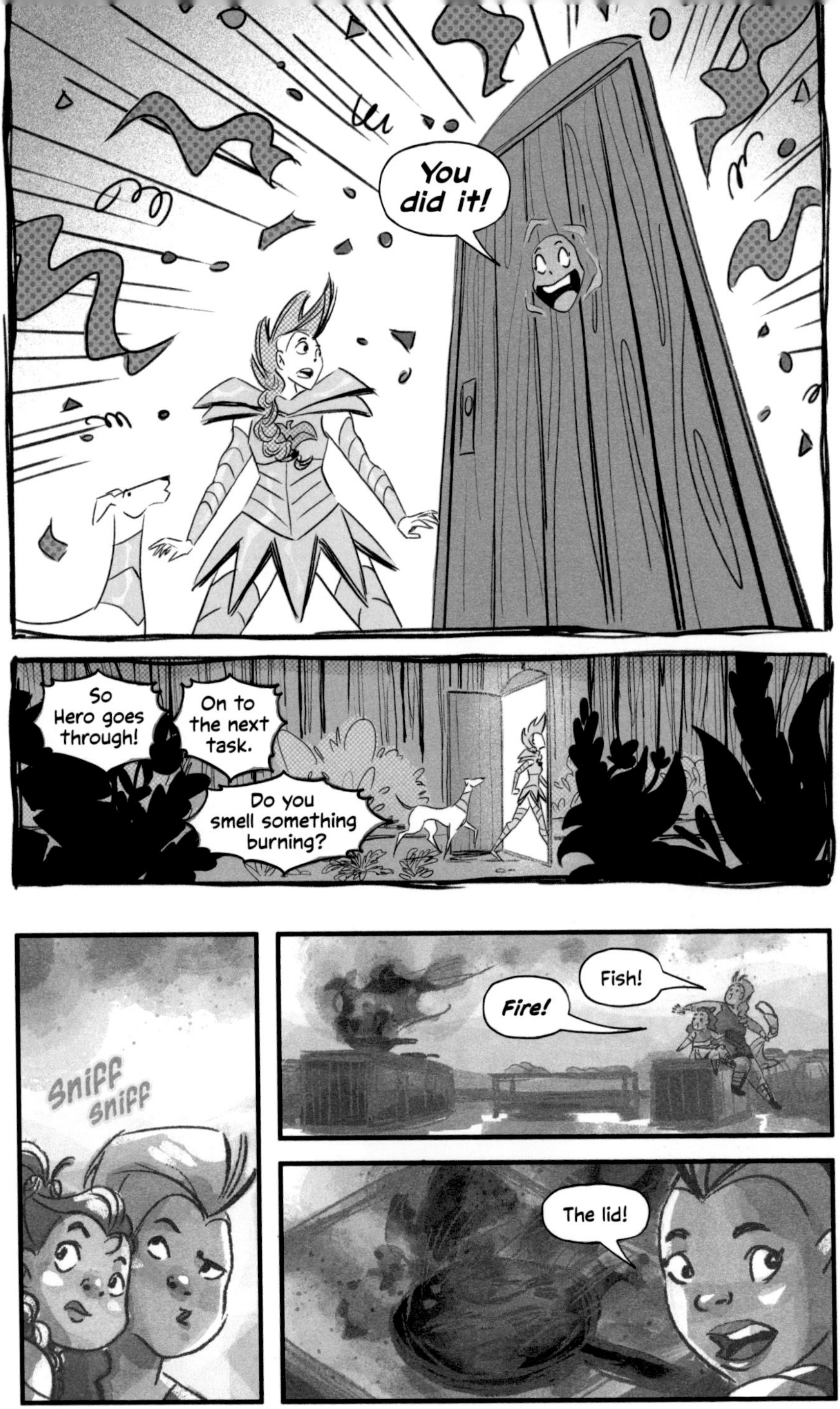
You did it!
So Hero goes through!
On to the next task.
Do you smell something burning?
Sniff sniff
Fish!
Fire!
The lid!

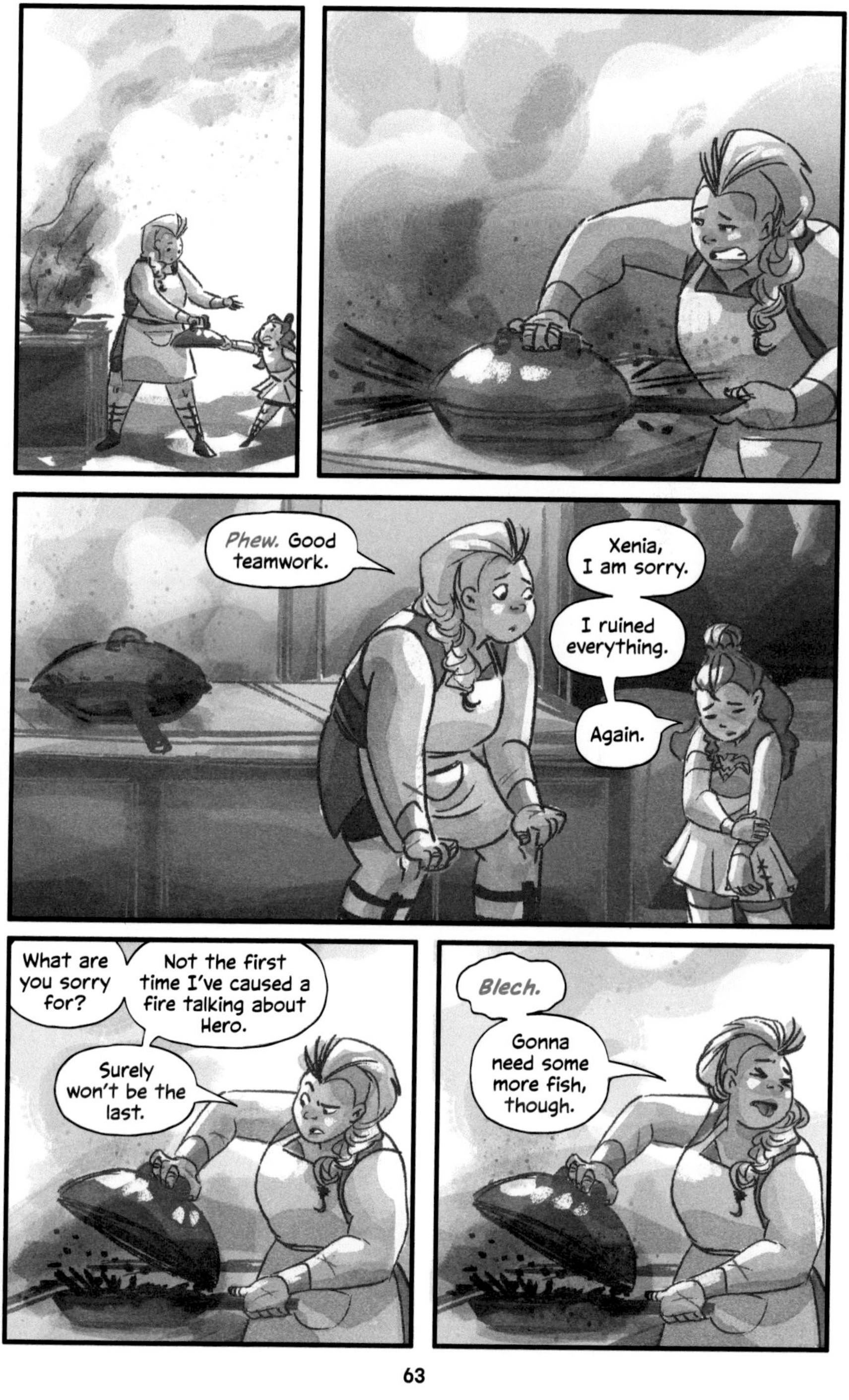
Phew. Good teamwork.
Xenia, I am sorry.
I ruined everything.
Again.
What are you sorry for?
Not the first time I've caused a fire talking about Hero.
Surely won't be the last.
Blech.
Gonna need some more fish, though.

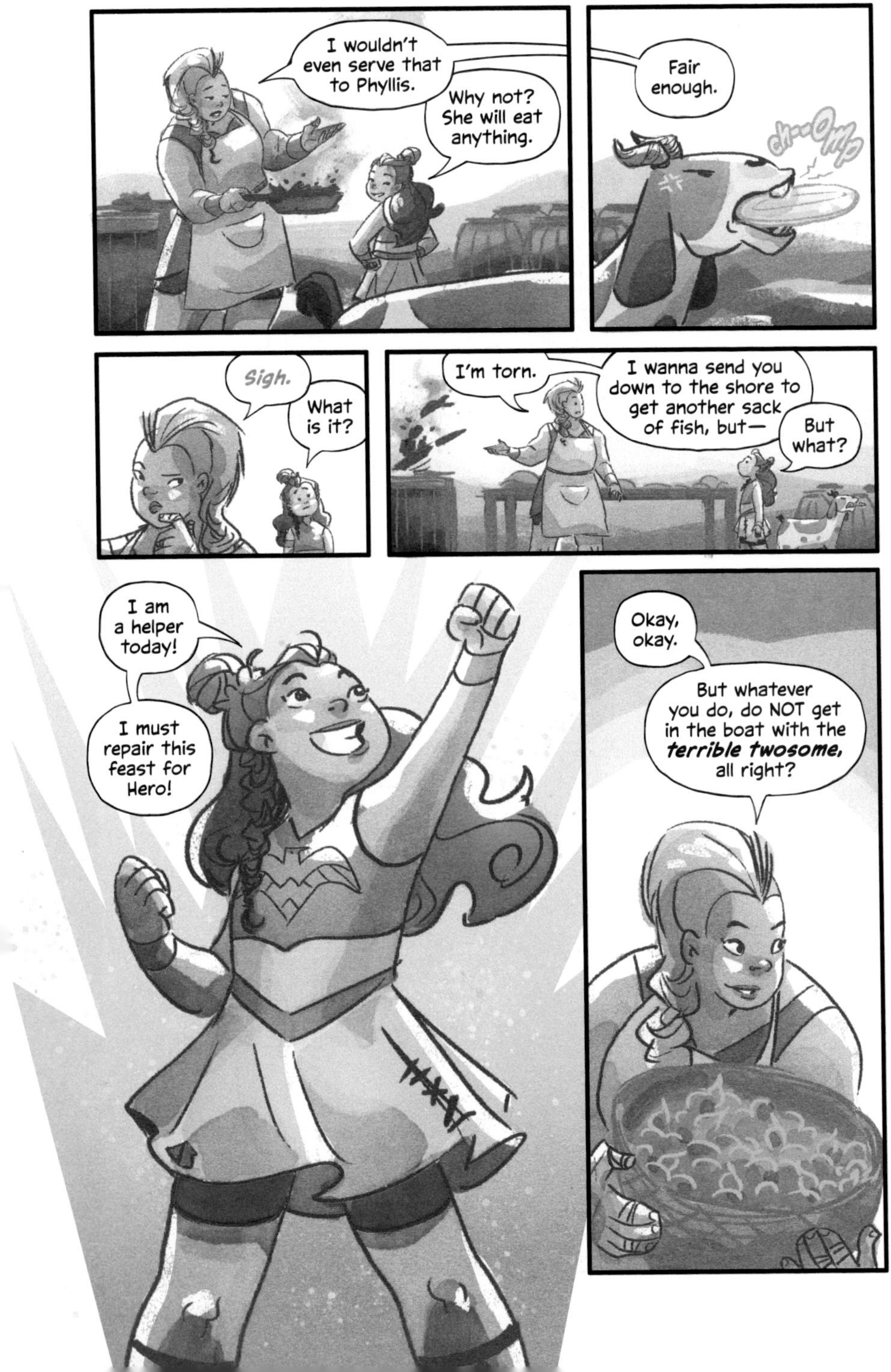
I wouldn't even serve that to Phyllis.
Why not? She will eat anything.
Fair enough.
ch--OMP
Sigh.
What is it?
I'm torn.
I wanna send you down to the shore to get another sack of fish, but—
But what?
I am a helper today!
I must repair this feast for Hero!
Okay, okay.
But whatever you do, do NOT get in the boat with the ***terrible twosome,*** all right?

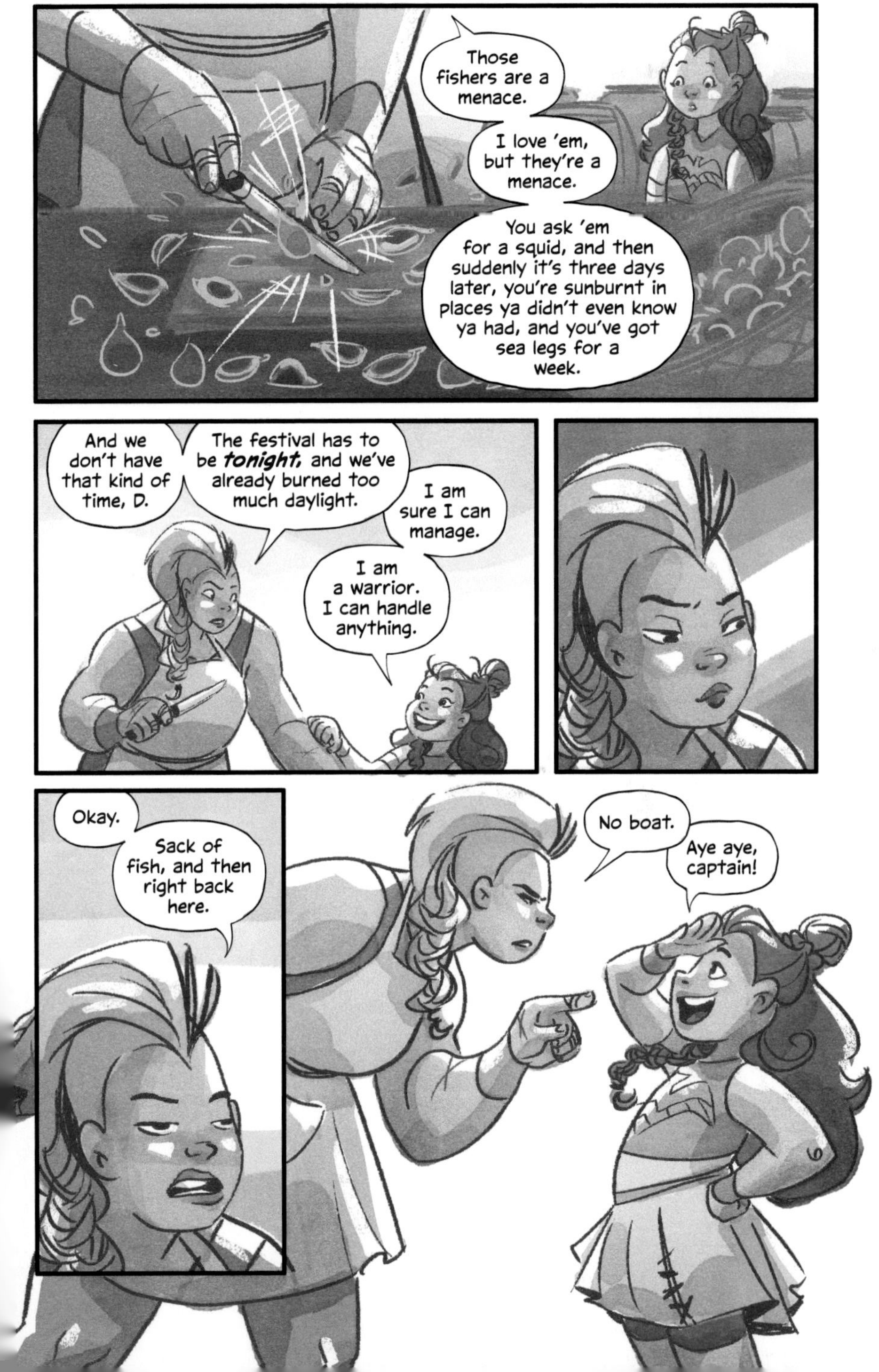

Those fishers are a menace.
I love 'em, but they're a menace.
You ask 'em for a squid, and then suddenly it's three days later, you're sunburnt in places ya didn't even know ya had, and you've got sea legs for a week.
And we don't have that kind of time, D.
The festival has to be *tonight,* and we've already burned too much daylight.
I am sure I can manage.
I am a warrior. I can handle anything.
Okay.
Sack of fish, and then right back here.
No boat.
Aye aye, captain!

CHAPTER 3

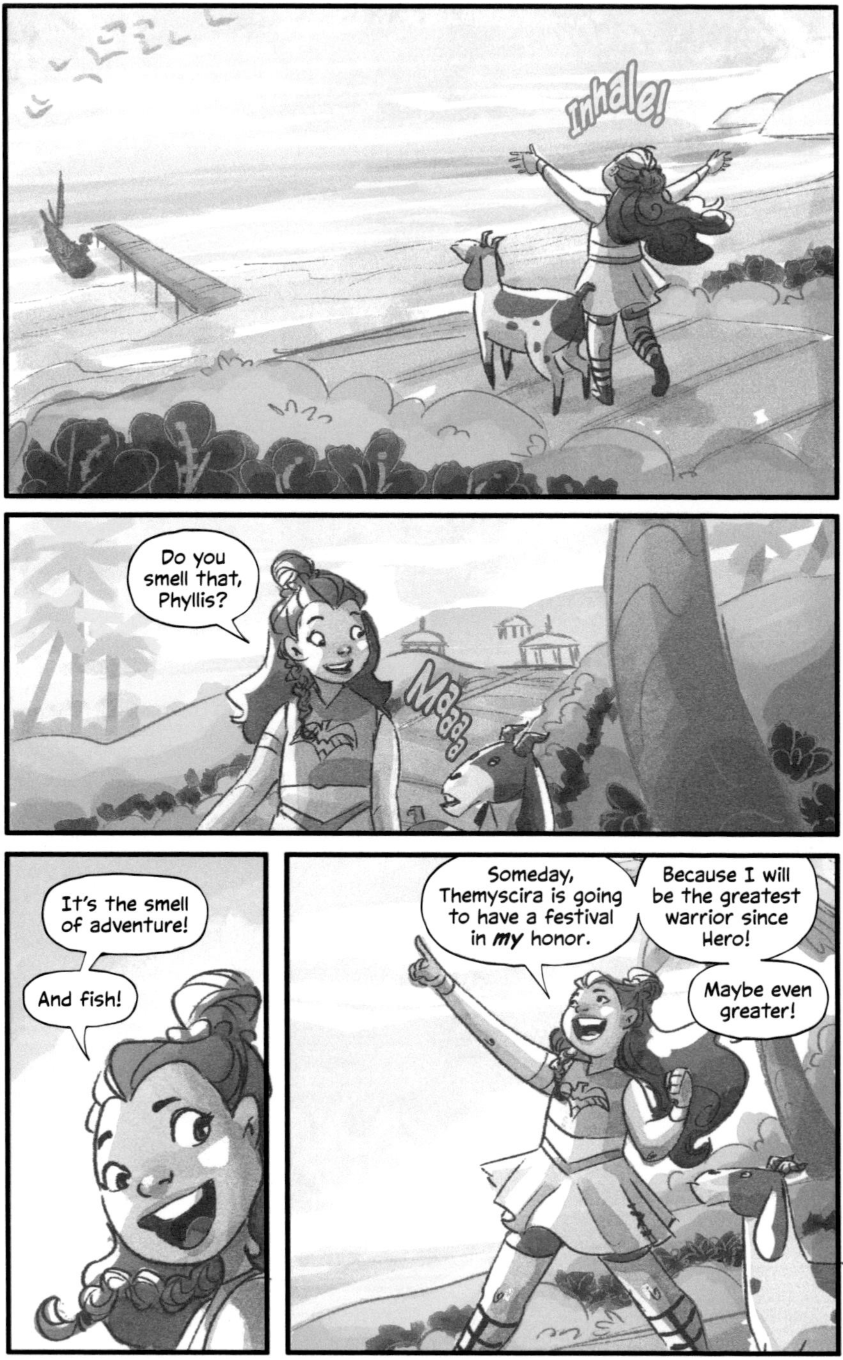
Inhale!
Do you smell that, Phyllis?
Maaa
It's the smell of adventure!
And fish!
Someday, Themyscira is going to have a festival in *my* honor.
Because I will be the greatest warrior since Hero!
Maybe even greater!

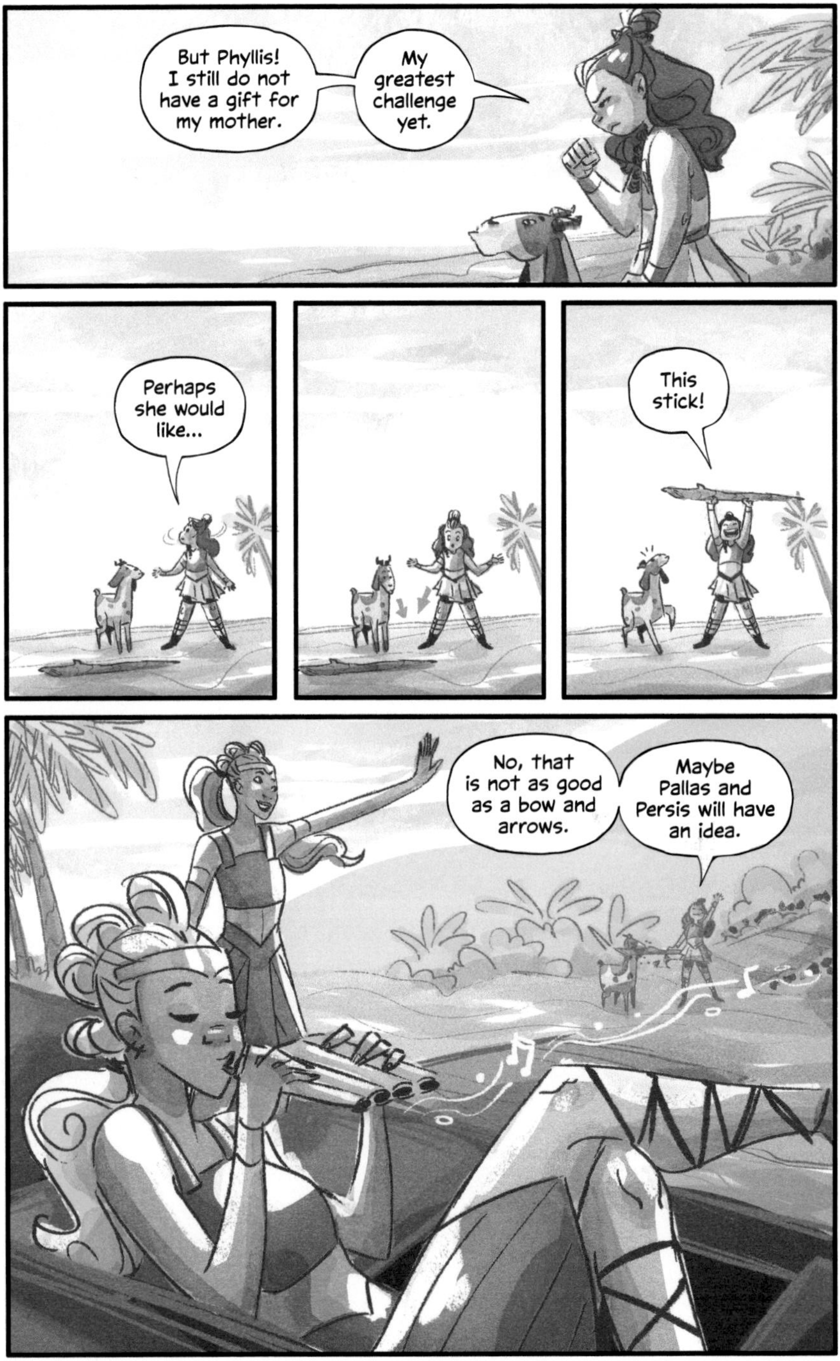
But Phyllis! I still do not have a gift for my mother.
My greatest challenge yet.
Perhaps she would like...
This stick!
No, that is not as good as a bow and arrows.
Maybe Pallas and Persis will have an idea.

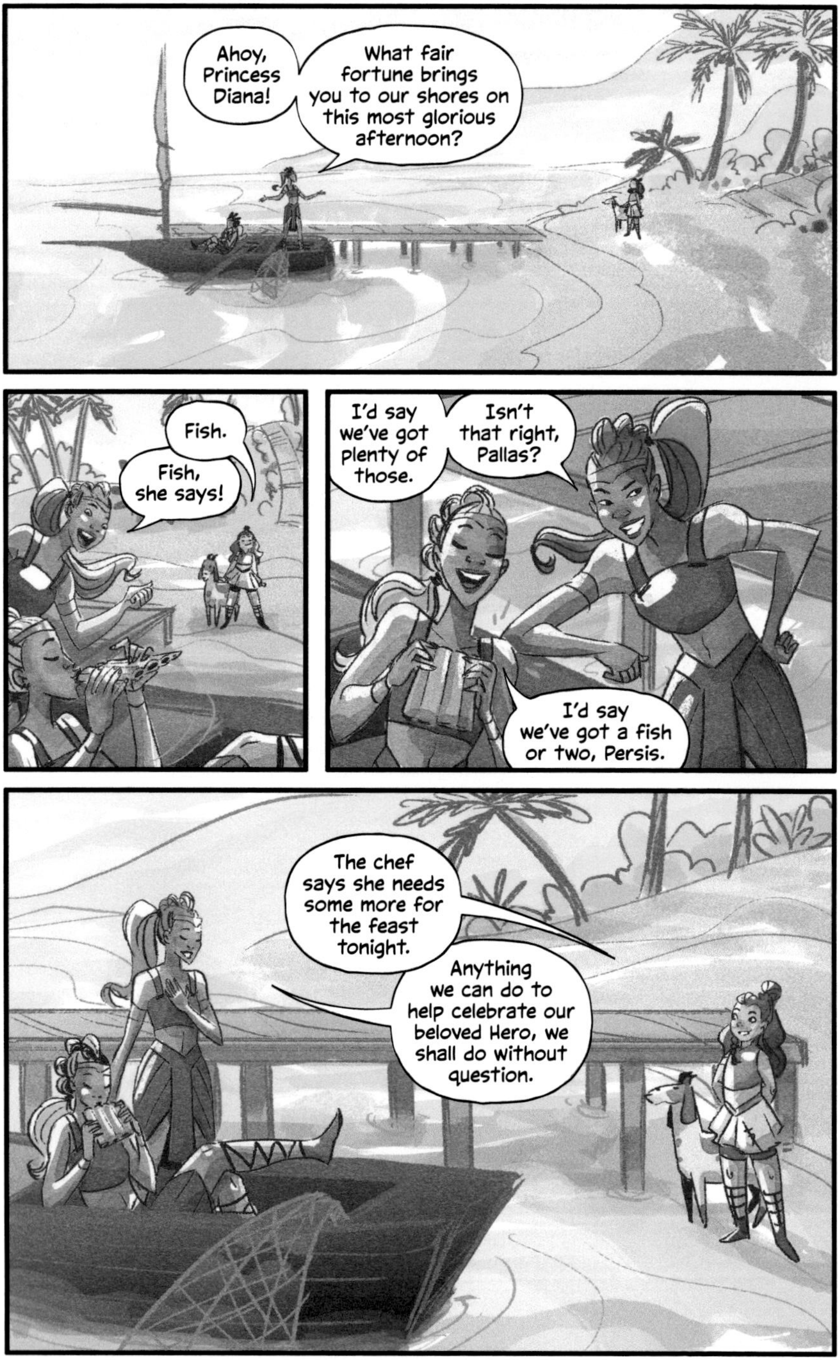
Ahoy, Princess Diana!
What fair fortune brings you to our shores on this most glorious afternoon?
Fish.
Fish, she says!
I'd say we've got plenty of those.
Isn't that right, Pallas?
I'd say we've got a fish or two, Persis.
The chef says she needs some more for the feast tonight.
Anything we can do to help celebrate our beloved Hero, we shall do without question.

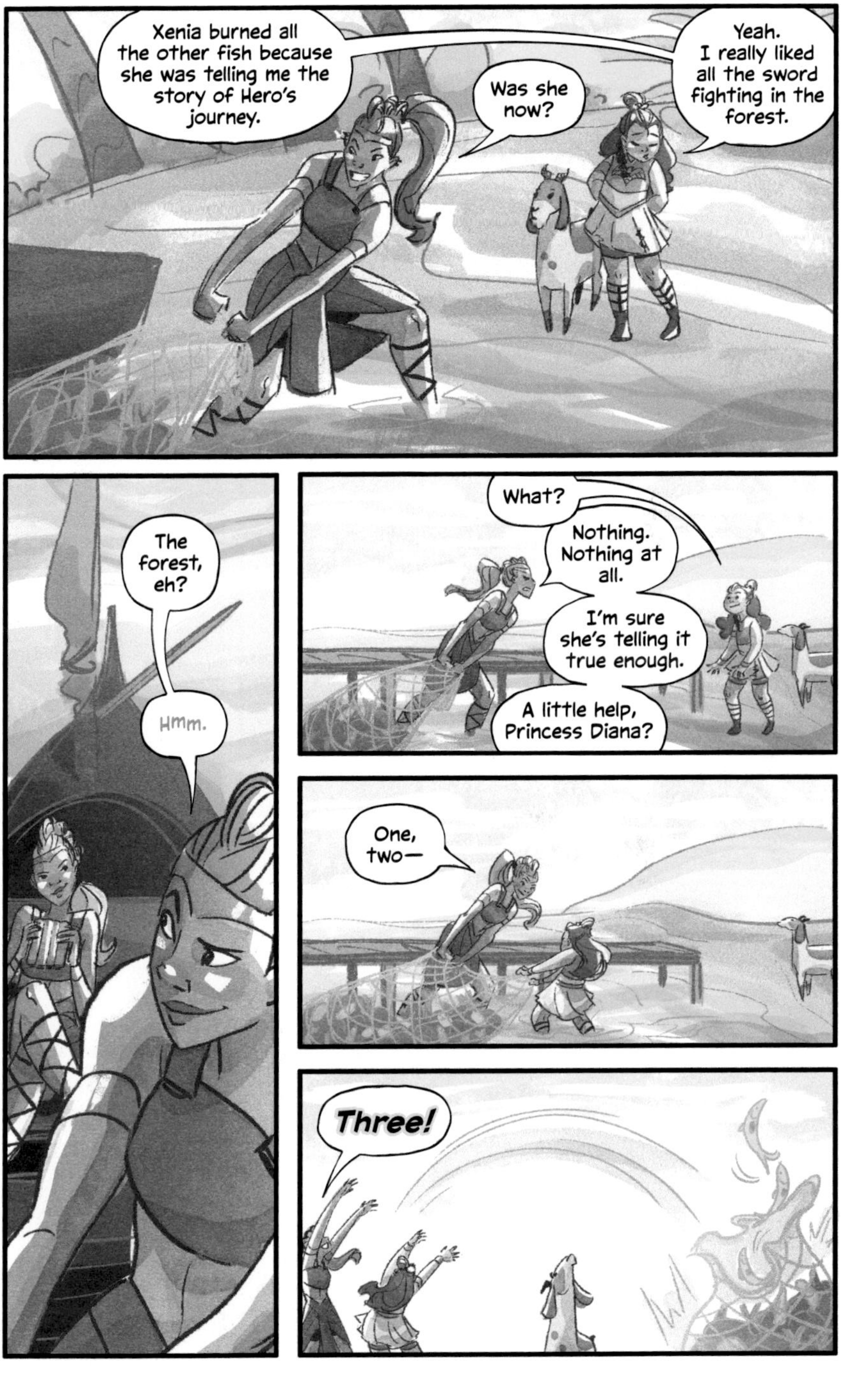
Xenia burned all the other fish because she was telling me the story of Hero's journey.
Was she now?
Yeah. I really liked all the sword fighting in the forest.
The forest, eh?
Hmm.
What?
Nothing. Nothing at all.
I'm sure she's telling it true enough.
A little help, Princess Diana?
One, two—
Three!

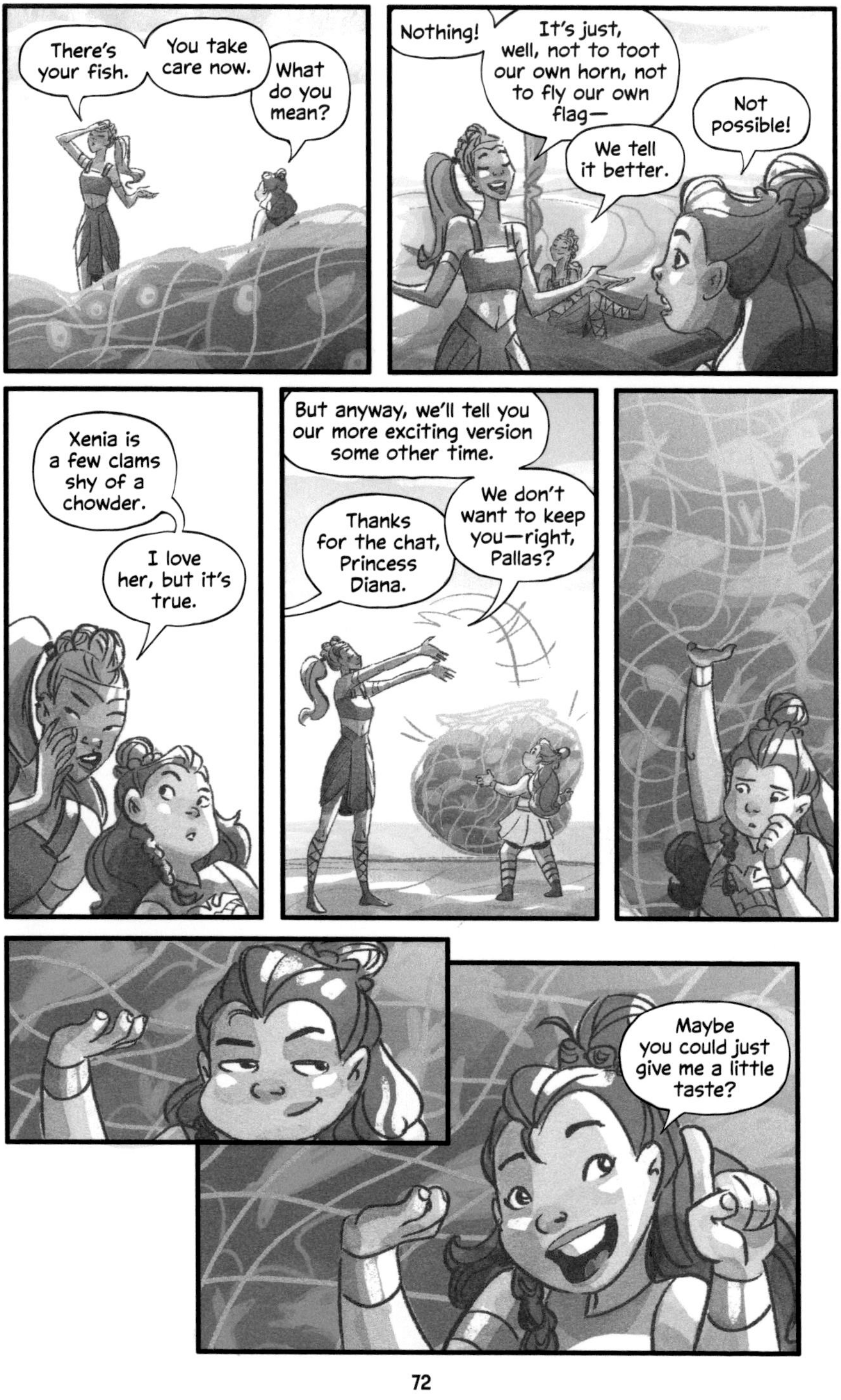
There's your fish.
You take care now.
What do you mean?
Nothing!
It's just, well, not to toot our own horn, not to fly our own flag—
We tell it better.
Not possible!
Xenia is a few clams shy of a chowder.
I love her, but it's true.
But anyway, we'll tell you our more exciting version some other time.
Thanks for the chat, Princess Diana.
We don't want to keep you—right, Pallas?
Maybe you could just give me a little taste?

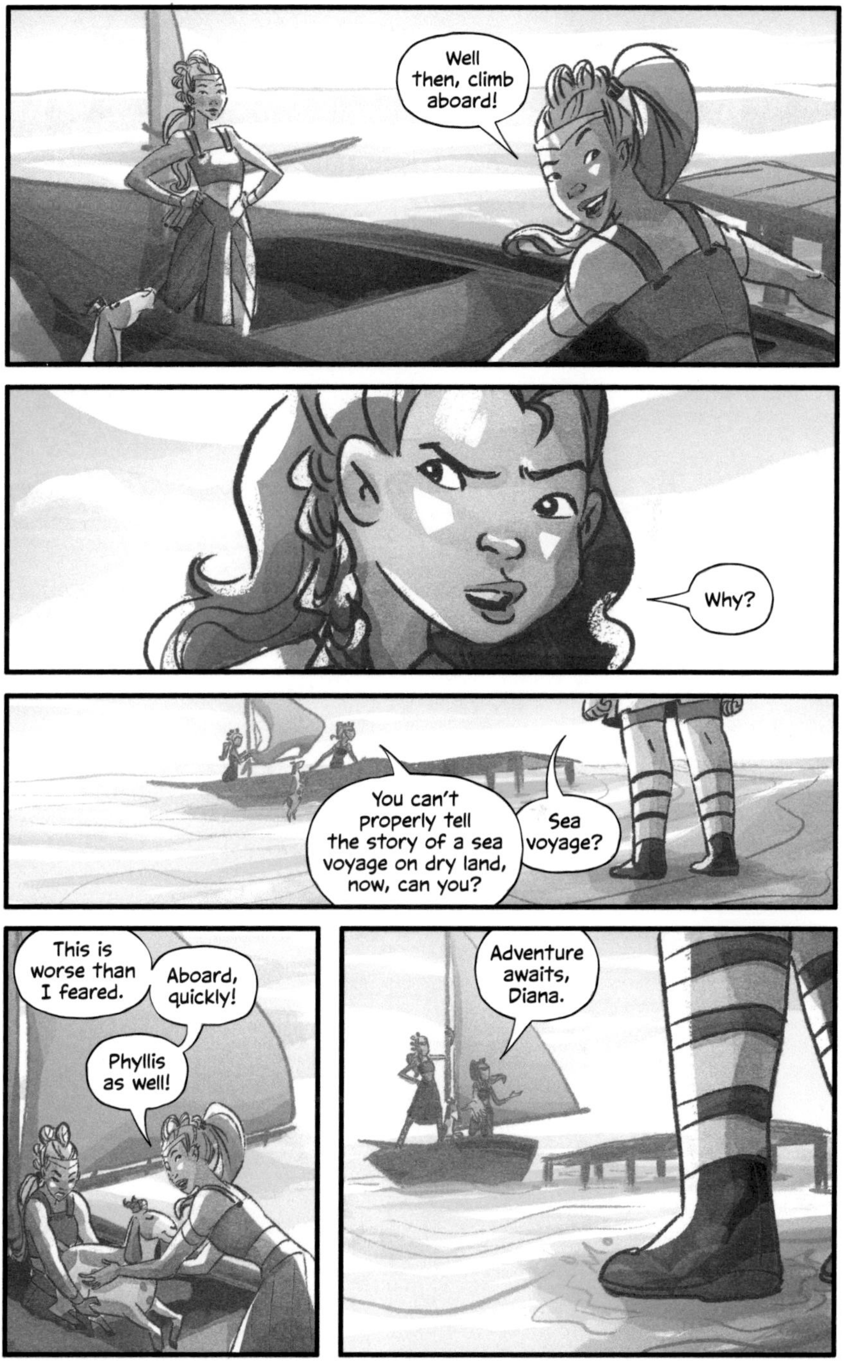
Well then, climb aboard!
Why?
Sea voyage?
You can't properly tell the story of a sea voyage on dry land, now, can you?
This is worse than I feared.
Aboard, quickly!
Phyllis as well!
Adventure awaits, Diana.

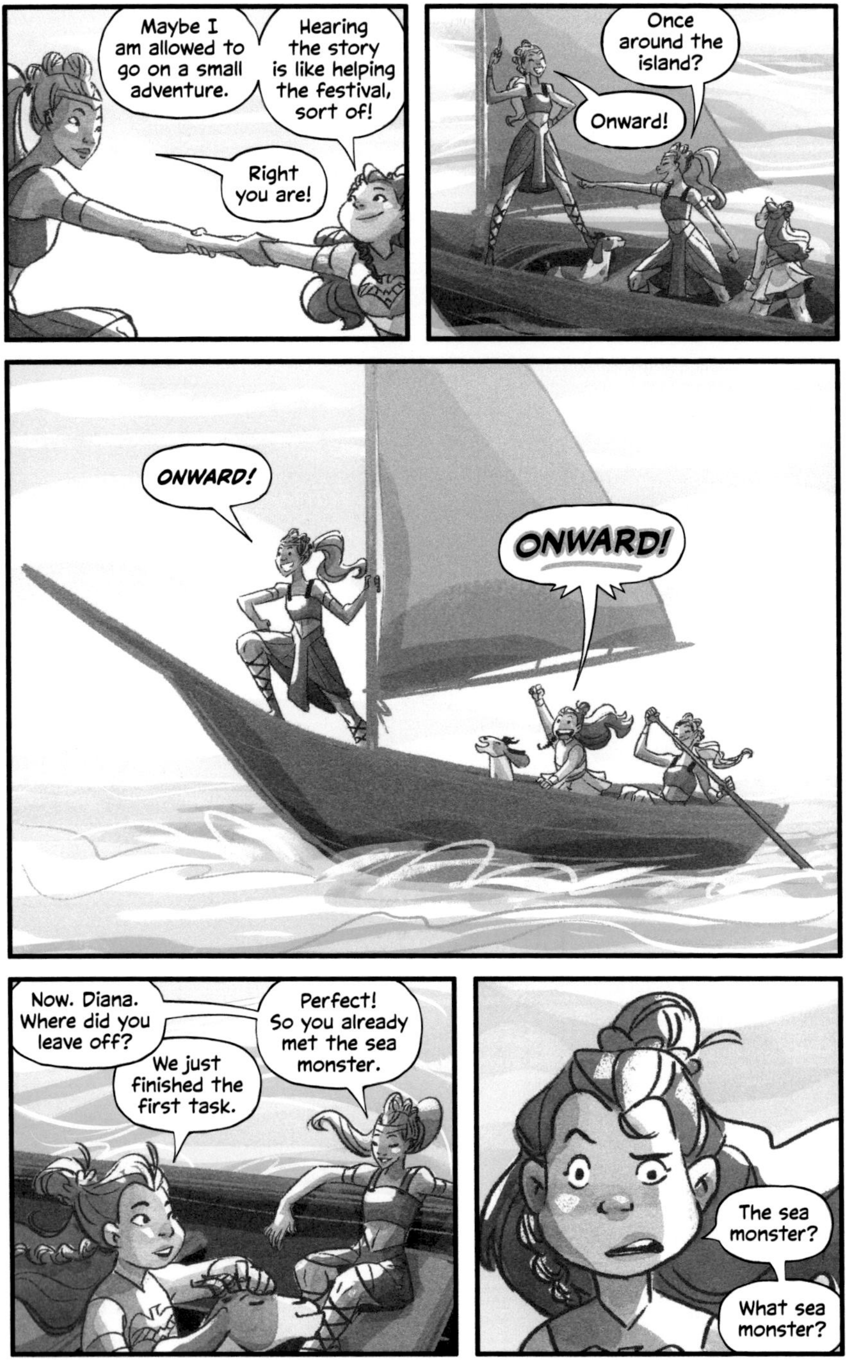
Maybe I am allowed to go on a small adventure.
Hearing the story is like helping the festival, sort of!
Right you are!
Once around the island?
Onward!
ONWARD!
ONWARD!
Now. Diana. Where did you leave off?
We just finished the first task.
Perfect! So you already met the sea monster.
The sea monster?
What sea monster?

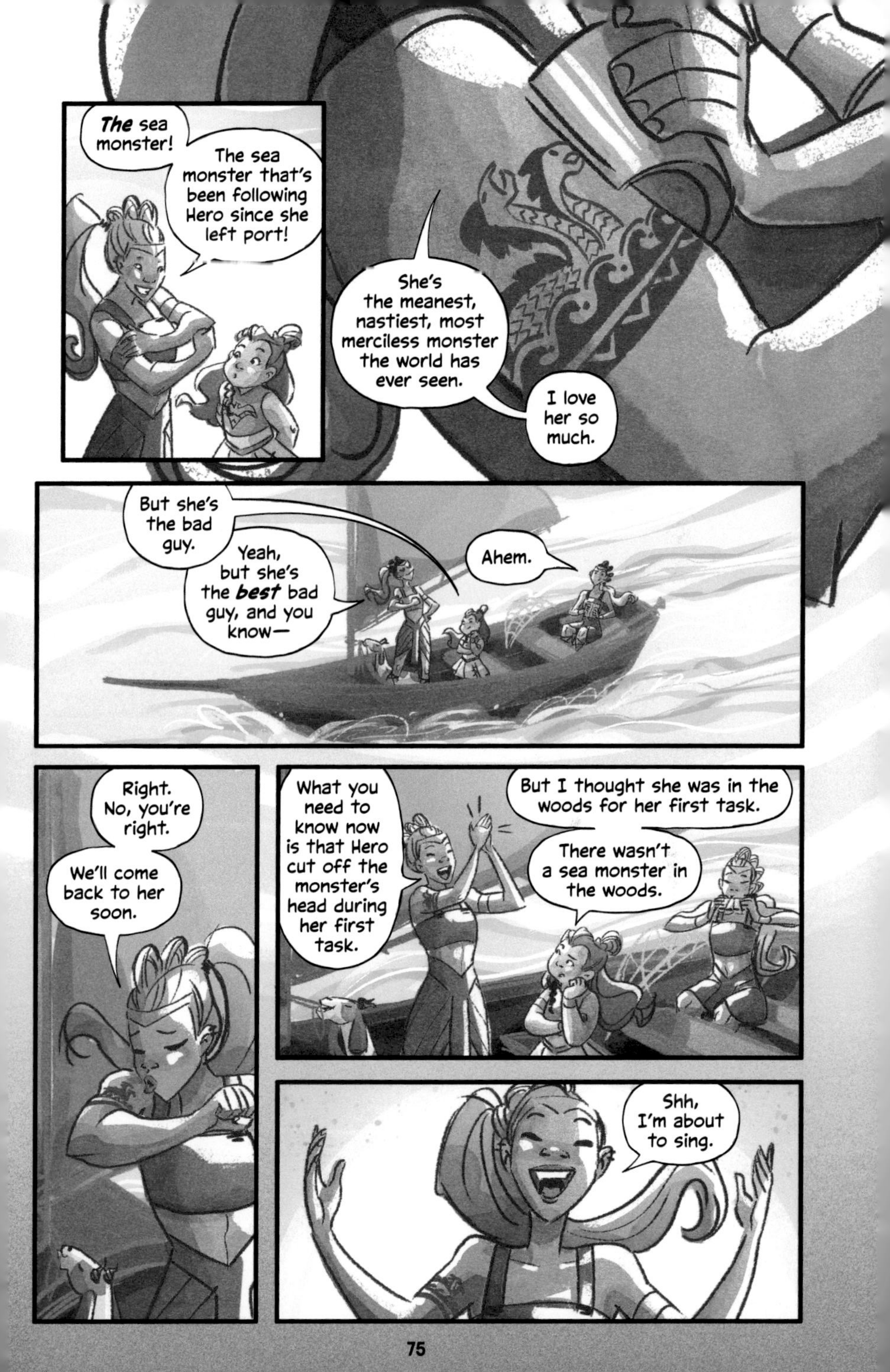

The sea monster!
The sea monster that's been following Hero since she left port!
She's the meanest, nastiest, most merciless monster the world has ever seen.
I love her so much.
But she's the bad guy.
Yeah, but she's the ***best*** bad guy, and you know—
Ahem.
Right. No, you're right.
We'll come back to her soon.
What you need to know now is that Hero cut off the monster's head during her first task.
But I thought she was in the woods for her first task.
There wasn't a sea monster in the woods.
Shh, I'm about to sing.

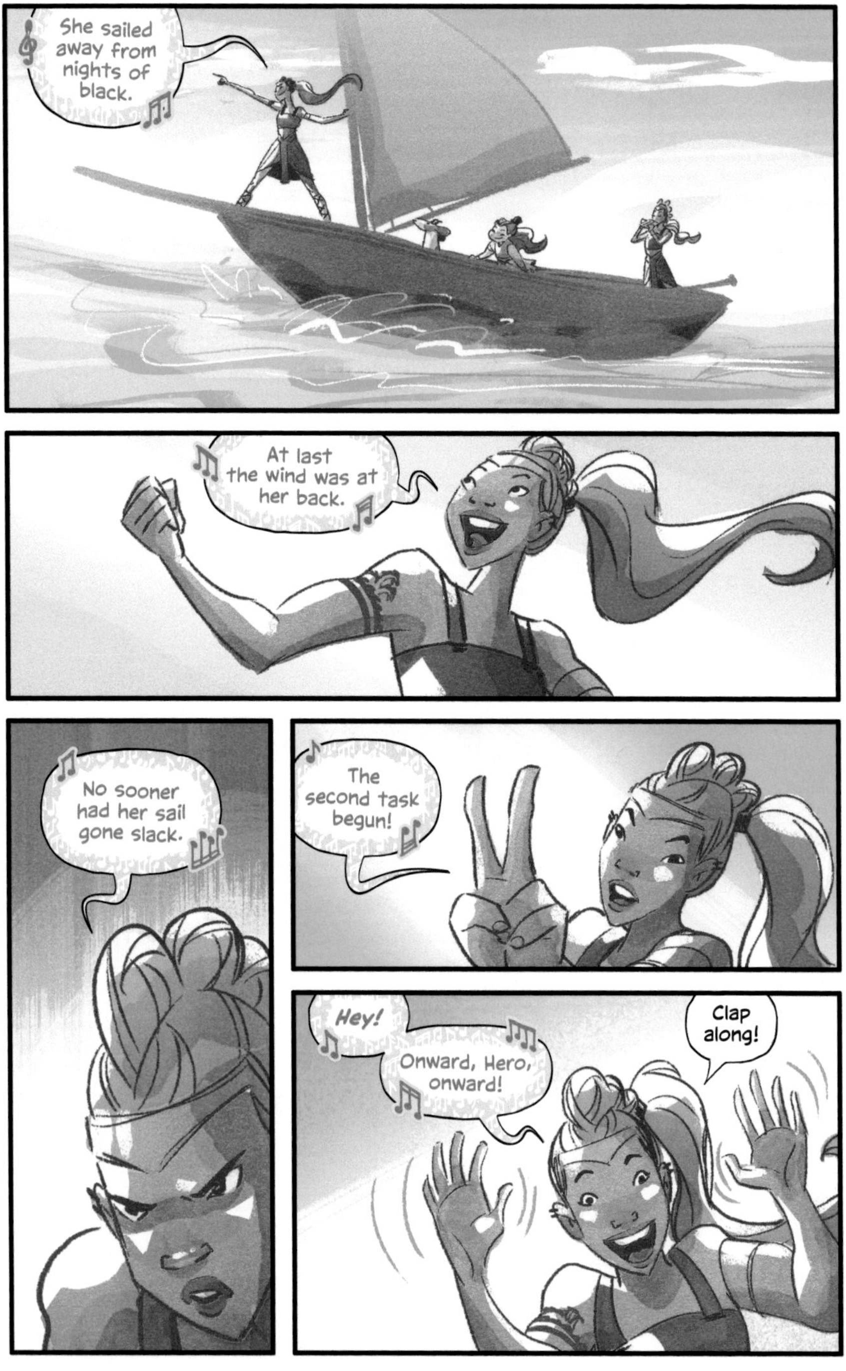
She sailed away from nights of black.
At last the wind was at her back.
No sooner had her sail gone slack.
The second task begun!
Hey!
Onward, Hero, onward!
Clap along!

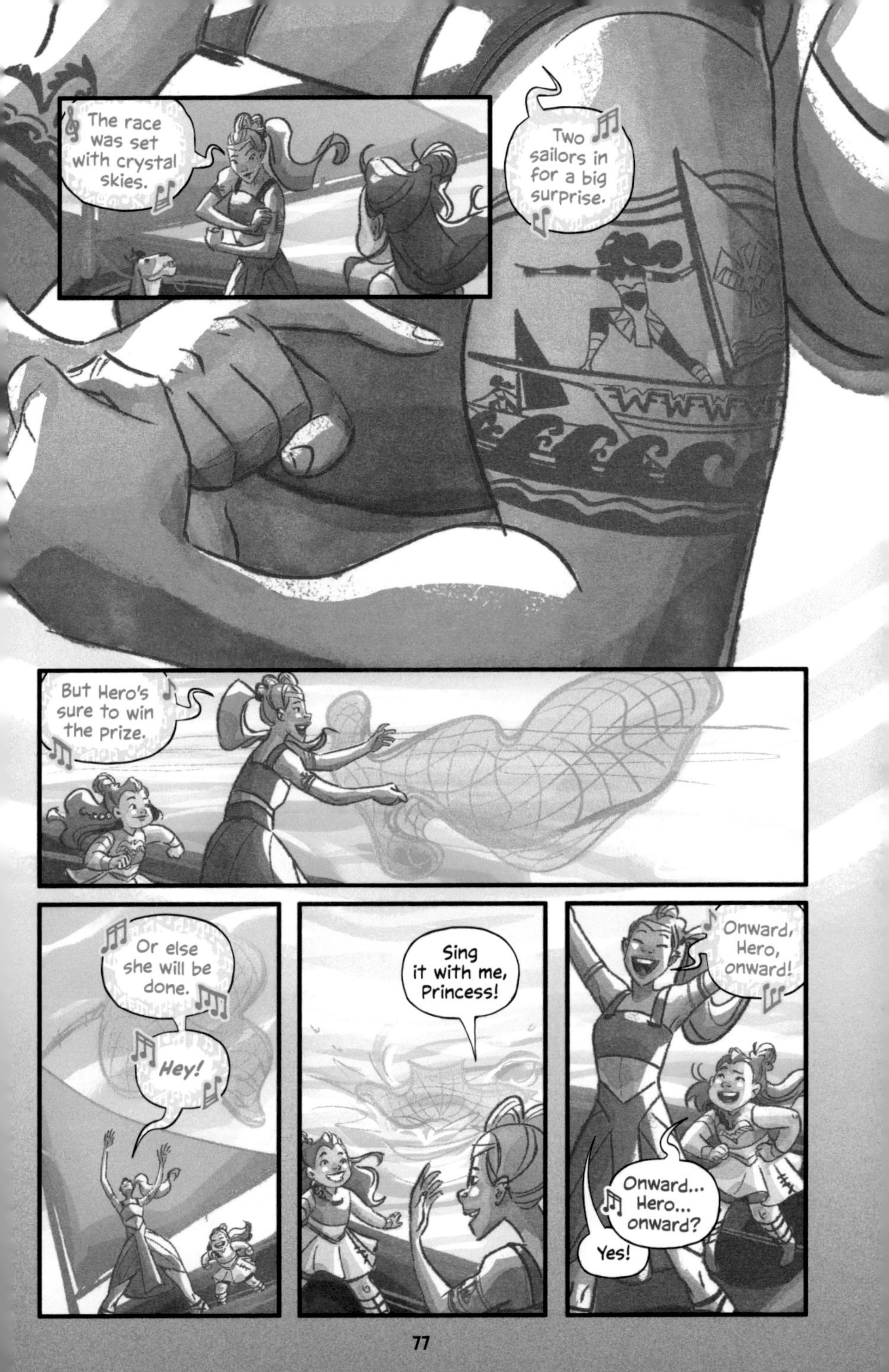
The race was set with crystal skies.
Two sailors in for a big surprise.
But Hero's sure to win the prize.
Or else she will be done.
Hey!
Sing it with me, Princess!
Onward, Hero, onward!
Onward... Hero... onward?
Yes!

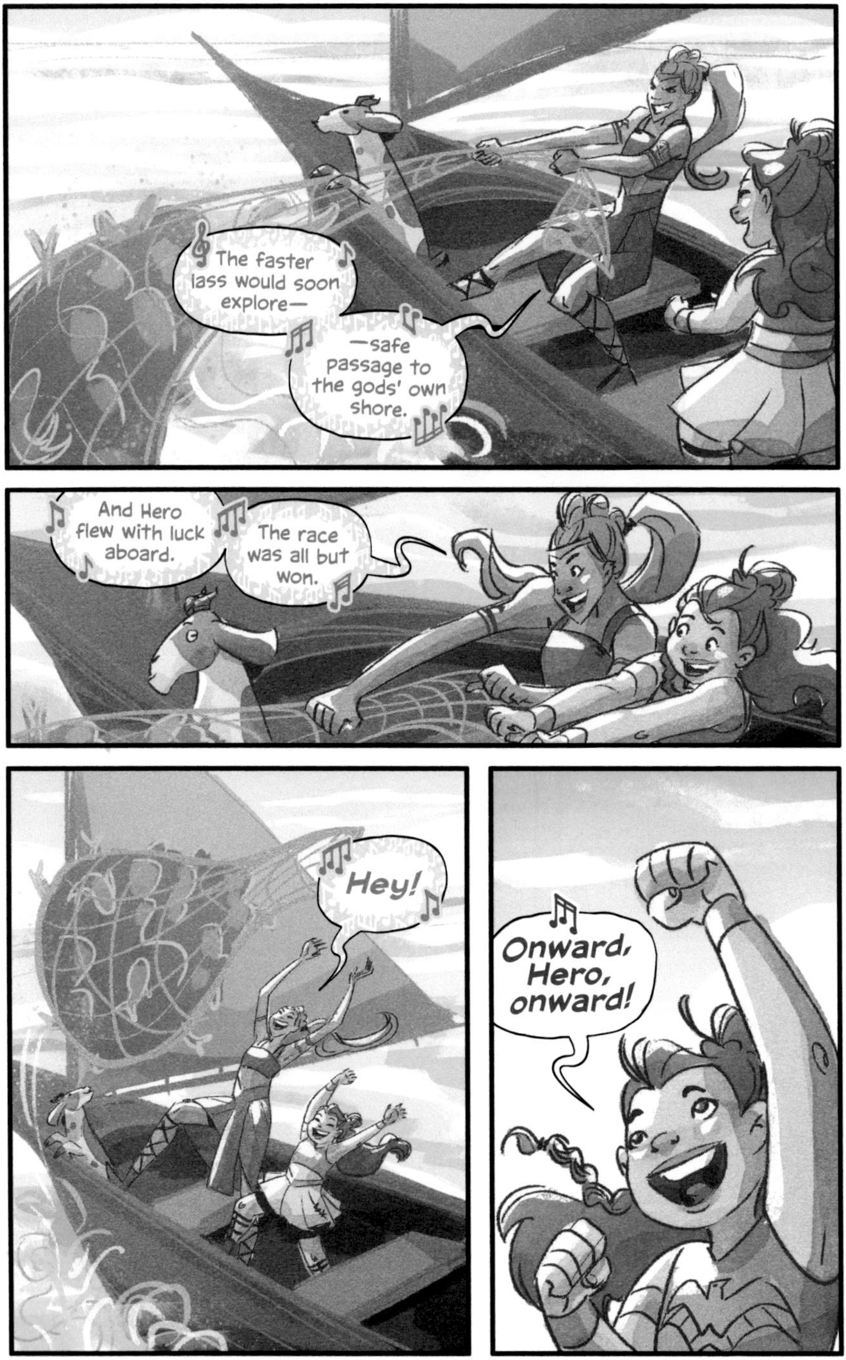
The faster lass would soon explore—
—safe passage to the gods' own shore.
And Hero flew with luck aboard.
The race was all but won.
Hey!
Onward, Hero, onward!

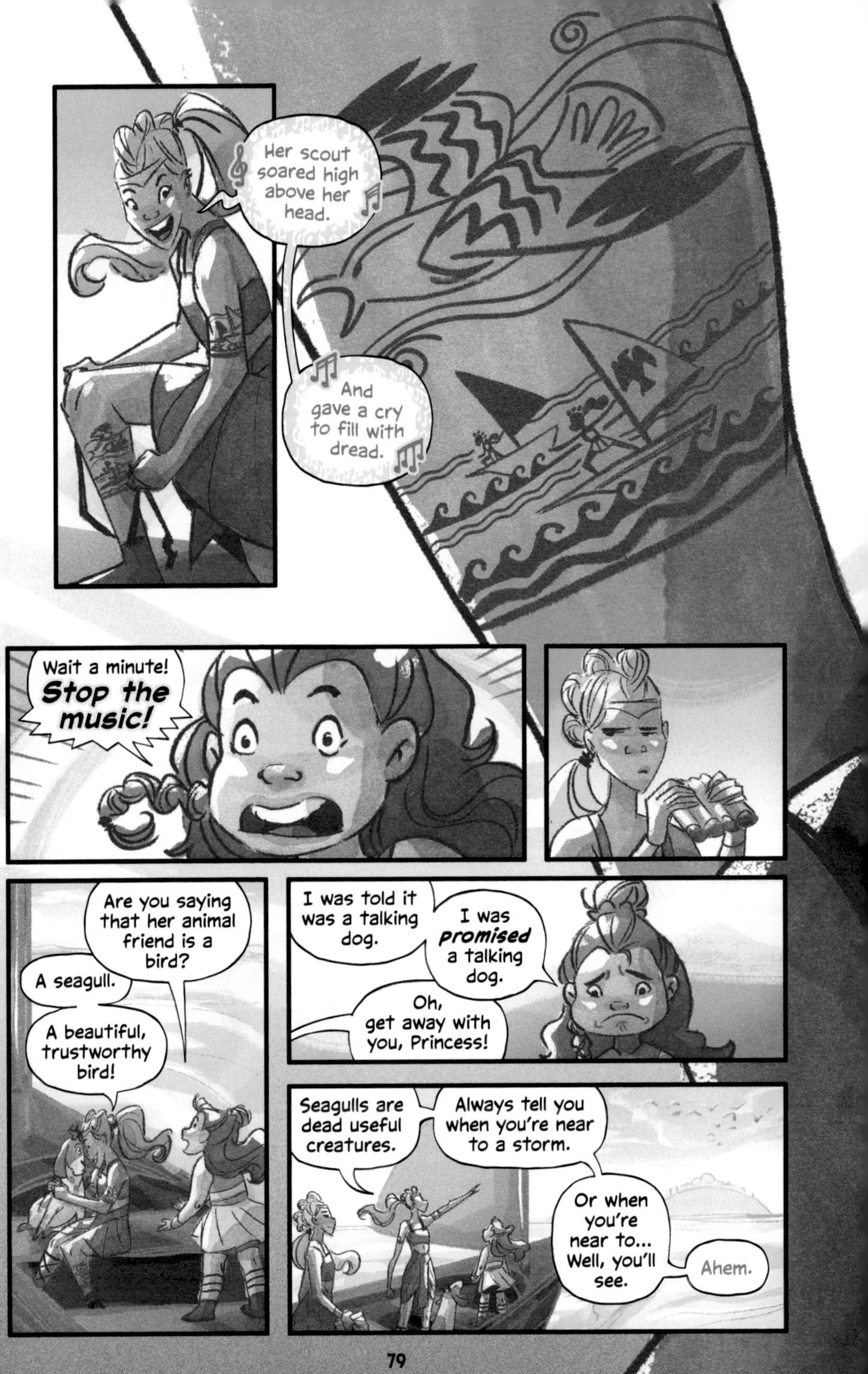
Her scout soared high above her head.
And gave a cry to fill with dread.
Wait a minute! Stop the music!
Are you saying that her animal friend is a bird?
A seagull.
A beautiful, trustworthy bird!
I was told it was a talking dog.
I was promised a talking dog.
Oh, get away with you, Princess!
Seagulls are dead useful creatures.
Always tell you when you're near to a storm.
Or when you're near to... Well, you'll see.
Ahem.

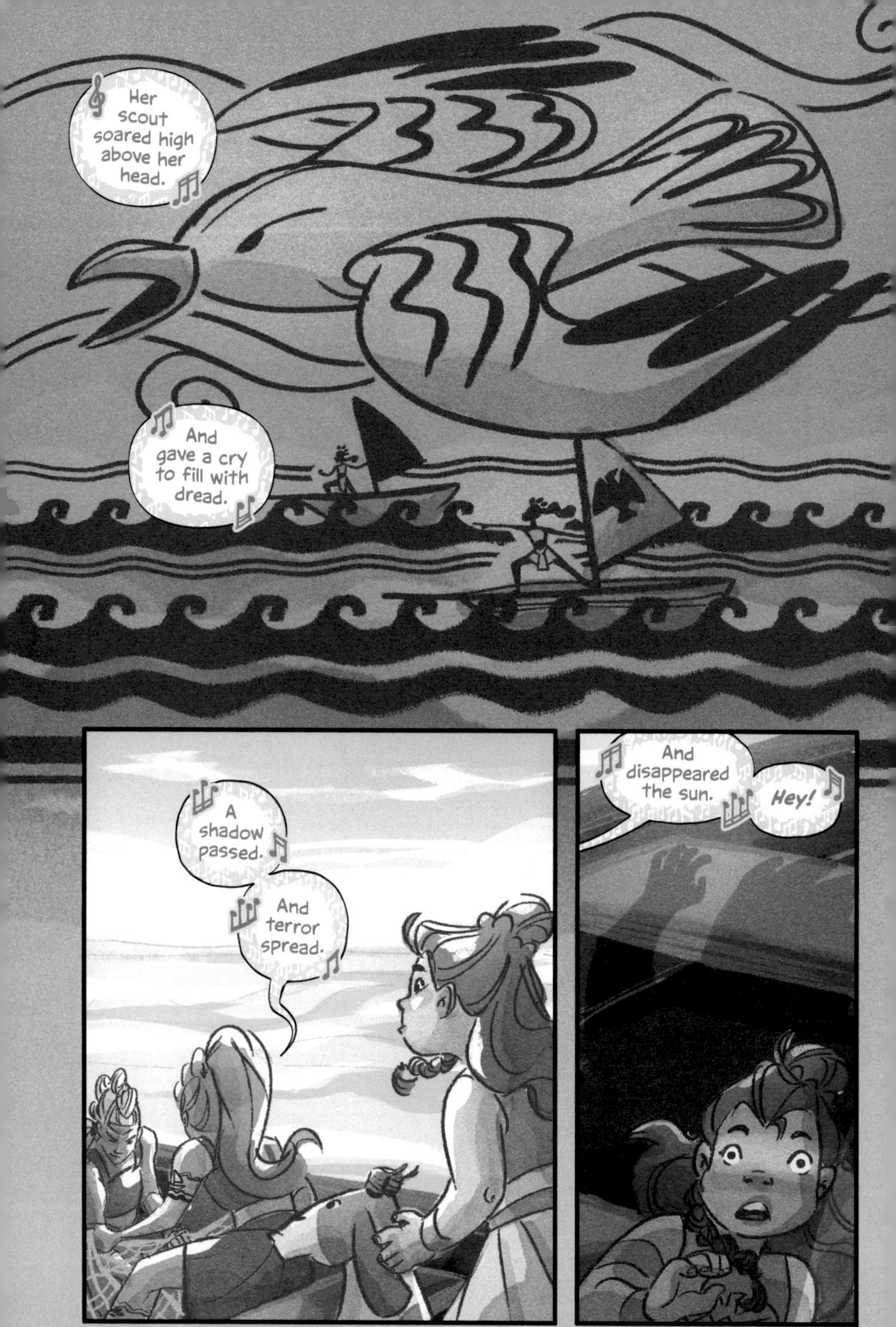
Her scout soared high above her head.
And gave a cry to fill with dread.
A shadow passed.
And terror spread.
And disappeared the sun.
Hey!

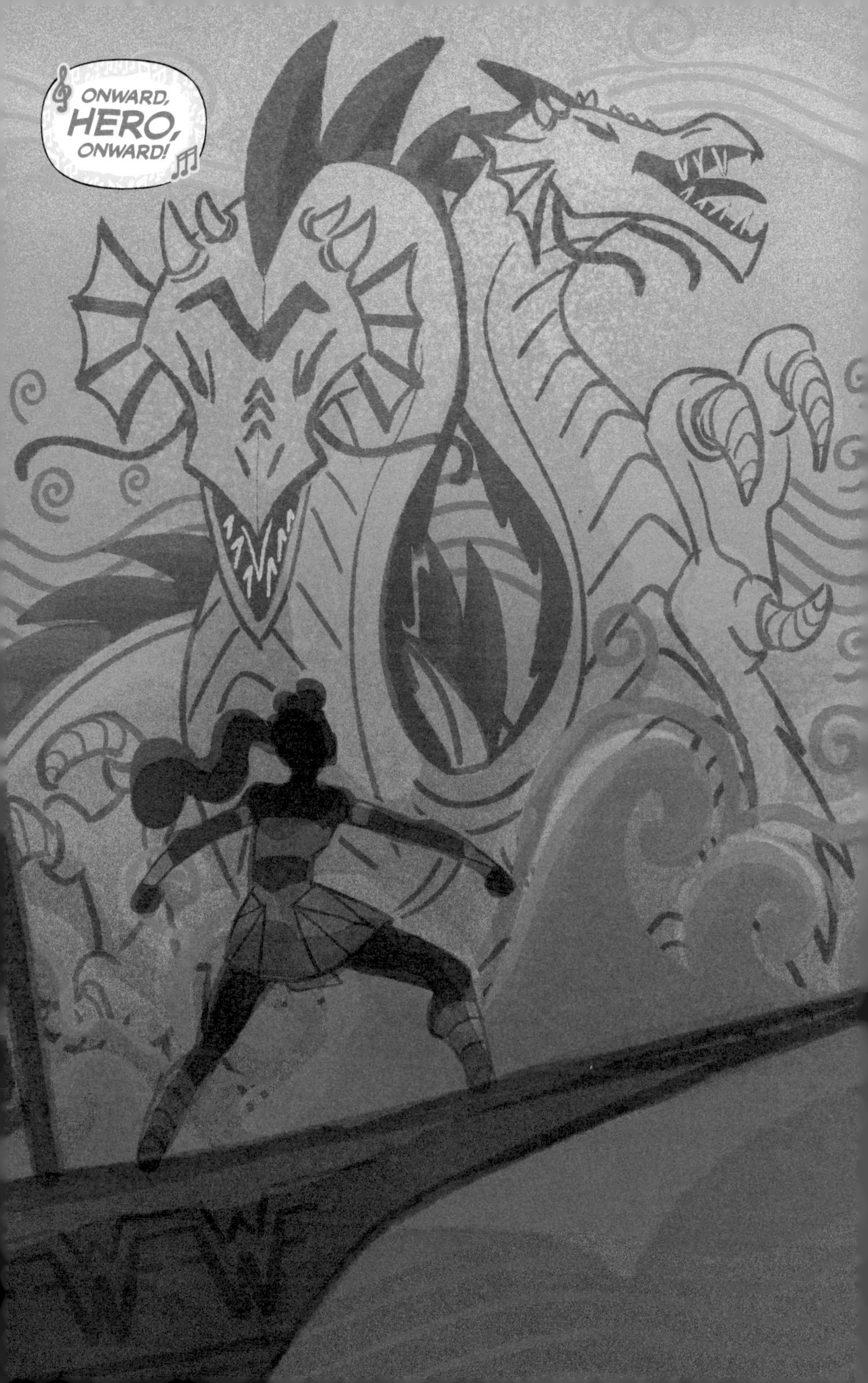
ONWARD, HERO, ONWARD!

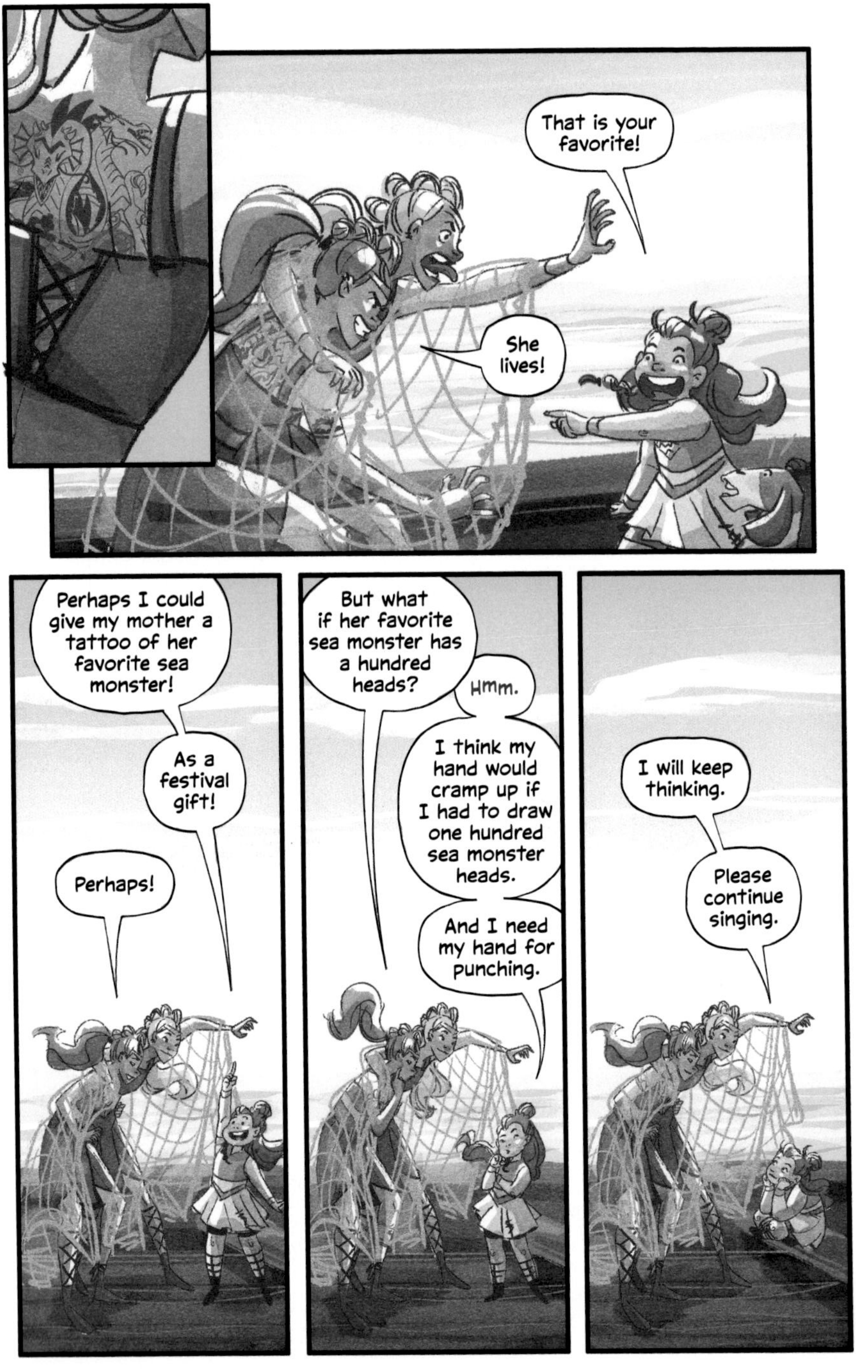
That is your favorite!
She lives!
Perhaps I could give my mother a tattoo of her favorite sea monster!
As a festival gift!
Perhaps!
But what if her favorite sea monster has a hundred heads?
Hmm.
I think my hand would cramp up if I had to draw one hundred sea monster heads.
And I need my hand for punching.
I will keep thinking.
Please continue singing.

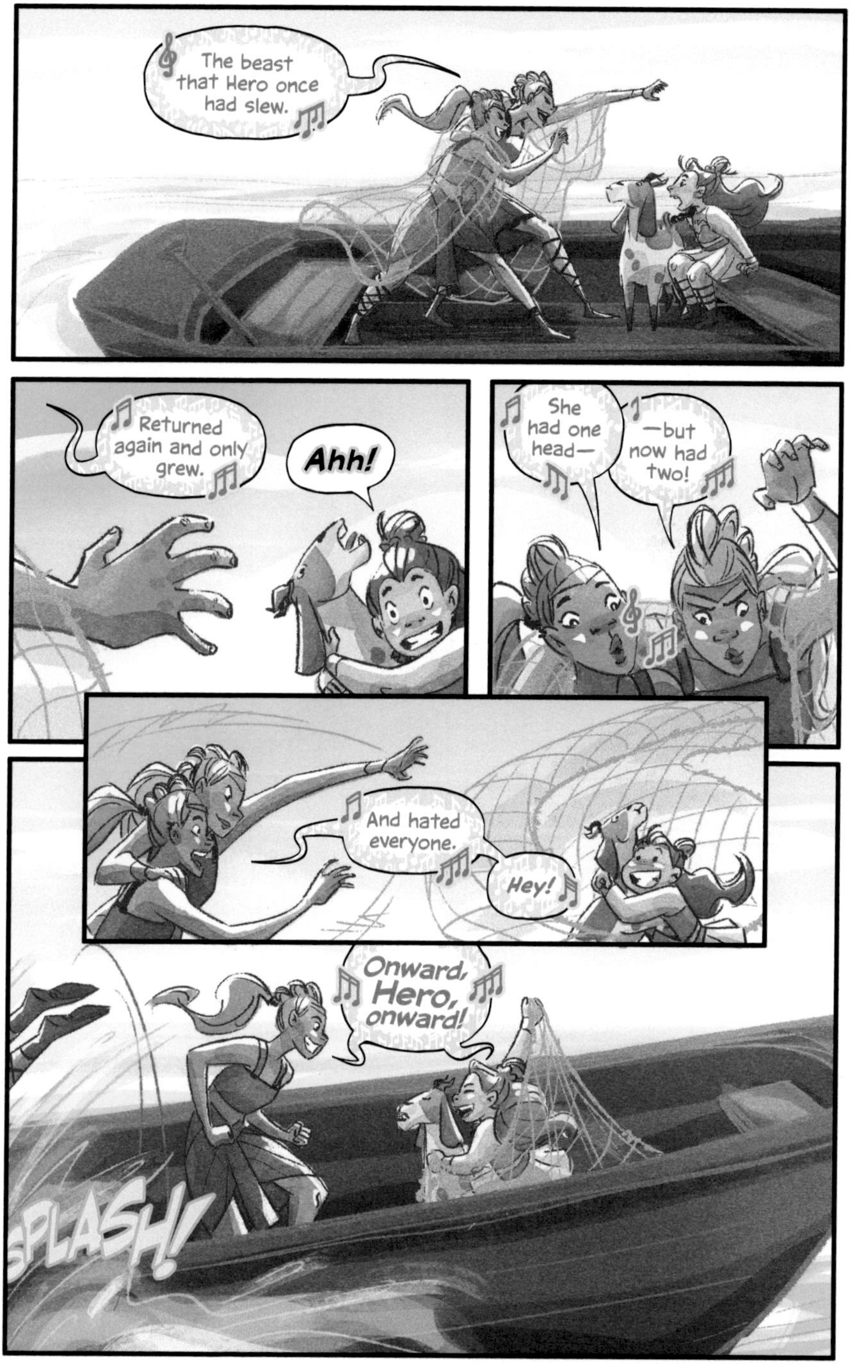
The beast that Hero once had slew.
Returned again and only grew.
Ahh!
She had one head—
—but now had two!
And hated everyone.
Hey!
Onward, Hero, onward!
SPLASH!

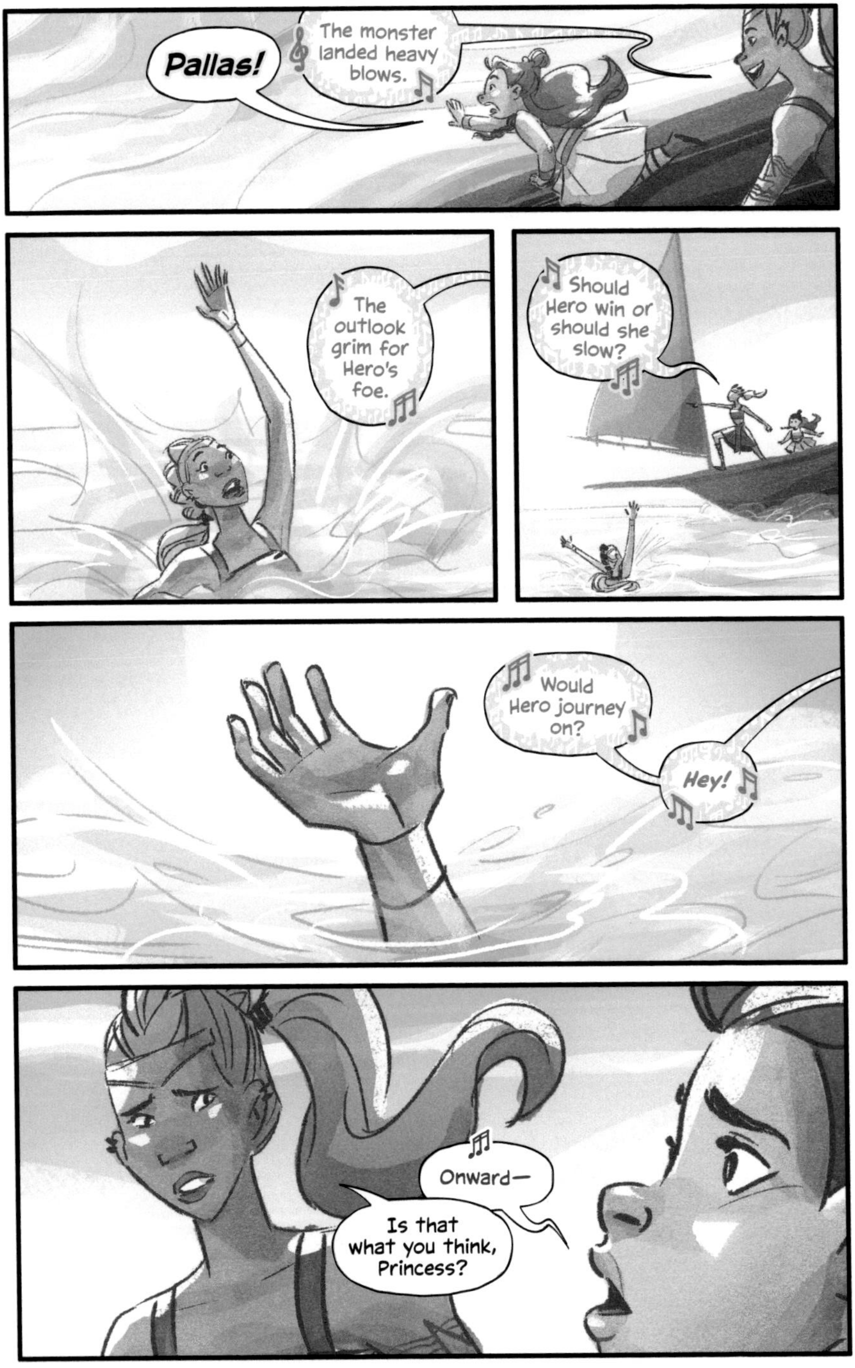
Pallas!
The monster landed heavy blows.
The outlook grim for Hero's foe.
Should Hero win or should she slow?
Would Hero journey on?
Hey!
Onward—
Is that what you think, Princess?

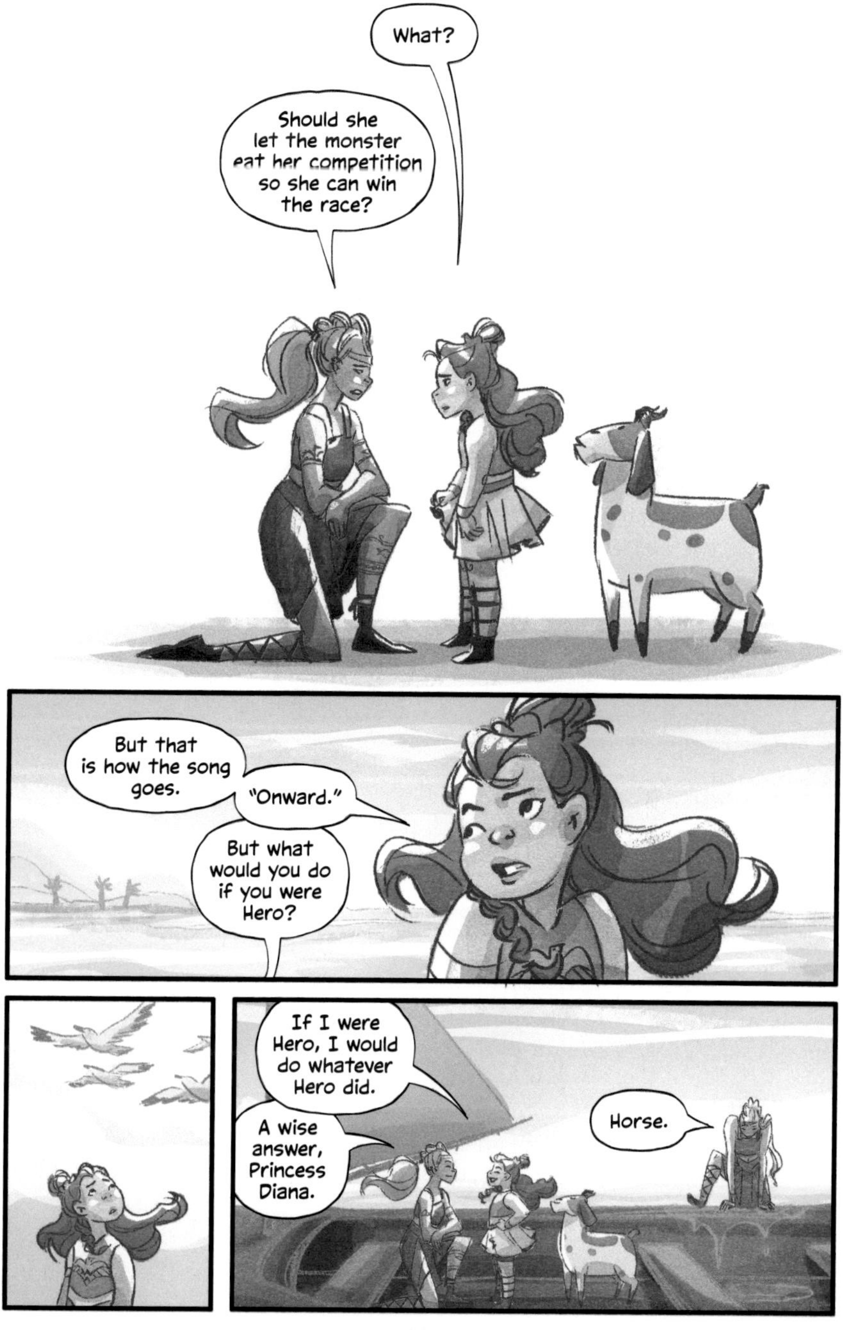
What?
Should she let the monster eat her competition so she can win the race?
But that is how the song goes.
"Onward."
But what would you do if you were Hero?
If I were Hero, I would do whatever Hero did.
A wise answer, Princess Diana.
Horse.

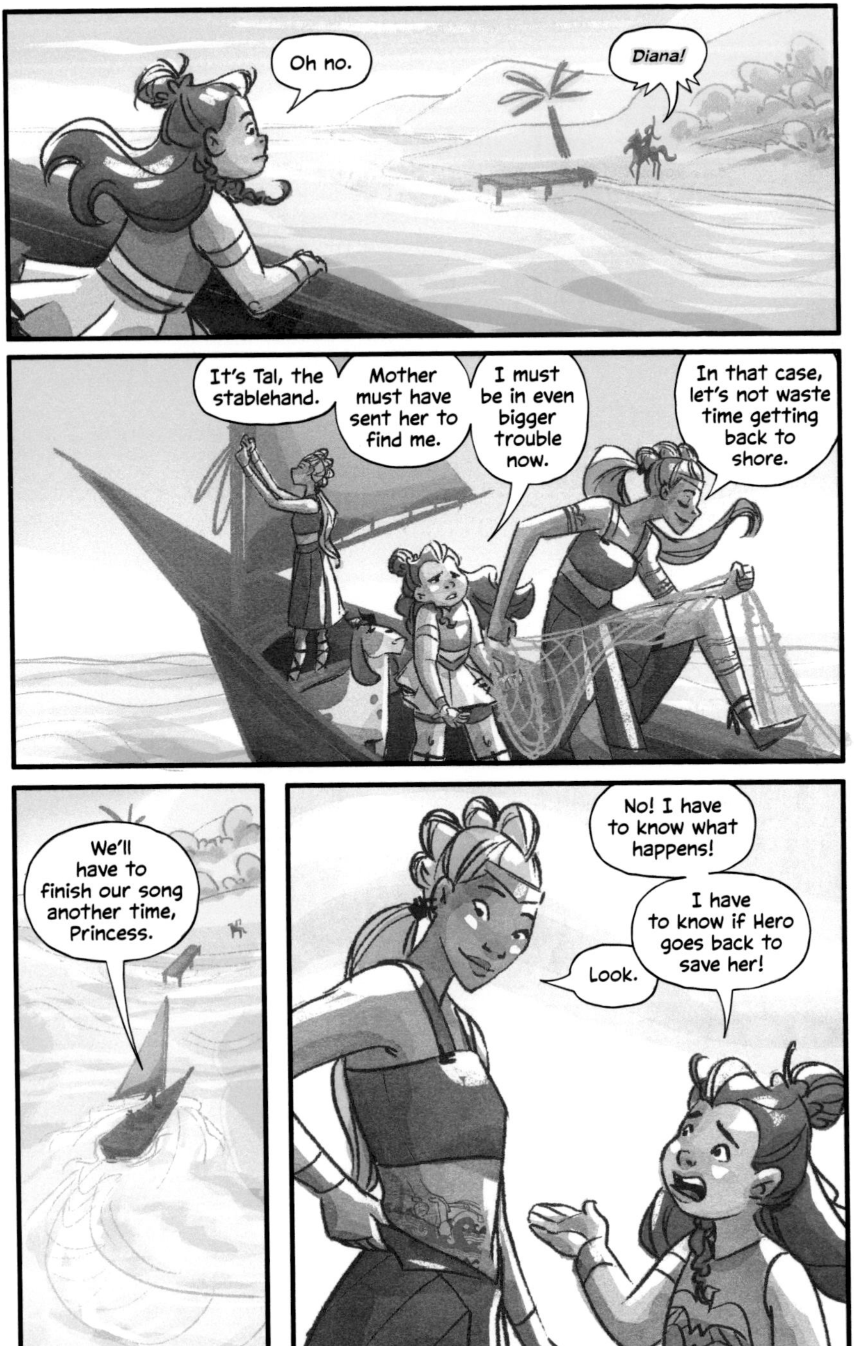
Oh no.
Diana!
It's Tal, the stablehand.
Mother must have sent her to find me.
I must be in even bigger trouble now.
In that case, let's not waste time getting back to shore.
We'll have to finish our song another time, Princess.
No! I have to know what happens!
I have to know if Hero goes back to save her!
Look.

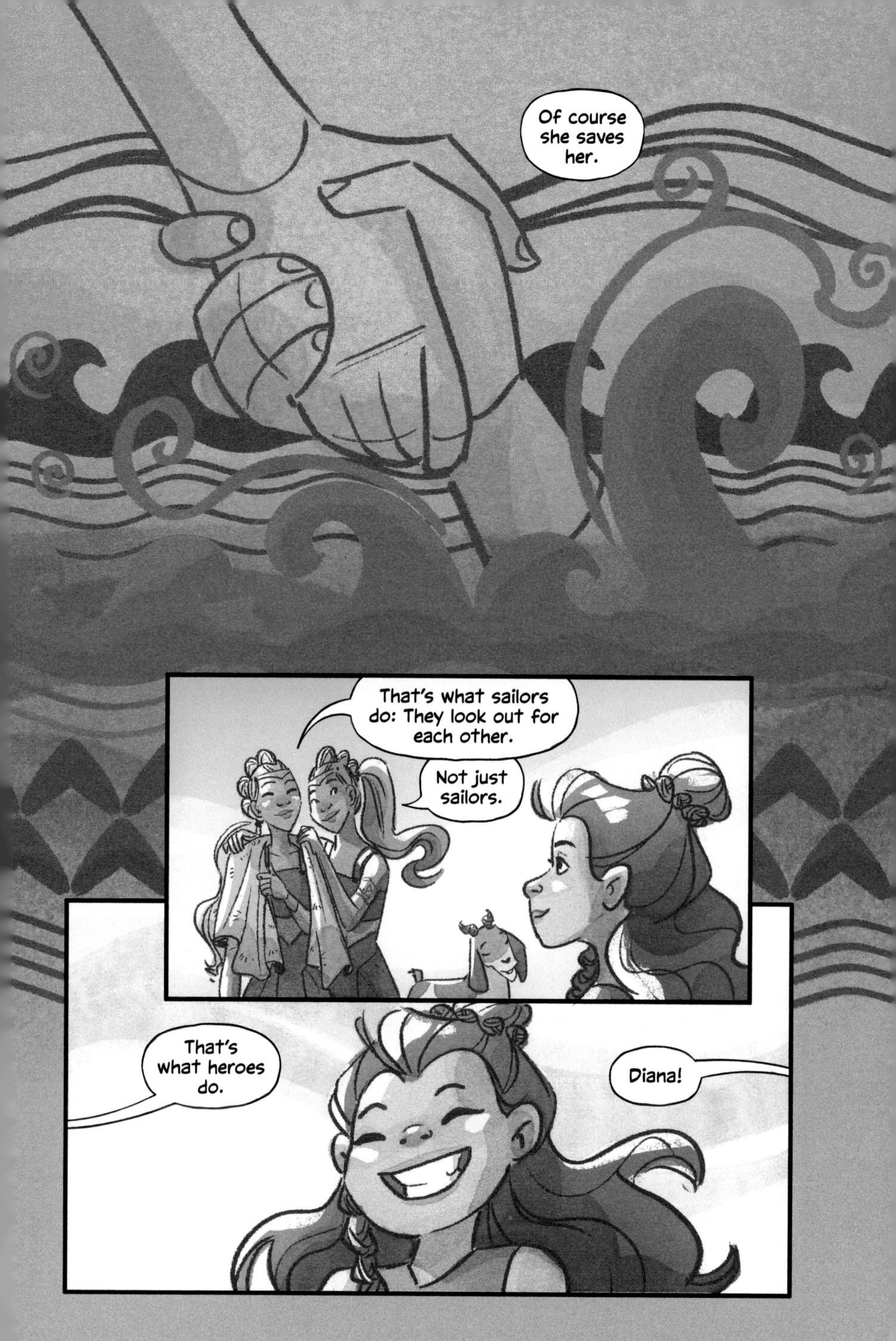
Of course she saves her.
That's what sailors do: They look out for each other.
Not just sailors.
That's what heroes do.
Diana!

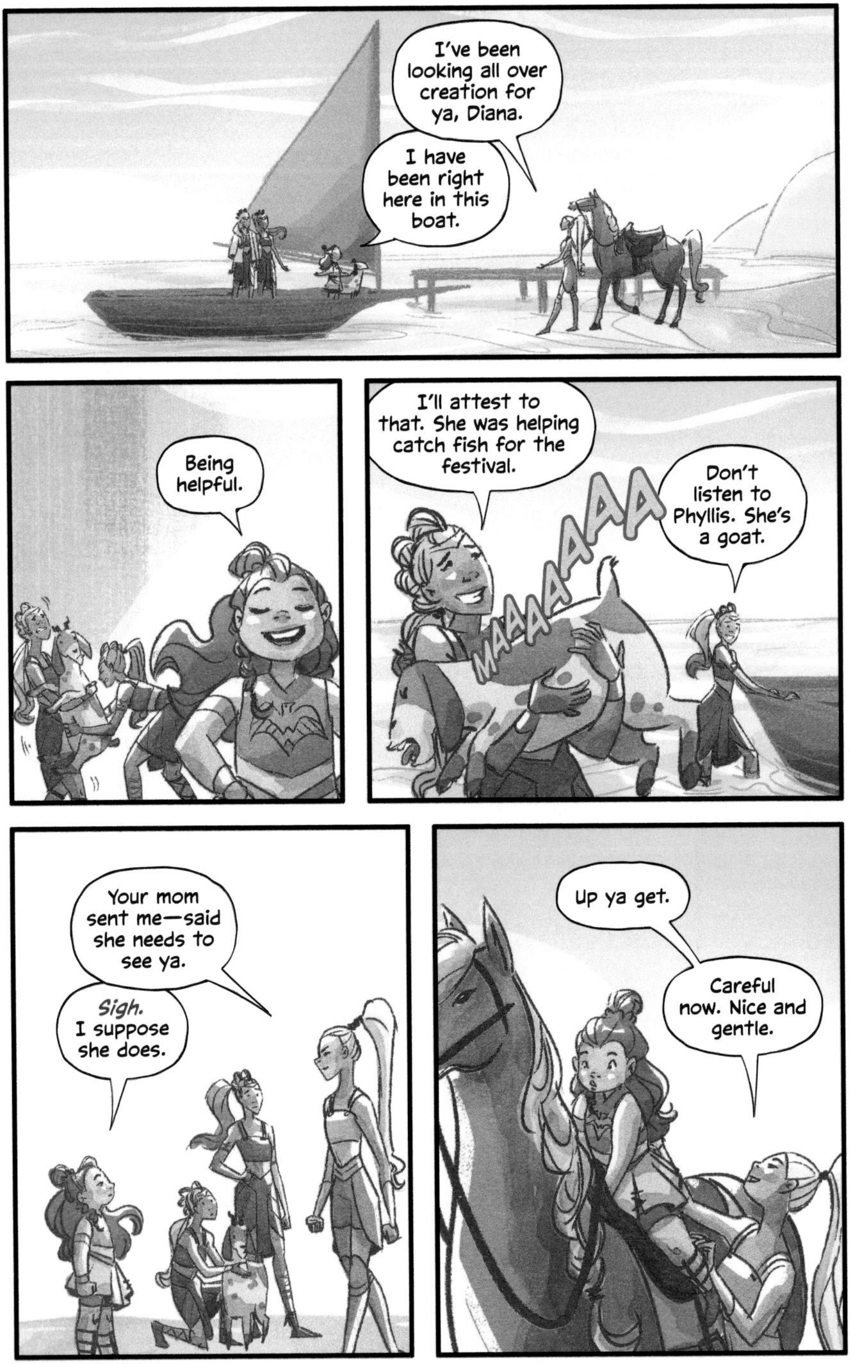
I've been looking all over creation for ya, Diana.
I have been right here in this boat.
Being helpful.
I'll attest to that. She was helping catch fish for the festival.
MAAAAAAA
Don't listen to Phyllis. She's a goat.
Your mom sent me—said she needs to see ya.
Sigh. I suppose she does.
Up ya get.
Careful now. Nice and gentle.

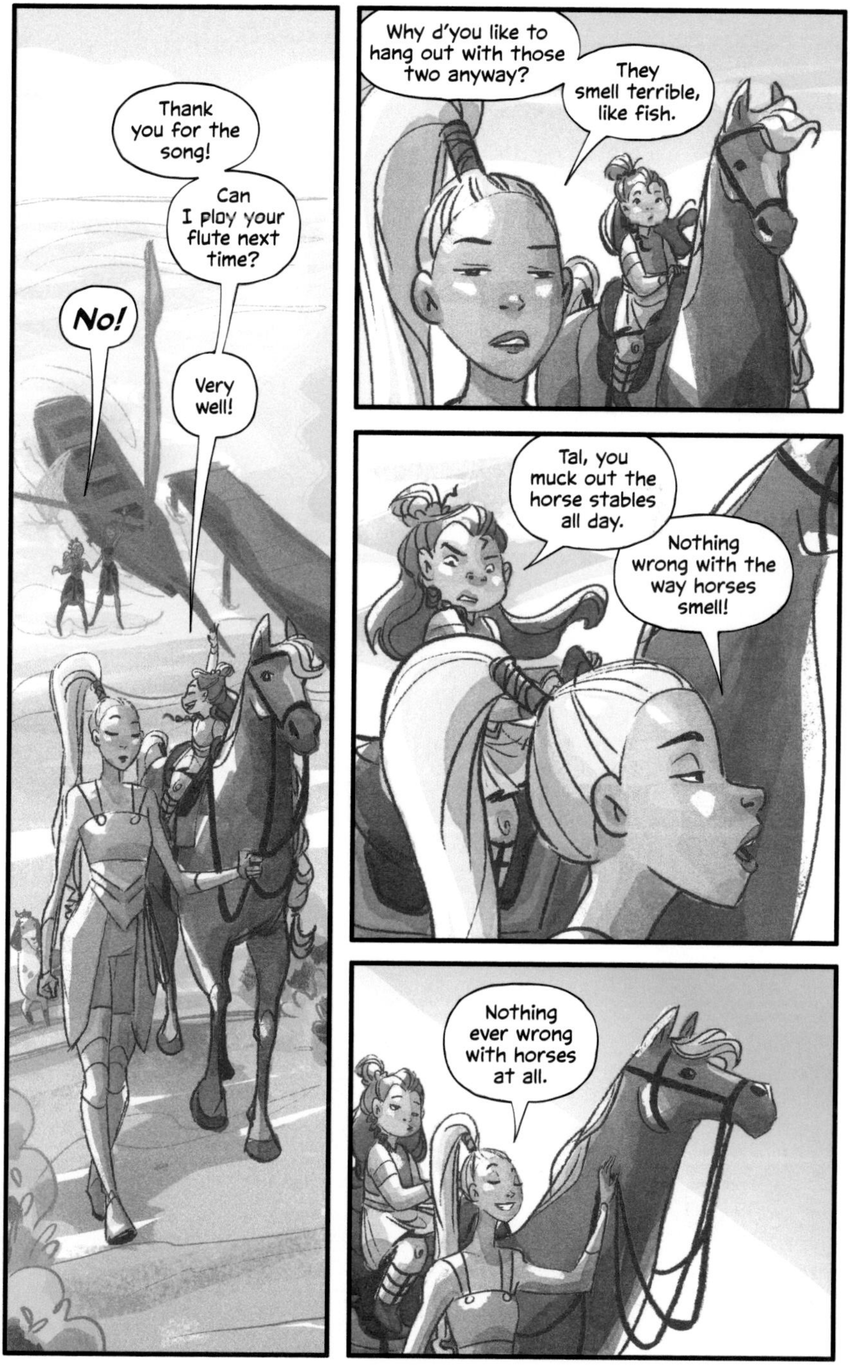
Thank you for the song!
Can I play your flute next time?
No!
Very well!
Why d'you like to hang out with those two anyway?
They smell terrible, like fish.
Tal, you muck out the horse stables all day.
Nothing wrong with the way horses smell!
Nothing ever wrong with horses at all.

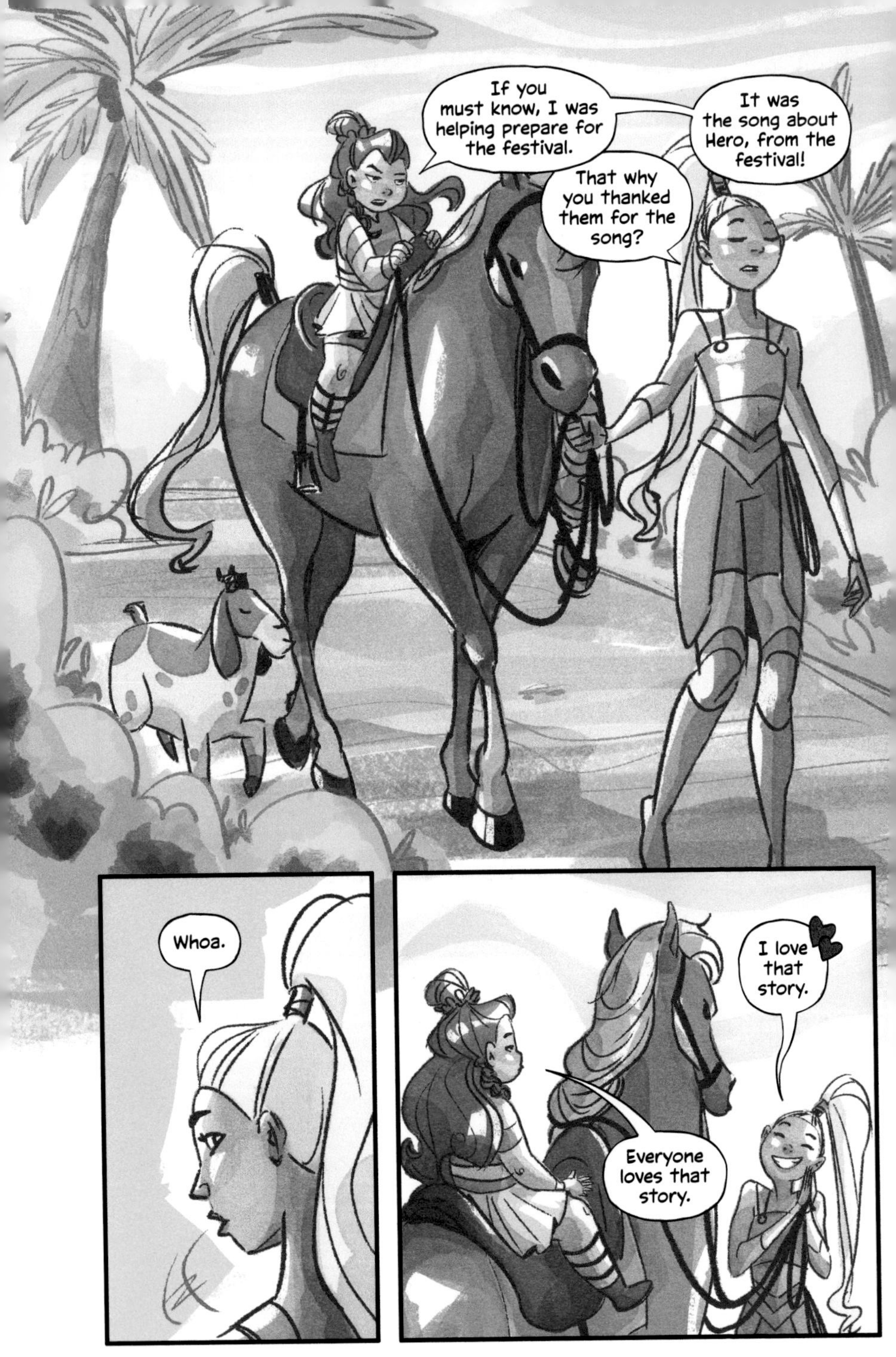
If you must know, I was helping prepare for the festival.
That why you thanked them for the song?
It was the song about Hero, from the festival!
Whoa.
I love that story.
Everyone loves that story.

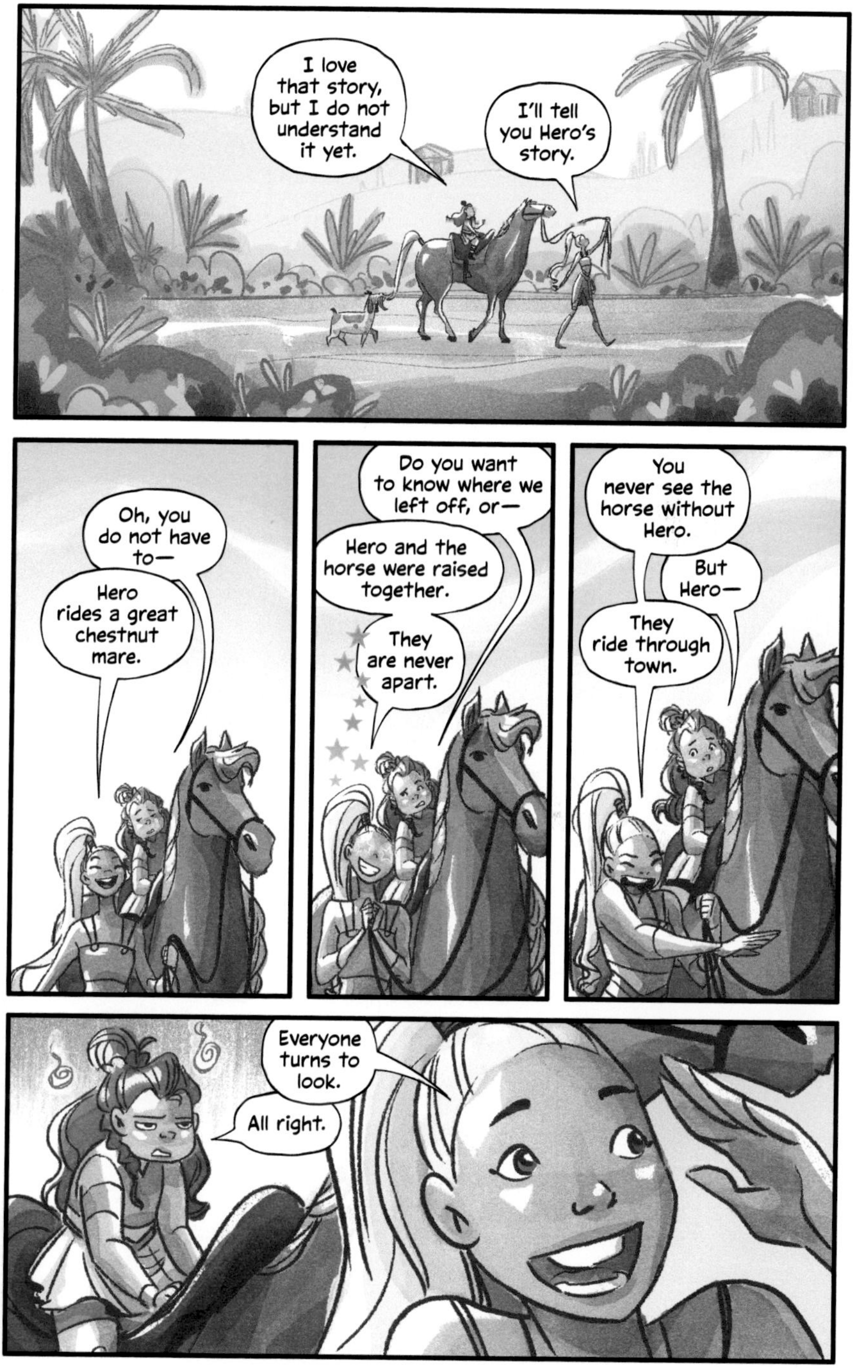
I love that story, but I do not understand it yet.
I'll tell you Hero's story.
Oh, you do not have to—
Hero rides a great chestnut mare.
Do you want to know where we left off, or—
Hero and the horse were raised together.
They are never apart.
You never see the horse without Hero.
But Hero—
They ride through town.
Everyone turns to look.
All right.

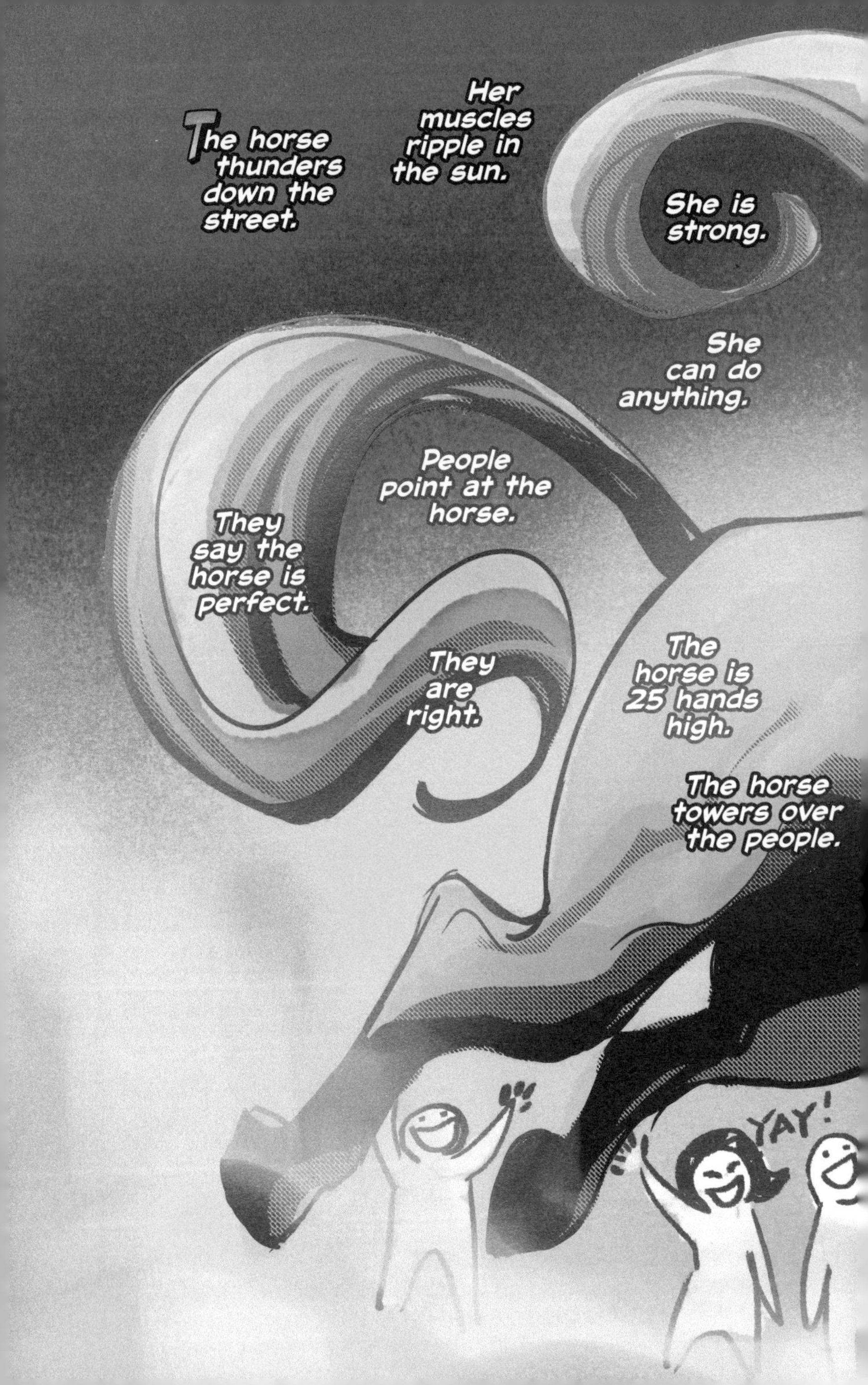
The horse thunders down the street.
Her muscles ripple in the sun.
She is strong.
She can do anything.
People point at the horse.
They say the horse is perfect.
They are right.
The horse is 25 hands high.
The horse towers over the people.
YAY!

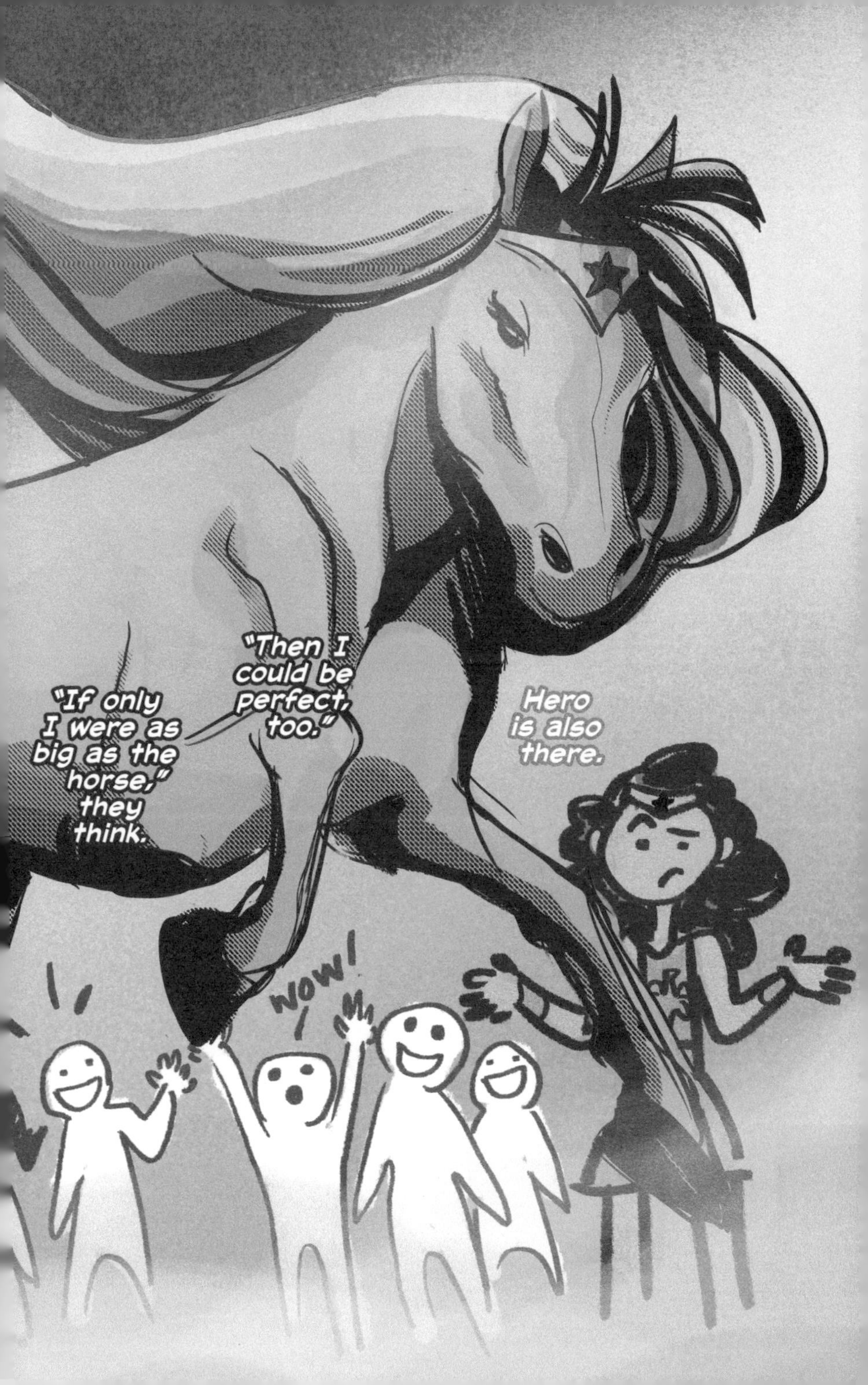
"If only I were as big as the horse," they think.
"Then I could be perfect, too."
Hero is also there.
WOW!

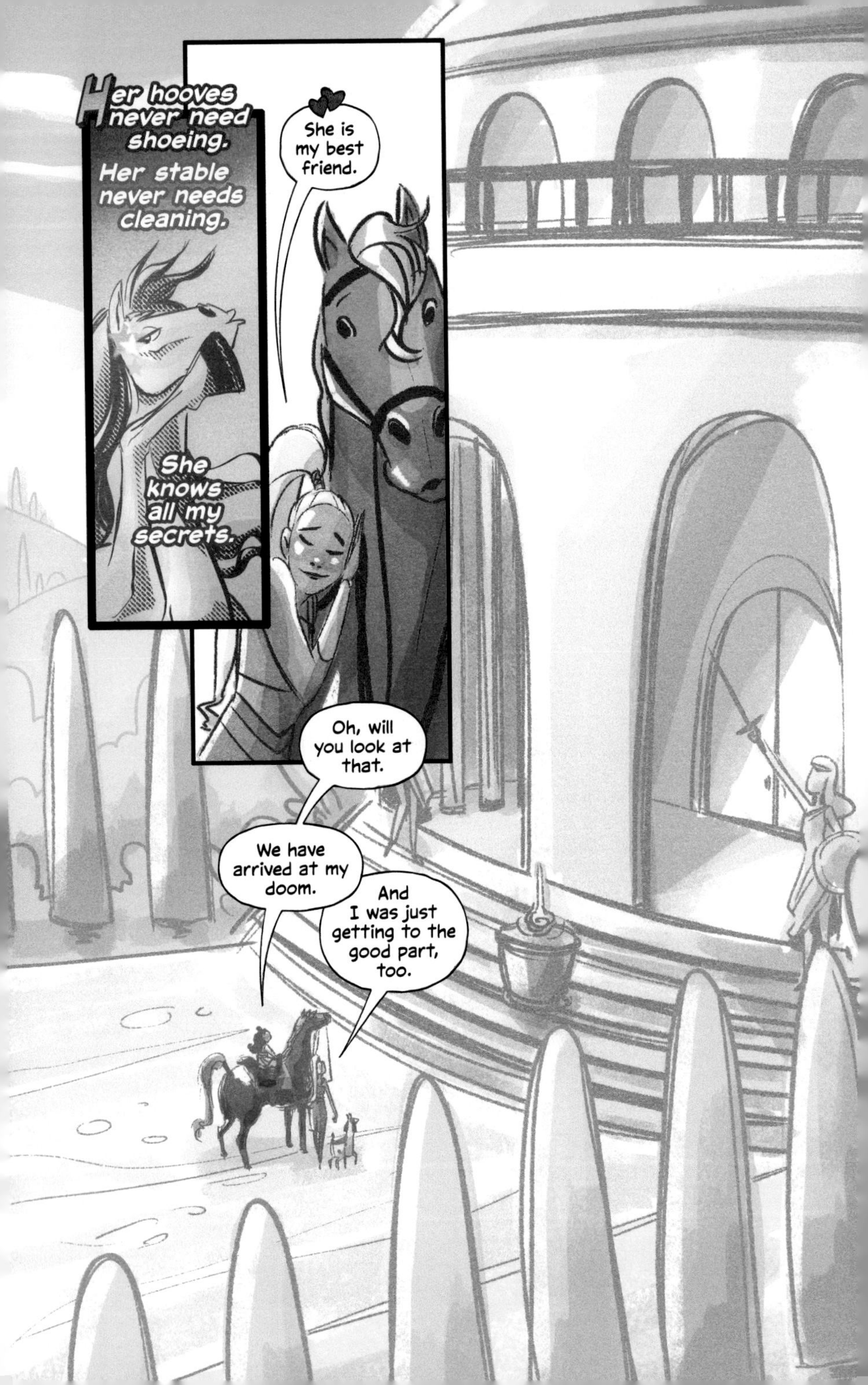
Her hooves never need shoeing.
Her stable never needs cleaning.
She knows all my secrets.
She is my best friend.
Oh, will you look at that.
We have arrived at my doom.
And I was just getting to the good part, too.

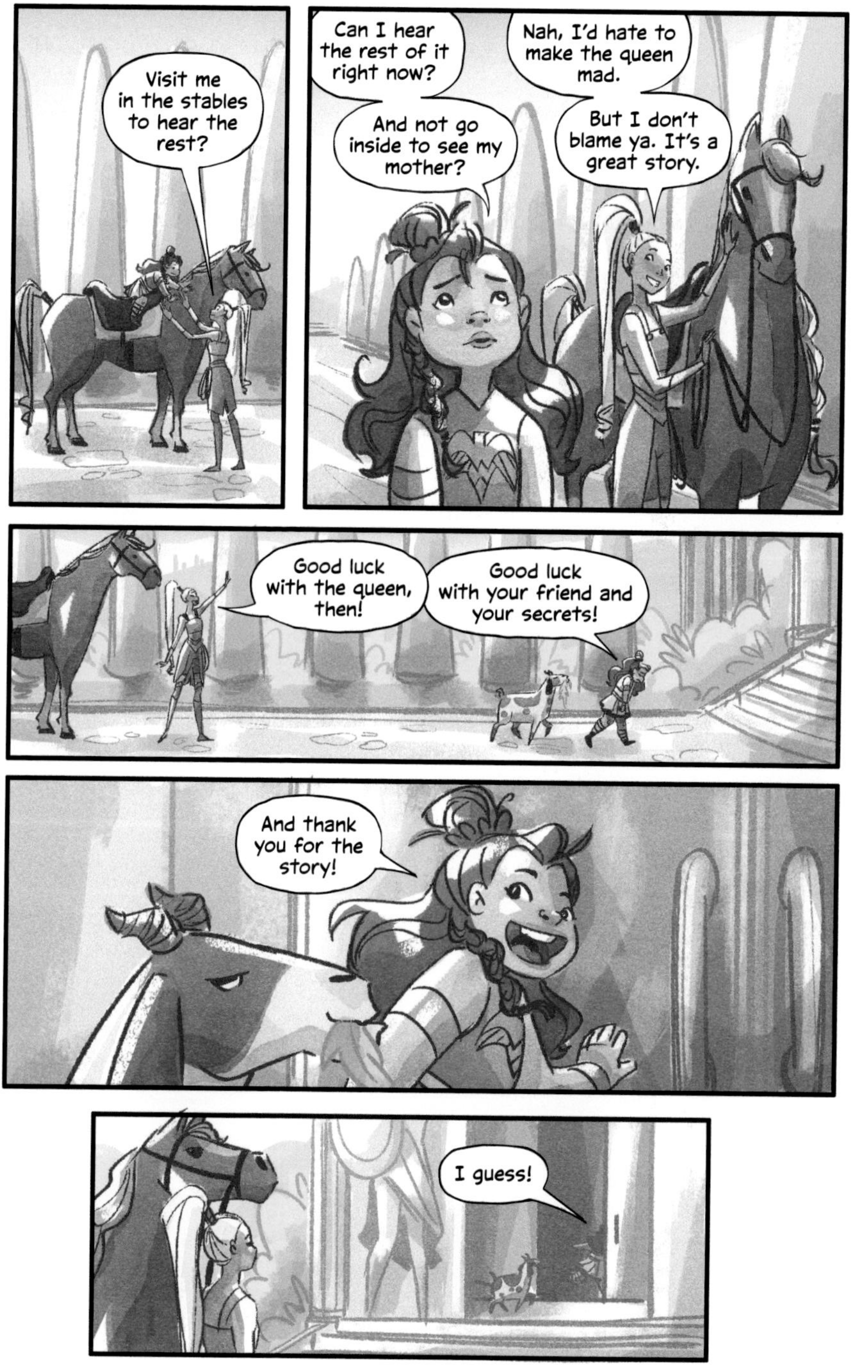
Visit me in the stables to hear the rest?
Can I hear the rest of it right now?
And not go inside to see my mother?
Nah, I'd hate to make the queen mad.
But I don't blame ya. It's a great story.
Good luck with the queen, then!
Good luck with your friend and your secrets!
And thank you for the story!
I guess!

CHAPTER 4

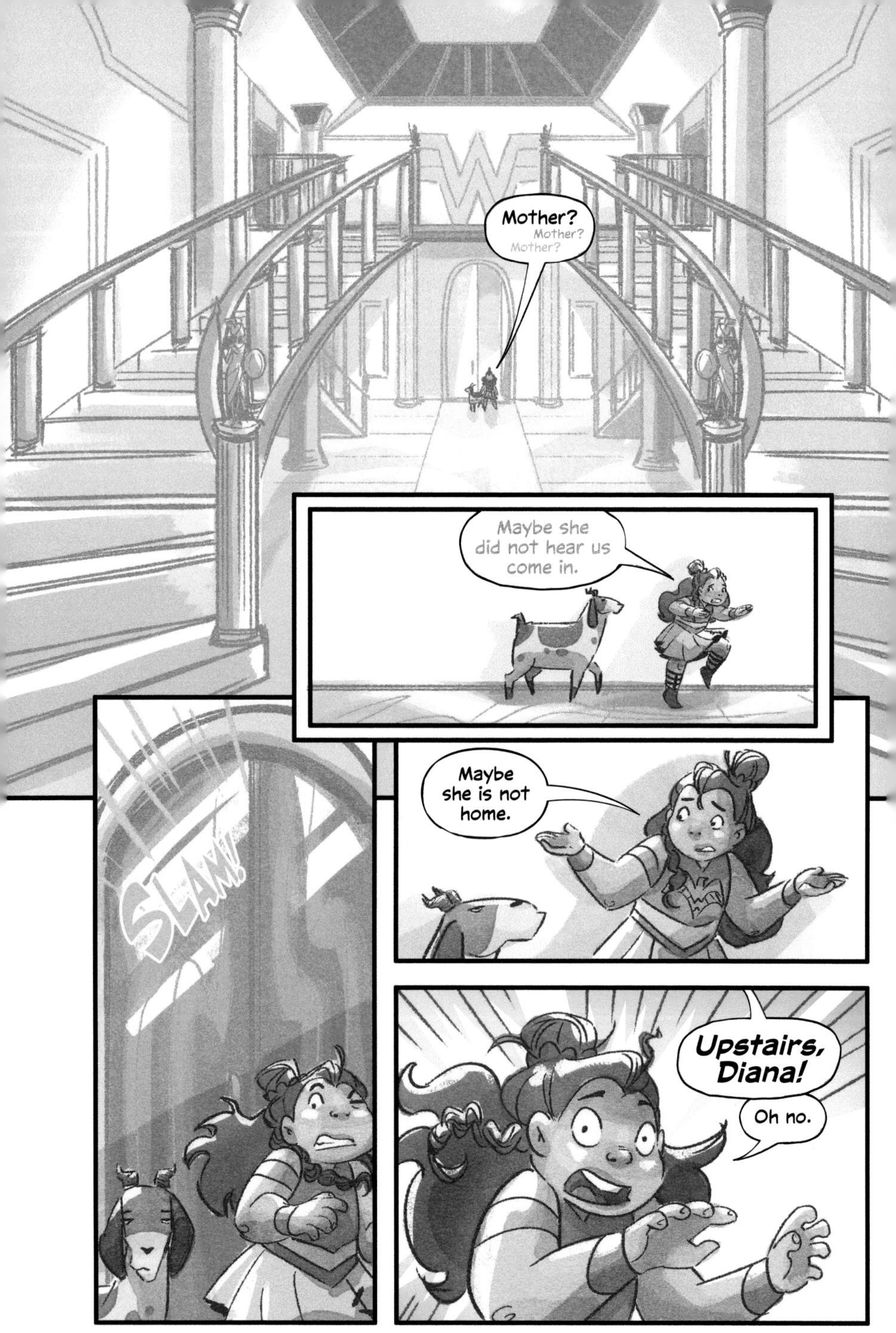
Mother? Mother? Mother?
Maybe she did not hear us come in.
SLAM!
Maybe she is not home.
Upstairs, Diana!
Oh no.

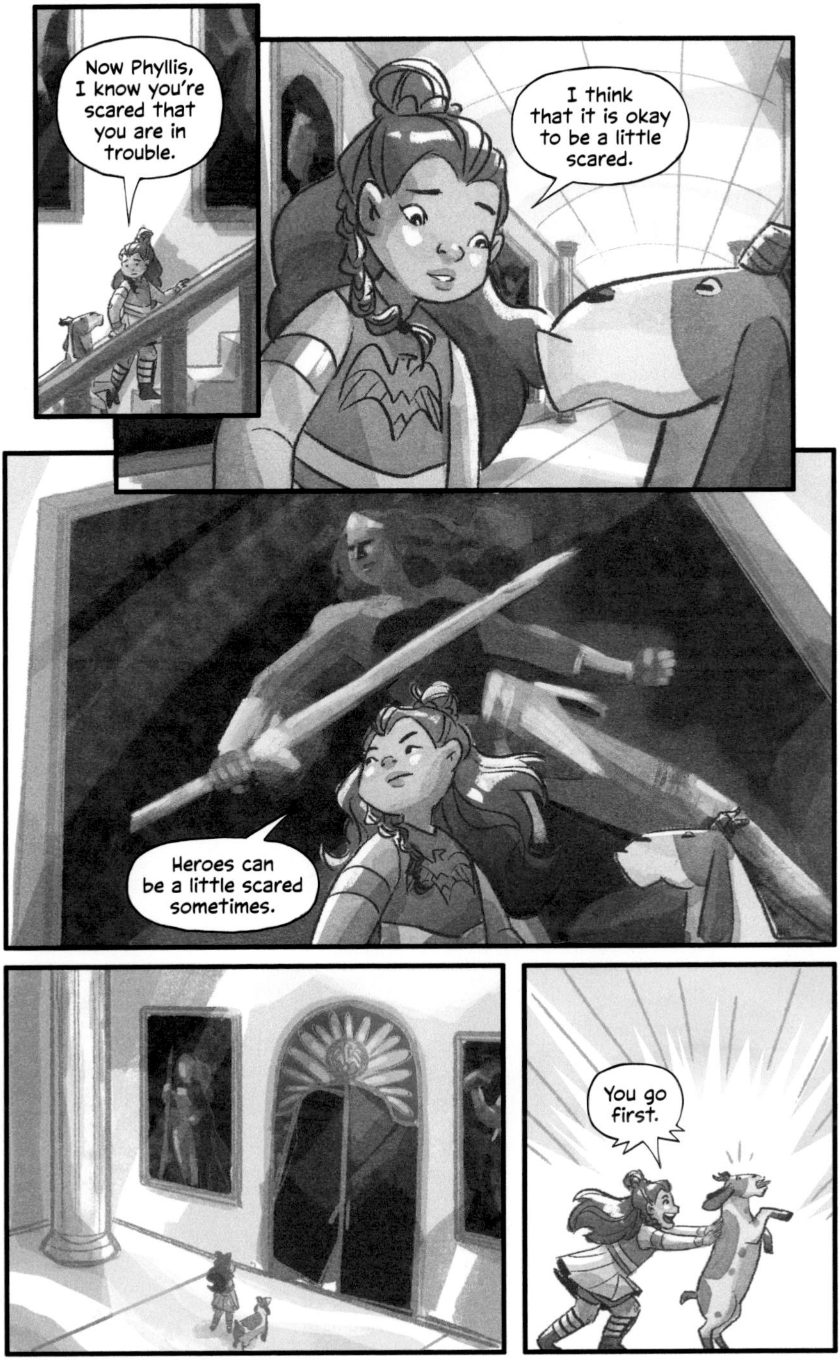
Now Phyllis, I know you're scared that you are in trouble.
I think that it is okay to be a little scared.
Heroes can be a little scared sometimes.
You go first.

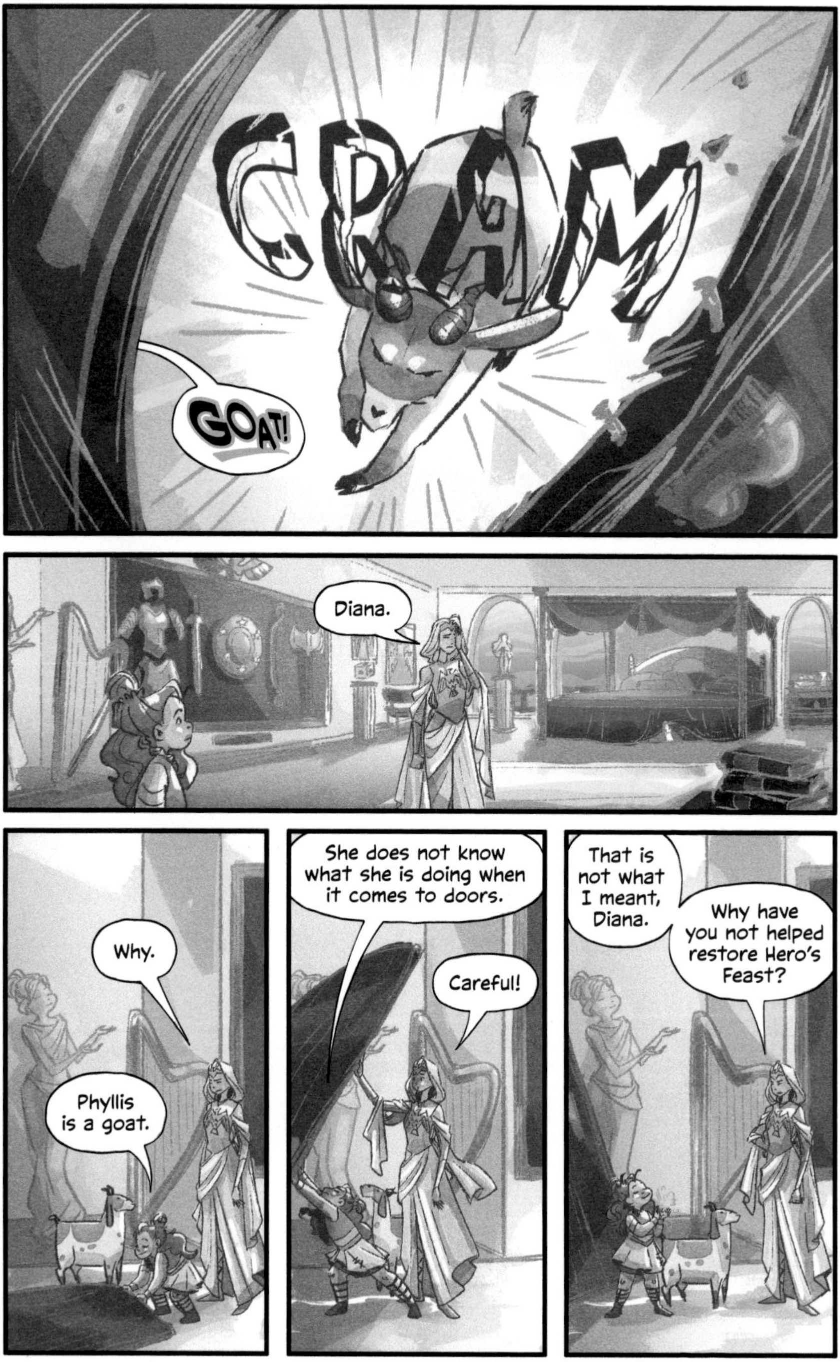
CRAM
GOAT!
Diana.
Why.
Phyllis is a goat.
She does not know what she is doing when it comes to doors.
Careful!
That is not what I meant, Diana.
Why have you not helped restore Hero's Feast?

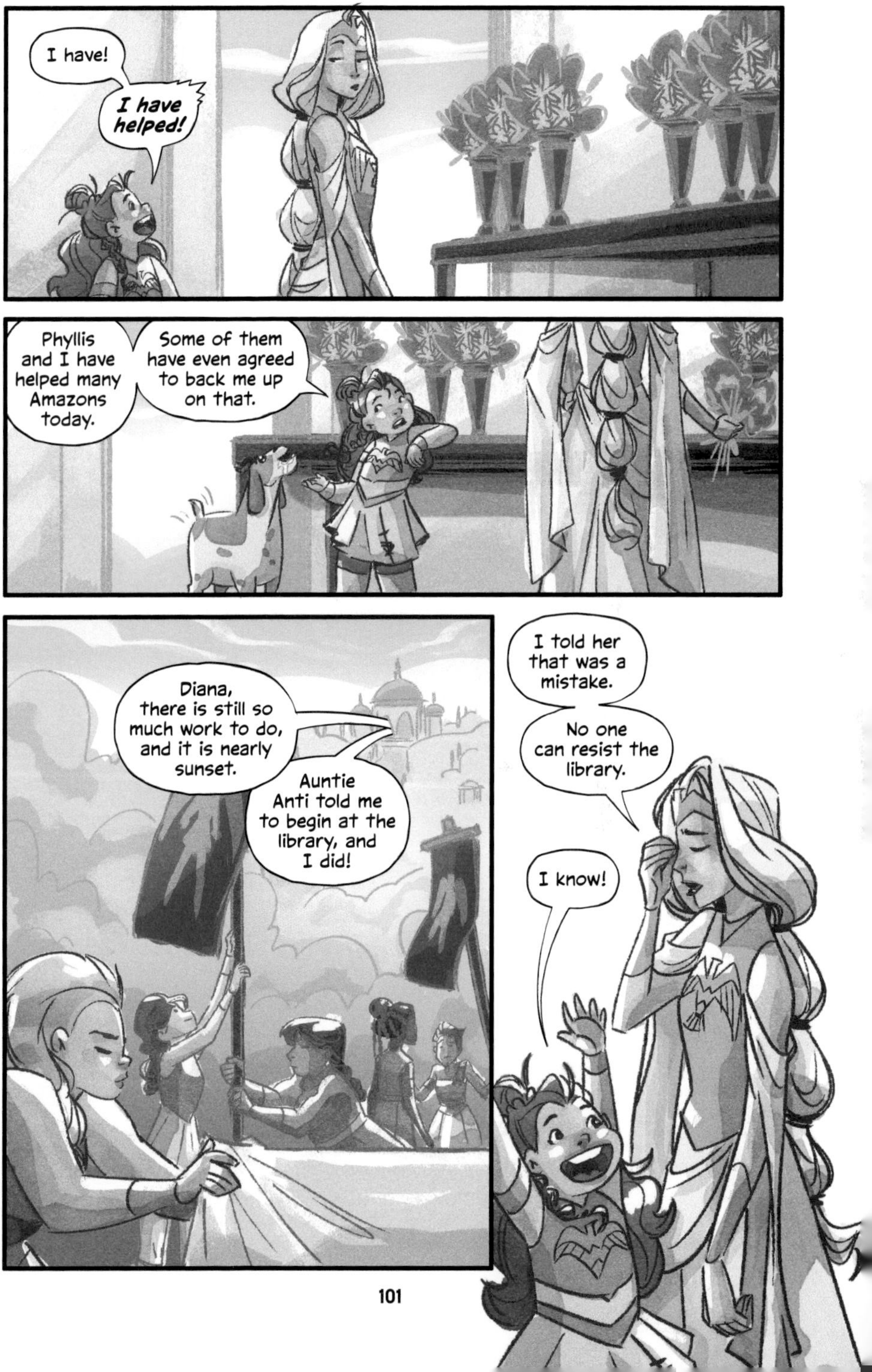
I have!
I have helped!
Phyllis and I have helped many Amazons today.
Some of them have even agreed to back me up on that.
Diana, there is still so much work to do, and it is nearly sunset.
Auntie Anti told me to begin at the library, and I did!
I told her that was a mistake.
No one can resist the library.
I know!

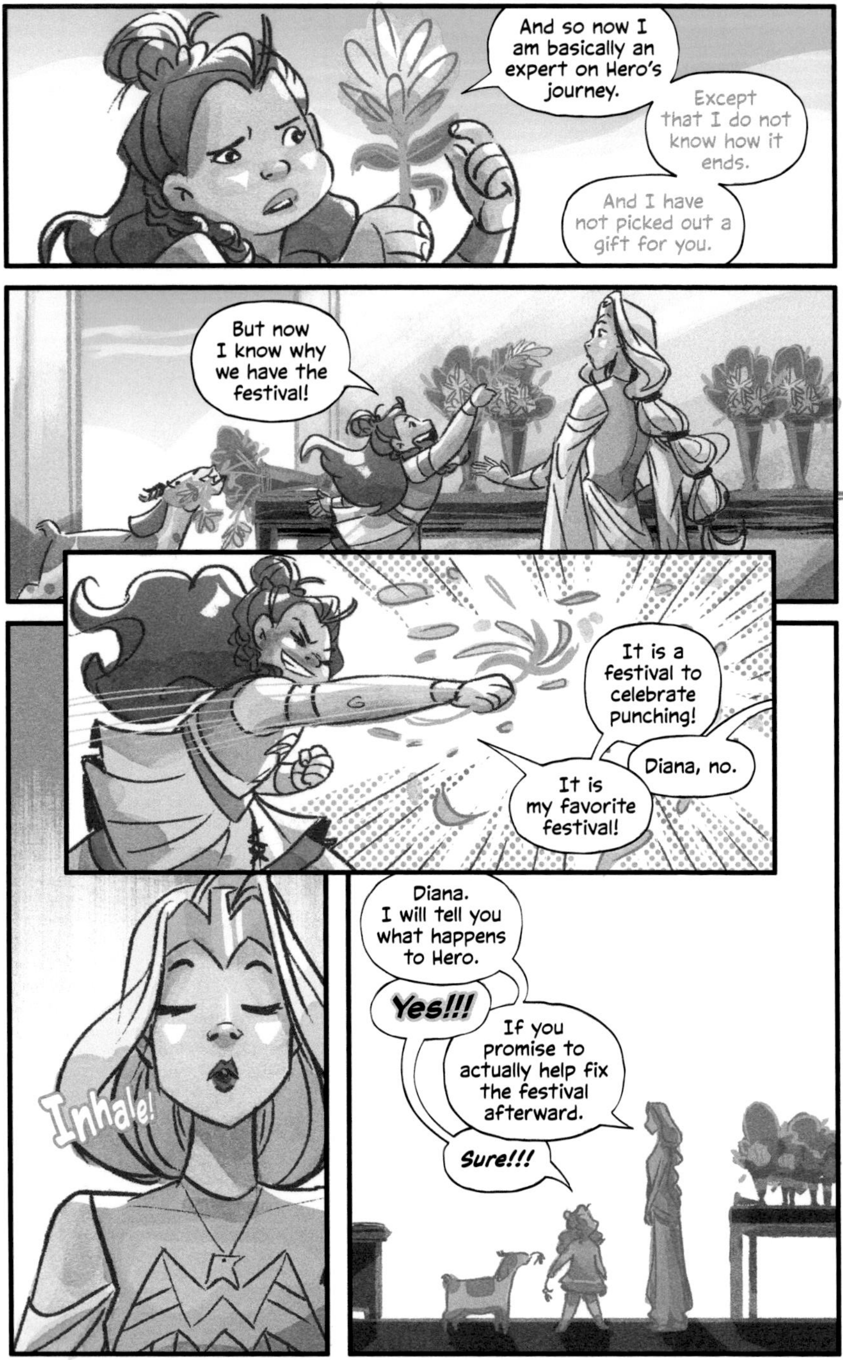

And so now I am basically an expert on Hero's journey.
Except that I do not know how it ends.
And I have not picked out a gift for you.
But now I know why we have the festival!
It is a festival to celebrate punching!
It is my favorite festival!
Diana, no.
Inhale!
Diana. I will tell you what happens to Hero.
Yes!!!
If you promise to actually help fix the festival afterward.
Sure!!!

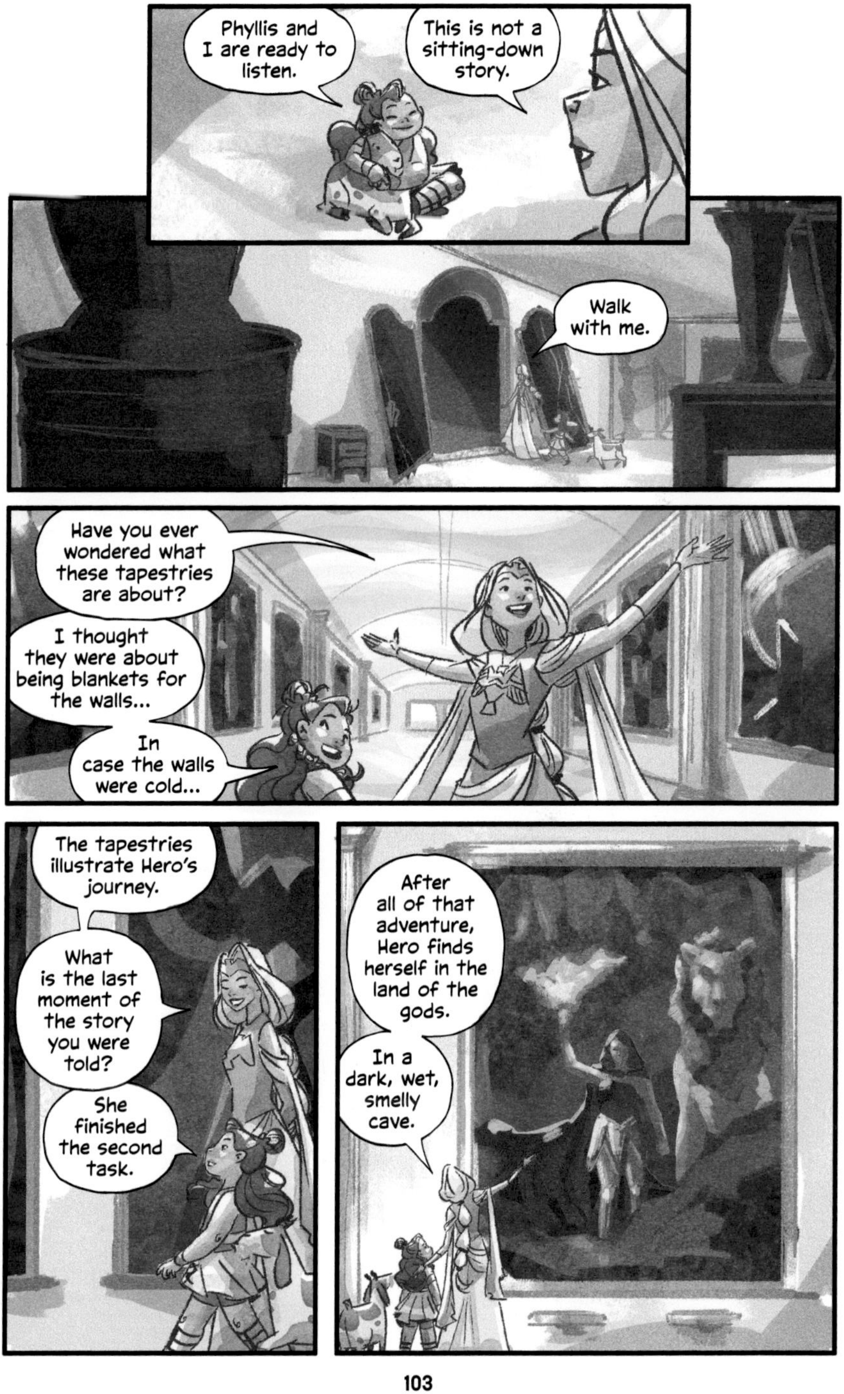
Phyllis and I are ready to listen.
This is not a sitting-down story.
Walk with me.
Have you ever wondered what these tapestries are about?
I thought they were about being blankets for the walls...
In case the walls were cold...
The tapestries illustrate Hero's journey.
What is the last moment of the story you were told?
She finished the second task.
After all of that adventure, Hero finds herself in the land of the gods.
In a dark, wet, smelly cave.

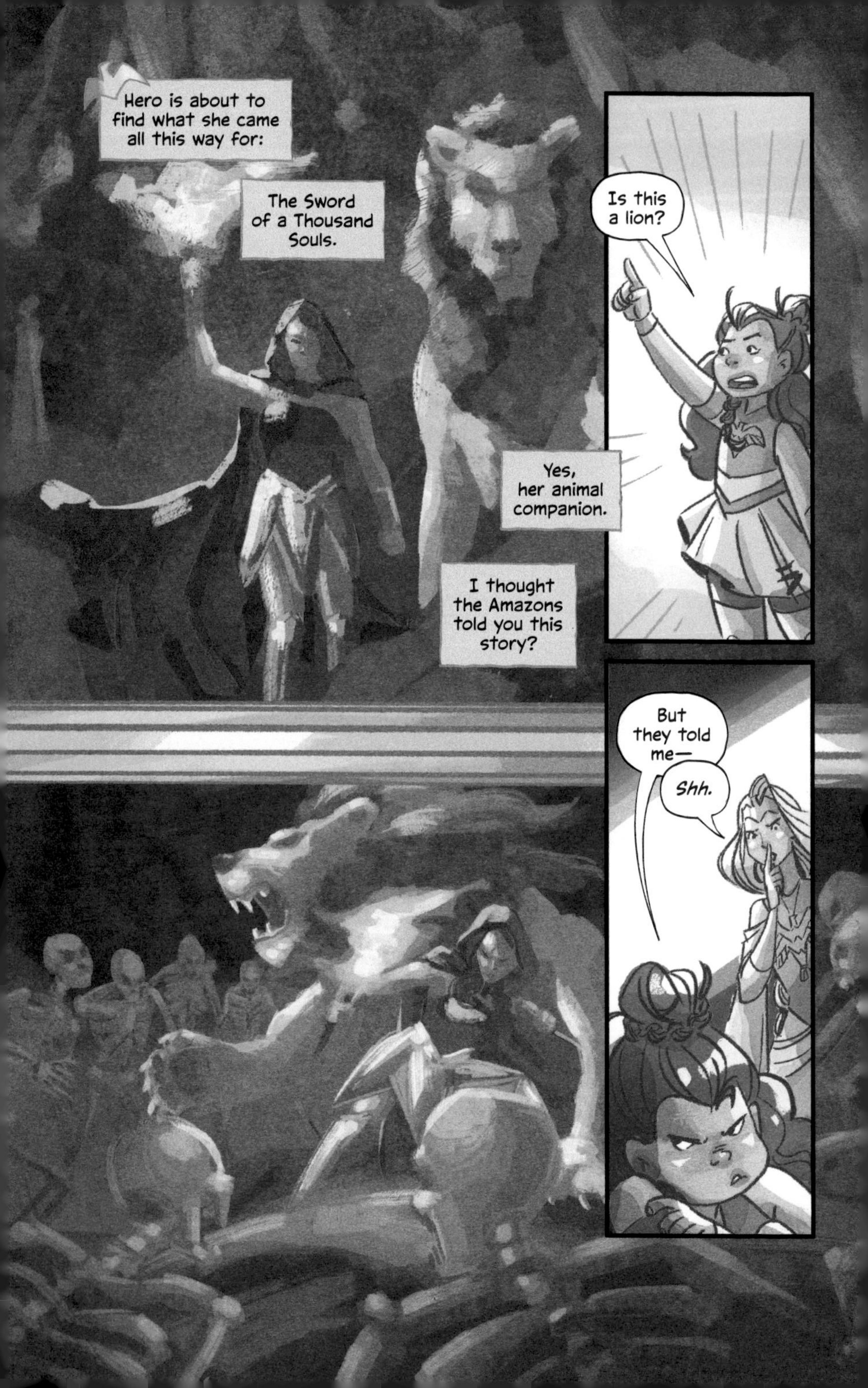
Hero is about to find what she came all this way for:
The Sword of a Thousand Souls.
Is this a lion?
Yes, her animal companion.
I thought the Amazons told you this story?
But they told me—
Shh.

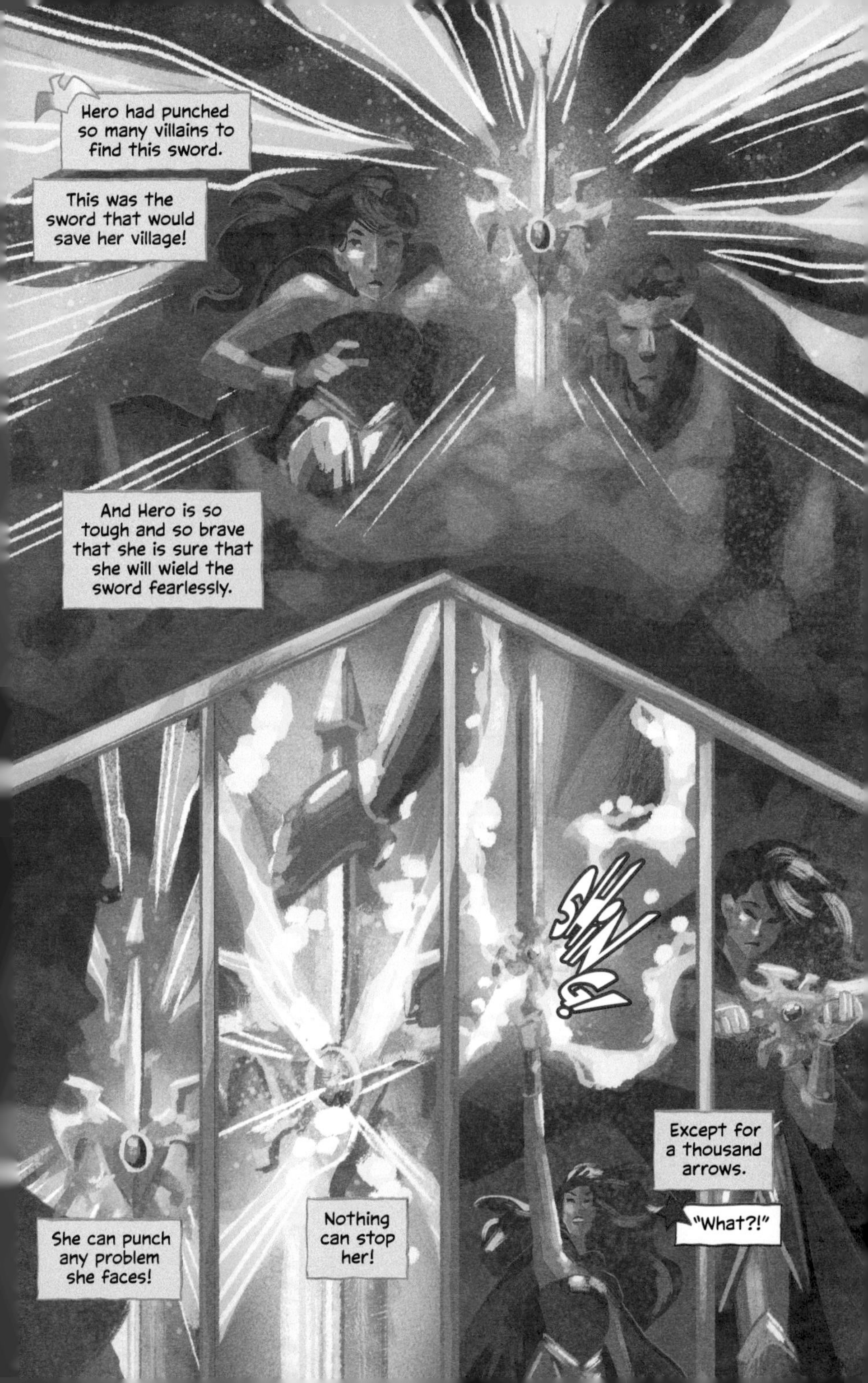
Hero had punched so many villains to find this sword.
This was the sword that would save her village!
And Hero is so tough and so brave that she is sure that she will wield the sword fearlessly.
She can punch any problem she faces!
Nothing can stop her!
SHING!
Except for a thousand arrows.
"What?!"

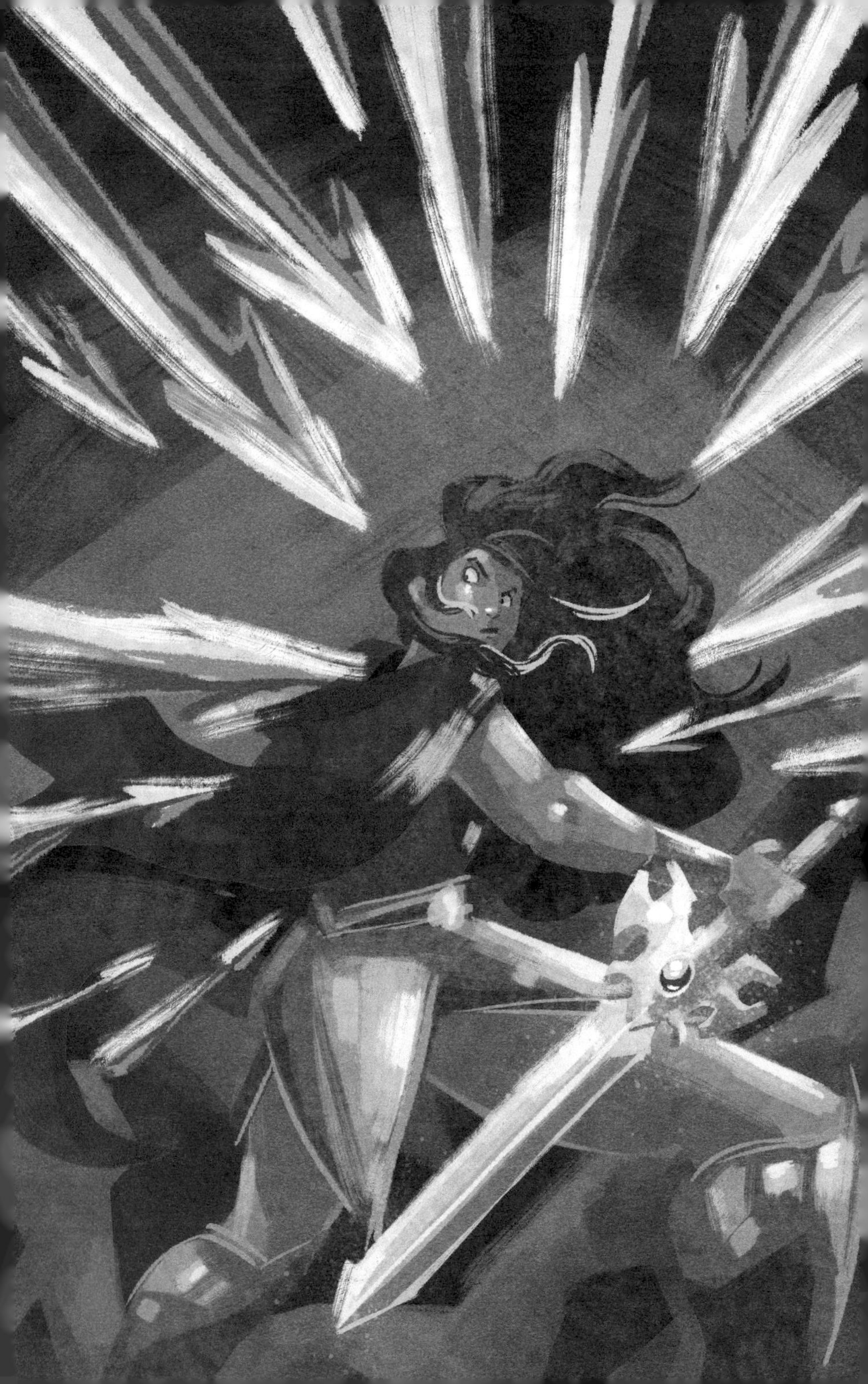

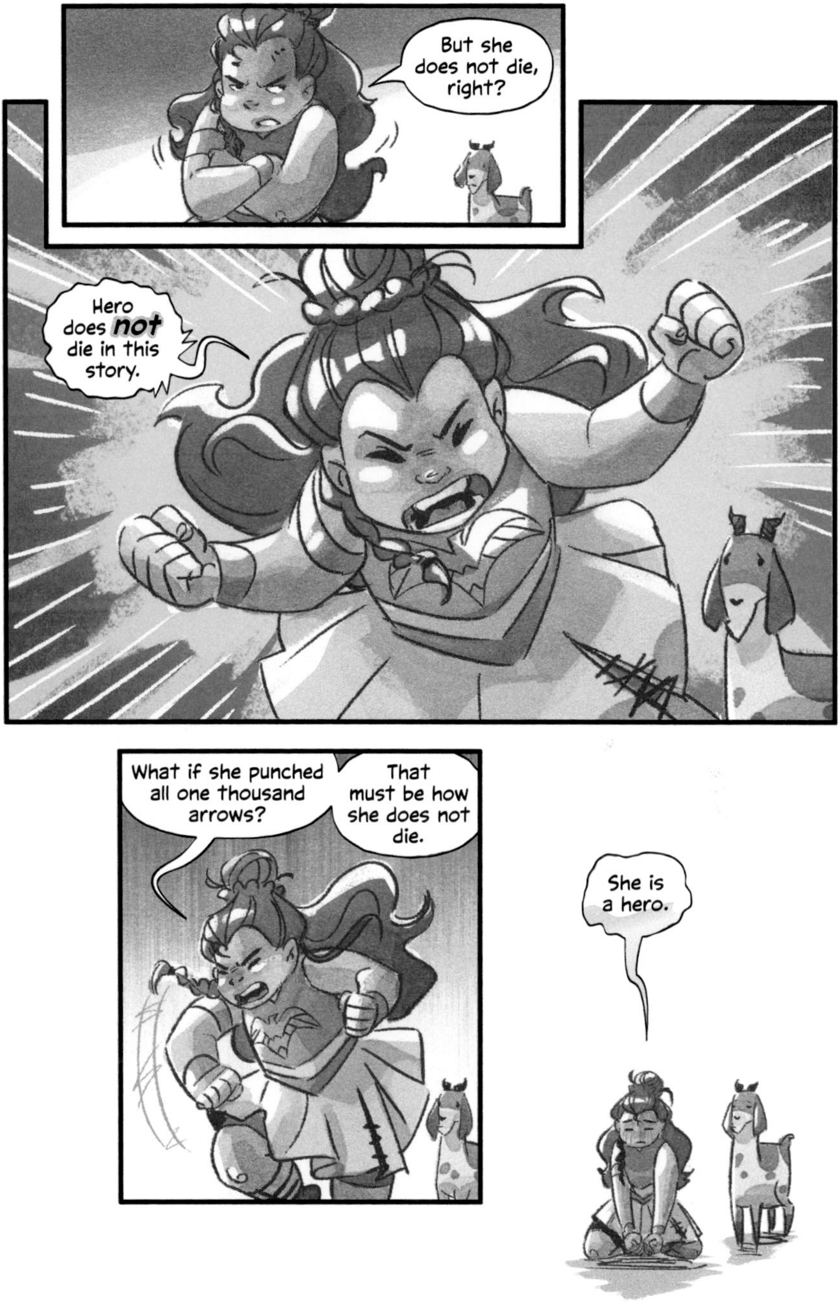

But she does not die, right?
Hero does **not** die in this story.
What if she punched all one thousand arrows?
That must be how she does not die.
She is a hero.

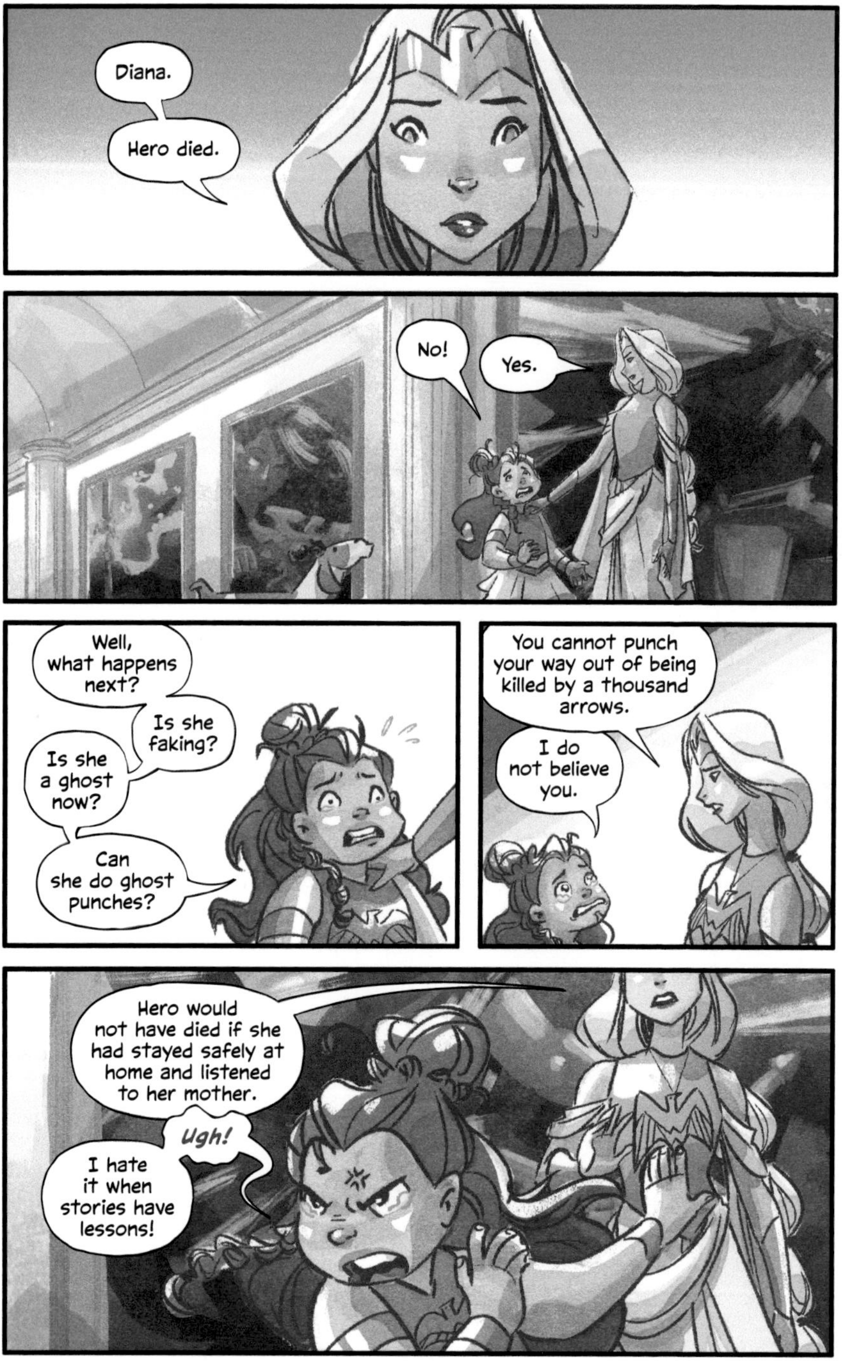
Diana.
Hero died.
No!
Yes.
Well, what happens next?
Is she faking?
Is she a ghost now?
Can she do ghost punches?
You cannot punch your way out of being killed by a thousand arrows.
I do not believe you.
Hero would not have died if she had stayed safely at home and listened to her mother.
Ugh!
I hate it when stories have lessons!

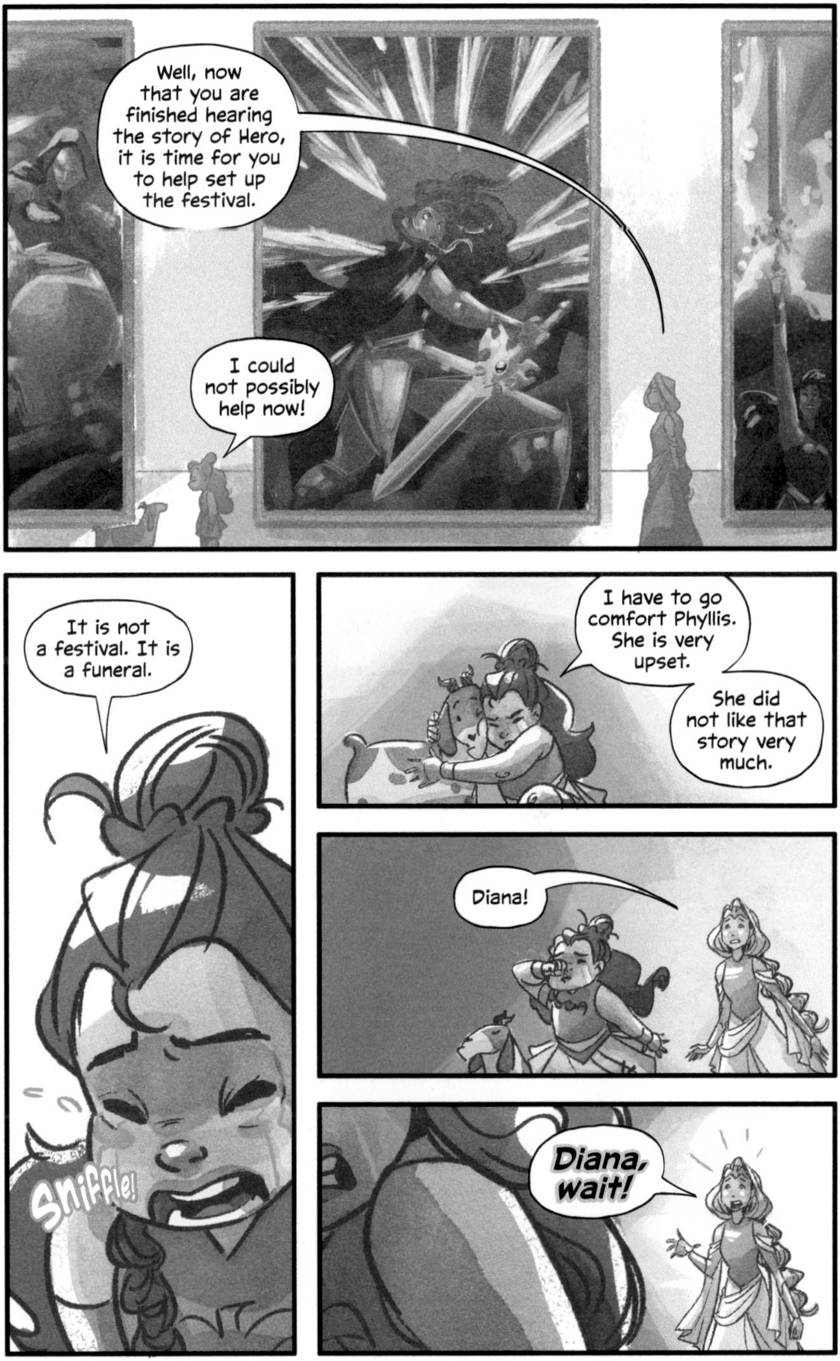
Well, now that you are finished hearing the story of Hero, it is time for you to help set up the festival.
I could not possibly help now!
It is not a festival. It is a funeral.
Sniffle!
I have to go comfort Phyllis. She is very upset.
She did not like that story very much.
Diana!
Diana, wait!

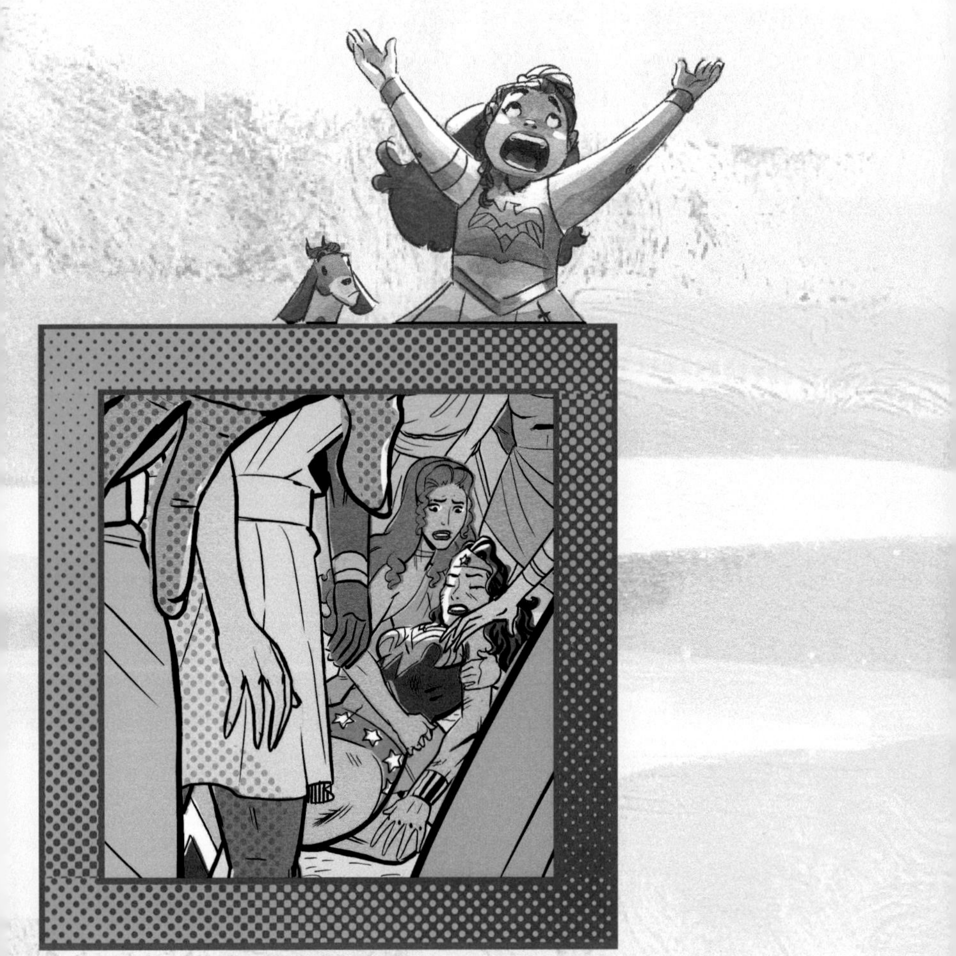

CHAPTER 5

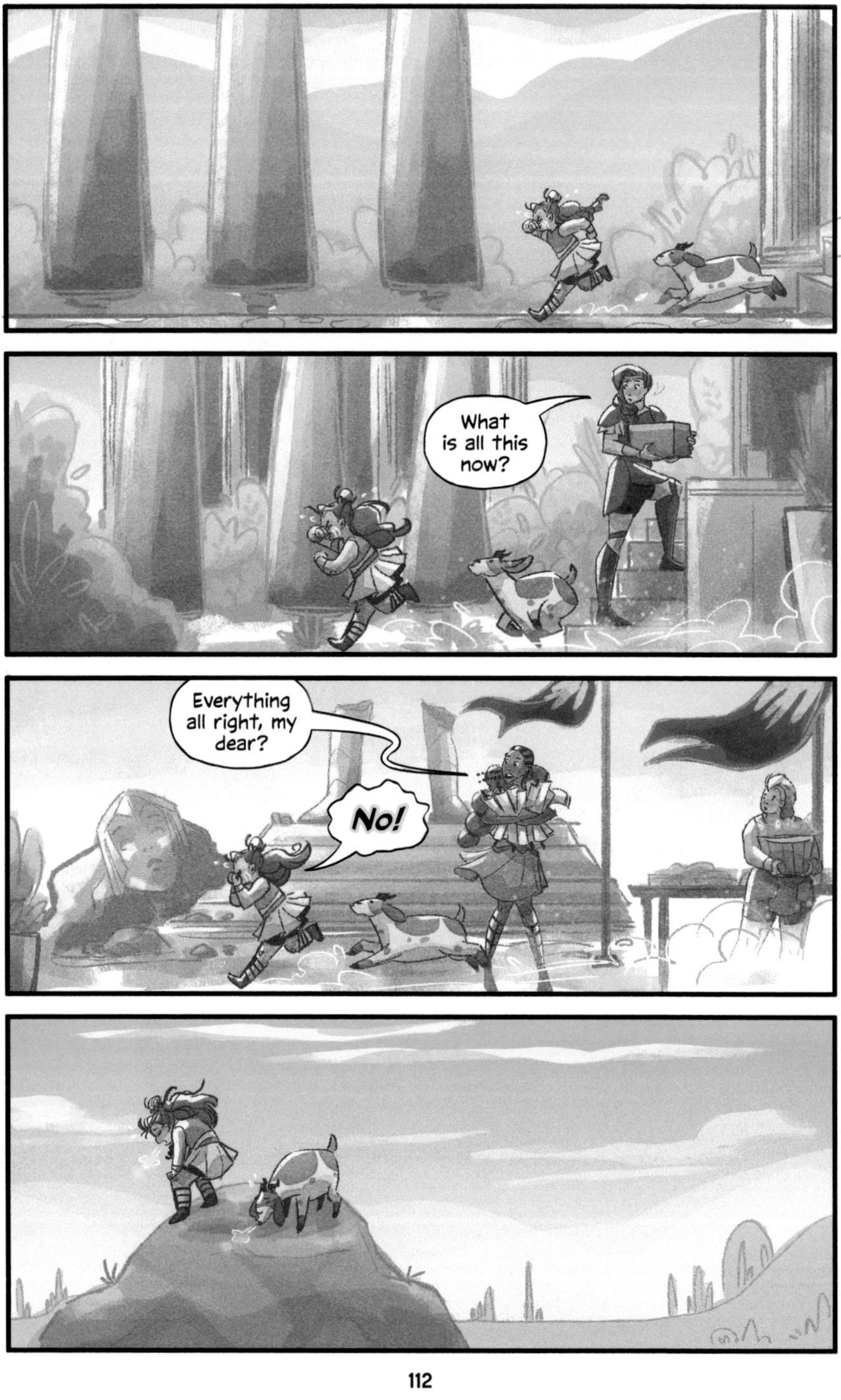
What is all this now?
Everything all right, my dear?
No!

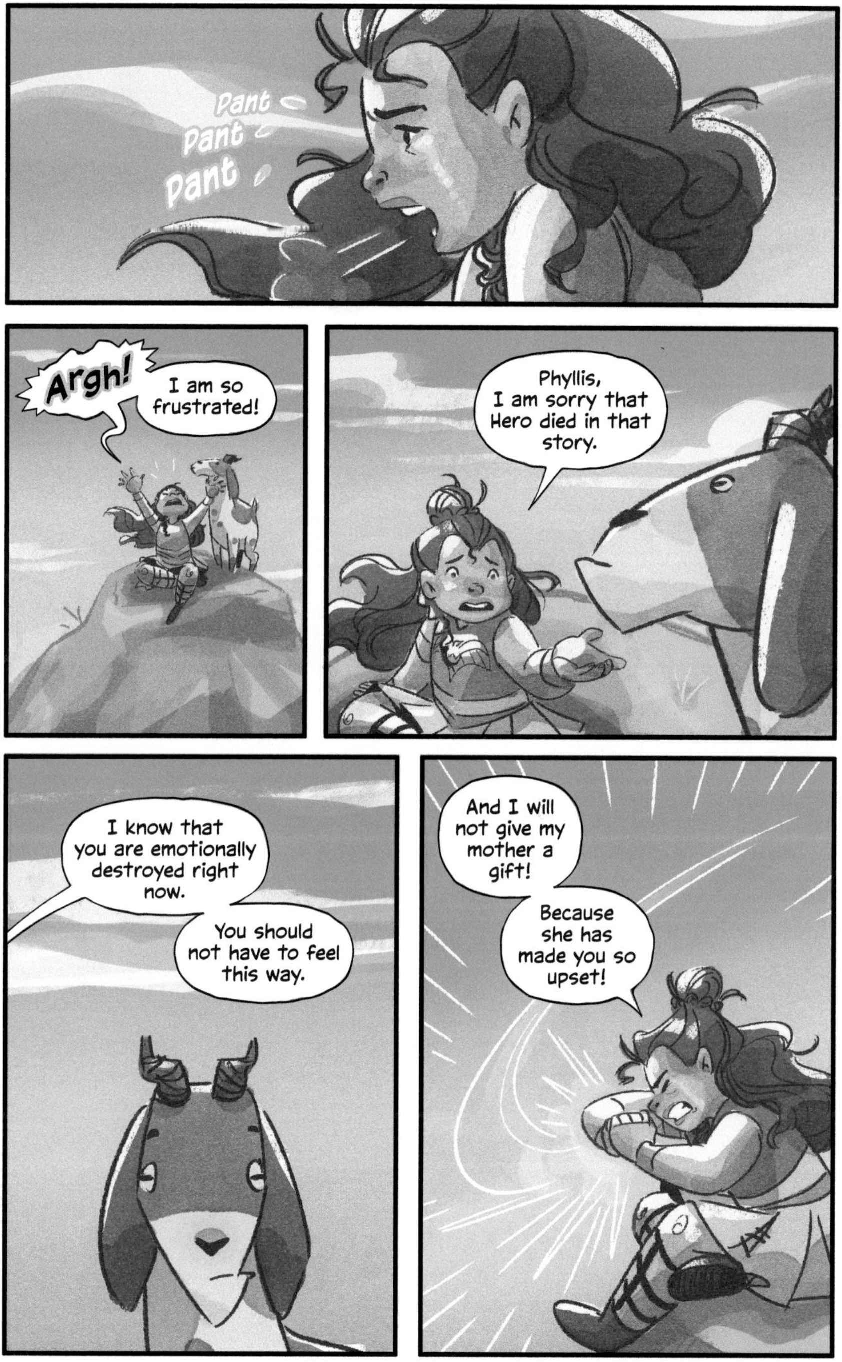
Pant
Pant
Pant
Argh!
I am so frustrated!
Phyllis, I am sorry that Hero died in that story.
I know that you are emotionally destroyed right now.
You should not have to feel this way.
And I will not give my mother a gift!
Because she has made you so upset!

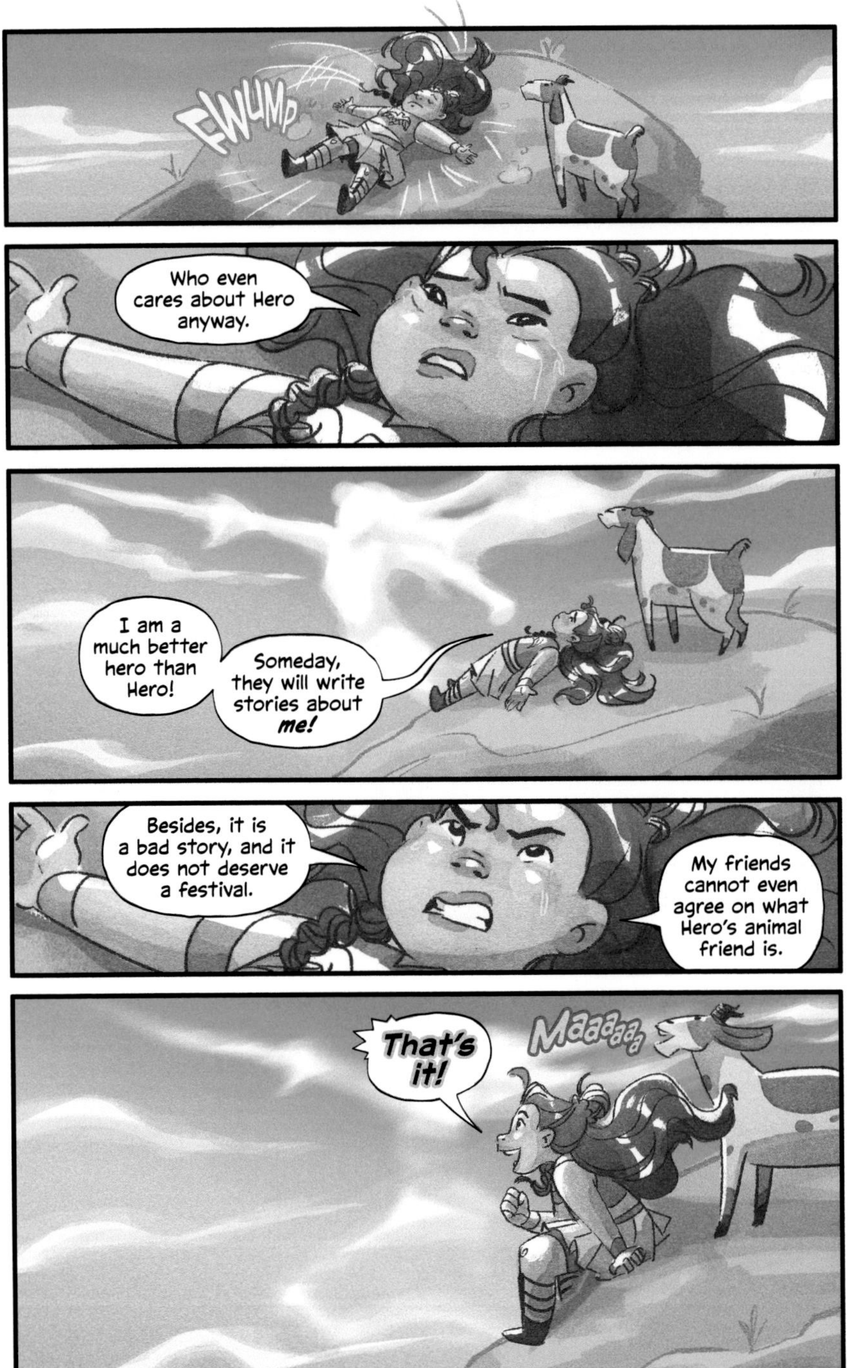
FWUMP
Who even cares about Hero anyway.
I am a much better hero than Hero!
Someday, they will write stories about *me!*
Besides, it is a bad story, and it does not deserve a festival.
My friends cannot even agree on what Hero's animal friend is.
That's it!
Maaaaaa

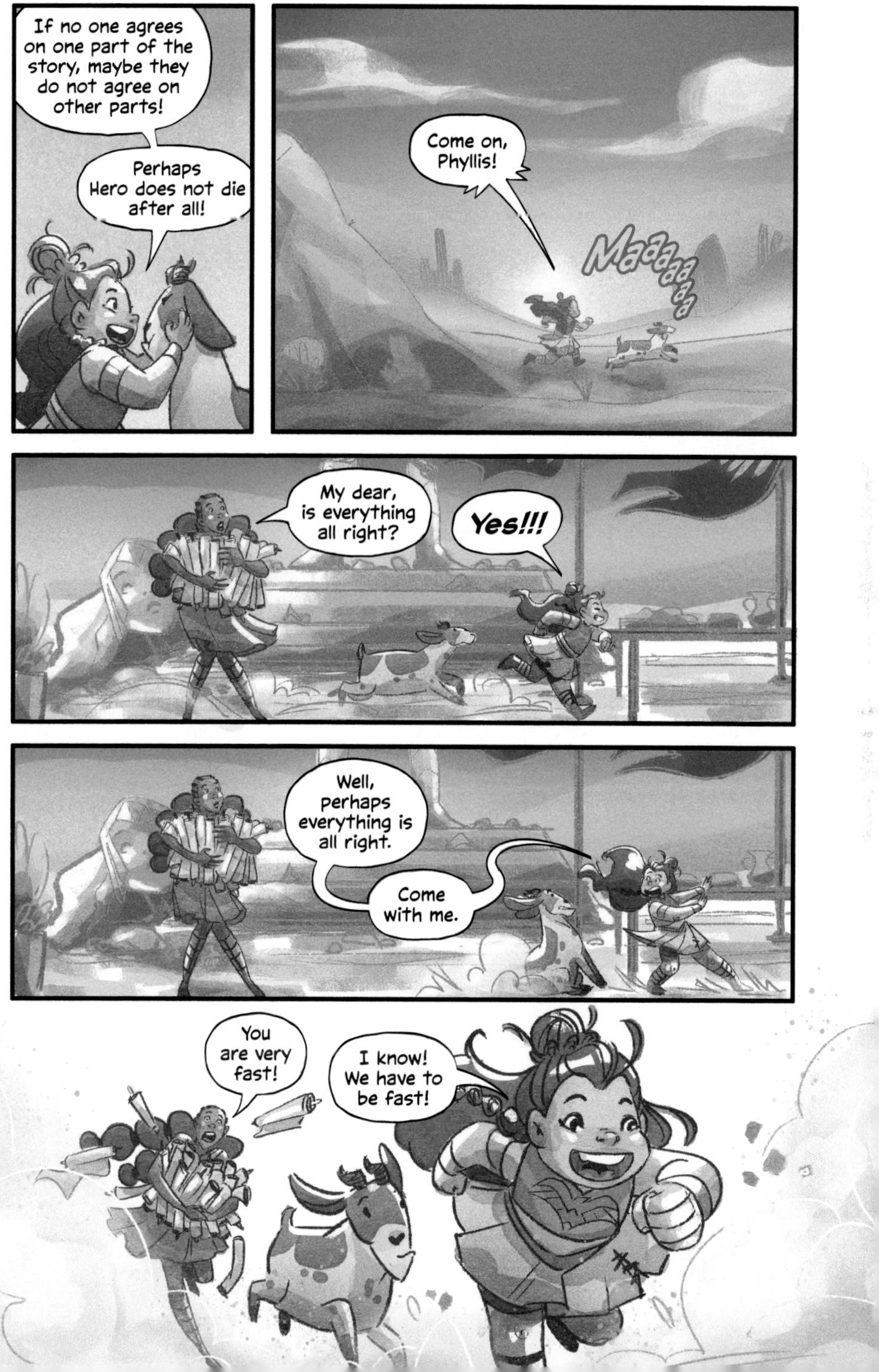
If no one agrees on one part of the story, maybe they do not agree on other parts!
Perhaps Hero does not die after all!
Come on, Phyllis!
Maaaaaa
My dear, is everything all right?
Yes!!!
Well, perhaps everything is all right.
Come with me.
You are very fast!
I know! We have to be fast!

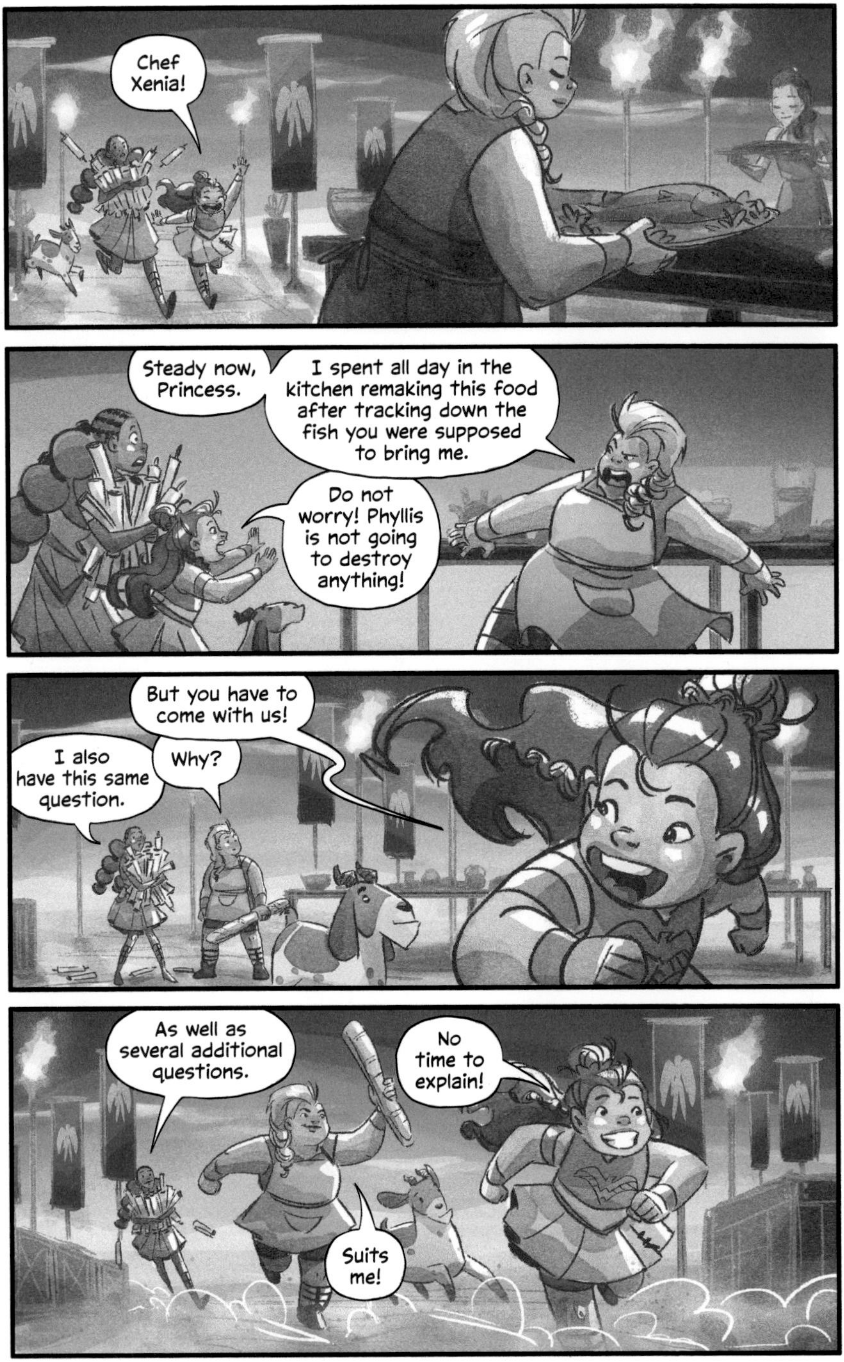
Chef Xenia!
Steady now, Princess.
I spent all day in the kitchen remaking this food after tracking down the fish you were supposed to bring me.
Do not worry! Phyllis is not going to destroy anything!
But you have to come with us!
Why?
I also have this same question.
As well as several additional questions.
No time to explain!
Suits me!

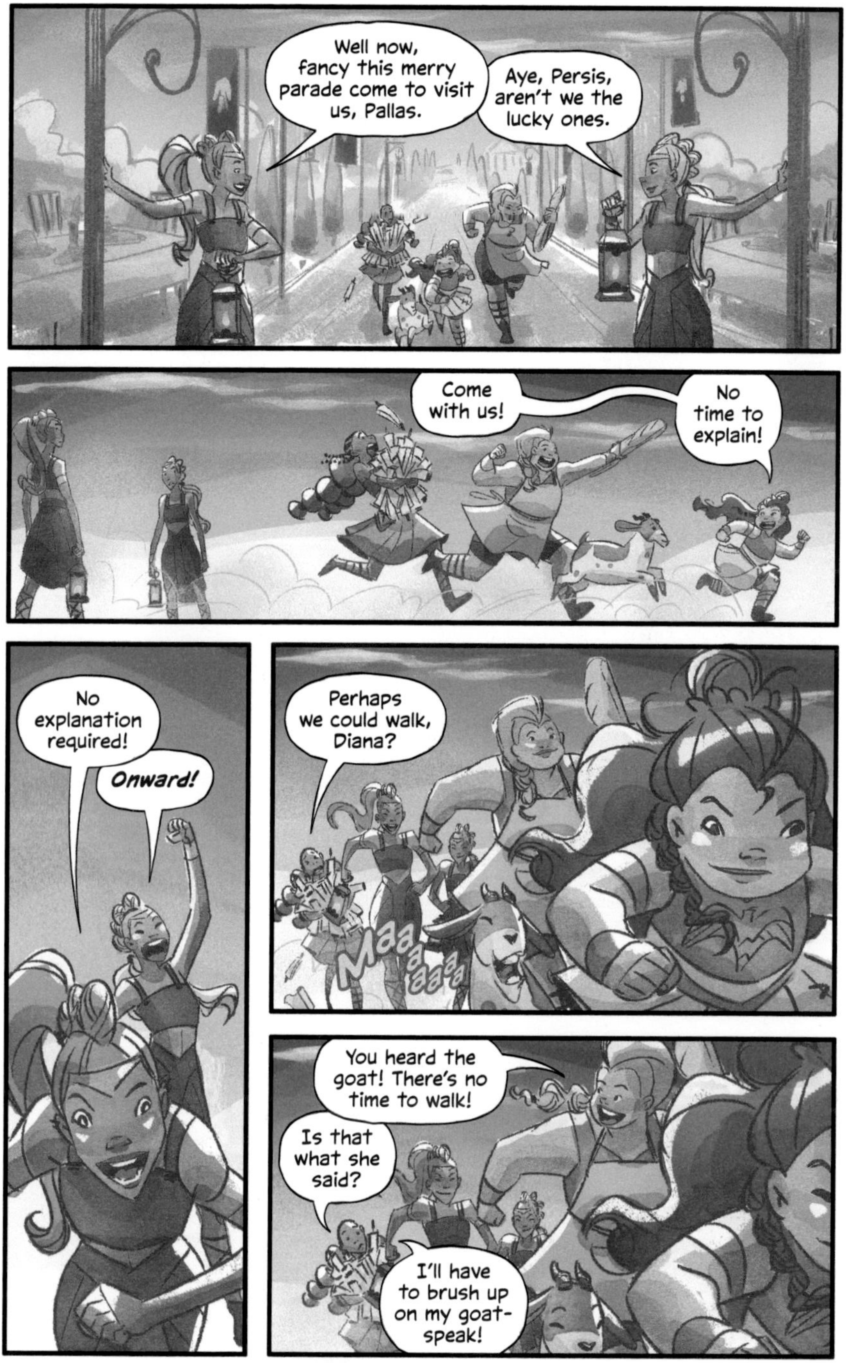
Well now, fancy this merry parade come to visit us, Pallas.
Aye, Persis, aren't we the lucky ones.
Come with us!
No time to explain!
No explanation required!
Onward!
Perhaps we could walk, Diana?
Maaaaaa
You heard the goat! There's no time to walk!
Is that what she said?
I'll have to brush up on my goat-speak!

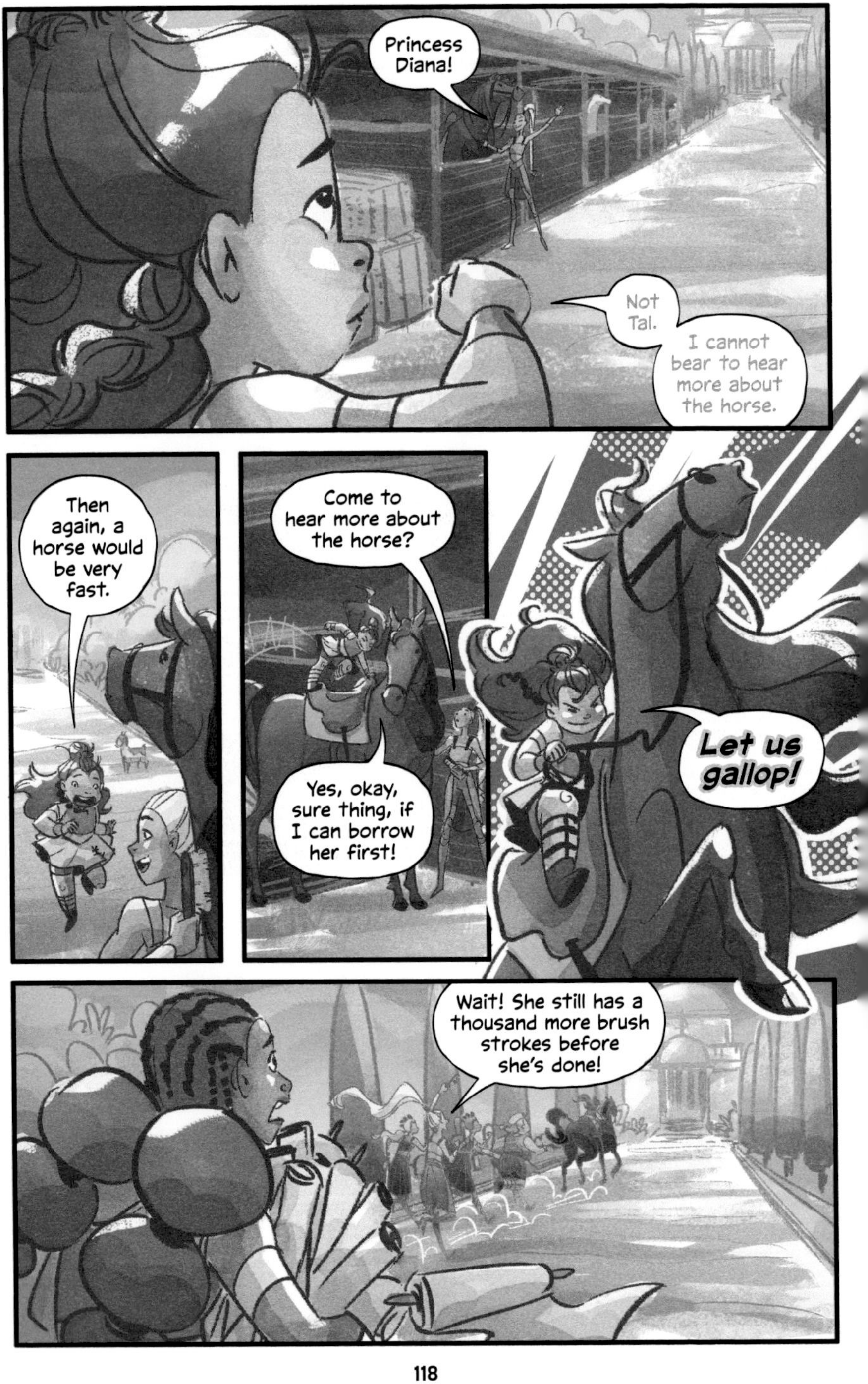
Princess Diana!
Not Tal.
I cannot bear to hear more about the horse.
Then again, a horse would be very fast.
Come to hear more about the horse?
Yes, okay, sure thing, if I can borrow her first!
Let us gallop!
Wait! She still has a thousand more brush strokes before she's done!

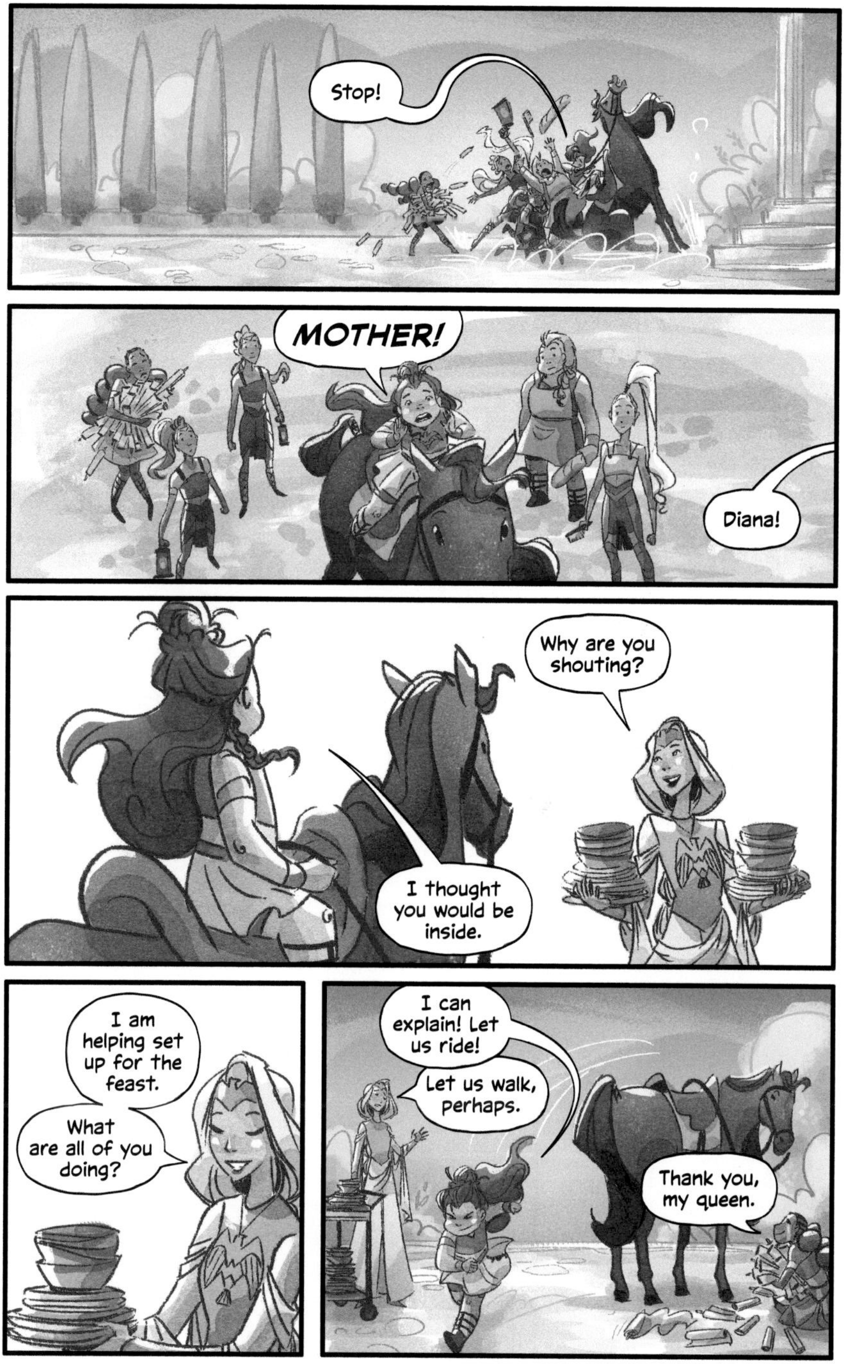
Stop!
MOTHER!
Diana!
Why are you shouting?
I thought you would be inside.
I am helping set up for the feast.
What are all of you doing?
I can explain! Let us ride!
Let us walk, perhaps.
Thank you, my queen.

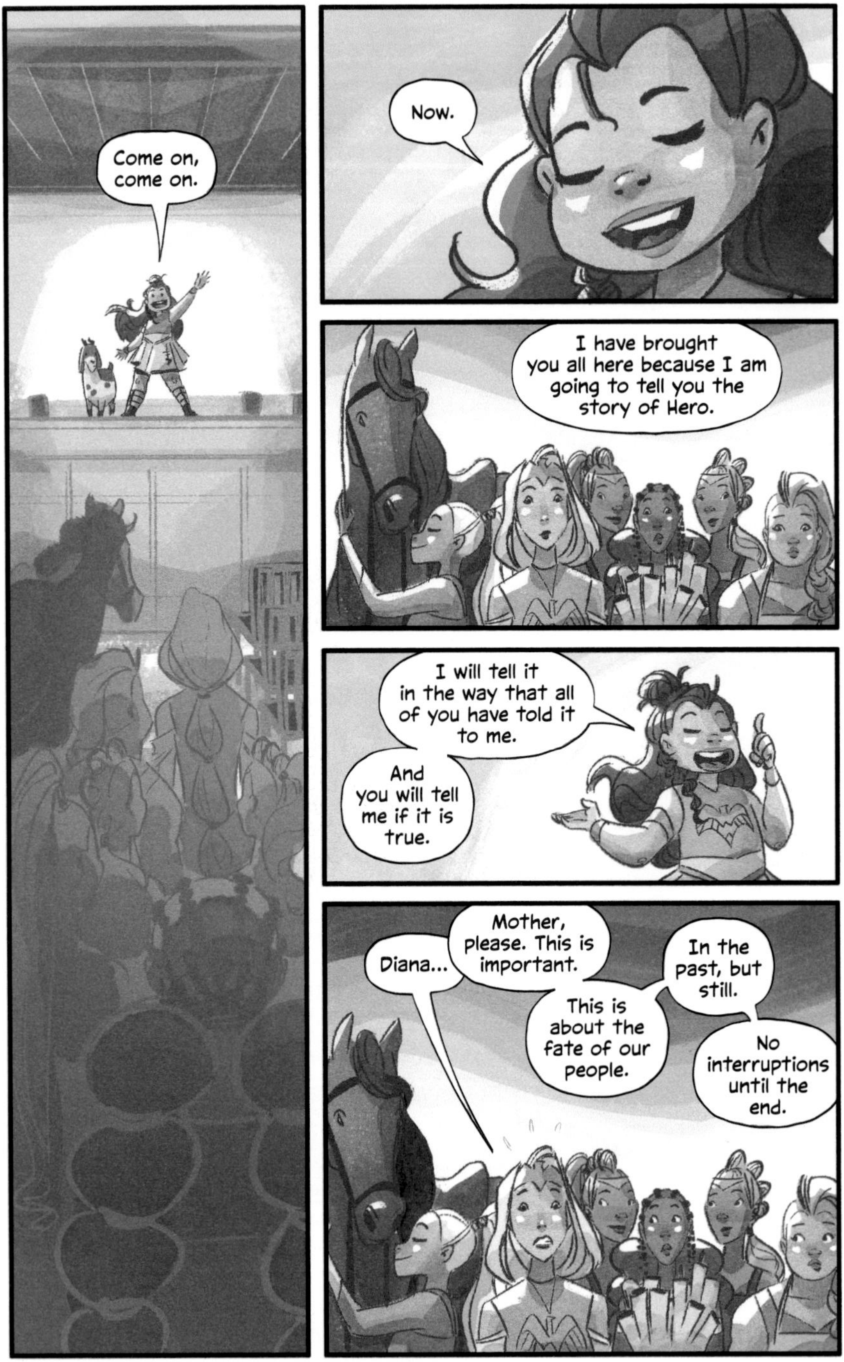
Come on, come on.
Now.
I have brought you all here because I am going to tell you the story of Hero.
I will tell it in the way that all of you have told it to me.
And you will tell me if it is true.
Diana...
Mother, please. This is important.
This is about the fate of our people.
In the past, but still.
No interruptions until the end.

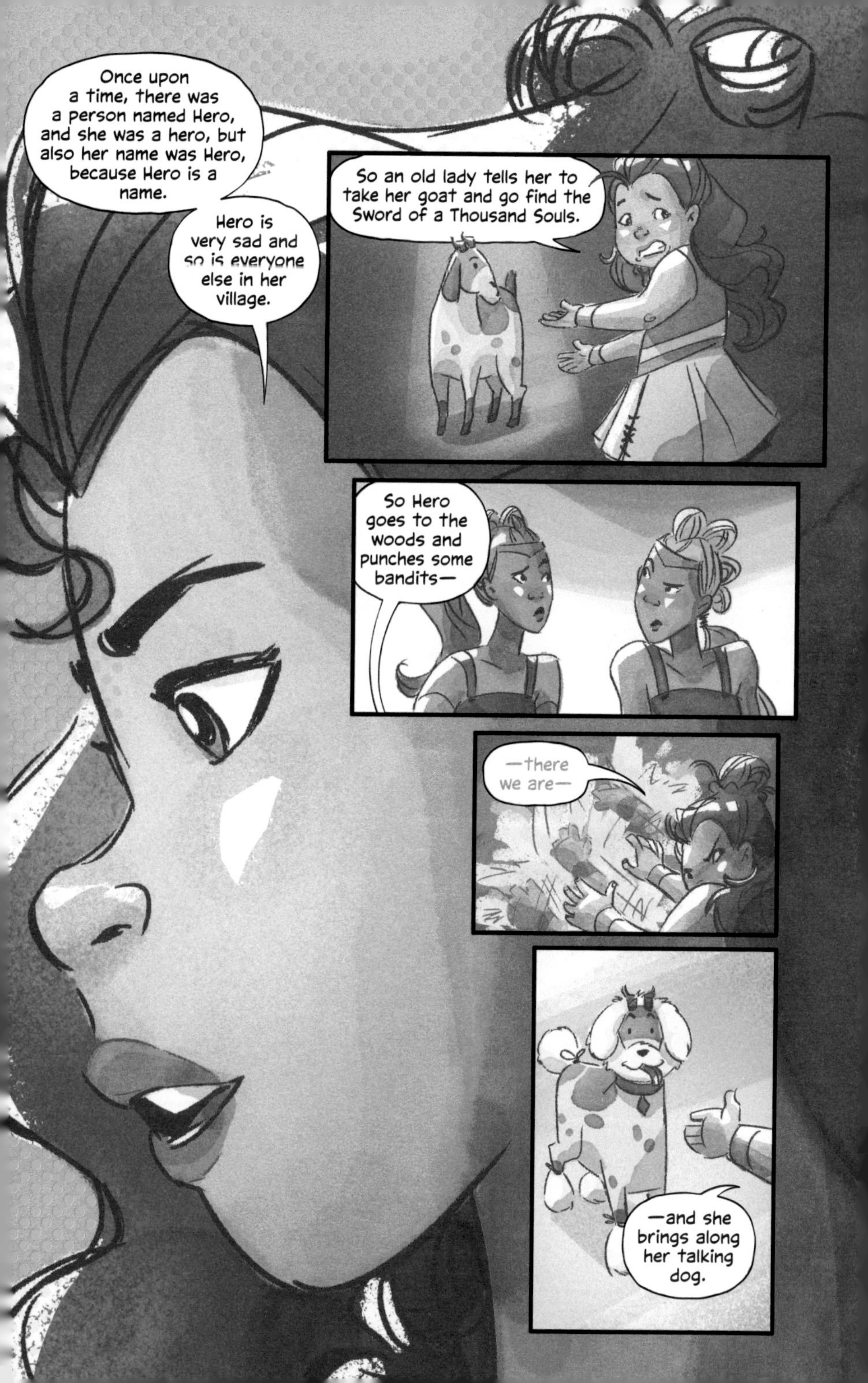
Once upon a time, there was a person named Hero, and she was a hero, but also her name was Hero, because Hero is a name.
Hero is very sad and so is everyone else in her village.
So an old lady tells her to take her goat and go find the Sword of a Thousand Souls.
So Hero goes to the woods and punches some bandits—
—there we are—
—and she brings along her talking dog.

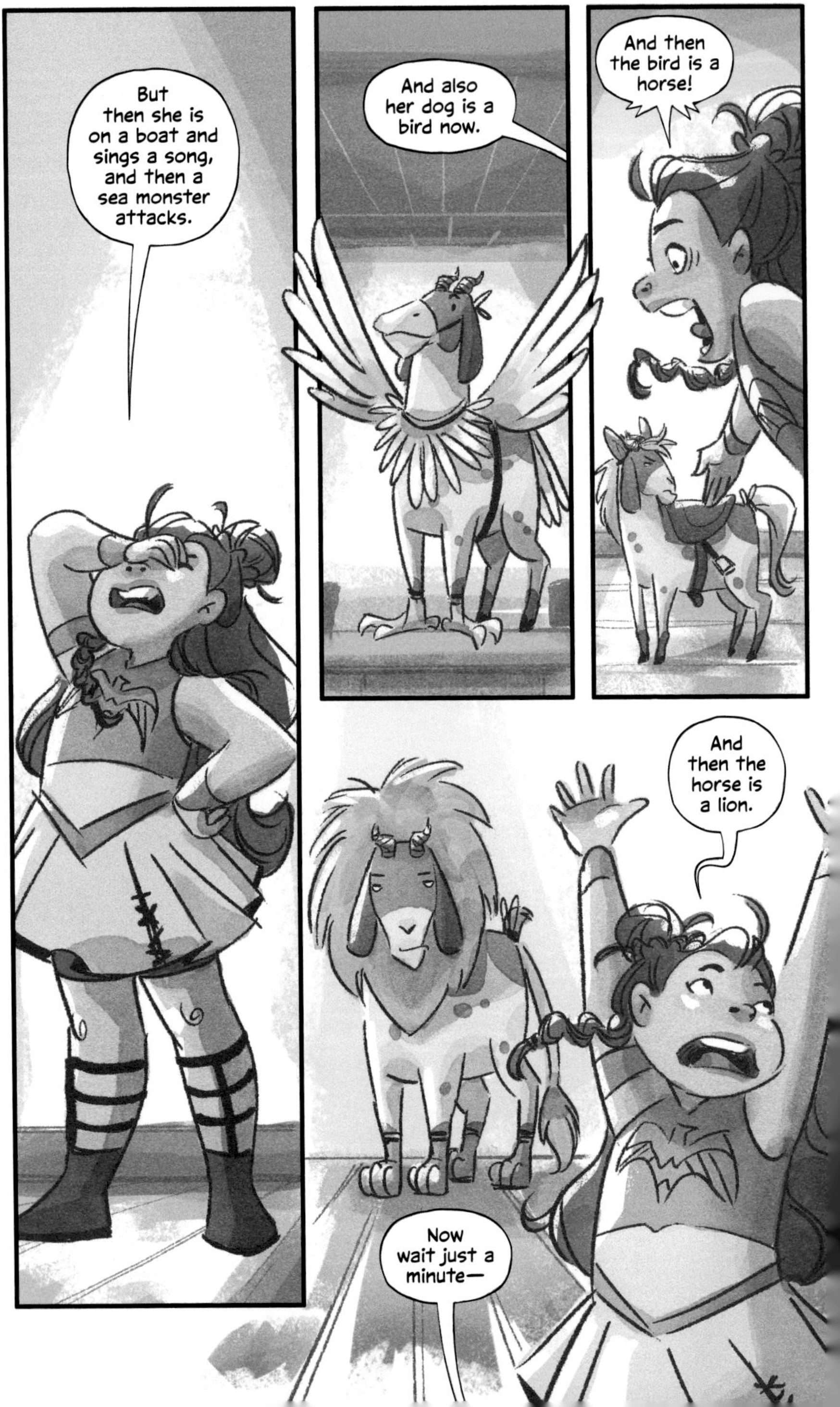
But then she is on a boat and sings a song, and then a sea monster attacks.
And also her dog is a bird now.
And then the bird is a horse!
And then the horse is a lion.
Now wait just a minute—

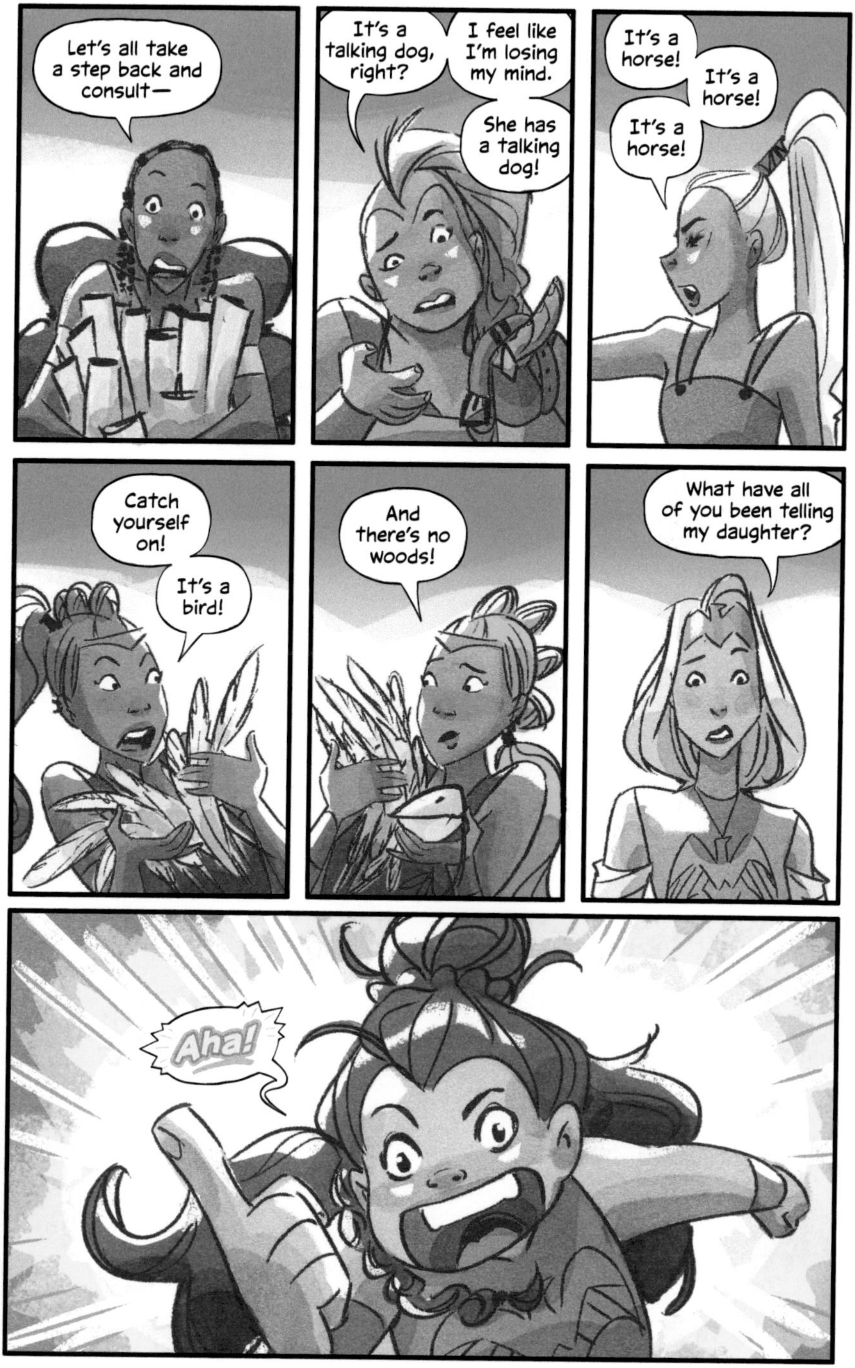
Let's all take a step back and consult—
It's a talking dog, right?
I feel like I'm losing my mind.
She has a talking dog!
It's a horse!
It's a horse!
It's a horse!
Catch yourself on!
It's a bird!
And there's no woods!
What have all of you been telling my daughter?
Aha!

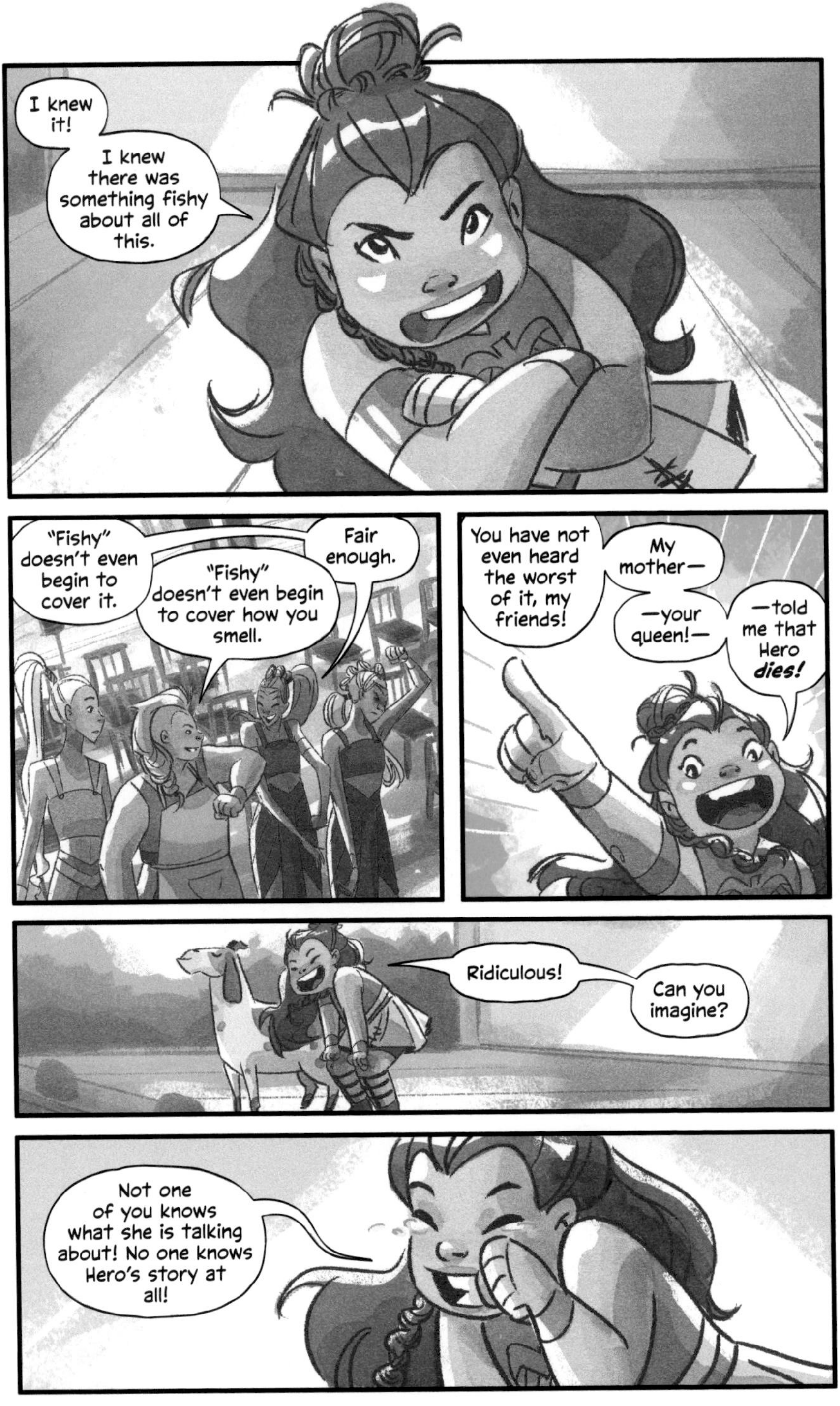
I knew it!
I knew there was something fishy about all of this.
"Fishy" doesn't even begin to cover it.
"Fishy" doesn't even begin to cover how you smell.
Fair enough.
You have not even heard the worst of it, my friends!
My mother—
—your queen!—
—told me that Hero *dies!*
Ridiculous!
Can you imagine?
Not one of you knows what she is talking about! No one knows Hero's story at all!

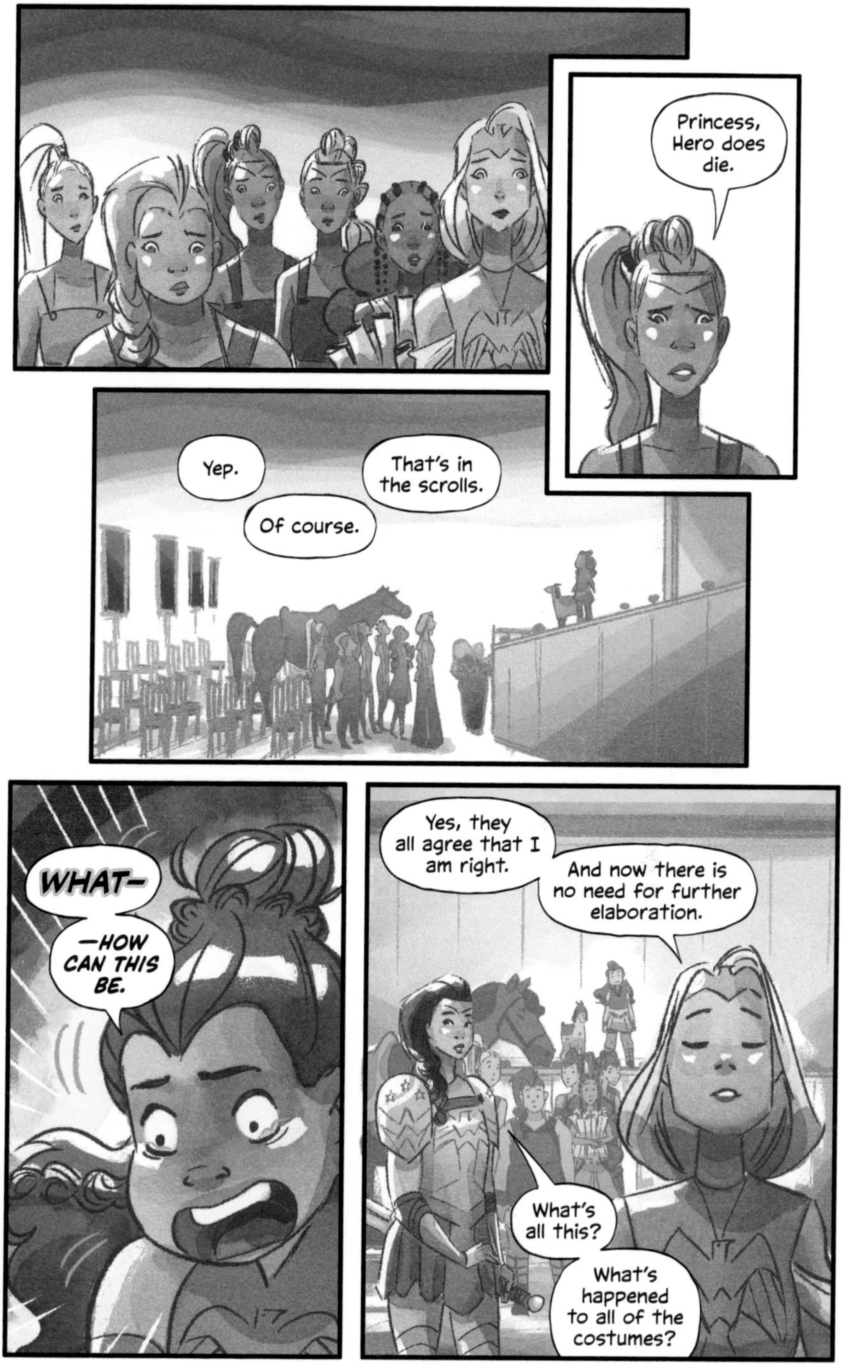

Princess, Hero does die.
Yep.
That's in the scrolls.
Of course.
WHAT–
–HOW CAN THIS BE.
Yes, they all agree that I am right.
And now there is no need for further elaboration.
What's all this?
What's happened to all of the costumes?

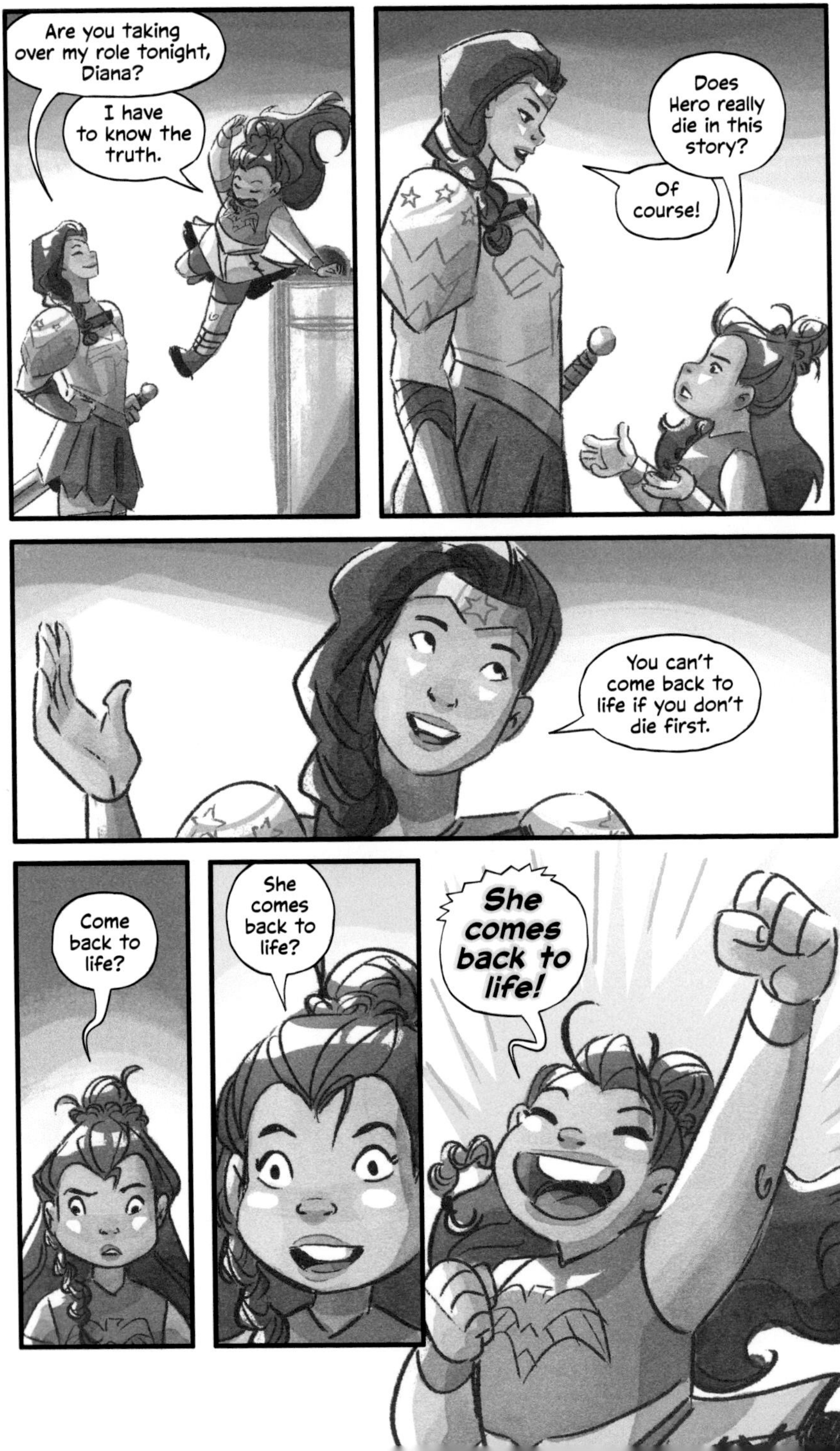
Are you taking over my role tonight, Diana?
I have to know the truth.
Does Hero really die in this story?
Of course!
You can't come back to life if you don't die first.
Come back to life?
She comes back to life?
She comes back to life!

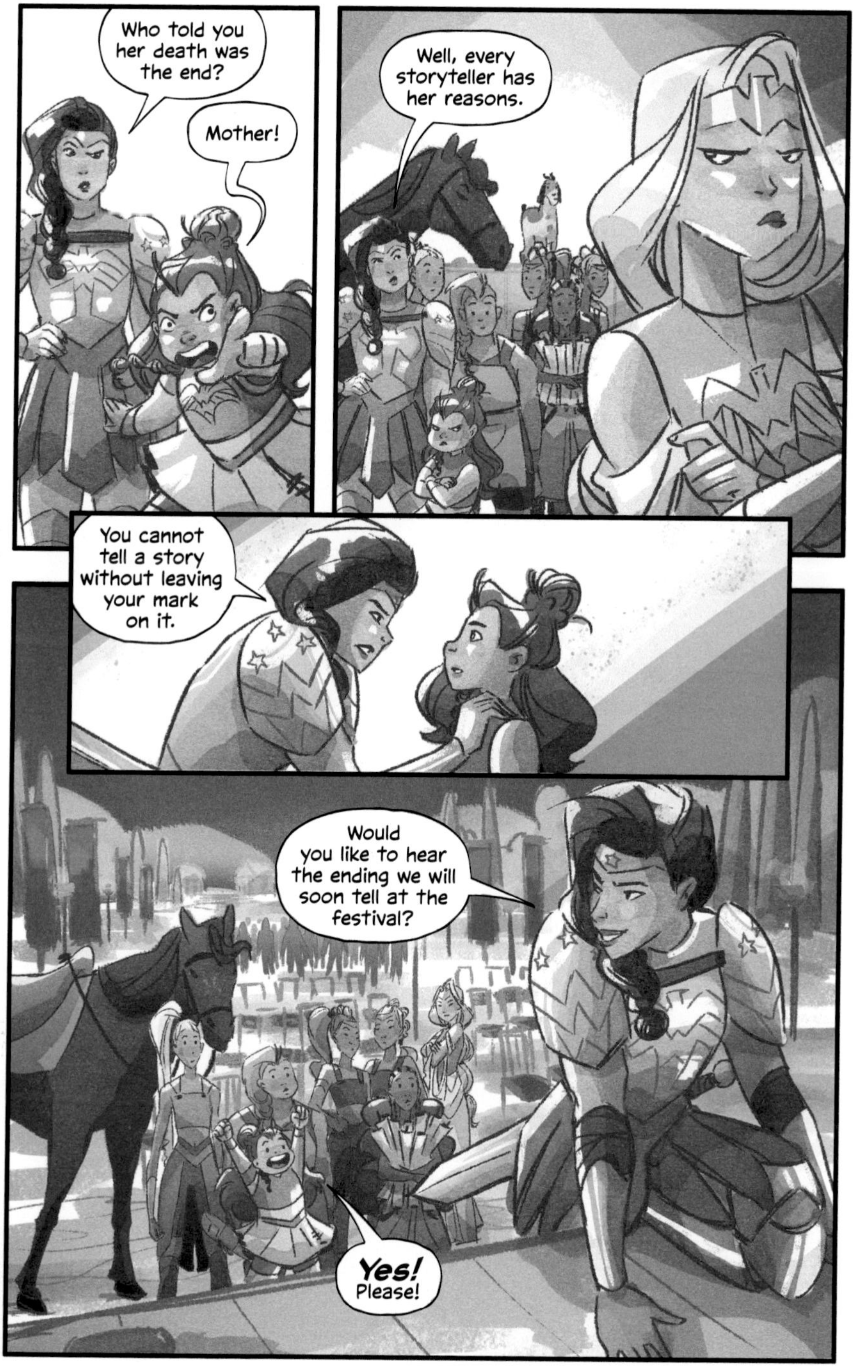
Who told you her death was the end?
Mother!
Well, every storyteller has her reasons.
You cannot tell a story without leaving your mark on it.
Would you like to hear the ending we will soon tell at the festival?
Yes! Please!

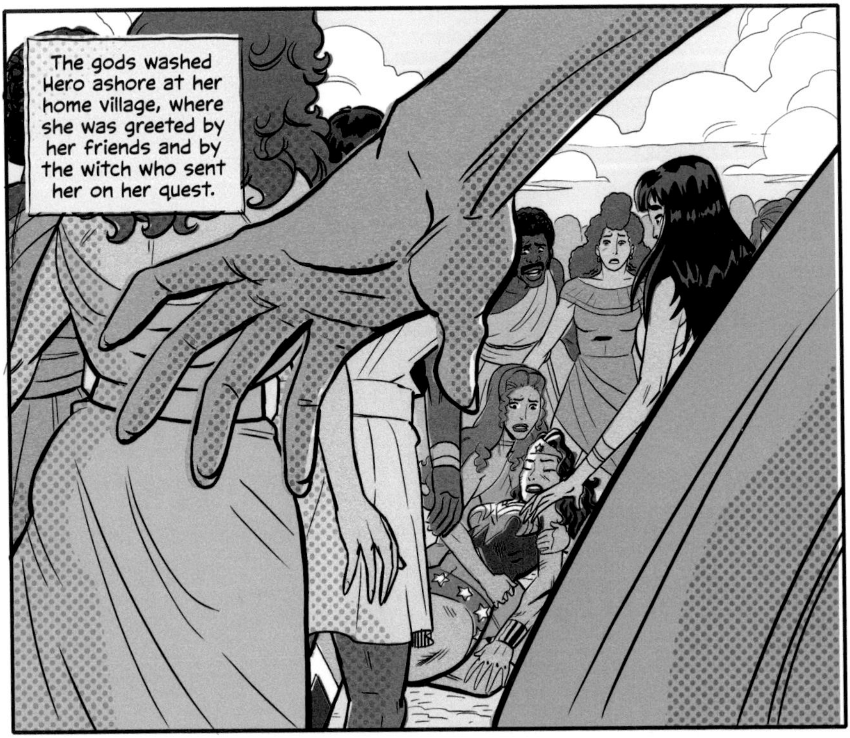
The gods washed Hero ashore at her home village, where she was greeted by her friends and by the witch who sent her on her quest.

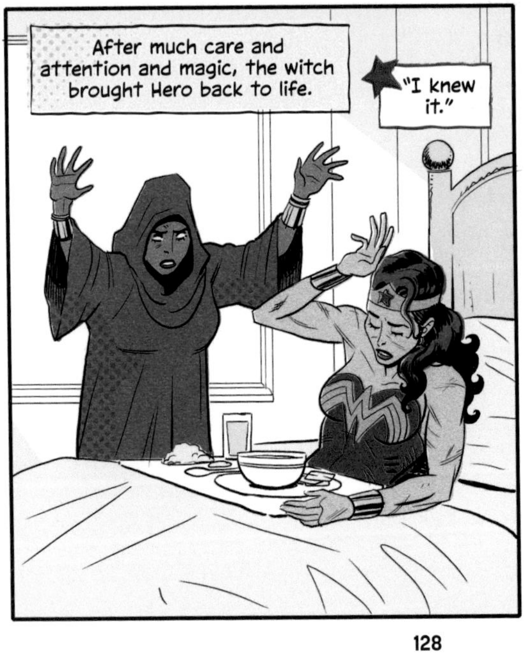
After much care and attention and magic, the witch brought Hero back to life.
"I knew it."

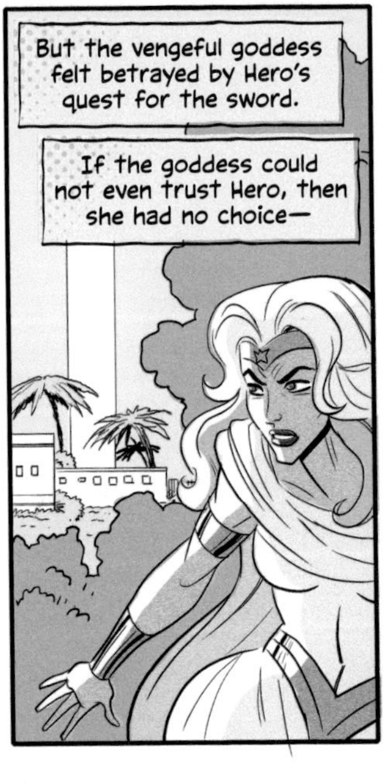
But the vengeful goddess felt betrayed by Hero's quest for the sword.
If the goddess could not even trust Hero, then she had no choice—

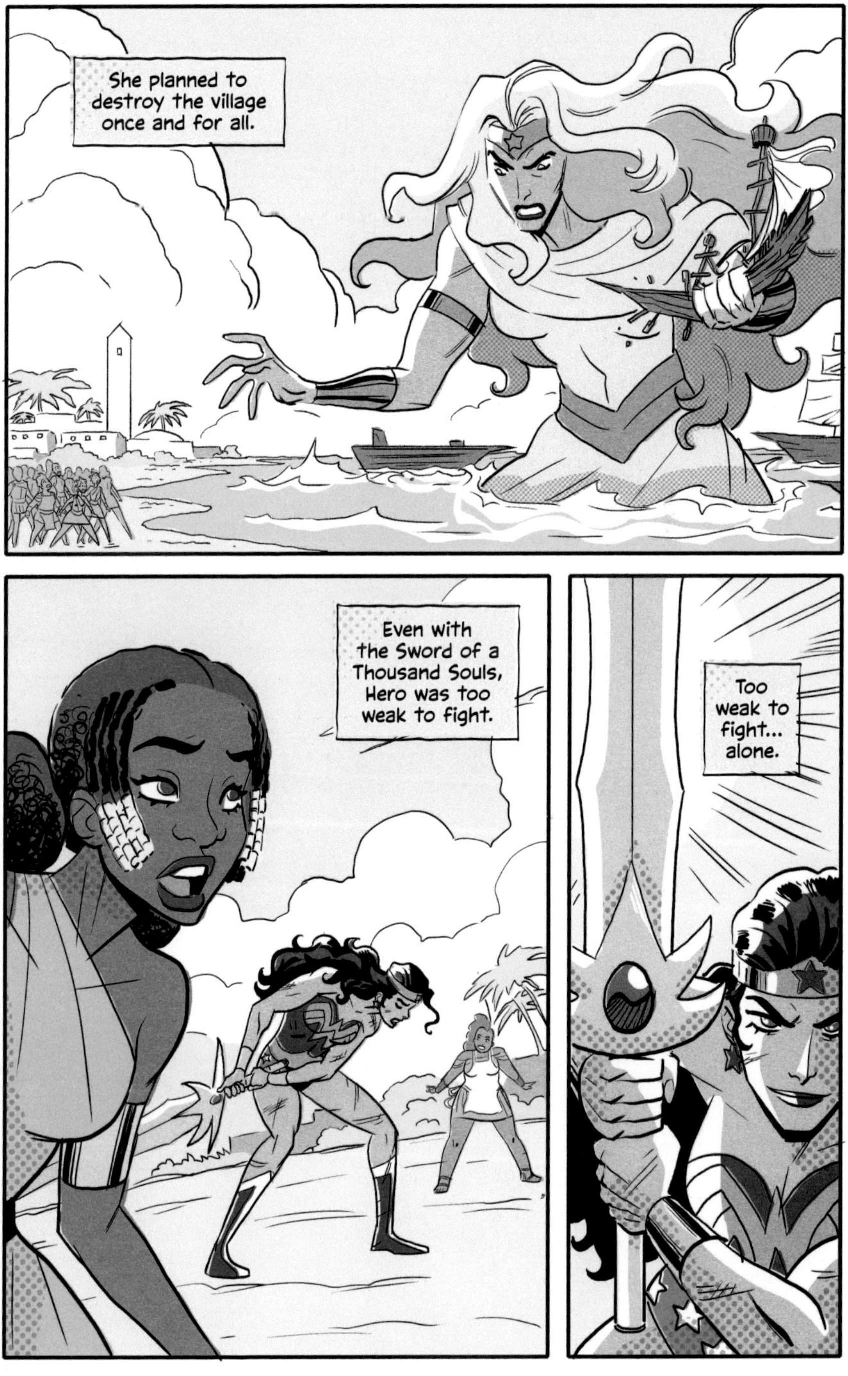
She planned to destroy the village once and for all.
Even with the Sword of a Thousand Souls, Hero was too weak to fight.
Too weak to fight... alone.

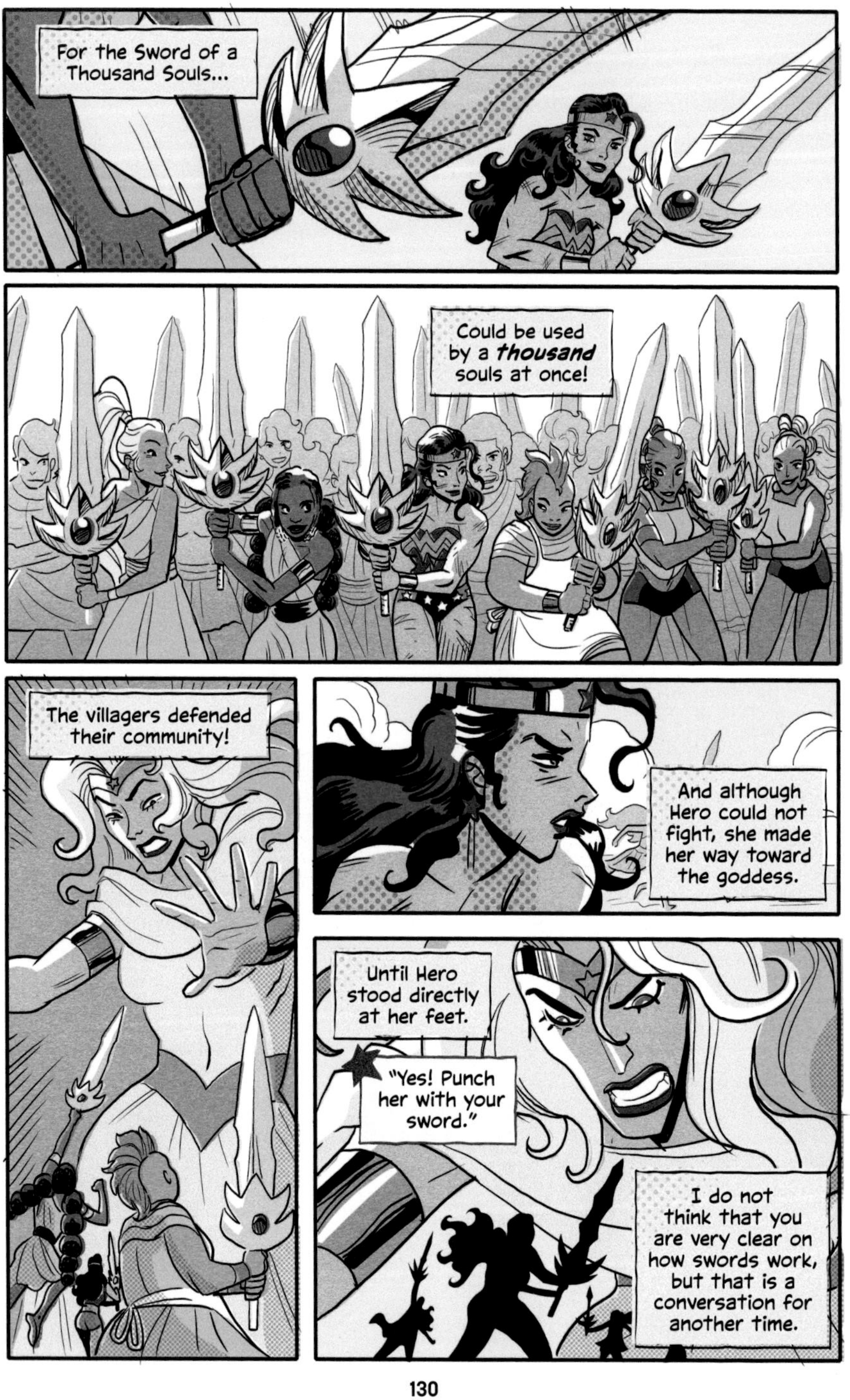
For the Sword of a Thousand Souls...
Could be used by a *thousand* souls at once!
The villagers defended their community!
And although Hero could not fight, she made her way toward the goddess.
Until Hero stood directly at her feet.
"Yes! Punch her with your sword."
I do not think that you are very clear on how swords work, but that is a conversation for another time.

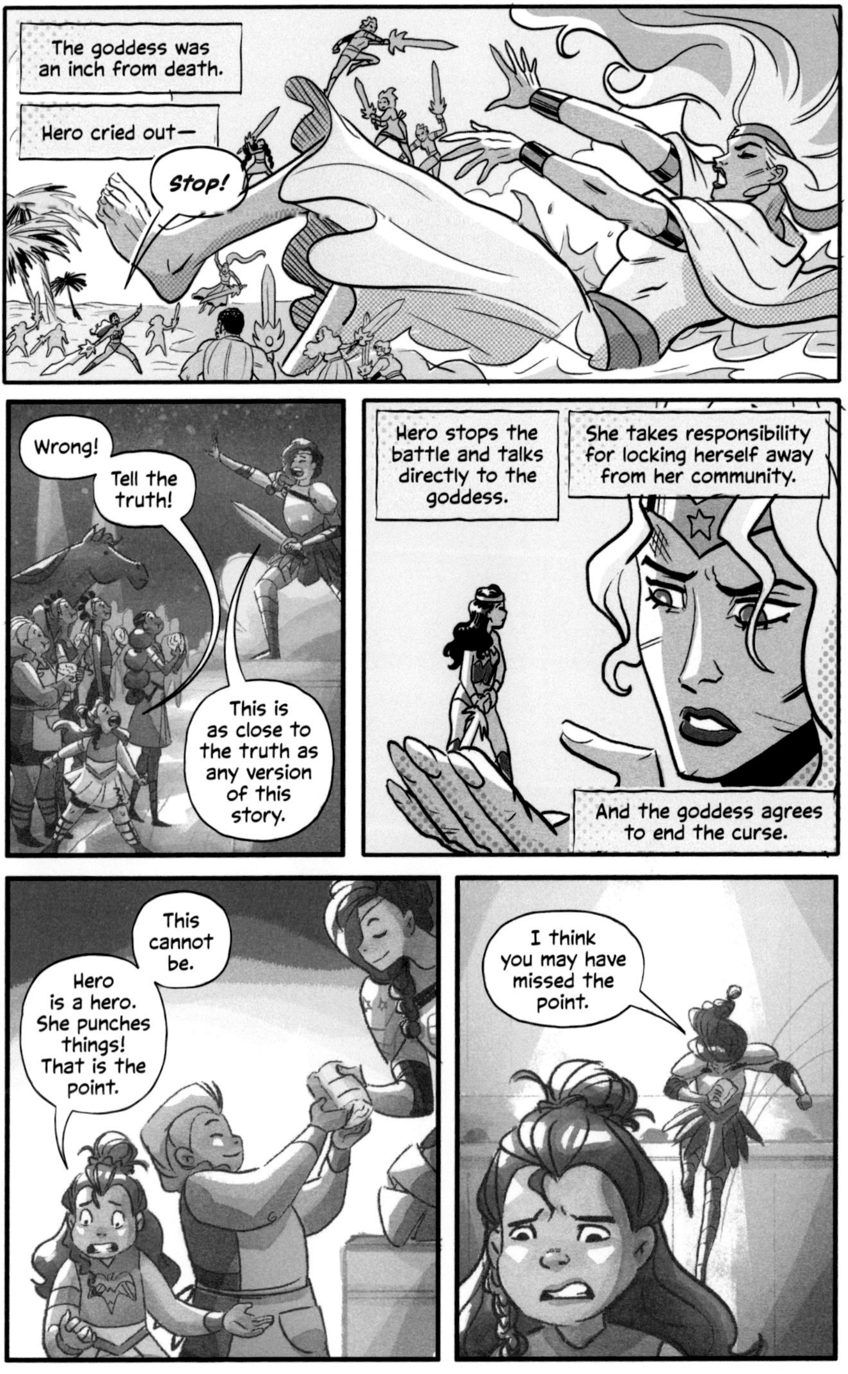
The goddess was an inch from death.
Hero cried out—
Stop!
Wrong!
Tell the truth!
This is as close to the truth as any version of this story.
Hero stops the battle and talks directly to the goddess.
She takes responsibility for locking herself away from her community.
And the goddess agrees to end the curse.
This cannot be.
Hero is a hero. She punches things! That is the point.
I think you may have missed the point.

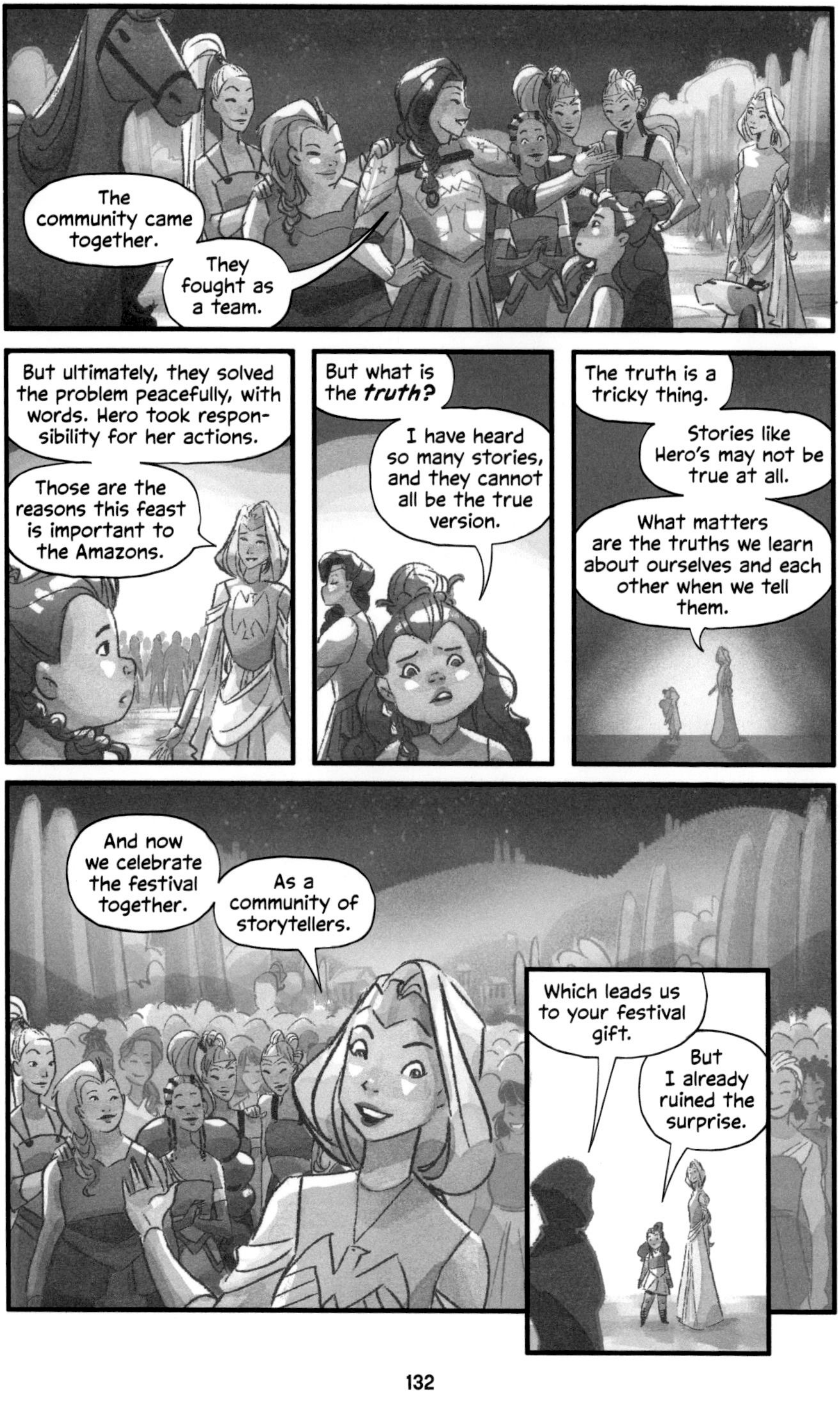
The community came together.
They fought as a team.
But ultimately, they solved the problem peacefully, with words. Hero took responsibility for her actions.
Those are the reasons this feast is important to the Amazons.
But what is the *truth?*
I have heard so many stories, and they cannot all be the true version.
The truth is a tricky thing.
Stories like Hero's may not be true at all.
What matters are the truths we learn about ourselves and each other when we tell them.
And now we celebrate the festival together.
As a community of storytellers.
Which leads us to your festival gift.
But I already ruined the surprise.

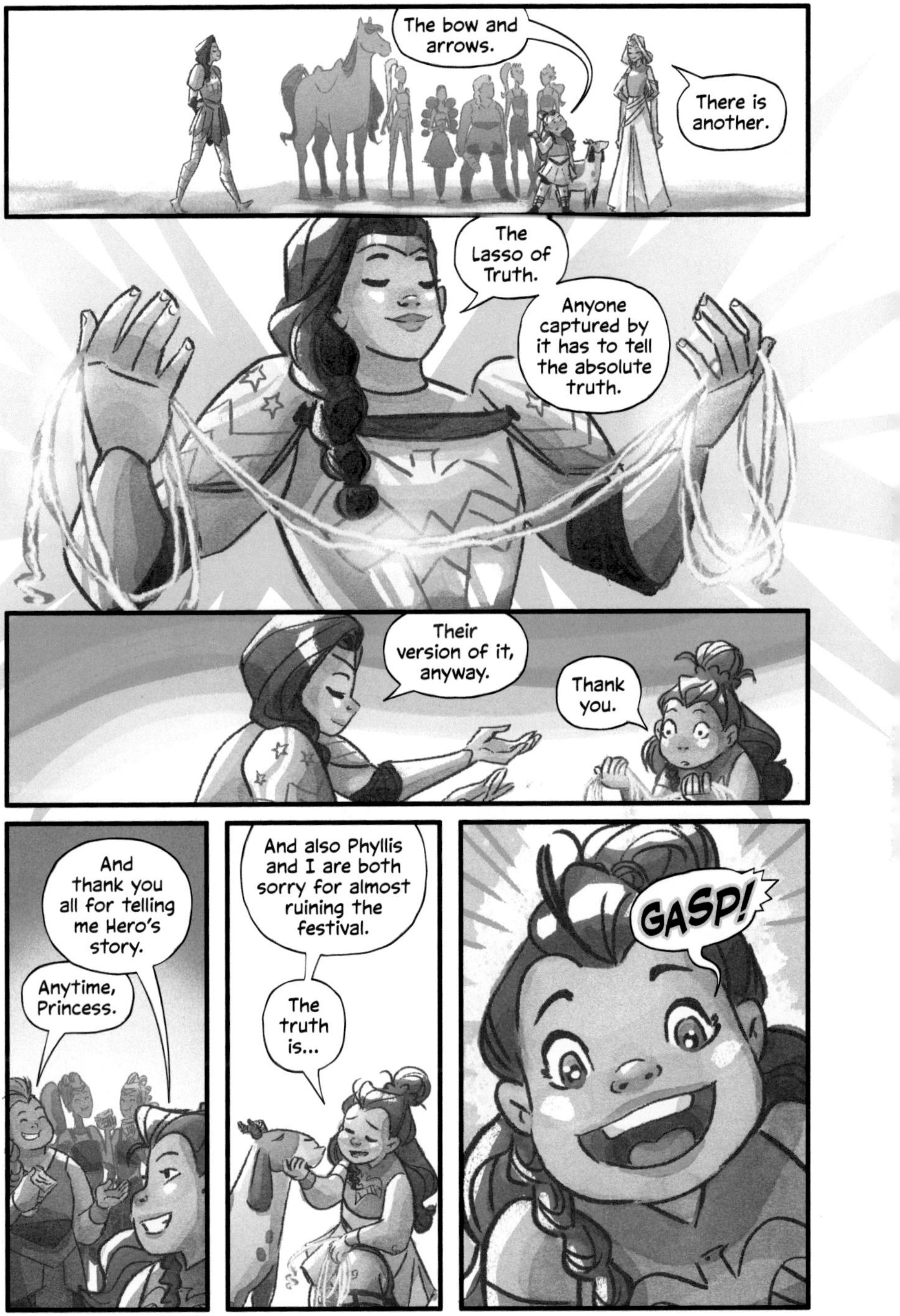
The bow and arrows.
There is another.
The Lasso of Truth.
Anyone captured by it has to tell the absolute truth.
Their version of it, anyway.
Thank you.
And thank you all for telling me Hero's story.
Anytime, Princess.
And also Phyllis and I are both sorry for almost ruining the festival.
The truth is...
GASP!

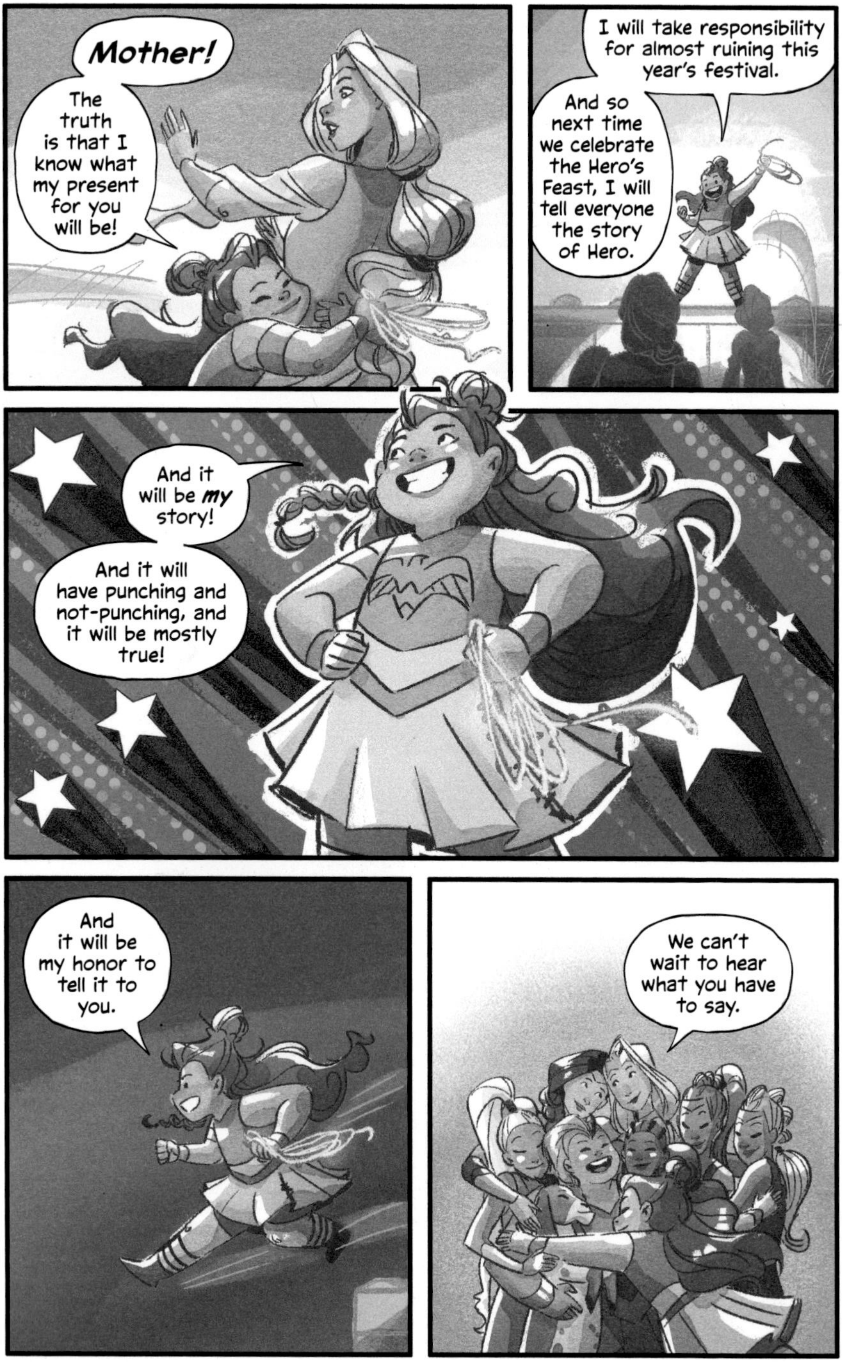
Mother!
The truth is that I know what my present for you will be!
I will take responsibility for almost ruining this year's festival.
And so next time we celebrate the Hero's Feast, I will tell everyone the story of Hero.
And it will be *my* story!
And it will have punching and not-punching, and it will be mostly true!
And it will be my honor to tell it to you.
We can't wait to hear what you have to say.

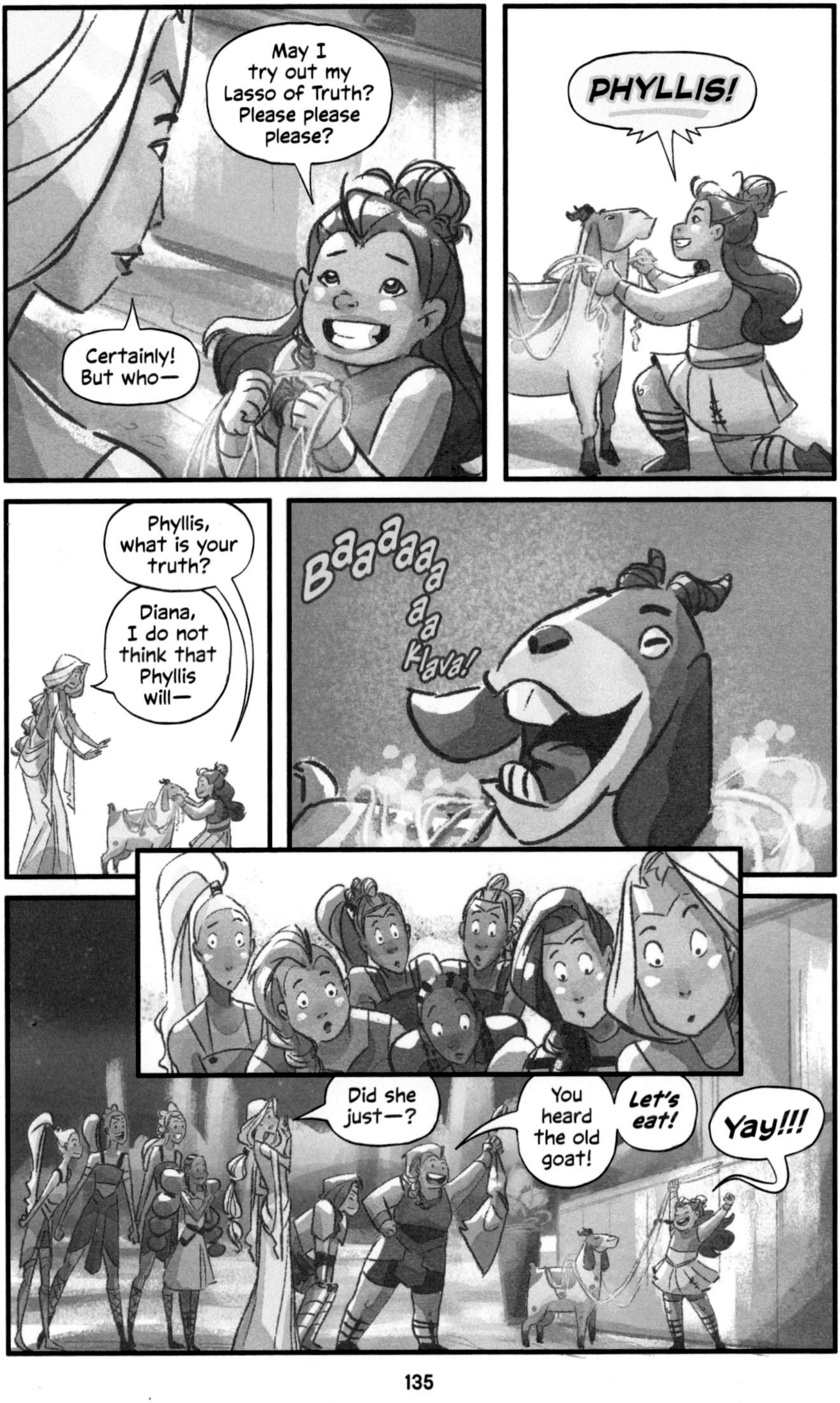
May I try out my Lasso of Truth? Please please please?
Certainly! But who—
PHYLLIS!
Phyllis, what is your truth?
Diana, I do not think that Phyllis will—
Baaaaaaaaa Klava!
Did she just—?
You heard the old goat!
Let's eat!
Yay!!!

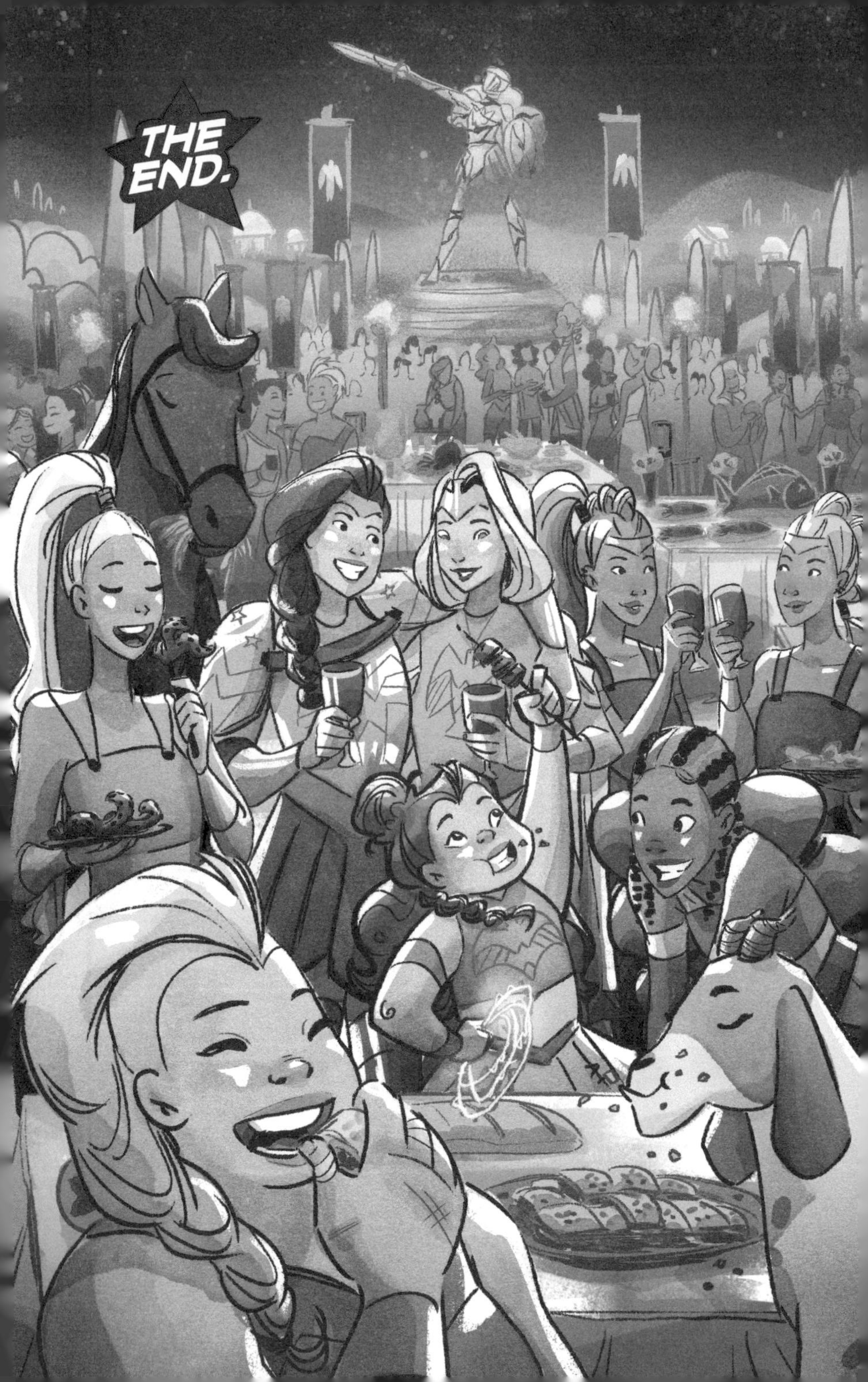
THE END.

Grace Ellis is a script writer whose comic books include *Moonstruck*; the Eisner-nominated *Flung out of Space*; and the Eisner- and GLAAD Award-winning, *New York Times*-bestselling series *Lumberjanes*. She has written some favorite DC Comics characters including Batwoman, Harley Quinn, and Lois Lane in the middle grade graphic novel *Lois Lane and the Friendship Challenge*. Grace lives in Columbus, Ohio, where she can often be found attending a play or petting a cat.

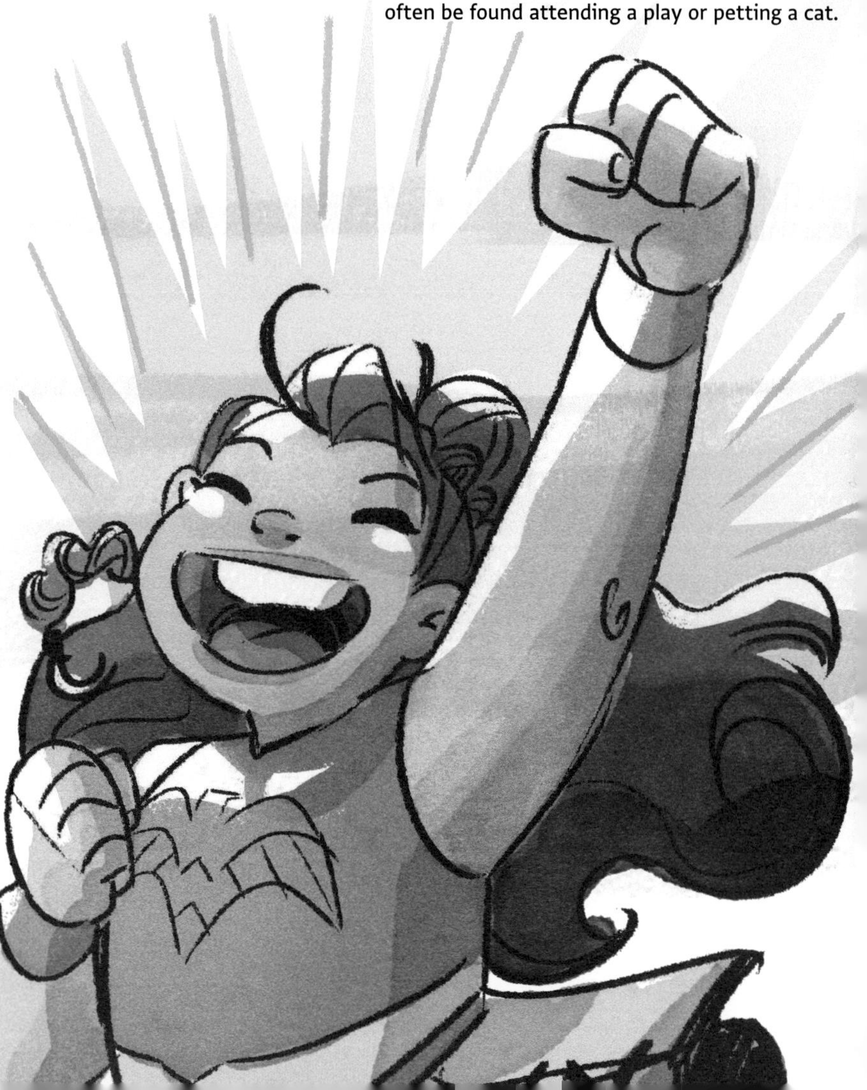

Photo by Emma Parker

Penelope Rivera Gaylord is an illustrator and visual development artist based in the Los Angeles area. She started her professional career in comics but has since transitioned into the animation industry, creating stories and characters for studios like Cartoon Network, Imagine Entertainment Kids + Family, and 9B Collective. She illustrated the *Captain Marvel* Little Golden Book and the *Avengers: Battle on the Moon* Little Golden Book for Penguin Random House. Born in the Philippines, Penelope grew up in the Washington, DC area. She and her husband, Jerry, moved to LA to pursue their dreams of bringing their stories to life in cartoon form—also to live that cowabunga lifestyle.

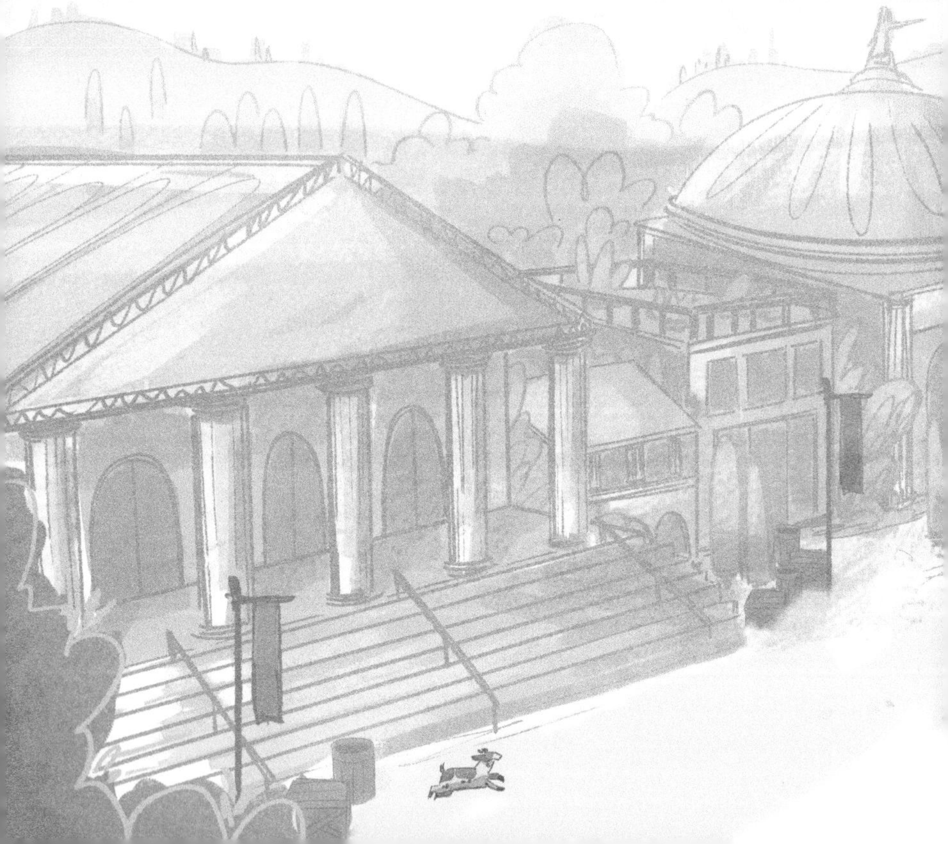

THE STORY OF HERO

The people who lived in ancient Greece are known for the stories they liked to tell, which included everything from family dramas to epic, heroic journeys to the land of the gods. In fact, the English word "hero" originally comes from a similar Greek word. That's how important heroes were in ancient Greece!

One of the popular stories that the ancient Greeks liked to tell was the story of Hero and Leander. It goes like this:

> Once upon a time, in two cities across the sea, lived two friends named Hero and Leander. Even though they lived far apart, Hero and Leander were in love. This was a problem, because Hero was a priestess, which meant she wasn't allowed to fall in love. But Hero and Leander were so in love that they came up with a way to see each other in secret: Every night, Hero would light a torch on her tower, and Leander would swim across the sea to see her, guided by the light.
>
> One stormy night, Leander made his journey across the sea to see Hero, but the storm was so fierce that it blew out Hero's torch. Leander got lost in the dark and was swept away by the waves, never to be seen again.

That's where the traditional story ends, but as you know, that's only the beginning of the Amazons' version. In their telling, Hero sets out on a grand journey, faces a series of challenges, and returns home to fight alongside her friends.

So why do the Amazons tell their own version instead of sticking to the original? The Amazons are a community that values courage, resilience, and independence. They seek out adventure, and they believe that it takes a whole village—not just one person—to keep everyone safe. This is what it takes to be a hero.

When Diana grows up to become Wonder Woman, she'll remember the lessons and legends she learned when she was a kid. She carries with her not only the spirit of Hero but also the spirit of the friends who told her Hero's story.

We all have stories that we love to tell. What's your favorite story and how has it shaped you into the hero you are?

Want more graphic novels from the writer behind *Diana and the Hero's Journey*?
Keep reading for a special preview of *Lois Lane and the Friendship Challenge*!

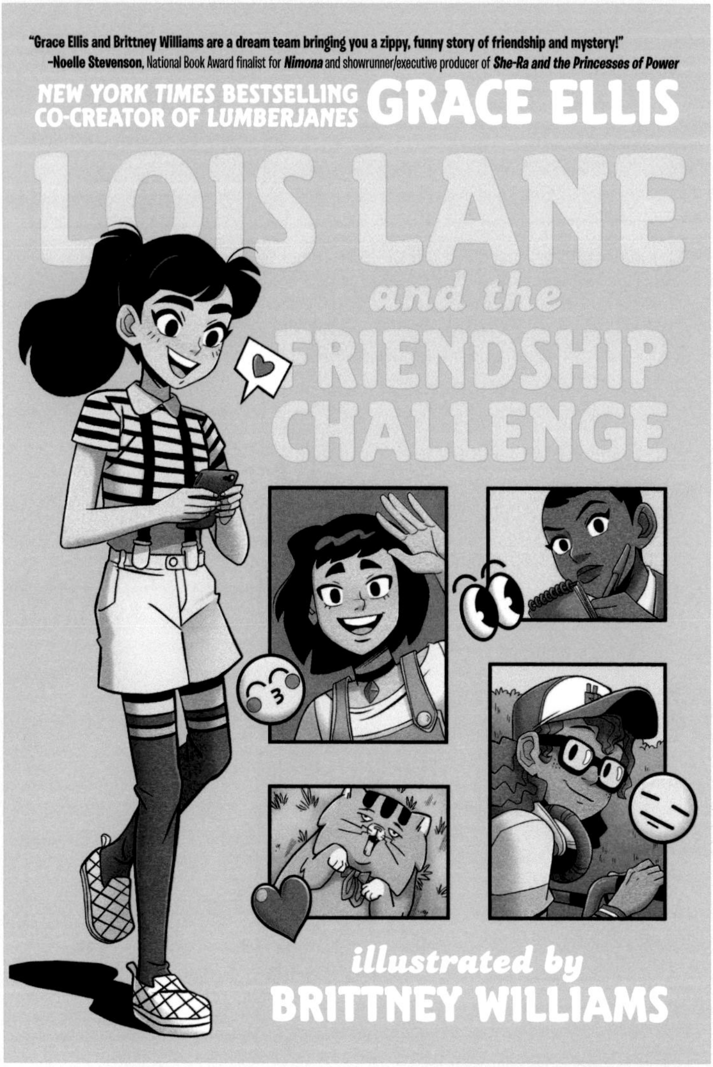
"Grace Ellis and Brittney Williams are a dream team bringing you a zippy, funny story of friendship and mystery!"
–Noelle Stevenson, National Book Award finalist for Nimona and showrunner/executive producer of She-Ra and the Princesses of Power
NEW YORK TIMES BESTSELLING CO-CREATOR OF LUMBERJANES
GRACE ELLIS
LOIS LANE
and the
FRIENDSHIP CHALLENGE
illustrated by
BRITTNEY WILLIAMS

Who knew friendship could be such a #challenge?

From *New York Times* bestselling author **Grace Ellis** and with expressive art by **Brittney Williams** (*Girl on Fire*) comes a fun new adventure about 13-year-old Lois Lane as she navigates the confusing worlds of social media and friendship.

In stores now!

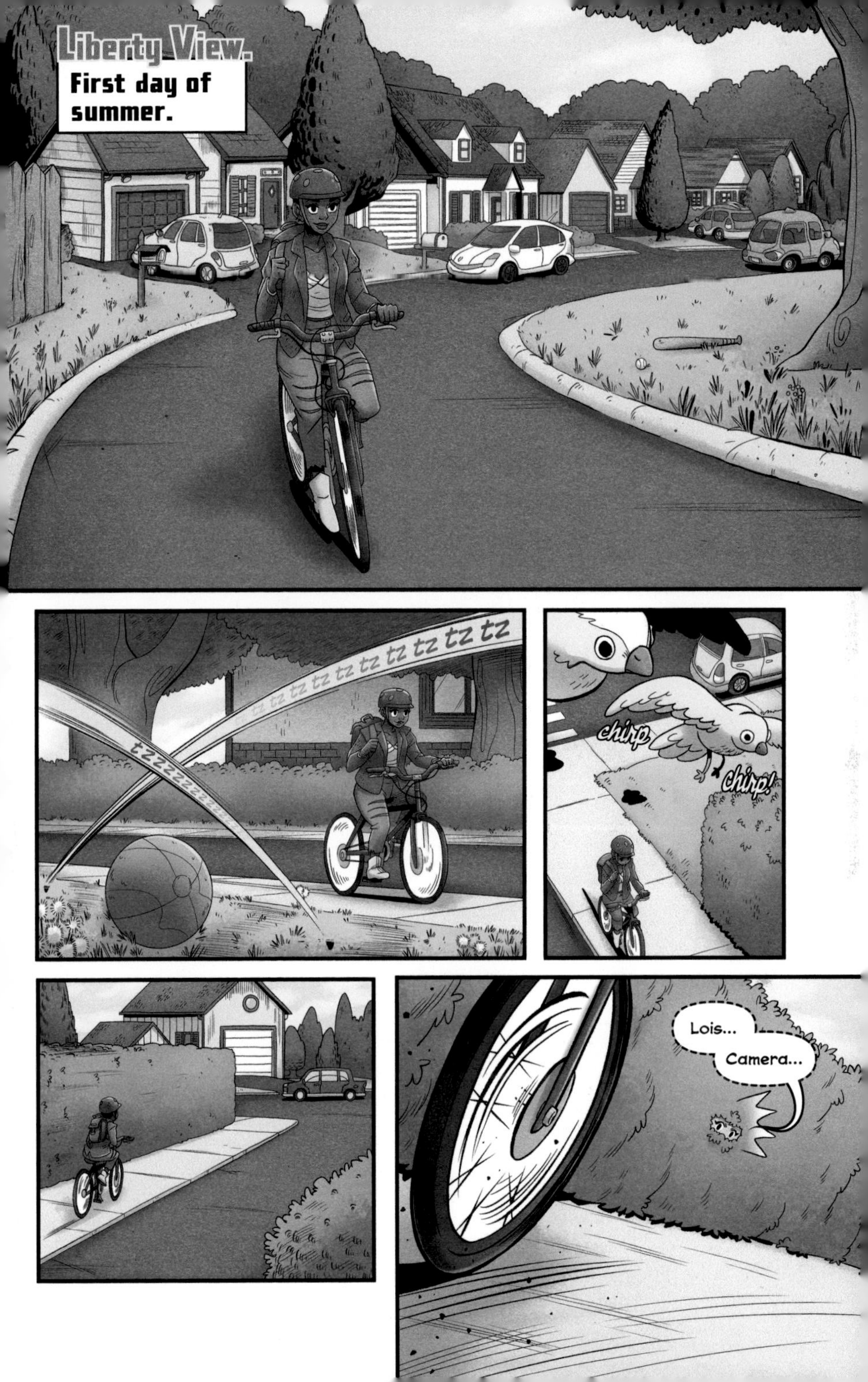
Liberty View.
First day of summer.
tz tz tz tz tz tz tz tz tz tz tz
tzzzzzzzz
chirp
chirp!
Lois...
Camera...

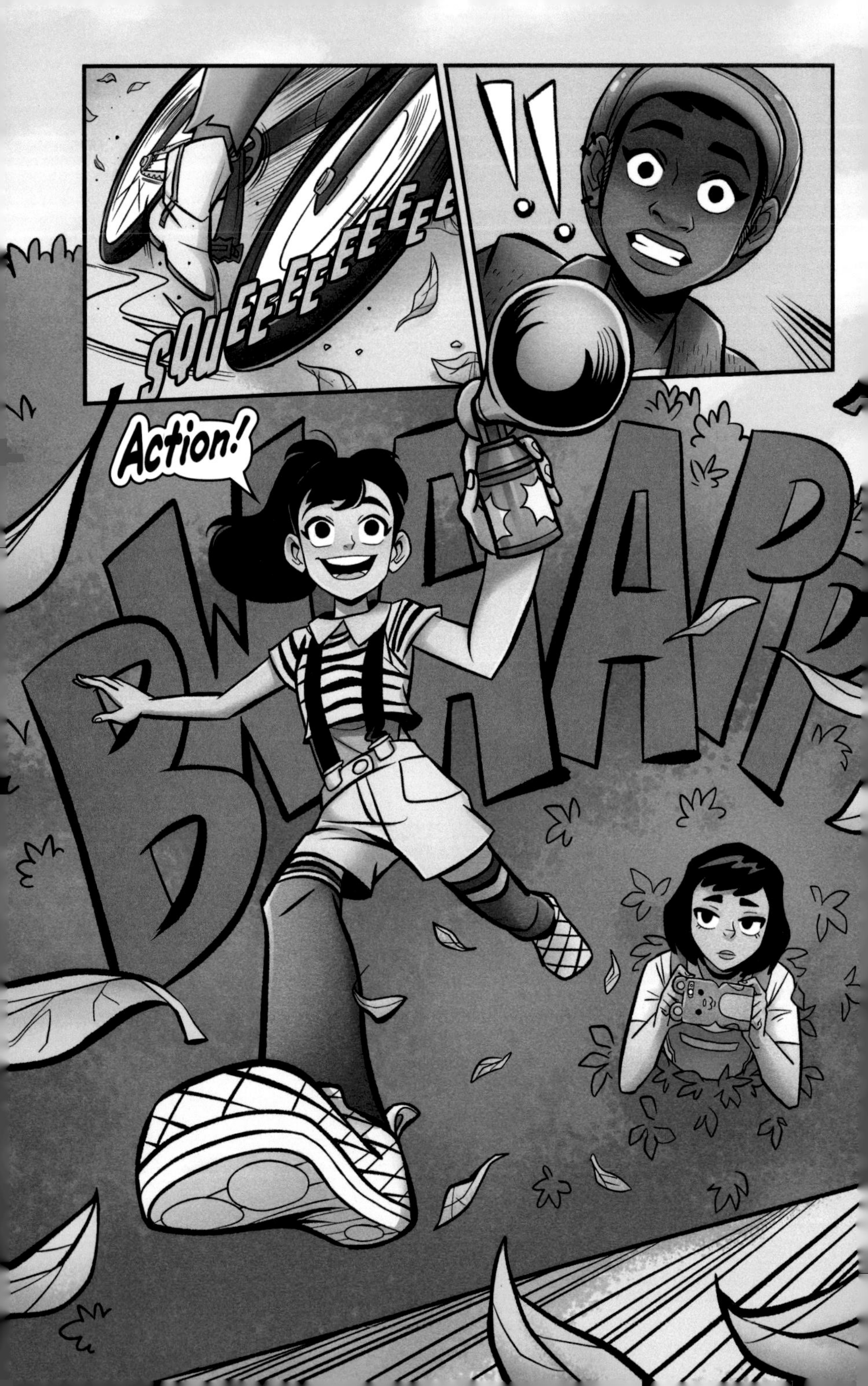
SQUEEEEEEEEEEE
!!
Action!
BWAAR

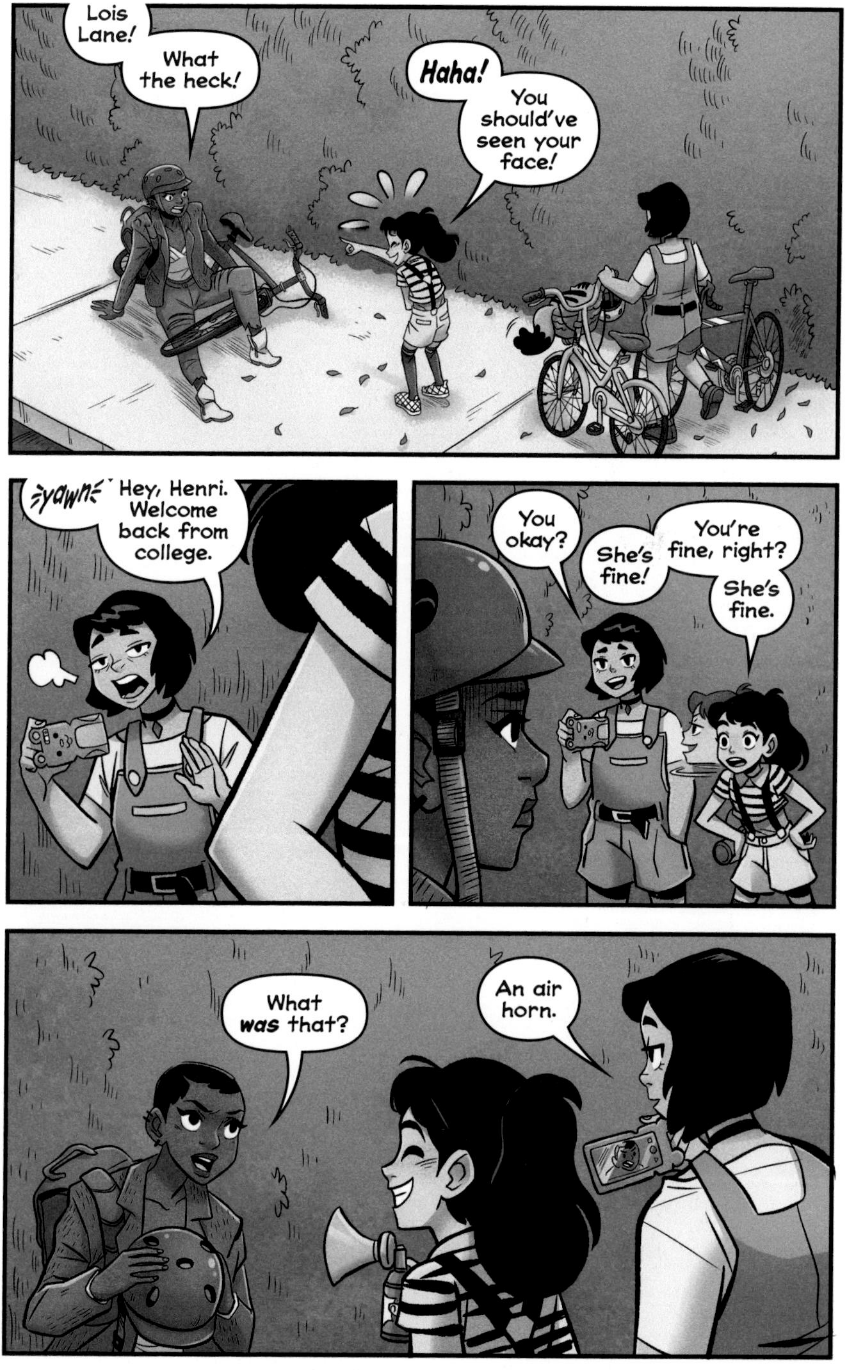
Lois Lane!
What the heck!
Haha!
You should've seen your face!
yawn
Hey, Henri. Welcome back from college.
You okay?
She's fine!
You're fine, right?
She's fine.
What was that?
An air horn.

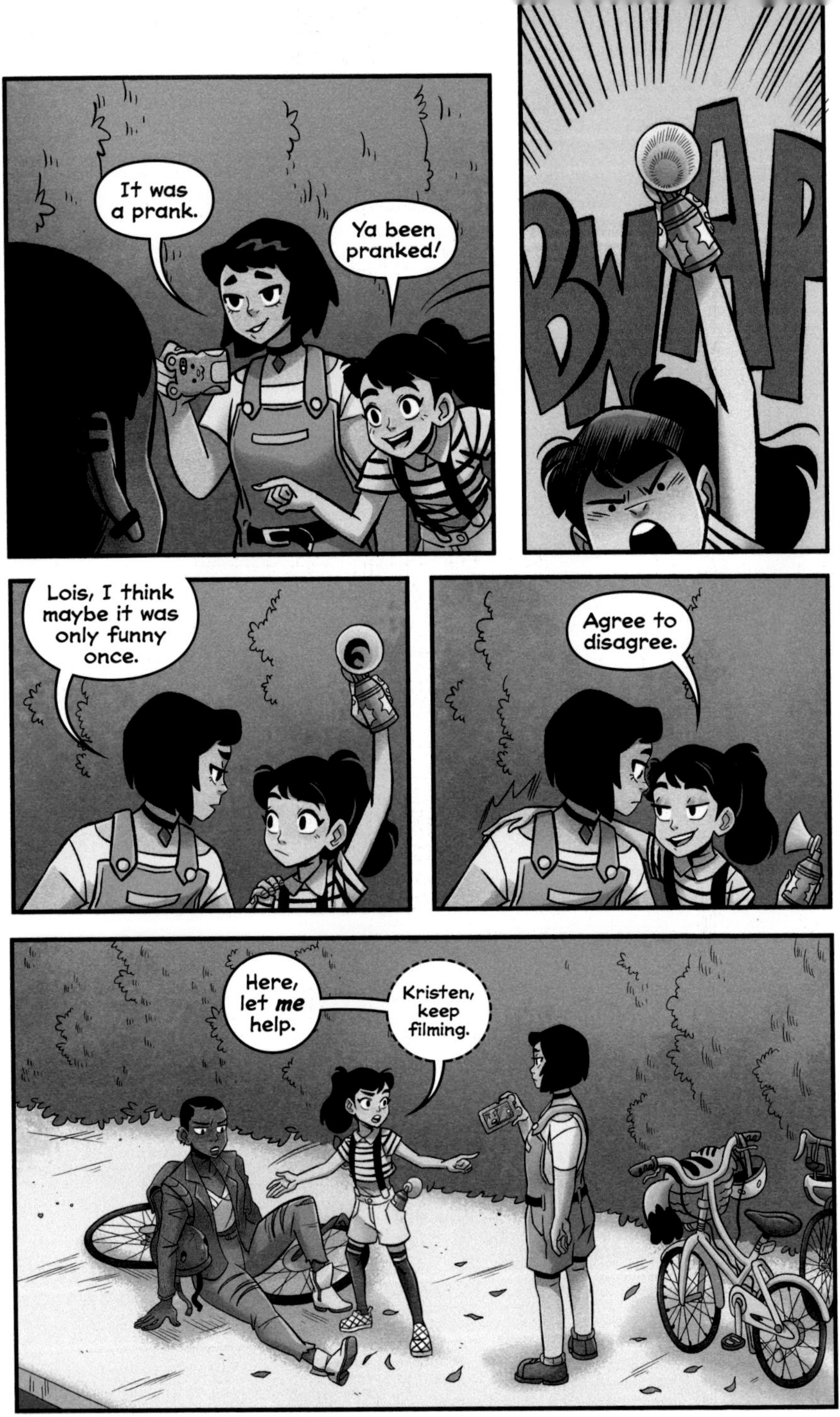
It was a prank.
Ya been pranked!
BWAP
Lois, I think maybe it was only funny once.
Agree to disagree.
Here, let *me* help.
Kristen, keep filming.

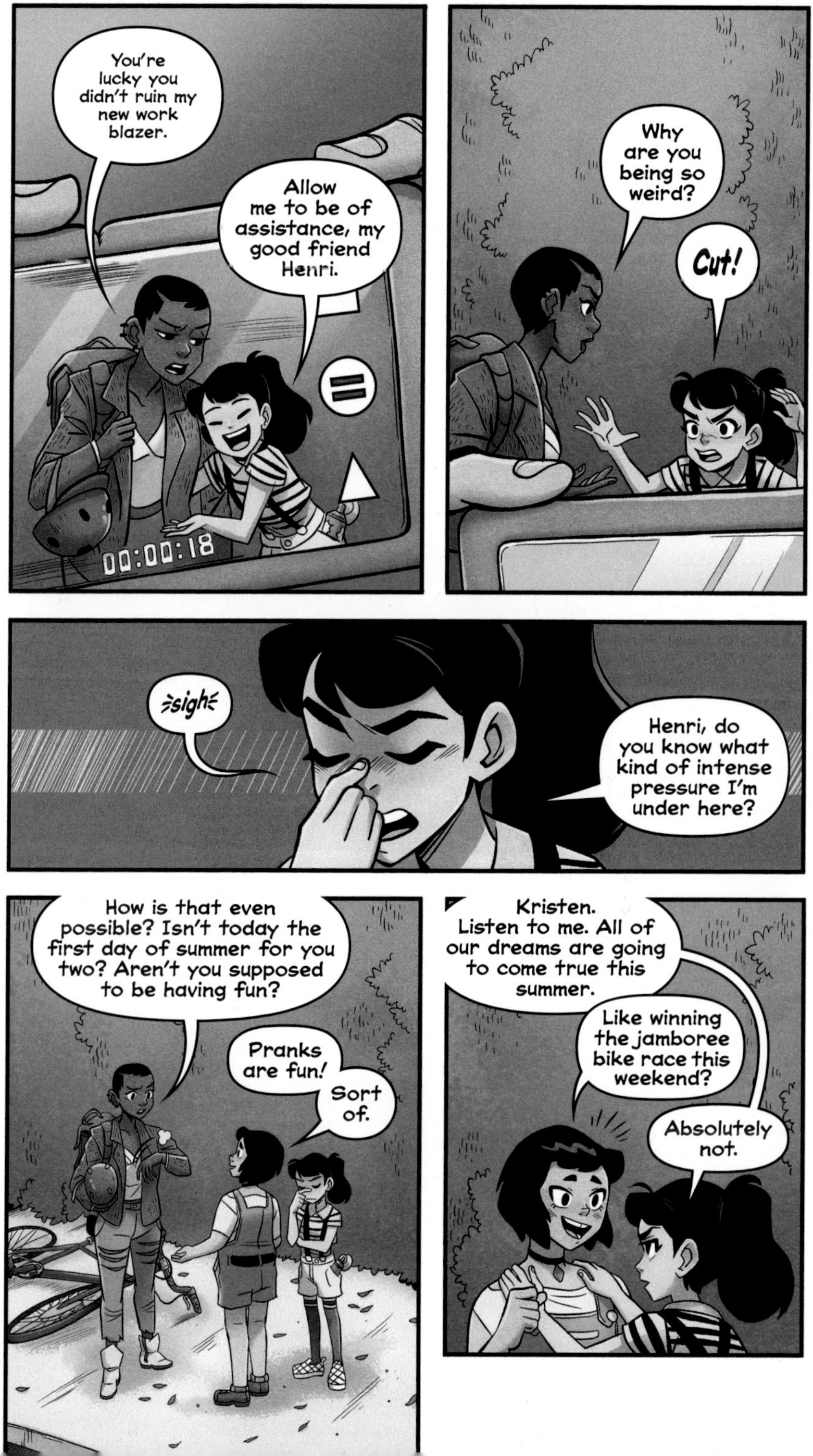

You're lucky you didn't ruin my new work blazer.
Allow me to be of assistance, my good friend Henri.
00:00:18
Why are you being so weird?
Cut!
sigh
Henri, do you know what kind of intense pressure I'm under here?
How is that even possible? Isn't today the first day of summer for you two? Aren't you supposed to be having fun?
Pranks are fun!
Sort of.
Kristen. Listen to me. All of our dreams are going to come true this summer.
Like winning the jamboree bike race this weekend?
Absolutely not.

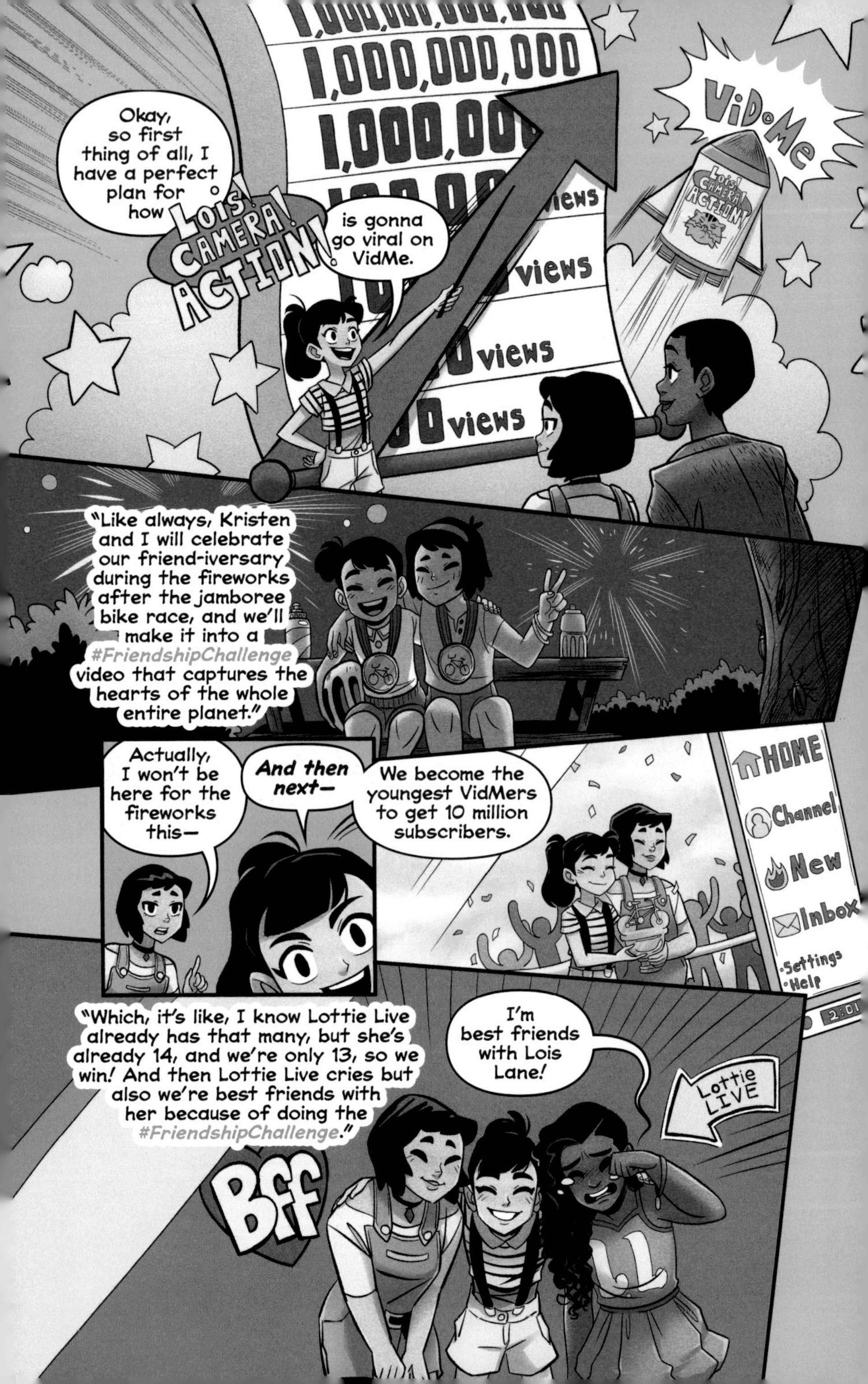
1,000,000,000
1,000,000
views
views
views
views
Okay, so first thing of all, I have a perfect plan for how
LOIS! CAMERA! ACTION!
is gonna go viral on VidMe.
ViD•Me
LOIS! CAMERA! ACTION!
"Like always, Kristen and I will celebrate our friend-iversary during the fireworks after the jamboree bike race, and we'll make it into a #FriendshipChallenge video that captures the hearts of the whole entire planet."
Actually, I won't be here for the fireworks this—
And then next—
We become the youngest VidMers to get 10 million subscribers.
HOME
Channel
New
Inbox
•Settings
•Help
2:01
"Which, it's like, I know Lottie Live already has that many, but she's already 14, and we're only 13, so we win! And then Lottie Live cries but also we're best friends with her because of doing the #FriendshipChallenge."
I'm best friends with Lois Lane!
Lottie LIVE
Bff

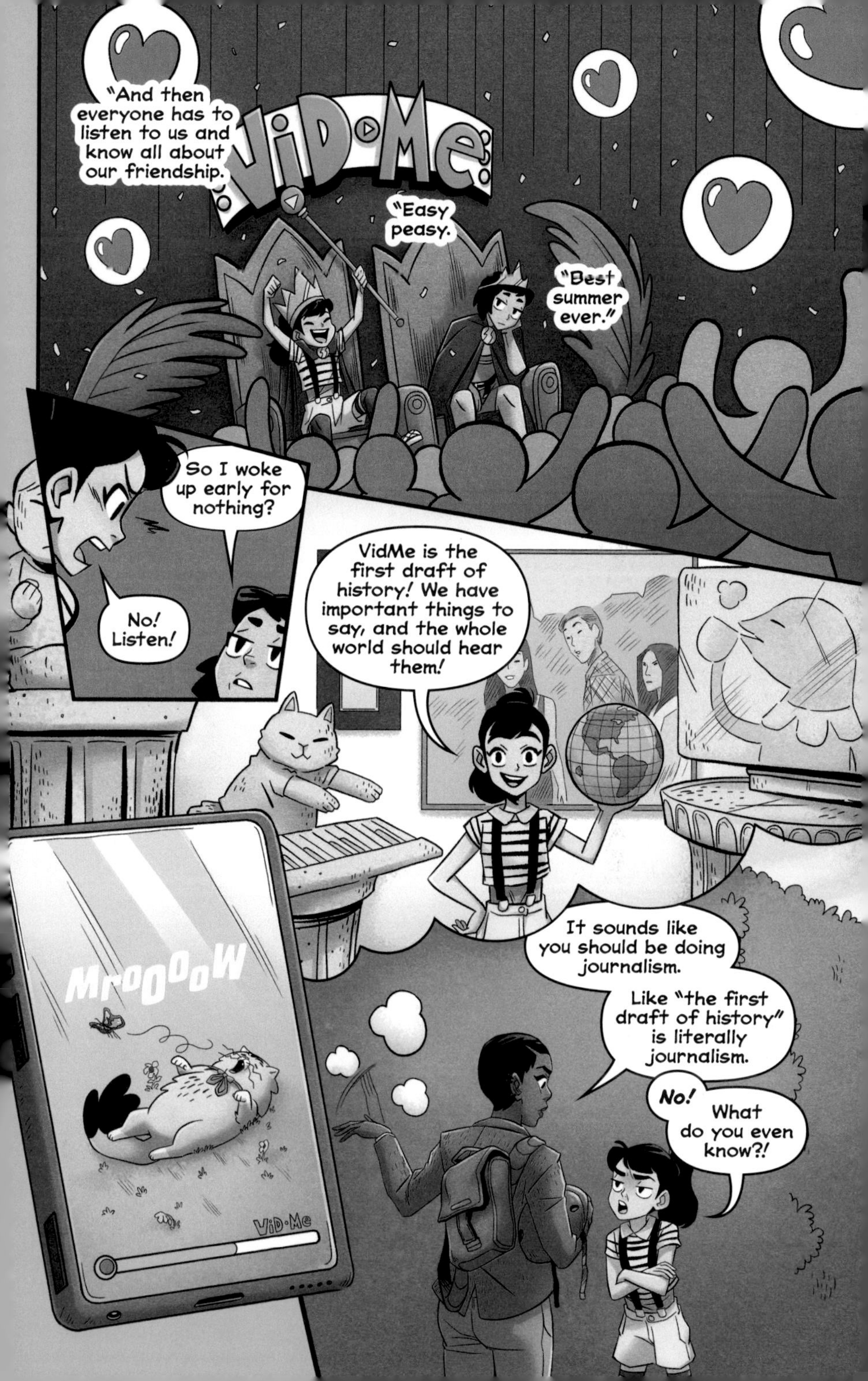
"And then everyone has to listen to us and know all about our friendship.
VidMe
"Easy peasy.
"Best summer ever."
So I woke up early for nothing?
No! Listen!
VidMe is the first draft of history! We have important things to say, and the whole world should hear them!
MroOooW
VidMe
It sounds like you should be doing journalism.
Like "the first draft of history" is literally journalism.
No! What do you even know?!

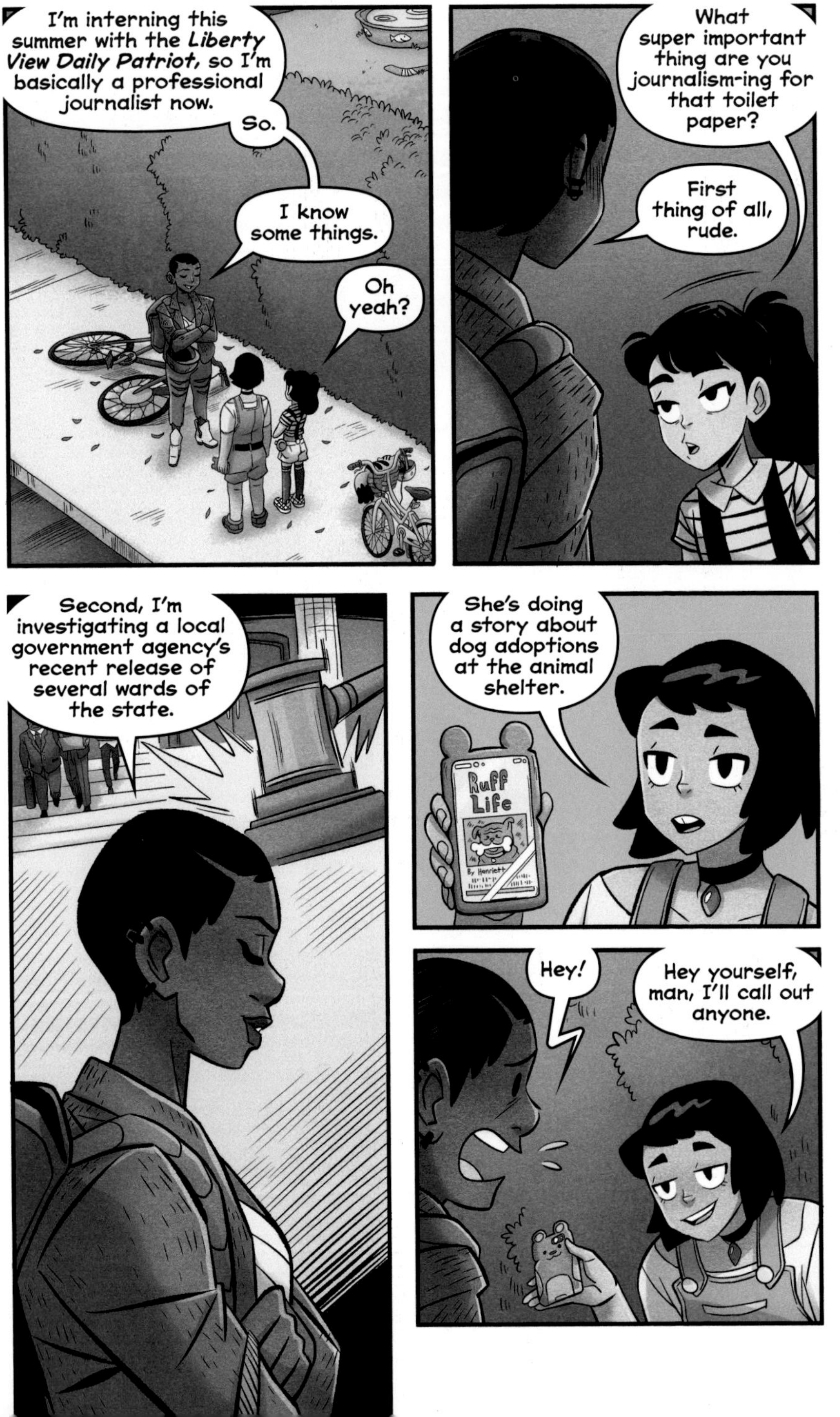
I'm interning this summer with the *Liberty View Daily Patriot*, so I'm basically a professional journalist now.
So.
I know some things.
Oh yeah?
What super important thing are you journalism-ing for that toilet paper?
First thing of all, rude.
Second, I'm investigating a local government agency's recent release of several wards of the state.
She's doing a story about dog adoptions at the animal shelter.
Ruff Life
Hey!
Hey yourself, man, I'll call out anyone.

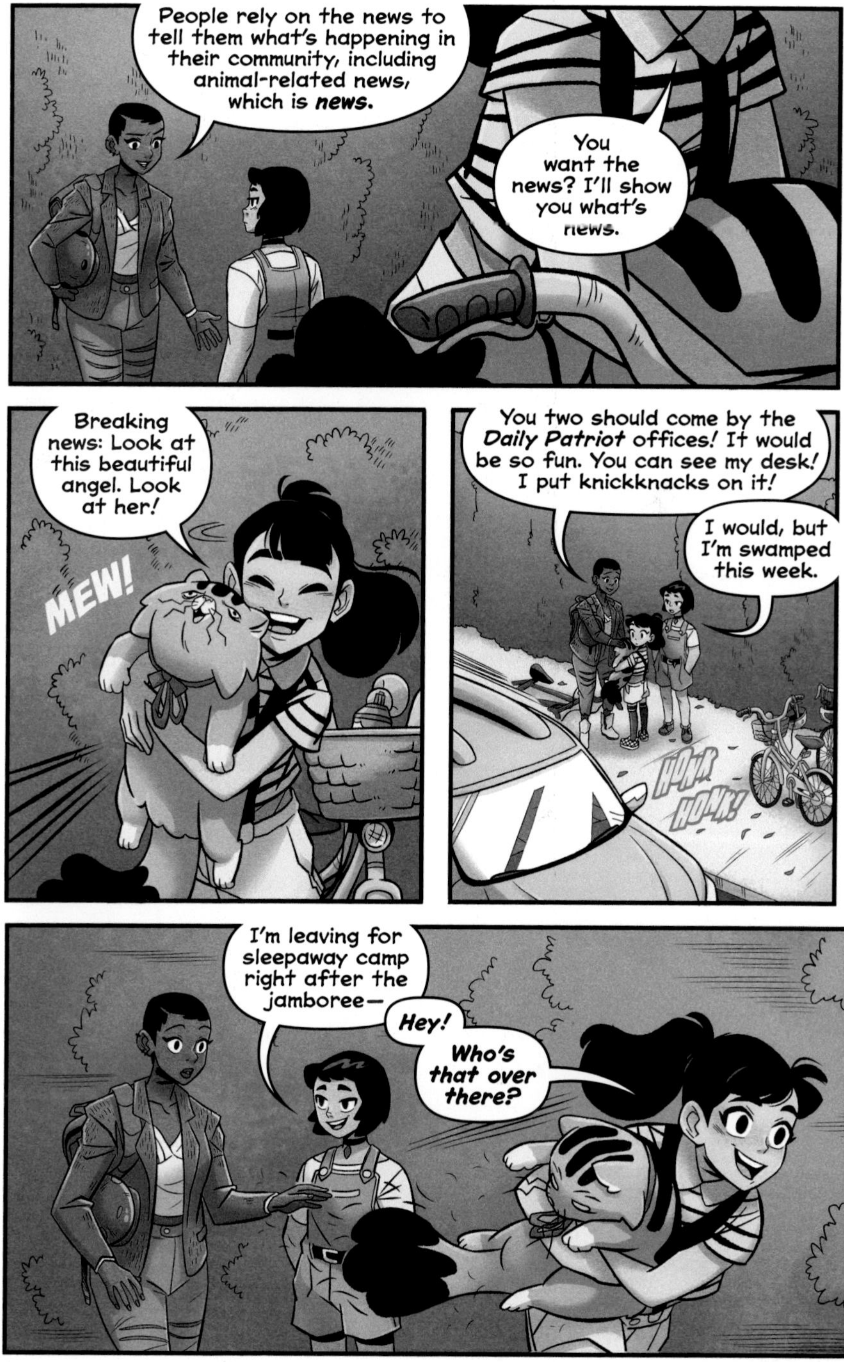
People rely on the news to tell them what's happening in their community, including animal-related news, which is *news.*
You want the news? I'll show you what's news.
Breaking news: Look at this beautiful angel. Look at her!
MEW!
You two should come by the *Daily Patriot* offices! It would be so fun. You can see my desk! I put knickknacks on it!
I would, but I'm swamped this week.
HONK HONK!
I'm leaving for sleepaway camp right after the jamboree—
Hey!
Who's that over there?

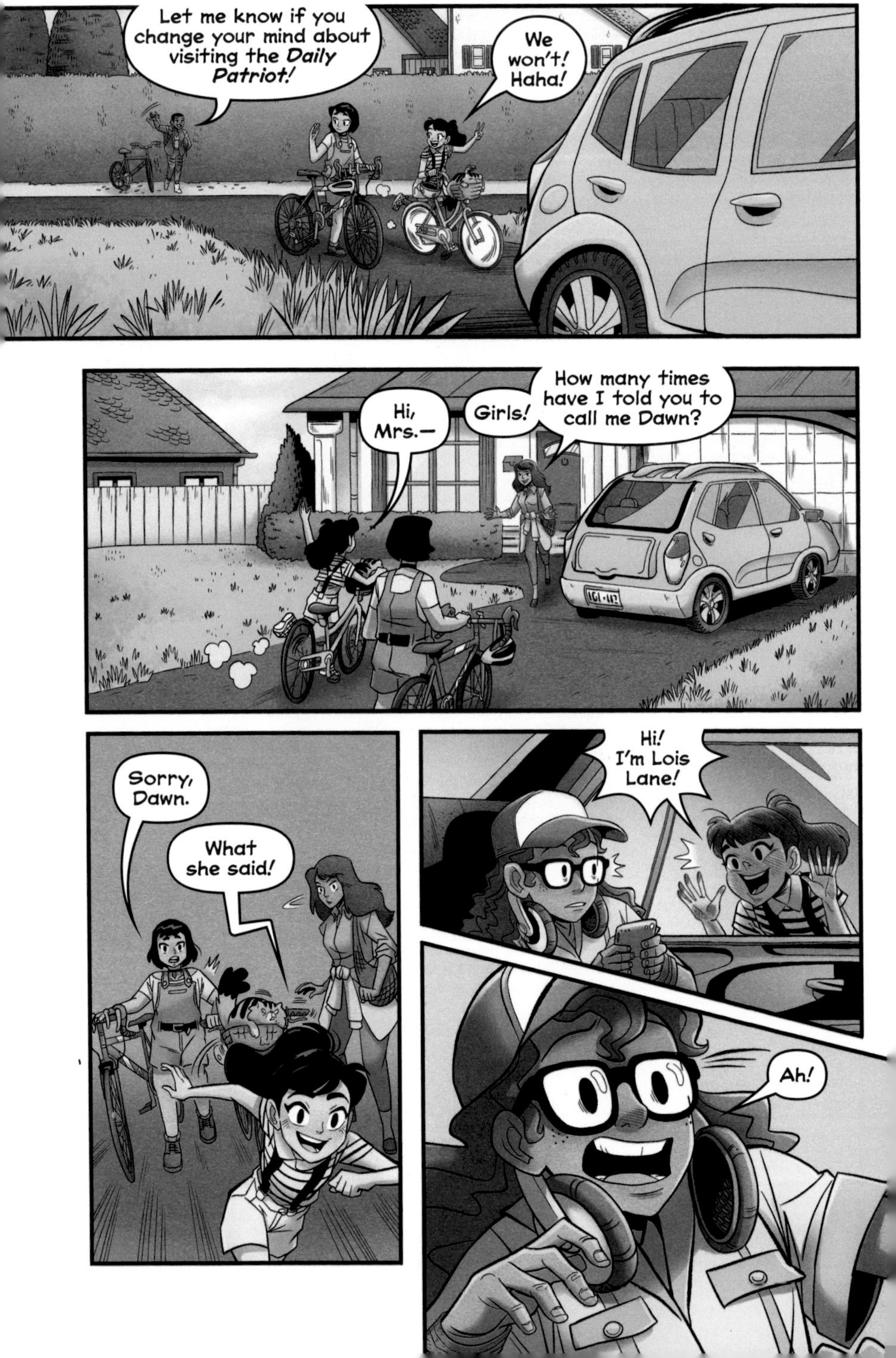

Let me know if you change your mind about visiting the *Daily Patriot!*
We won't! Haha!
Hi, Mrs.—
Girls!
How many times have I told you to call me Dawn?
Sorry, Dawn.
What she said!
Hi! I'm Lois Lane!
Ah!

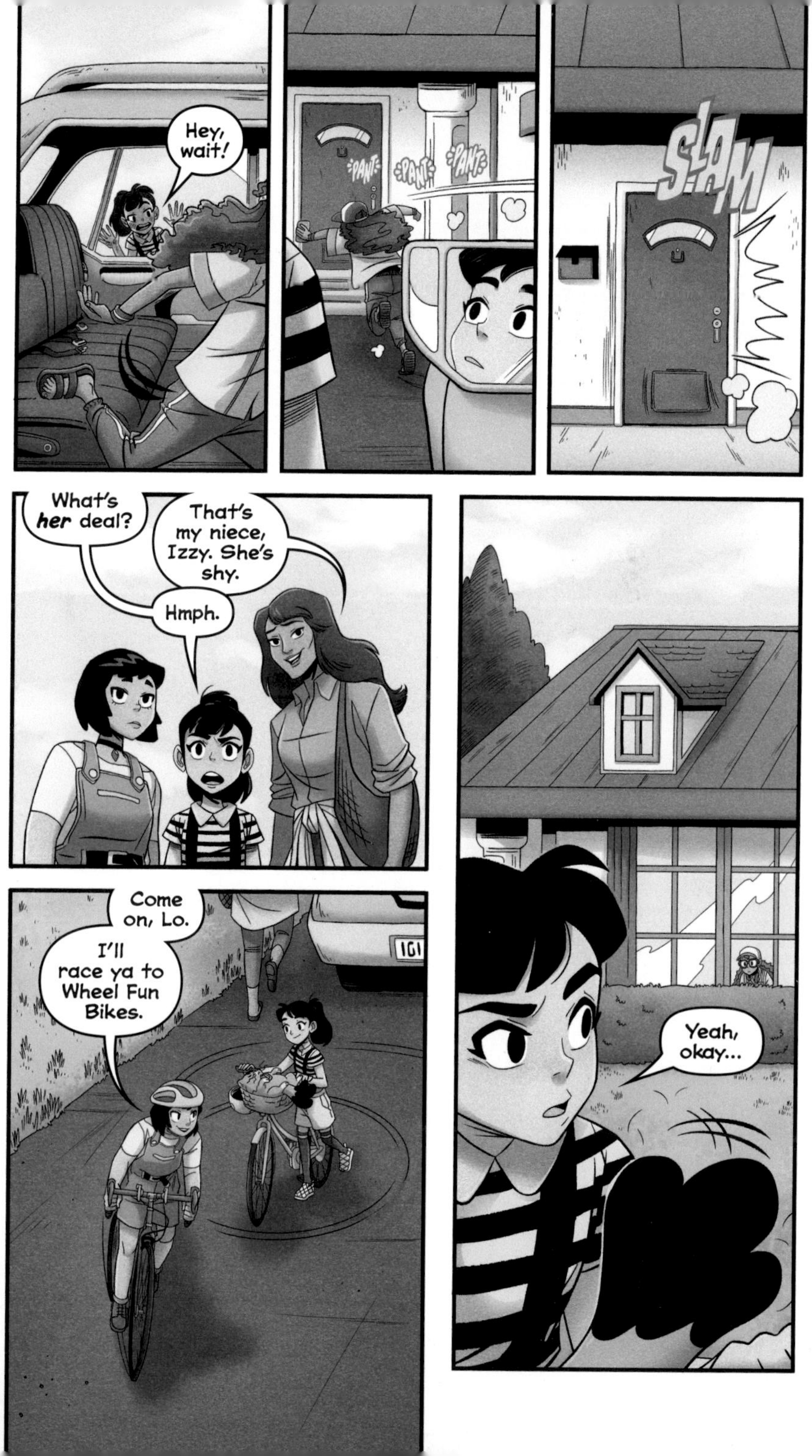
Hey, wait!
PANT
PANT
PANT
SLAM
What's *her* deal?
That's my niece, Izzy. She's shy.
Hmph.
Come on, Lo.
I'll race ya to Wheel Fun Bikes.
Yeah, okay...

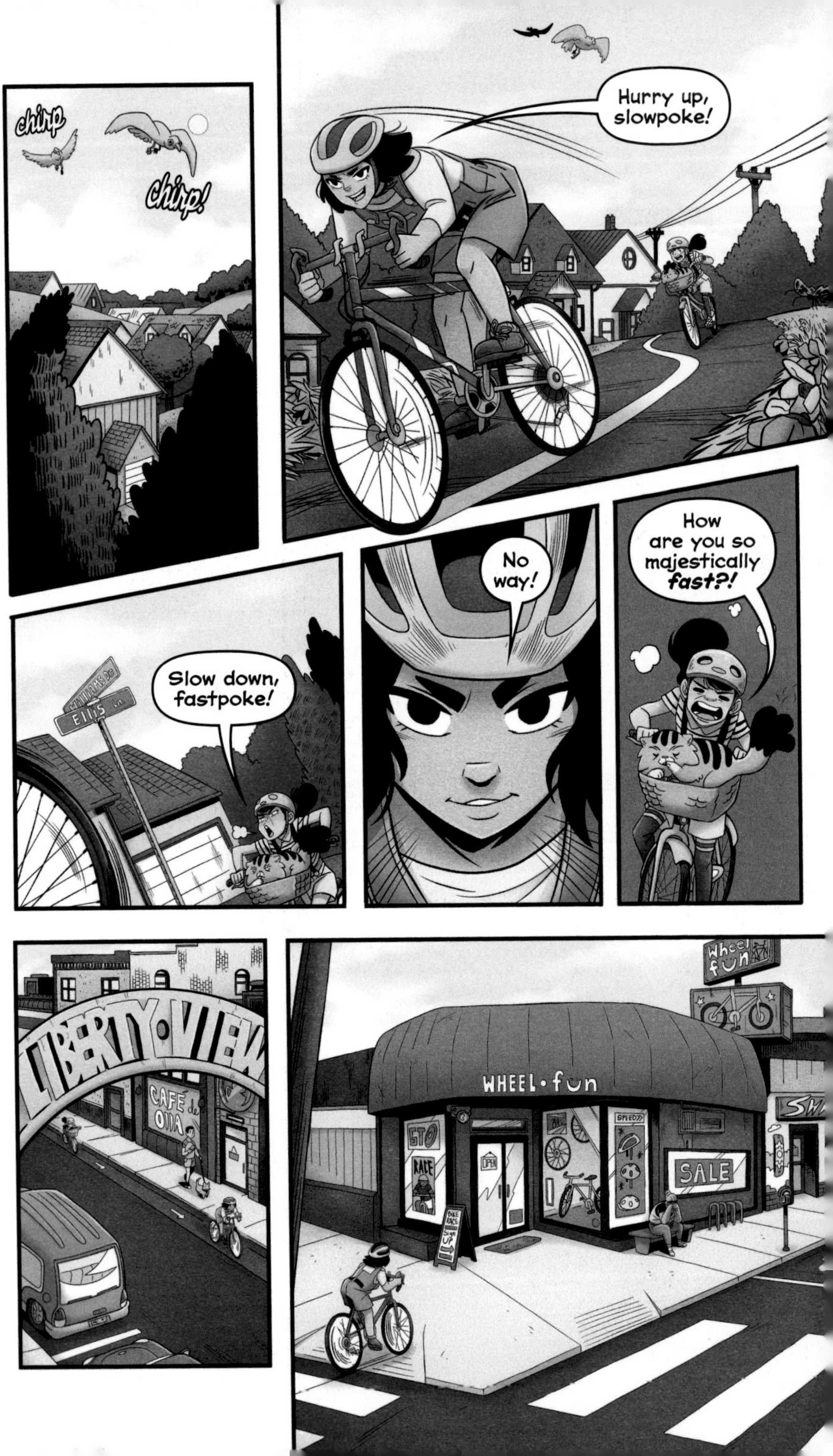
chirp
chirp!
Hurry up, slowpoke!
Slow down, fastpoke!
No way!
How are you so majestically fast?!
LIBERTY VIEW
WHEEL • fun
SALE
OPEN
BIKE RACE Sign UP

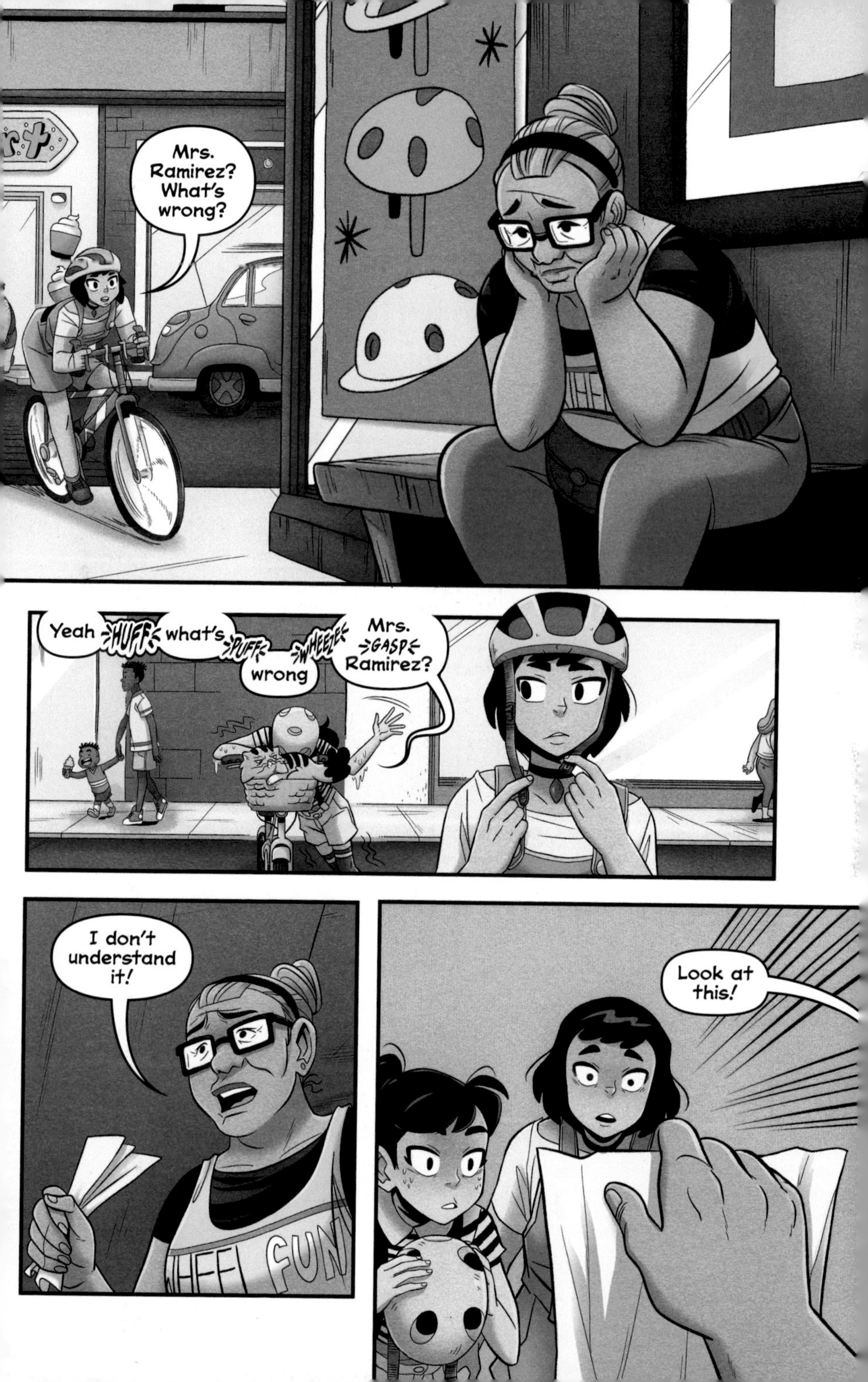
Mrs. Ramirez? What's wrong?
Yeah
HUFF
what's
PUFF
wrong
WHEEZE
Mrs.
GASP
Ramirez?
I don't understand it!
Look at this!
WHEEL FUN

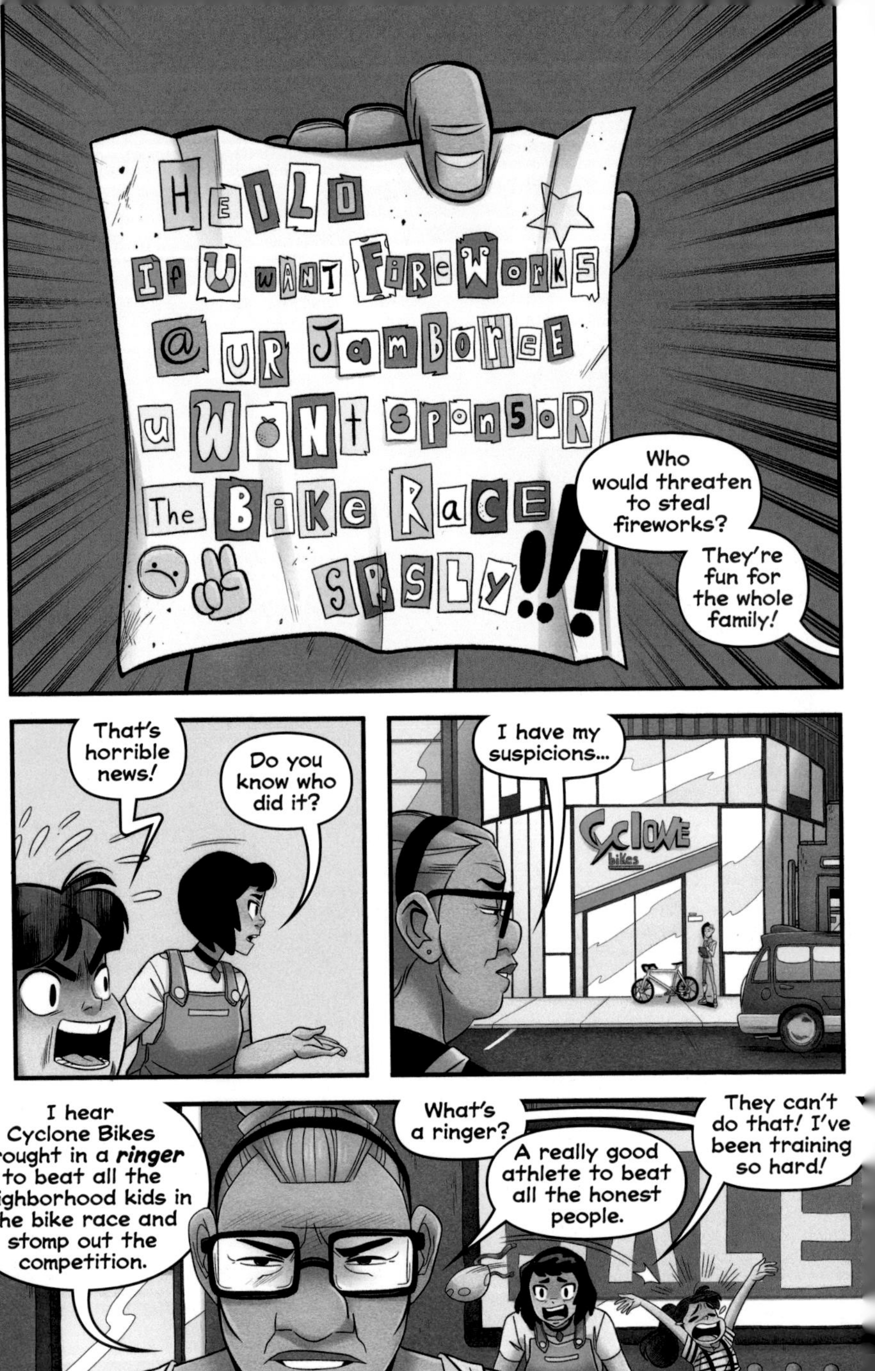
HELLO
If U want FireWorks
@ UR Jamboree
u WONt spon5oR
The Bike RaCE
SRSLy!!!
Who would threaten to steal fireworks?
They're fun for the whole family!
That's horrible news!
Do you know who did it?
I have my suspicions...
Cyclone bikes
I hear Cyclone Bikes brought in a *ringer* to beat all the neighborhood kids in the bike race and stomp out the competition.
What's a ringer?
A really good athlete to beat all the honest people.
They can't do that! I've been training so hard!

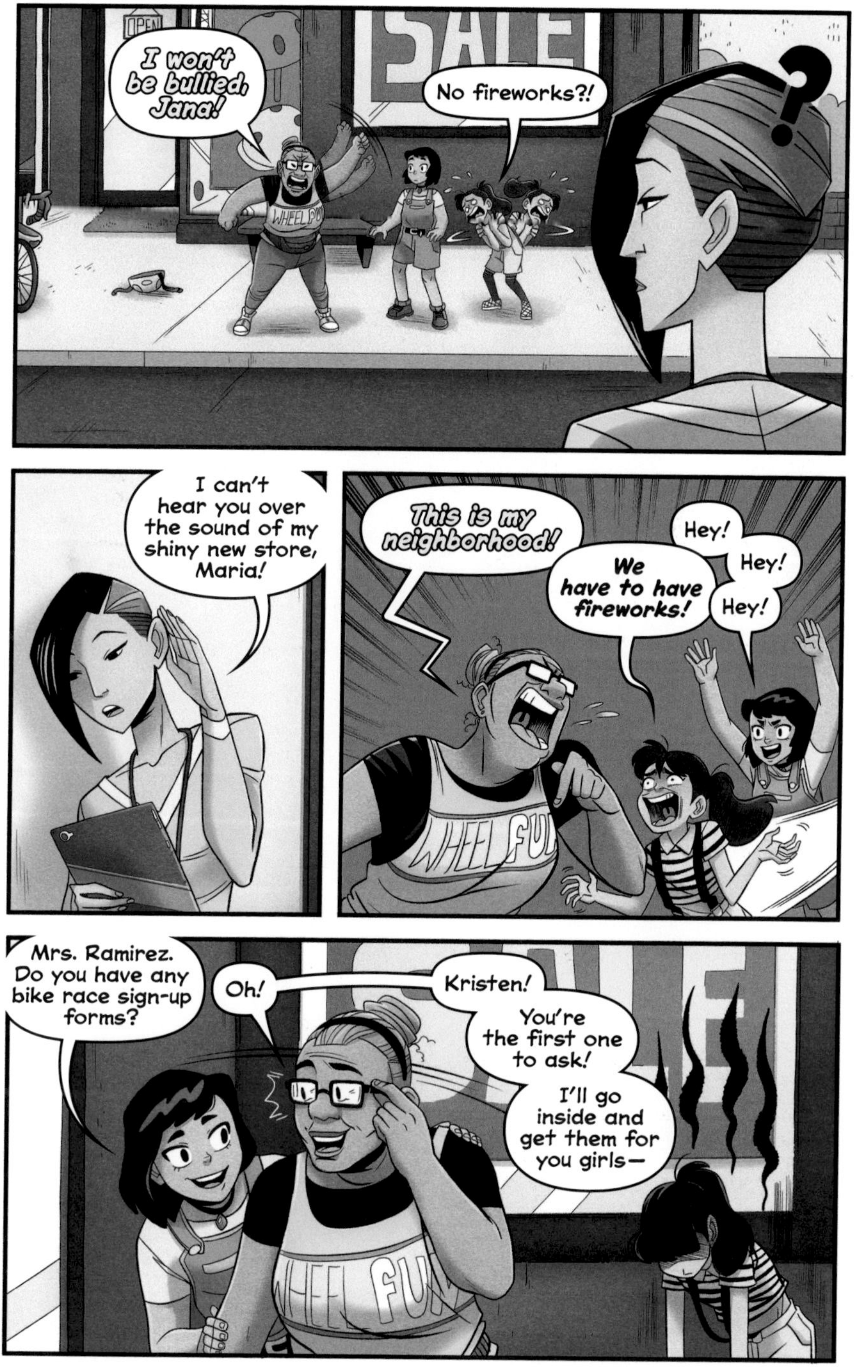
I won't be bullied, Jana!
No fireworks?!
?
I can't hear you over the sound of my shiny new store, Maria!
This is my neighborhood!
We have to have fireworks!
Hey!
Hey!
Hey!
Mrs. Ramirez. Do you have any bike race sign-up forms?
Oh!
Kristen!
You're the first one to ask!
I'll go inside and get them for you girls—

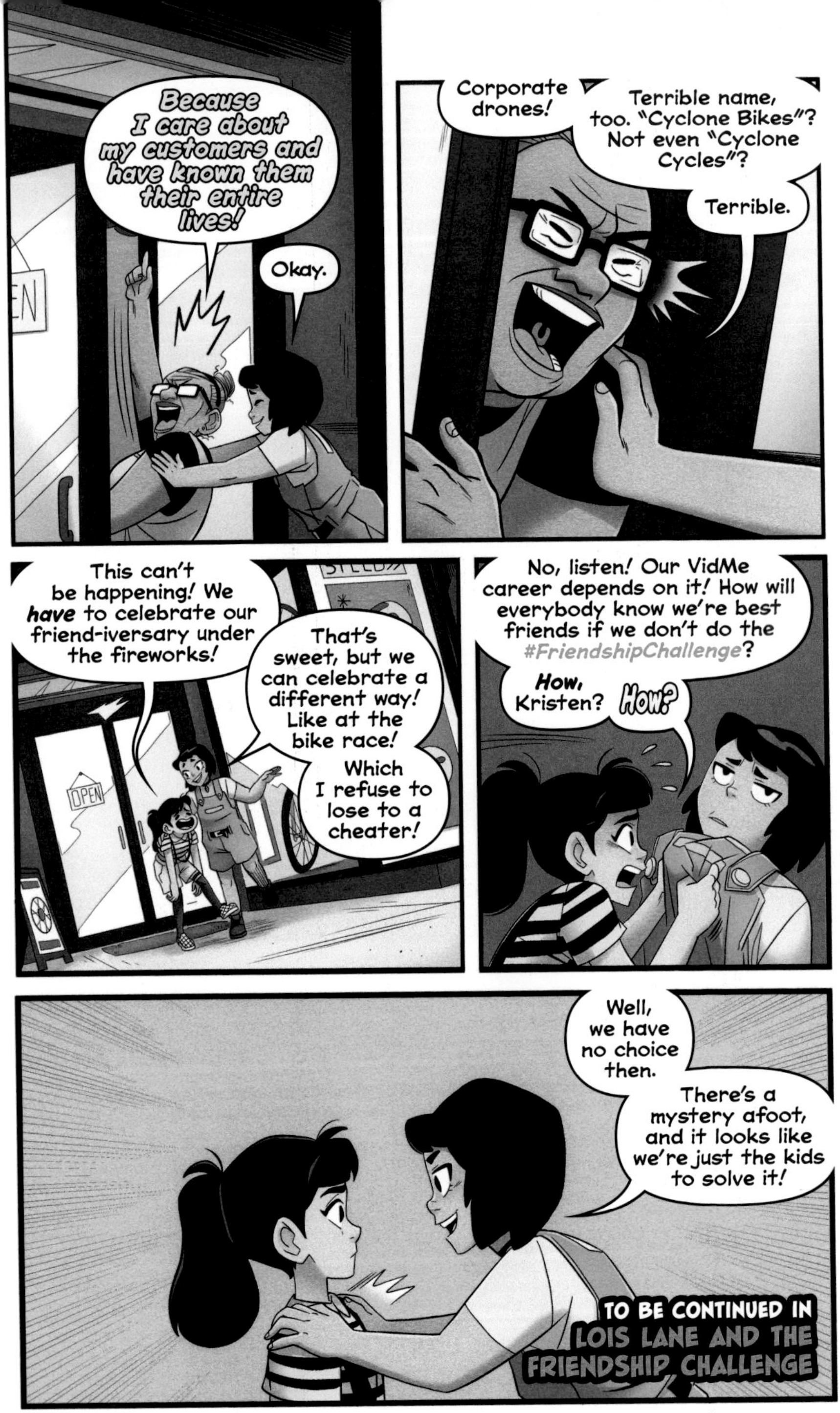
Because I care about my customers and have known them their entire lives!
Okay.
Corporate drones!
Terrible name, too. "Cyclone Bikes"? Not even "Cyclone Cycles"?
Terrible.
This can't be happening! We *have* to celebrate our friend-iversary under the fireworks!
OPEN
That's sweet, but we can celebrate a different way! Like at the bike race!
Which I refuse to lose to a cheater!
No, listen! Our VidMe career depends on it! How will everybody know we're best friends if we don't do the #FriendshipChallenge?
How, Kristen?
HOW?
Well, we have no choice then.
There's a mystery afoot, and it looks like we're just the kids to solve it!
TO BE CONTINUED IN LOIS LANE AND THE FRIENDSHIP CHALLENGE

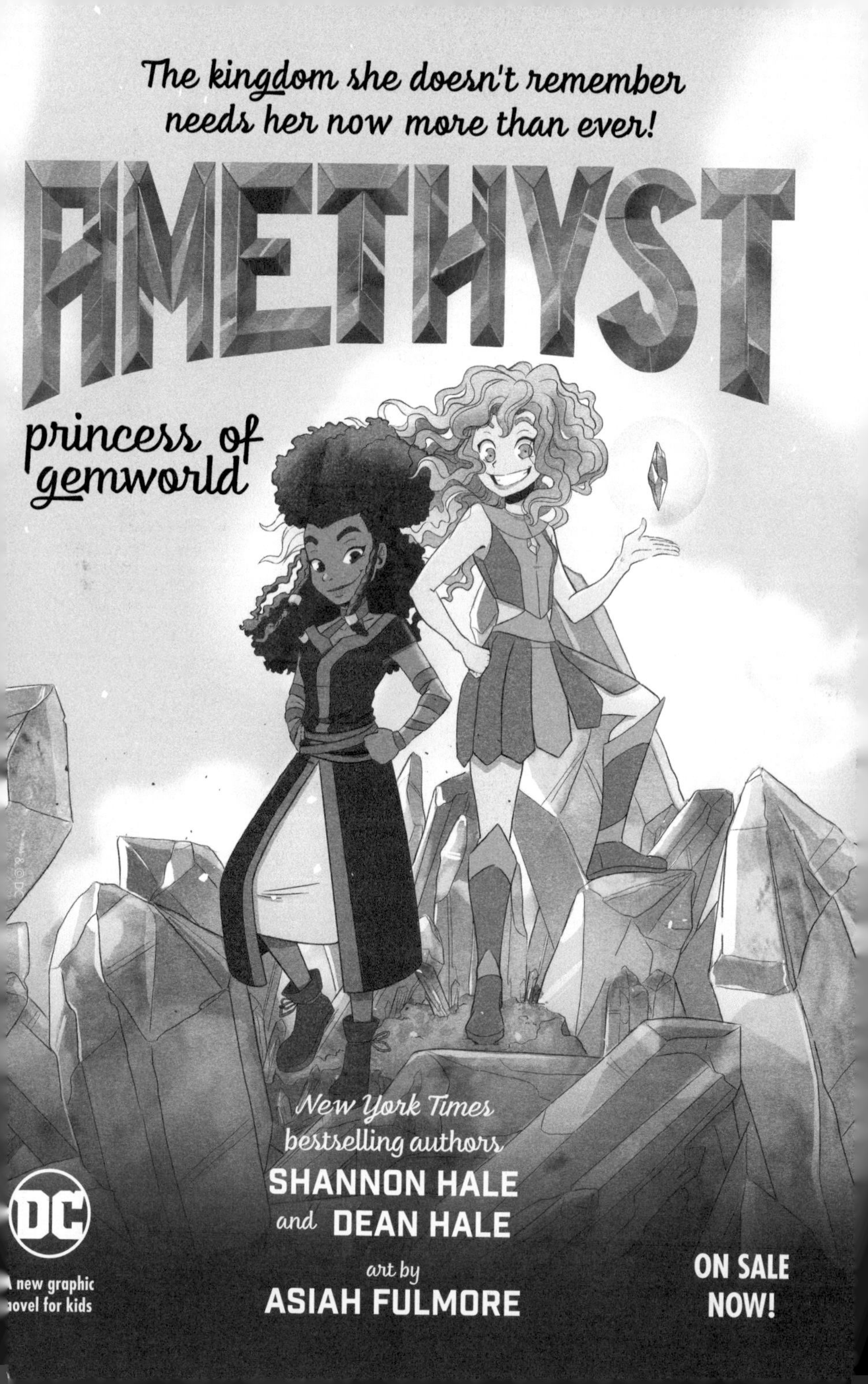
The kingdom she doesn't remember
needs her now more than ever!
AMETHYST
princess of gemworld
New York Times
bestselling authors
SHANNON HALE
and DEAN HALE
art by
ASIAH FULMORE
A new graphic
novel for kids
ON SALE
NOW!

Diana: Princess of the Amazons
Shannon Hale, Dean Hale,
Victoria Ying
ISBN: 978-1-4012-9111-2

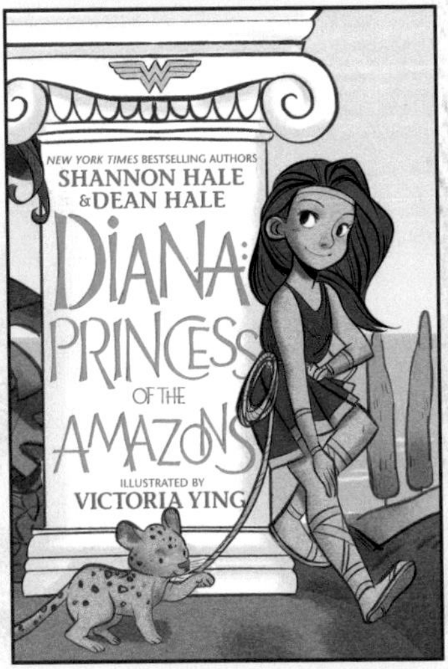
NEW YORK TIMES BESTSELLING AUTHORS
SHANNON HALE
& DEAN HALE
DIANA:
PRINCESS
OF THE
AMAZONS
ILLUSTRATED BY
VICTORIA YING

Diana and Nubia: Princesses of the Amazons
Shannon Hale, Dean Hale,
Victoria Ying
ISBN: 978-1-77950-769-3

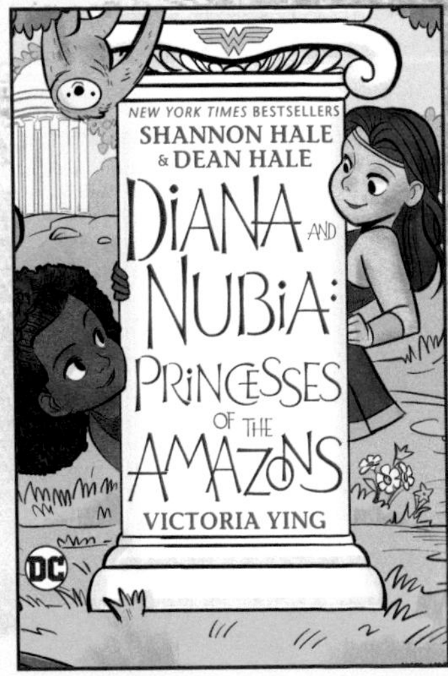
NEW YORK TIMES BESTSELLERS
SHANNON HALE
& DEAN HALE
DIANA AND
NUBIA:
PRINCESSES
OF THE
AMAZONS
VICTORIA YING
DC

More DC Books for Young Readers!

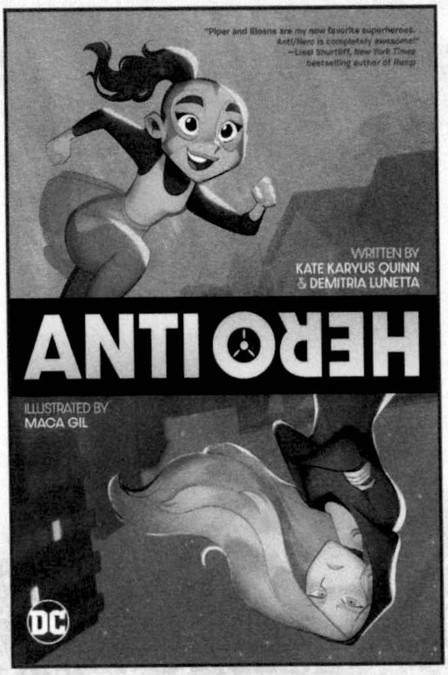
WRITTEN BY
KATE KARYUS QUINN
& DEMITRIA LUNETTA
ANTI/HERO
ILLUSTRATED BY
MACA GIL
DC

Anti/Hero
Kate Karyus Quinn,
Demitria Lunetta, Maca Gil
ISBN: 978-1-4012-9325-3

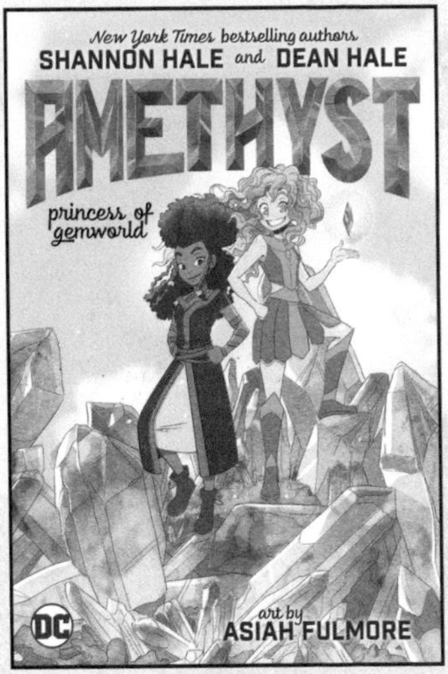
New York Times bestselling authors
SHANNON HALE and DEAN HALE
AMETHYST
princess of gemworld
art by
ASIAH FULMORE
DC

Amethyst: Princess of Gemworld
Shannon Hale, Dean Hale,
Asiah Fulmore
ISBN: 978-1-77950-122-6